CROWNLESS
KING

PART 2

MARINA SIMCOE
THE RIVER OF MISTS

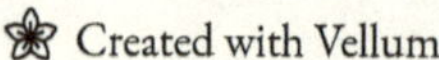 Created with Vellum

Crownless King

PART 2

MARINA SIMCOE

To all who need no wings to fly.

Chapter One

SPARROW

It was dark when I opened my eyes. Dark and warm.

I remembered riding with Voron, tucked into his chest under his soft, velvet cloak. I remembered feeling cold, even as my body burned with heat. Someone had given me a fragrant tea to drink. I recalled a warm, wet cloth against my skin, wiping the filth of the dungeon off my body.

All these memories were fuzzy except for the feeling of overwhelming exhaustion. It was so heavy, I couldn't even open my eyes when people washed and changed me. And after a few more sips of the tea, I remembered nothing at all.

I lay in bed now. In a dark room dimly lit by pale blue crystals entrapped in the semi-transparent black walls. The charcoal-gray vines holding the black wall panels reminded me of Elaros, but it didn't look like any room I'd seen in the Sky Palace.

Rising on my elbows, I took a better look at the space. It appeared to be a huge bedroom. The bed alone was almost as big as my entire room back in Elaros. A tall fireplace opposite the bed would comfortably fit a whole pickup truck inside it. It was unlit. Which was good, as it felt warm without a fire in here.

A couple of dark blue couches in carved black frames, a chair, and a low table were arranged into a sitting area in front of the fireplace. One of the tall windows was open. A light breeze gently moved the thin white curtains that glistened with *firrian* beetles.

My arms trembled from the effort of supporting my body, and I lay back into the pillows. Rolling to my side, I found a high-backed armchair by my bed. Voron slouched in it. His long legs bent, knees apart, his head dropped to one shoulder, he appeared asleep.

There was something tragic and vulnerable about his position, like he'd been so exhausted, he'd just crashed into the chair and fallen asleep immediately without bothering to arrange his limbs comfortably first.

I had lots of questions, but I didn't want to wake him to demand the answers.

The familiar staccato of hooves hitting the floor sounded from the distance. I rose from the cushions again as the door opened and Brebie trotted in with a small tray in her hands.

"Oh, you're up? Good, good. Drink your water." She set the tray on the bedside table, then handed me a wide crystal glass. "I'll go fetch your dinner."

She sounded cheerful and energetic like always. And just as loud.

"Shhh." I pressed a finger to my lips. "You'll wake Voron."

"Him?" She waved her hand toward her lord. "Nothing can wake him when he's this tired, only Magnus maybe. But I locked the bird in the library so Voron can get some rest. He was up all night, pacing here like a man possessed. It's a miracle he hasn't worn a hole in the floor yet."

"Why was he up? Was he worried?"

She nodded. "Out of his mind. He read somewhere that humans are extremely fragile and was worried sick about you. But look at you." Her voice lifted. "You did just fine, like I told him you would."

"How long did I sleep?" Words scratched my dry throat. I drank the water, emptying the glass.

"You arrived late last night. And you weren't really awake when you got here, falling asleep right after we put you to bed. So, you slept for a night and a day. It's your second night here."

"Where's *here?* What is this place?"

"Oh, this is Vensari, Voron's family home."

His family home?

I took another look around. It suited him. Granted, I'd only seen this one room, but the rich yet subdued colors of black, dark-gray, and royal blue seemed to be Voron's preferred palette both in clothes and furnishings.

Brebie grabbed my empty glass. "I'll get your dinner now. You need to eat to regain your strength. Poor thing, you couldn't even walk when you got here. Voron had to carry you like a baby."

That must have been the fever that knocked me out so badly. It wasn't surprising I caught something, considering the horrible conditions in the royal dungeon.

I smoothed a hand down the sleeveless satin nightshirt I was wearing.

"Did you change my clothes?"

"Voron and I did. You were like a rag doll. It was like handling dead weight. I needed some help to maneuver you. There was no way I would've let you into the bed as filthy as you were." She shuddered.

My face warmed with gratitude and a whiff of shame for putting them both through all that trouble.

"Thank you."

I debated asking Brebie about the queen and my planned execution, but the matter was probably best discussed with Voron. Before I could make up my mind, Brebie rushed out of the room. She returned in a few minutes with a steaming bowl of soup and a slice of fragrant sourdough bread. I brought the bread to my nose, inhaling its fresh scent without even a hint of mold.

"It smells so good and looks actually edible." I tried to smile, but judging by Brebie's expression, failed at it miserably.

She patted my shoulder sympathetically. "King Tiane's dungeon is a horrible place I've heard. It's mostly empty, though. The king far prefers executions to imprisonment. I'm glad you're out, Sparrow. Safe and sound."

I placed my hand on top of hers. "Me too. I'm really happy to be here instead."

Good food, soft silky sheets, clean air—I'd never take any of it for granted for as long as I lived.

After I'd eaten most of the soup and drank some of the tea she'd given me, Brebie was satisfied to leave me alone. She tucked the sheets around me, gathered the dishes, and left, wishing me a good night.

I turned to my side and faced the sleeping Voron again. He really didn't look comfortable, like a broken mannequin dumped into the chair. It bugged me.

I crawled to the edge of the bed and straightened his legs, arranging them in front of him. Then I took a small cushion from the pile of pillows behind me. Climbing out of bed, I carefully stepped between his knees and took his head in my hands with the intention of lifting it and sticking the cushion between his cheek and shoulder.

With a soft snort, he jerked and woke up, blinking at me.

"Sorry," I mumbled, still holding his head between my hands. "I didn't mean to wake you."

"Were you trying to wring my neck in my sleep, little vixen?" Despite his biting words, a smile quivered his lips. "How are you feeling?"

"Better."

It was safe to assume he was capable of holding his head up on his own, so I let go of it. I tried to step back but tripped over his leg and plopped my butt down on his knee.

"Shit." I made a move to get up, but he stopped me by placing a hand on the small of my back.

"Not that much 'better,' I see." He clicked his tongue disapprovingly. "You're not naturally clumsy like that."

"It's that tea that Brebie made me drink. It makes me sleepy."

He moved a strand of my hair back over my shoulder, then went to stroke my bare arm, but before his skin touched mine, he jerked his hand away.

"You should be in bed."

"You should be, too. It can't be comfortable sleeping in this chair."

"Well, you took my bed." He splayed his hand on my thigh over my nightshirt. Apparently, touching me through the fabric didn't bother him as much as grazing my bare skin.

I decided to test his touching limits by covering his hand with mine. He didn't shake it off.

"Don't tell me this is the only bedroom you have in your house," I said. "I'm happy to sleep anywhere else."

He grunted, getting up with me in his arms. "All right, little bird. Too much chirping when you should be resting."

Walking around the bed, he placed me on the sheets, then drew the covers over me.

"Voron, I have questions."

"I know. But they'll have to wait until morning. It'll suffice to say that you're safe here. Safe enough to rest for as long as you need."

"You have to get some rest, too." I patted the mattress next to me. "If you insist on both of us staying in the same room, this bed is huge. I could easily have three men here with me."

"There is no way I'll ever let you roll around my bed with three random men," he muttered under his breath, kicking off his shoes.

I smiled, watching him take off his leather belt and his black vest. He loosened the collar of his white shirt and climbed onto the bed with me but stayed over the covers.

"Here." He stifled a yawn. "I'm in bed. Will you go to sleep now?"

"Now, I will." I giggled, which earned me an amused glance from him. Come to think of it, I didn't remember ever giggling before, not since I came to Sky Kingdom at least.

He turned with his back to me and stuffed a pillow under his head. "Good night, Sparrow."

But there was one question I needed to know the answer to before I could even think about sleeping.

"Voron?"

"Hmm?

He didn't turn around, so I kept talking to his back.

"What do you want for hiding me here?"

"What do you mean?" Now, he turned. His eyes looked dark blue in the night, reflecting the deep glow of the crystals.

"Nothing is for free," I explained. "In Sky Kingdom, everything has its price. I learned that much."

"Right. Well..." He rubbed the back of his neck. "If you absolutely insist on paying me, I'll take another one of those meringue swans. With a neck to snap," he added with a cold glint in his eyes.

"That may be difficult to do, since I probably won't see the head chef any time soon. How about I'll make you a meringue with whipped cream instead? Without a neck to snap?"

I'd ask Brebie to show me how to make meringue. It might take me all day to make it, but I would learn.

"Fine." He turned back around again. "I'll find a way to wring *his* neck instead."

I didn't clarify whose neck he meant, but it was safe to assume it wasn't the head chef's.

"It's a deal then." I shifted a little closer to him. We were in the same position we had taken a nap in the woods once. Only this time, I had no intention of running anywhere.

Pressing my forehead to his back, I closed my eyes. "Good night, Voron."

Chapter Two

SPARROW

When I woke up in the morning, Voron was gone. Brebie came in to help me get dressed and brush my hair. She told me Voron wished to have breakfast with me on the patio off his library. Then, she showed me the way through the wide corridors of Voron's elegant home.

When I came out onto a wide stone patio shaded by overhanging vines dripping with pink and silver flowers, Voron was already there, waiting for me at a small table set with breakfast dishes.

"Did you sleep well?" I asked, taking a seat across the table from him.

He gave me one of his infrequent half-smiles.

"Splendid. Thank you for asking. How about you?"

I'd woken a couple of times through the night. Voron proved to be a restless sleeper. He tossed and turned. Once, he'd made a strangled noise in his throat—a half-moan, half-whimper. He'd sounded in pain, and I'd gotten up to see if he was okay, wondering if I should shake him awake. But he'd just rolled over onto his side and blindly found me by patting around. Tucking me into his chest, he'd calmed down, sleeping more soundly after that.

"I'm fine," I assured him. "I've slept close to thirty hours in the past day and a half. I definitely got a lot of rest."

I drank my tea and ate most of my porridge. This one didn't have any maggots, of course, but just thinking about the food in the dungeon made me lose my appetite. I smeared the last remaining spoonful of the porridge over the plate, poking at it without eating.

With a soft caw, Magnus landed on a branch nearby. I smiled, as if meeting an old friend.

"Hi, buddy. We didn't part well last time, did we?"

"Last time?" Voron tilted his head.

"He knows what I'm talking about. I stole your horse, and he woke you up to send you after me."

Voron laughed, tossing his head back, and this time, I got to see it, not just hear it. The corners of his eyes crinkled in mirth. Creases winged the corners of his mouth, making his smile look even wider and his laugh appear even heartier.

I loved the sight of Voron in a cheerful mood way too much. It left me defenseless. I could fall for him. I could fall for him so hard, and I wouldn't even know when exactly I stepped off the cliff.

He flashed me a teasing look. "Oh yes, that one time I let you trick me."

"You didn't *let* me! I did trick you. Fair and square." I leaned back in my chair with a triumphant smirk. "Admit it. You lost that one."

"All right. You did catch me off guard," he confessed, shaking his head in disbelief. "Waking up with my feet tied up and my horse and my boots gone was a surprise."

My smile grew wider in satisfaction. Sure, I hadn't made it far in escaping him. All my victories had been temporary at best. I tended to win battles when Voron won wars. But if all that had brought me here to the patio of his family home, enjoying a breakfast in his company, I was not going to complain.

Magnus eyed me with heightened suspicion in his black, glossy eyes, like he expected me to take off with Voron's silverware any minute.

I scooped up the remaining oatmeal off my plate onto my finger.

"Come here, Magnus." I extended my porridge topped finger toward the bird as a peace offering. "Have breakfast with me. Let's be friends."

"He already had his breakfast." Voron didn't seem pleased with my attempt to spoil his pet.

"This will be his snack, then. Does he like oatmeal?"

Voron huffed. "He likes everything. I saw him gut a frog in the garden earlier this morning."

"Eww. The porridge is so much better than a gutted frog. Please, Voron, let him have it."

He released a long-suffering sigh.

"Why is it so fucking hard to say no to you? Fine." With a hand gesture, he allowed Magnus to come to me.

The bird hopped onto my hand eagerly and scooped the blob of porridge with his beak.

"Ouch," I hissed at the sting of his talons.

"You asked for it." Voron shook his head disapprovingly, even as his lips quivered with a smile.

I laughed as Magnus took off with his loot for the second breakfast, or third, if we counted the gutted frog. The air stirred by his wings blew out my hair, and I smoothed my hand over it once the bird was gone.

"Do you think he'll like me more now?" I watched Magnus disappear into the tall trees of the luscious grounds of Voron's estate, probably to eat his oatmeal in peace or to hide it for later.

"He liked you too much already when he let you steal my horse," Voron scoffed.

I licked the buttery trace of the oatmeal off my finger, giving him a look from under my windblown locks. "Then, there is hope for us still."

"Us?"

"Magnus and me," I clarified.

"Right." He took a sip of his tea.

I eyed Voron's breakfast—a plate of thinly sliced roasted white meat, fluffy egg soufflé, and grilled vegetables with a roll of flaky pastry. It looked so much better than my oatmeal. My appetite returned with a vengeance.

He intercepted my stare. "Would you like more food? You shouldn't eat anything too heavy after your ordeal in the dungeon cell. But I can ring for some more porridge."

"No. I'm good. Thanks."

I refilled my porcelain cup with tea from the equally delicate teapot, trying not to dip the lacy ruffles of my sleeves into the liquid. The dress Brebie had gotten for me was made from the lightest spider silk, which was the perfect material for the warmer weather we were finally having.

The summer had barely started, but the heat was setting in already. It had rained overnight, which made the air stifling and muggy this morning.

My lace trimmed sleeves reached down to my wrists, but the long slits from the shoulder to the cuff made them cooler. The single-layer skirt wasn't transparent. And there was no corset, just a soft, cobalt-blue bodice stitched with lily-of-the-valley flowers. Laced with a white ribbon in the front, it also provided full support for my breasts in lieu of a bra.

Another big change in my clothing was underwear. Back in Elaros, with a brief exception once a month, I was expected to provide easy access to my body at all times in case the king felt like pawing at me. In Vensari, Brebie had supplied me with a drawer full of panties. They were all pretty, lacy things, thin like air, but I had more than enough of them to wear every day of the month.

With the thought of the king, worries returned.

"Any news from Elaros?" I asked. "Is the queen looking for me?"

Voron cut off a small piece of meat on his plate. It looked so moist and succulent, the juices glistening on it in a most appetizing way.

"I decided against reporting to the queen in person about what I've done," he said, his tone breezy. "Instead, I sent her a message, explaining that I had to fulfill the promise I'd given to you to allow you to return to the human world."

"You never gave me such a promise."

"You're right. I didn't." He glanced at me slyly. "But the queen doesn't need to know that. She thinks I promised you'd leave Nerifir, and I went against her wishes to deliver on that promise out of fear of ending up as one of the cursed if I didn't. Fear is a powerful motivator and one that the queen understands well."

"So, she didn't punish you?"

"Oh yes, she did. Just because she believed me didn't mean she forgave me. In fact, she was furious." He lifted his teacup to his lips, giving me an amused look over the rim. "She was really looking forward to your public execution."

So much for my hopes for royal leniency.

"I can't say I'm sorry to disappoint her on that one." I fidgeted with the edge of the tablecloth, eyeing his plate. "What will happen now?"

"Now, Queen Pavline thinks you're gone from this world."

"As good as dead," I echoed his words from before.

"Right. There's no reason for the crown to search for you."

"But how about you?"

"Oh, the queen knows exactly where I am. She ordered me to stay away from Elaros, which is just as well."

"You've been banished?"

He put another morsel of food into his mouth, then gestured with his fork at the luscious, colorful gardens surrounding his sprawling, one-story mansion of black marble, blue crystals, and graceful vines.

"Not the worst place to be exiled to, don't you think?"

I took in the tall trees, the vines dripping with flowers, and the fountains with a large pond in the distance and agreed, "It's gorgeous."

"Most of the estate is treed," Voron added. "You don't have to fear the queen's people spotting you from the air. Just make sure you stay under the canopies and use the treed alleys to walk in the park and the gardens."

I wondered if he had the trees planted that way, specifically to conceal himself from those who had wings and could spy on him from above.

"All right," I agreed, without realizing that my eyes flickered to his breakfast plate once again.

He smirked and shoved it my way.

"Fine. Help yourself. Just don't tell Brebie I let you have anything other than porridge."

If I had any restraint or self-respect, I'd refuse. I wasn't even that hungry after having eaten most of my oatmeal. But his food smelled and looked so good, I had no willpower to say no.

"Oooh, thanks." I quickly swiped a slice of meat off his plate and stuffed it into my mouth. "Mmm, this is so good," I moaned, and closed my eyes, savoring the delicious flavors. They seemed especially intense after the rotten dungeon food.

When I opened my eyes again, Voron was staring at me with an odd expression. His dark-gray eyes glistened with silver from behind the bi-colored strands hanging over his forehead.

The air around us seemed hotter somehow, sweltering under the thick clouds above. His foot slid between mine under the table, and I felt his leg press to the inner side of my knee.

His gaze heated. I reached to brush his hair out of his face, but he grabbed my wrist before I could touch him.

"Sparrow." There was so much in my name slipping from his lips. His voice rang with passion, torment, and plea—all at once.

Only what was he pleading with me for? Not to touch him? Then why did he keep holding my arm, his thumb gently gliding over the sensitive skin inside my wrist?

Mesmerized, I couldn't take my eyes off his long, deft fingers, thinking about the one and only time he'd had them between my legs and how amazing it had felt. With a soft sound deep inside my throat, I squirmed in my chair, pressing my thighs together.

"Don't," he exhaled sharply, suddenly rising to his feet.

Letting go of me, he turned around and promptly left the patio, leaving me drowning in confusion.

What had just happened?

Did I do something wrong?

I hadn't done anything that didn't feel right at that moment. Did he not feel the same?

The cheerful clicking of Brebie's hooves against the patio stones announced her arrival.

"Good girl, you ate all your breakfast." She started gathering the dishes from the table.

"Brebie? Do you think Voron is angry with me for something?"

Voron had never been easy to read. He made sure of it, putting a lot of effort into remaining unreadable. But lately, he acted outright confusing. One minute he was gentle with me, almost affectionate even. The next, he'd push me away like he resented me fiercely.

Brebie paused. "What? Why would he be? Did he say something?"

"No, but..." There were some valid reasons for Voron to resent me. "He prefers Elaros to this place, doesn't he? And now, he's stuck here because of me."

He'd rescued me from the royal dungeon, and I would be forever grateful to him for that. But maybe he was having second thoughts now, having been faced with the consequences of that decision?

"Pff." Brebie made a face. "Who in their own mind would

prefer a bunch of spoiled nosy nobles to the serenity of the countryside?"

Not me. But Voron was one of those nobles. The court was where he belonged.

"Shouldn't the High General be at the palace, next to the ruling monarch? But he's exiled here, out of favor with the queen."

"Voron isn't the High General anymore," she blurted out.

"What?

That I could not imagine. In my mind, there could never be another High General but Voron, for as long as he lived.

"The queen stripped him of the rank," Brebie explained. "She took away his position at the court and all of his properties except this one."

"Why not this one?"

"Vensari belonged to Voron's mother," she said. "The queen couldn't just take it from him, even if he'd gone against her wishes. The rest of his estates and palaces were given to him by the crown for his service to the king. Those have all been taken back."

I focused on helping her clean the dishes rather than face the fact that Voron had some grave reasons to hate my guts right now. He'd paid dearly for his act of kindness toward me.

"But don't you worry, honey." Brebie patted my shoulder reassuringly. "Voron knew the risks before he made the decision to get you out. I'm sure he isn't blaming you for what happened."

I wished she was right. But there was a difference between knowing the consequences and actually facing them. Voron was an ambitious man. He'd worked hard, literally risking his life for everything he'd gained. He sold his freedom for the power he had.

And now, he'd lost it all.

He'd avoided breaking his promises to the crown, obeying all direct orders from the queen. But by ignoring her wishes, he still caused her displeasure. I didn't know the exact terms of Voron's deal with the royals, but it must have some clause about him disappointing them, because the queen clearly found a way to make him pay.

She had his freedom, and now she'd taken away his power too.

I could only imagine what it must feel like for him to lose it all. It'd be no wonder if some of that bitterness and disappointment ended up being directed at me as a result.

Chapter Three

SPARROW

I spent that afternoon making meringue with Brebie in the kitchen.

"What do you need this for?" She asked as I arranged the airy pieces on a plate, trying to glue them with whipped cream into some resemblance of a swan without the pulled sugar neck.

"I promised Voron a dessert in exchange for him saving me from the queen."

My "swan" ended up looking more like a sheet-wearing ghost. But from the taste tests I'd done while making it, I knew it was delicious.

Voron avoided me for the rest of the day, however, and didn't meet me for breakfast the following morning, either.

I had no idea where he slept that night, but it wasn't in his bedroom. The chair was empty when I went to bed, and it remained unoccupied every time I opened my eyes through the night.

The next day, I asked Brebie to move me to another room.

She tried to brush off my concerns. "Voron put you here. He's fine with it."

"He did it on impulse," I insisted. "It was late when we arrived here. I was barely conscious. He thought he had to keep an eye on me. But I'm much better now. There is no reason for me to occupy his bedroom. It's bad enough that he's now forced to share his one and only house with me." When she still didn't look convinced, I threatened, "I'll sleep on the breakfast patio or on the couch in the library, but I'm not keeping him out of his bedroom for another night."

That did it. Brebie relocated me to one of the spare bedrooms. Either on purpose or by accident, my new room was in the furthest wing away from Voron's. Combined with his clear efforts to avoid me, I didn't see Voron at all for the next three days.

Brebie delivered my meringue contraption to him to close our deal. But I never even knew whether he liked it or even ate it.

I spent this time mostly alone.

Since there was no need for me to impress anyone anymore, I would get myself ready in the morning with no assistance from the maids. I wore dresses similar to those of Brebie's. They had fewer pieces and their bodices laced in the front, which I could easily do up on my own. I brushed and braided my hair, too.

I ate either in my room or in the library, which Voron seemed to avoid, too, now. Other than an occasional servant in the hallway or Brebie, who brought me food, I spent days hardly seeing anyone.

To pass time, I read. Voron's library was stocked with long manuscripts on Nerifir history, governance, detailed recounts of wars, and in-depth analysis of battle strategies. But I found a section with fables. These were shorter, fictional stories that helped me take my mind off things and fed my imagination with beautiful imagery.

As much as I enjoyed the peaceful existence at Vensari, after three days of almost complete solitude, I craved interaction. Brebie was kind enough to join me on a walk in the gardens the next morning. She showed me the main alleys and the way to the pond with huge lily pads floating on its surface.

"You can swim here. The water is clean with a nice sandy bottom," she said.

As we walked back to the house, I complimented the well-kept grounds.

"A lot of work must go into maintaining these."

"Oh yes, Voron employs a team of gardeners."

"Is Kanbor one of them now?"

Her face fell. She blinked, glancing aside.

"No. Kanbor had to stay in Elaros. He's employed by the king." She sighed.

Guilt pinched my heart. So many lives had been disrupted because of me.

"I'm sorry," I said softly.

She patted my arm. "It's not your fault, honey."

But it was. I didn't plan for any of this to happen, but I felt responsible nevertheless. If it wasn't for me, Voron would still be the powerful High General, living in the Sky Palace, and Brebie would be there with him, together with Kanbor.

They had made sacrifices for me. People I cared about were now worse off because of me, and I had no idea how to fix it.

The muggy heat was exceptionally hard to deal with in the afternoon. Every day, the weather seemed bloated with storm, but the relief never came. Since the king's mood affected the weather in the Sky Kingdom, I wondered if King Tiane's spirit was brewing with anger against me, not finding a relief in vengeance—not yet, at least.

My bathroom in Vensari came with a water feature that served as a bathtub. It was a round pool, shallow on the edges that allowed me to lie down. Deeper in the middle, it had a short fountain like a low bubbling geyser in a hot spring. However, the water in the tub was warm, too warm for the sweltering afternoon.

Brebie was too busy to join me on a walk this time. As I strolled alone past the pond in the gardens, the dark water called to me. I descended the narrow path toward it, then toed off my shoes, and waded in. The water was warm but not cooler than in my bathtub.

My skin was sticky with sweat. Brebie had told me I could swim here, but I had nothing in my wardrobe that would serve as a bathing suit.

With a quick glance around to make sure no one was close enough to see me, I untied the laces of the bodice of my dress, then took the whole thing off over my head, staying only in a thin, knee-length undershirt and a pair of panties. These would have to do as a bathing suit.

Wading knee-deep into the pond, I wondered if I could swim. A few days ago, I'd been ready to find it out by taking a plunge into the River of Mists. This pond seemed like a less extreme way to answer that question.

I waded in up to my waist. The water was cooler than the air and felt pleasantly refreshing against my heated skin. Bending my knees, I let the water come all the way up to my chin. Then I pushed off the sandy bottom, stretching in the water horizontally, and made a few strokes with my arms.

My mind didn't remember, but my body retained the necessary movements. I swam. And it felt exhilarating.

I moved along the shore, careful to stay in an area shallow enough for me to touch the bottom with my feet. After a little while, I had to stop to catch my breath.

It turned out I wasn't the strongest swimmer. Neither was I very confident about my technique. But I could swim.

This was a thrilling discovery. My memories were gone, but the skills I'd gained in my past were still there. I wondered what else I could do, suddenly feeling excited to try everything and anything under the sky, just to test it all.

Not willing to get out of the water yet, I eyed the giant lily pads on the other side of the pond. I gauged the distance to the first pad under the canopy of a sprawling willow tree and decided I could make it.

I waded in that direction, walking until the water reached my chin. Then I pushed off the bottom and swam. I was nearly out of breath by the time I made it to the lily pad, but I made it.

Up close, the leaf appeared even bigger. It was as large as my bed, surrounded by floating pale-blue flowers the size of dinner plates. The underside of the thick pad was spongy and felt like velvet. The top was glossy and dark. It looked strong and big enough to hold my weight.

Gripping its edge, I kicked my feet and climbed onto the pad. It held, only rocking a little on the surface of the pond.

"Oh, this is lovely," I muttered to myself, surveying this newfound place.

The branches of the willow tree swayed above me, their leaves rustling softly. This would make a wonderful place for an afternoon nap, had I been tired. But I wasn't.

I felt restless. Swimming in the cool water energized me. My wet clothes felt refreshing against my flushed skin. I wrung the water out of my hair, then spread over the lily pad to dry as I lay on my back, watching the tree branches swing gently in the barely-there breeze.

A splash of water jolted me with alarm. The sound seemed too loud for a fish or a frog.

I sat up promptly.

A head broke through the surface of the pond next to my lily pad. Water sluiced down the hair—ink-black with a few thick, silver-white strands in the front.

"Voron! What are you doing here?"

He shook the water out of his hair and rested his bent arms on the edge of the pad.

His eyes slowly traveled down my body as he replied, "Swimming to my doom, it appears."

I glanced down at my chest. My undershirt was still soaking wet. The thin material turned practically transparent, clinging to every curve of my body. It plastered around my breasts, displaying the pink of my areolas and the buds of my nipples that hardened instantly under his heated stare.

"Um..." I threw an arm over my chest.

"Don't," he rasped. "I won't touch. Just let me see you again. Please."

He'd been gone for days, suddenly re-surfacing, quite literally, out of nowhere. Without even saying hello, he now demanded I let him ogle me?

He sounded desperate, almost in pain, like a starving man begging for crumbs of food. But his torture was of his own making. I craved his touch, and there was no one in Vensari to stop us.

My heart sped up in my chest. My breathing turned shallow. Heat that had nothing to do with the weather rushed down my body, swelling into a pool of need low in my belly.

All it took was just one look from Voron—one intense, ravenous look—and my body was very much on board with whatever game he was playing. Desire buzzed under my skin, throbbing between my legs. No one had that power over me, no one but Voron. All I could do was to try playing his game on *my* terms.

I stretched a leg out toward him until my toes almost touched his elbow.

"You can only see if you touch me."

His eyes flashed with fire. But so infuriatingly stubborn, he shook his head. A wicked smirk quivered his lips.

"Touch yourself and let me watch."

"Ha!" I jerked my foot away. "In your dreams."

"In my dreams, I've already seen you do it all, Sparrow. You're all I've dreamed about ever since I first laid my eyes on you. Let me see you in real life now."

He shot out his arm, grabbed my ankle, and dragged my foot back to him. I gasped, propping both hands on the lily pad behind me to keep my balance.

"I bet you're as soaking wet as your clothes right now." His deep, low voice curled around me, coaxing. His gaze caressed me from my lips, down to my breasts, pausing on each nipple intently. "Soaking, drenched, and trembling with need. You need to come, little bird. And I want to see it happen."

I did need to come. Badly. The hot throbbing between my thighs grew so urgent, it spread through my entire body, making me shiver with need.

But I wanted more than just *my* touch. I needed Voron to be more than just a spectator. His stubborn refusal was only spurring my desire to break it.

I tipped my head, trailing the tips of my fingers along my collar bone.

"Why do you want to watch, Voron? Do you need more fuel for your wet dreams about me?"

He just grunted softly, his eyes following my hand closely, as if his life depended on it.

"Do you just *watch* me in your dreams, too?" I moved my hand down the swell of my right breast, then circled the nipple with my fingers, directing his gaze to it.

It was a dangerous game. The physical stimulation shot my desire up into a new gear. I risked getting desperate and losing control. But he was right there with me, too. Licking his lips, he flexed his fingers, his nails digging grooves in the glossy surface of the lily pad.

"Or do you touch me? At least in your dreams?"

I cupped my breast in my hand and squeezed it. The nipple peeked out between my fingers, and I pressed my fingers together, trapping the tightened bud. Heat surged through me, robbing me of breath. I released a strangled moan, my mind clouding with the overwhelming need for a release.

He stared at me with feral anticipation. Yanking my hand away, I balled it at my side. I couldn't let him win.

"Dammit, Voron. What do you do about *this* in your dreams?" I spread my legs open, presenting him with the view of my soaking wet underwear. "Do you just keep staring? Or do you fuck me so hard I forget the name you gave me?"

"Fuck," he gritted through his teeth, his look turning murderous.

His right hand clamped harder around my ankle. Grabbing my other leg with his left hand, he yanked me to him.

I lost my balance and fell on my back as his head ended up between my legs. Ravenous and unstoppable, he ripped through the flimsy material of my panties. His mouth landed on my sensitive flesh. I shivered with pleasure at the contact.

Finally.

His touch was punishing, almost angry, and at that moment, it was what I needed, what I craved.

I arched my back, pressing myself against his tongue. His teeth scraped against my clit, making me whimper, and he doubled his efforts at the sound. Digging his fingers into my skin, he gripped my thighs, sucking and lapping at me relentlessly.

I threw my arms aside, fully surrendering to him becoming undone. It was impossible to resist the hurricane of his unbridled passion. It swept me along, making my head spin and my body tremble.

Raising my hips, I pressed against his mouth, riding his tongue. He didn't stop, didn't even come up for air once, until I came. The orgasm rippled through every nerve in my body. My entire being seemed to dissolve on Voron's tongue, melting with pleasure.

I reached down to touch him and raked my fingers through his hair. He lifted his head. His lips glistened with my arousal. His eyes shined wildly—black, impossibly wide pupils, rimmed with only a thin ring of silver.

"Voron," I murmured, sitting up. "Come up here."

But he jerked away from me, as if I'd slapped him. Letting go of my thighs, he pushed off the lily pad with force. Cutting through the glassy surface of the pond, he swam back to shore in wide, powerful strokes.

My body was still quivering with the aftershocks of my climax. My limbs felt heavy, weighted down by the languid warmth of pleasure flowing through my muscles. I wanted to have him next to me. I longed to have his arms around me.

I'd won. He'd given in and touched me, but it didn't feel like a win. Despite being completely satisfied in one way, I felt robbed and bereft in another. I didn't just want sex, I realized, I needed his time and affection, too.

I felt like cursing, and I didn't hold back.

"What the fuck, Voron?" I yelled, watching him swimming away. "What do you want from me?"

The next morning, I woke up to the clopping of horse's hooves outside my window. Careful to stay out of sight, I drew the curtain aside and peeked out into the yard.

Voron was on horseback, riding toward the gate of the estate. Magnus soared above him. A few larger figures with wings flew ahead—Alcon and several others of Voron's trusted men.

He left Vensari without even saying goodbye.

At that moment I really hated him. Just as he wanted me to feel about him. Just what I should have felt for him all along.

Chapter Four

"Where is Alcon staying?" I asked Brebie at breakfast. By the time I got up, she'd already eaten. But I'd talked her into having tea with me while I ate my breakfast. I was so sick and tired of eating alone day after day.

Since we were no longer in Elaros, with its strict etiquette and expectations, the lines between us were blurred. I was hardly a lady, and Brebie had always been so much more than a servant. In a way, she was in charge of all of us here, even of Voron. He would never cross her on purpose.

She stirred a third spoonful of honey in her tiny cup of tea. "Staying? What do you mean by staying?"

"Well, Alcon used to practically live in Voron's rooms back in Elaros. And now, I don't see him at all. Except for this morning when he came to get Voron."

That was a long way around the one question I really wanted to ask. Where did Voron go, and how long would he be away?

"Alcon's estate isn't too far from here. About an hour or so to fly."

"I didn't know he had an estate."

"All of Voron's men are well off. Voron made sure of that."

"So, the queen didn't take their properties from them?"

She shook her head. "Voron took all the blame on himself, sparing them. Besides, the queen seems to be too busy to worry about your case at the moment."

"What is she so busy with?"

Brebie glanced around her shoulder, as if expecting to see a spy there—a habit she must've gained while living in Elaros. She then leaned closer, lowering her voice to the volume of gossip.

"The queen is not happy being married to a breathing corpse, which King Tiane is right now. I'm shocked she hadn't pulled that dagger out of his chest herself to send his spirit off and set herself free."

Brebie clearly was well informed about everything that had happened, even though she hadn't been present that night, and I hadn't spoken to her about what happened between the king and me. I doubted Voron would have told her. But the rumors must have been rampant in the palace while I was in the dungeon.

"Alcon arrived from Elaros this morning," she continued. "He said the queen has successfully petitioned both the Royal Council and the High Priest to declare King Tiane deceased."

"But he's not dead."

She shrugged. "His spirit is no longer in his body, and no one in the kingdom knows how to reunite the two. So, technically, he is very much gone, and Queen Pavline is already looking for a new king."

"Who will that be, you think?"

"The two favored candidates are rumored to be High Lord Caitore and High Lord Bussard. Though the queen hasn't confirmed her final choice yet."

"But how does Voron fit into the queen's love life? Where did Alcon take him?"

She huffed. "Love has nothing to do with royal marriages, honey. Both High Lords have a valid claim to the throne. They're also rivals and are on the verge of declaring war against each other.

The queen has been playing them both by giving each hope, which is keeping the peace in the kingdom for now. But there are a fair number of High Lords who oppose the two. A few have already united against them. So, there is an attack brewing from that direction, too."

"Highborn sure love to fight," I muttered.

"That's what they're good at." Brebie shook her head, "Poor things, they can do nothing else. Hunger for power consumes them."

"But what does Voron have to do with any of that?" I insisted. "He isn't a High Lord. He isn't even the High General anymore."

"But he's still a highborn. The queen might've stripped him of his position and possessions, but no one can take away his knowledge and expertise. He's won many wars for the king. And now, I suspect, the High Lords want him to do that for them."

"Which one of the High Lords is trying to recruit him?"

She smiled into her teacup. "All of them, I'm sure. The real question is which side he'll choose to support in all the mess that's coming."

Voron had been gone for ten days. Ten long, dragging days. As little as I'd seen of him before, it was even worse now. His absence rang through the walls of his house. The void of emptiness pressed on me acutely.

To occupy myself, I took up knitting. I'd been helping Brebie organize supplies in a storage room, and the moment I touched a piece of yarn, I felt the desire to do something with it. Just like with swimming before, there was a spark of confidence that I could do it.

My muscle memory kicked in. I formed a loop from the yarn, then threaded another through it, and another. Before long, I asked Brebie for a pair of knitting needles and some more yarn.

Then I started to knit a scarf between reading. I figured out a pattern that didn't make my scarf curl on the ends. It came out nice and thick but soft, even if a bit small.

"It's for a kid," I laughed, showing my work to Brebie.

"That's pretty good, Sparrow. Why don't we give it to the barber's family in the village? They have kids. Two of them."

"Who needs a scarf in this weather?" I smiled, flipping a thumb at the scorching hot day outside the window.

Brebie didn't return my smile, however. Her delicate features pinched into a worried expression.

"You never know what's coming, honey. With the current Sky King's bloodline ending and the new one not established yet, we may face years of turbulent weather ahead. Storms, blizzards, tornadoes... All of that may be coming."

The conversations about impending wars and storms made me set aside my light comfort reading and pick up a book about the most recent armed conflict. I chose the thinnest volume I could find to ease into the heavy subject. Still, I found the book dry and rather boring. It was a struggle to get through it without falling asleep, especially since I was reading it after lunch on a sweltering hot afternoon while reclining in the cushions piled up in the window seat in the library. Yet I persevered, even pinching myself awake once or twice.

The sound of hooves hitting the cobblestones of the yard around the corner reached me through the open window. It wasn't the rapid clicking of Brebie's hooves, but a much heavier thudding of a horse, carrying a rider.

I closed my book and pressed it to my chest, afraid to hope.

Was Voron coming home?

Of course, I wanted to know the news he might be bringing, about the war, the queen, and our future. But deep inside, I had to admit, I just missed him. I missed him so much, the feeling had gnawed a hole as big as this house inside me. I just needed to see his face again, even if it held a scowl.

The sound of hooves disappeared. I wondered if I should run

to the entrance hall. It would be polite to greet my host, wouldn't it? Maybe he'd missed me, too? At least a little bit? Enough to have dinner with me tonight and tell me all about his travels?

Before I had made up my mind, however, the door to the library burst open and Voron marched in. Still wearing a thin, long riding cloak with the dust of the road clinging to it, he looked weary and tense.

His eyes scanned the room, finding me. His chest fell with a long breath out and his shoulders dropped a little like the tension had drained from him.

A smile stretched across my face as I clutched my book to my chest.

"Hi. Welcome home."

"Home indeed." He sauntered my way, opening the closure of his cloak.

Dropping the cloak onto the chair by the fireplace, he came closer. I set the book down next to me and made a move to get up.

"Stay." He stopped me with a hand gesture. "You look too comfortable to disturb."

He tugged at the laces at the ruffled neckline of his white shirt, opening it up, then sat in the window seat next to me.

"How was your trip?" I asked.

He rubbed his chest.

"Good. Exhausting." He winced and finally confessed, "I hated it."

"Let's not talk about it, then."

His features relaxed. "Let's not."

He stretched his shoulders, looking like he was too tired even to sit up. Why did he not rest on the road? What was the rush to get back home?

I didn't want to make any assumptions, but since he was sitting here with me instead of having a meal, taking a bath, and going to bed, I believed his rushing might have something to do with the pull between us. I'd felt it from the day I met him, and it seemed he felt it, too. Even if he chose to fight it.

He leaned against the window frame. Exhaustion was etched into his handsome features. Yet he wouldn't leave.

"Do you want to lie down on the couch here?" I pointed at the sitting area by the fireplace.

"No." He turned with his back to me, then lay down right there in the window seat, putting his head into my lap. "I wish to stay right here." There was a challenge in his voice, like he was baiting me, expecting me to shove him off my lap.

But I didn't take the bait. Instead, I reveled in the chance to have him close, the chance I so rarely got.

"As you wish." I brushed his hair out of his face.

His ink-black hair, usually glossy, was a little matted today and more mussed than ever. He closed his eyes and breathed deeply as I combed through his hair with my fingers.

The sky was overcast, like usual, letting little sunlight through the window. For reading, I had several long candles lit in a large, floor standing candelabrum next to my seat. The candlelight broke through Voron's light locks in the front. And when I lifted the silvery strands, I could see my hand right through them.

An eerie feeling prickled down my spine. The images of the cursed impaled by the orders of King Tiane rose in my mind unbidden. Their bodies had been riddled with see-through patches. Some of their hair had turned transparent. Just like this.

"What does it mean, Voron? When the hair turns white, like yours?"

The peaceful expression slipped off his face, making me immediately regret my question.

"Not white. Transparent," he corrected softly.

He was right. It just looked white most of the time because of the way the light broke inside of each individual strand. And since the rest of his hair was so deeply black, the contrast was nearly as striking as between black and white.

"It's a sign of aging," he explained.

"Aging? But you aren't that old. For a fae."

Sky fae lived to be about five hundred years, I'd been told.

And they didn't start aging until only about the last decade of their lives. Voron was only one-hundred-and-eighty years old, not even half of his expected lifespan.

"Not old at all." He grinned. "I'm in my prime." He raked his hand through the hair over his forehead. "I've had these since I was ten."

"Ten? But you were just a boy."

Bending his legs, he placed his feet on the window seat to make himself more comfortable.

"Some say I was supposed to die that day. But really, I was supposed to die the day I was born. All my life has been borrowed time."

"Why do they say you were supposed to die?" I tilted my head to better see his face, and he raised his eyes to mine.

A gentle smile crossed his lips.

"Do you know why they call us highborn, Sparrow?"

"Because you are the noble caste? Because you reside above the rest? Or at least you put yourselves above the others." I laughed. "God knows, it'd be hard to find more arrogant people than some of the highborn I've met."

"No, Sparrow." He rolled his head in my lap. "The name for my kind is far more literal than that. We're born in the sky, little bird, high above the clouds."

"How?"

He rested his hands over his middle, lacing his fingers together.

"While giving birth, the mother flies over the Cloud River that connects the many islands of the Sky Kingdom. When the baby is born, it opens its wings as it takes its first breath. The baby flies, until the mother or someone else from her birthing party catches it."

I flinched at the picture created by his words in my mind. "It sounds dangerous."

He shrugged. "If everyone has wings, it's no more dangerous than giving birth on the ground."

"But what if not everyone has them? What if a baby is born without wings?"

"Then, the baby falls."

Chills trickled down my back. My fingers stilled in his hair.

"Falls where?"

"Through the Cloud River and down to the Below."

"How can anyone survive a fall like that?"

"They don't. Those born without wings die."

"No... That's barbaric. And cruel. Criminal." My heart just refused to accept or even comprehend something like that. "How long have people been doing this?"

"Since the beginning of time."

"But they say fae babies are so rare. They're treasured and loved. How could they get rid of them so cruelly? Just because they lack wings?"

He lifted a hand to my face and stroked my cheek with the back of his fingers. "Shhh, little bird. I didn't mean to upset you. A birth like mine doesn't happen very often."

"But if it does happen, it's not survivable. That's why there are no highborn alive that can't fly. Except for you."

"Except for me," he echoed.

Voron might not be as unique as I had thought. But his survival absolutely was.

"What happened, Voron? How did you live?"

He frowned.

"That I don't know. Either my mother gave birth on the ground, which is excruciatingly painful for highborn women and against tradition. Moving their wings alleviates the pain of child-birth. Or she or someone else caught me, not letting me fall."

"Your mother didn't tell you?"

"She never spoke about it. And while she was alive, I was too young to ask those questions. We lived here, in this house, with no stairs or upper floors. My mother and I were the only highborn in Vensari. I never felt like I was different. She never opened her wings in my presence. I don't even know what they looked like."

A wistful expression crossed his face. He rotated the slim silver ring around his left little finger. I always found that ring too small and delicate for him, but he never took it off.

"Was the ring hers?" I tipped my chin at his hand.

"Yes." He cleared his throat. "That's all I have left from her—the ring and this house."

That's all he had left. Period. He'd lost everything else because of me. But I didn't bring it up and didn't apologize. I didn't want to spoil this moment. Voron was telling me about his past, and I wished to listen.

"What was your mother's name?"

"Mulena." His voice remained even when he said it. It had been a hundred-and-seventy years since her passing—enough time for him to come to terms with his loss, or at least to learn to hide the pain of it.

"How did she die?" I asked softly.

He turned his head toward the window. "Royal guards came for her one fine morning. I was scared. But she told me to stay strong. She begged me to remember her." His throat bobbed with a swallow. "That was the last time I saw her. They told me she was accused of treason and executed."

I cradled his face in my hands. "I'm so sorry, Voron."

He covered my hand with his, silently accepting my sympathy.

"I always believed her 'treason' had something to do with me. There is no law against harboring wingless children, but only because there had been no need to have it before me. No one had kept a wingless baby before."

I drew in a shaky breath, and he took my hand in his, resting both on his chest.

"Please don't think about my people as heartless creatures, Sparrow. The birth of a wingless child is so rare, no one expects it. When it does happen, it happens quickly. People simply don't have a chance to react before it's too late."

"Yet here you are. *You* were saved somehow."

"My case must be a lucky accident," he said, then added with a humorless smile, "or an *unlucky* one, depending on one's point of view."

"Is there absolutely no one who could tell you what happened? Someone must know how you survived."

"Not *someone,* but *something*. And it's right here, in this house."

Chapter Five

SPARROW

I couldn't believe my ears.

"You have a record of your birth, Voron? Like a witness statement? What is it? A letter?"

He shifted on the window seat, turning his head in my lap to see my face.

"It's a book, Sparrow. Many houses of highborn keep family records. The records of the royal family are accessible to the public. Mine, however, are warded so no one can read them."

"Why the secrecy?"

He shrugged. "It happened before I can remember."

"If someone didn't want people to know what happened, why not just burn the book?"

"A family chronicle cannot be destroyed until the last of the bloodline dies, which is me. For as long as I live, the book is going to be where it is, in the room behind the fireplace here in the library of Vensari."

"Can I see it?"

"You can look, but you can't touch or read it. No one can.

The wards are impenetrable and hurt if you try to touch the book." He winced. "That's why it's stored out of sight."

I would love to take a look at the relic, even if from a distance. But Voron held my hand in his, his head was in my lap, we were having a conversation, he was finally opening up to me. There was nothing in this world that would make me move or leave him right now.

"What happened to you after your mother was taken?" I asked instead. "Who took care of you?"

He huffed a laugh without any mirth. "Magnus did. And a few soft-hearted gargoyles who shared my deficiency and couldn't fly."

"Gargoyles?"

"Mhmm. From the Dakath Kingdom in the Below," he explained. "King Herane, King Tiane's father, ruled that I didn't belong to Sky Kingdom. That since I was supposed to fall to the Below at birth, I should be there. Tossing me off the banks of the Cloud River at that point would've been a murder, according to both the law and tradition. So, he ordered the guards to fly me down and leave me in the Dakath Mountains."

"Alone? At ten years of age?" I gasped in horror.

He squeezed my hand gently.

"Not all was bad there. I met Magnus. He'd bring me acorns and buttons, but also an occasional coin sometimes. All he ever asked for in return was a pat on the head or a rub on the side of his neck. He loves that. Then, a group of wingless gargoyles found me. I grew up among them, viewing them as strong and capable. As part of their group, I also never thought the lack of wings was an impediment. It was only when we happened to go to the market for supplies or to a tavern for a drink when I learned what other people thought of us. Without wings, I was 'less than' either down in the Below or up here in Sky Kingdom." His grip on my hand tightened. "At some point, I decided if I were supposed to be an outcast all my life, I might as well be an outcast in the place where I came from. So, I returned here."

"How did you get back?"

His chest vibrated with an unexpected chuckle. "I traded a favor with the King of Dakath, and he personally flew me up to Sky Kingdom one fine afternoon."

"The king did that?"

That was so like Voron, though. He'd been kicked out of the kingdom and left to die. But he rose, higher than ever, and even got a royal escort to boot.

"He did." He smiled at the memory, but his smile didn't last long. "I had nothing when I got back here. No money, no power, no friends, not even a single person who cared to remember me. No one was waiting for me. But I had to start somewhere."

"What did you do?"

"A war was going on. King Herane was dead already. His son took the throne. But his cousin contested the succession with some powerful allies on his side. King Tiane needed highborn to fight for him. I joined his army as a foot soldier, literally, since all I could do was march on foot while the rest of them flew. I was put in charge of transporting supplies from camp to camp. It became clear early on, that was all they ever wanted me to do. I saw no advancement, no opportunities to ever move anywhere higher than where they wanted me to be—on the ground."

"How did you make it to the rank of the High General, then?"

He raised an eyebrow, flicking a sly glance my way.

"Not having wings actually helped me with that. Once, when left behind, I ran into a group of lords from the enemy side and overheard them talk about capturing King Tiane."

"Oh, did you warn the king to earn his favor?"

"No." His smile turned wicked. "I took Alcon and three other trusted men, and we waited near the area where they planned to kidnap the king. Then, we fought off the attack when it happened. The king never learned it was just a kidnapping plot. I convinced him it was an assassination attempt."

"Why?"

"Because being saved from what he thought was an imminent death left a far more lasting impression on the king than escaping a kidnapping would have. As soon as he recovered from terror, he offered me anything I desired."

"And you asked for the position of the High General?"

"No," he chuckled. "I highly doubt the king would've given it to me at that point, not without a strong opposition from everyone in his army. But I also didn't just need the position. I needed to become indispensable, irreplaceable, someone who was powerful regardless of the position he held."

"What did you ask him for, then?"

"A year of opportunities. I asked the king to give me a year with no obstacles, with no one holding me back. For twelve months, I was allowed to be a part of every military campaign. I participated in strategy meetings. I planned the logistics, not just moved the supply wagons around. I had a high platform constructed specifically for me, from where I could observe the battle being on the same level as the commanders who had wings. Within that year, I moved up two ranks."

"Just two?" I teased.

He laced his fingers with mine on his chest. "Just two, little bird. But within the next decade, I made it to the High General. By then, I had earned it, with a proven record of winning battles, making smart decisions, and commanding the respect of men and women in the army."

"That's why all those High Lords want you on their side now, even without you having any rank or titles."

He focused his gaze on me. "Who told you that?"

"Brebie."

"And how does she know?" he asked, then waved his hand before I could answer. "Never mind. It's impossible to hide anything from that woman."

"She wouldn't have talked about it if you told her not to."

"I know. Brebie can be trusted, despite her love for gossip. That's why I keep her around."

"So, what's happening now?"

"Now?" he asked slowly and with some added meaning.

I was about to clarify my question, to ask which of the High Lords he chose to support. But my hand was splayed flat against his chest. With his hand on top of it, Voron moved it into the opening of his shirt. My palm connected with his bare skin. I flexed my fingers, lightly scraping him with my nails.

"Now..." he exhaled, closing his eyes briefly, like a cat enjoying a warm day.

He turned his head, pressing his face into my lower stomach, and wrapped the arm around my hips, bringing me closer.

"Now, little bird, you're going to kick me off this seat." His voice was muffled by my dress. His breath seeped through the material, warming my skin just below my belly button.

With his hands propped on the seat, he rose over my lap in one determined movement.

"You'll pick up your book and slap me with it, Sparrow. Then, you'll yell at me to keep my hands to myself."

He slid one hand up my side, gently squeezing my breast on the way up to my neck.

"You'll have to save me," he rasped. "Because I don't know how long I can last on my own." He caressed the side of my face, sliding his thumb over my lower lip. "You're the first war I fear I'm not going to win. With you, I've been losing each and every battle."

He fitted his knee between my legs, hovering over me as I sank back into the cushions.

"Help me, Sparrow," he pleaded. "Stop me."

I lifted the book he'd implored me to hit him with and held it between us. The focus in his eyes sharpened as he flicked them between the book and my face. Waiting.

Slowly, to make a point, I moved my arm aside and opened my hand, dropping the book to the floor.

Voron was so badly mistaken. I wasn't the one to save him. I couldn't stop it. I was already falling myself. Rapidly.

"Cruel, cruel little bird," he groaned and dropped his head, burying his face between my breasts.

He yanked at the laces of my bodice, untying them.

"So be it." He pulled the fabric aside, exposing my right breast. "Gods know, I've wanted so long to do this..." He kissed the top of my breast, gently at first, then with ever-growing passion as he moved down and finally sucked in my nipple.

I couldn't focus on any one physical sensation. My entire body was alight. My mind was still reeling that Voron was here, with me, touching me and letting me touch him back.

Tenderness overtook me. Sinking my fingers into his hair, I wanted to lift him higher up my body, to nuzzle his hair, to kiss his lips, to look into his eyes. But he slipped out of my hold, shifting down.

He found the hem of my skirt, then slid his hands up my bare legs, lifting my skirt up to my waist.

"Let me look at you again," he groaned softly, sliding my underwear down my legs.

His attention filled me with warm excitement. He kissed the inside of my thigh, gently and ever so slowly trailing his kisses up to my core.

This was different from him practically devouring me on the lily pad ten days ago. I'd dreamed about that day while he was away. But I refused to touch myself in his absence. I wanted *his* hands on me, not mine.

Now, every nerve in my body sprang to life. The heat of intense arousal throbbed between my legs, spurred by the glide of his fingers.

He spread me open, admiring the view for a moment before dipping his tongue inside me. Slowly, languidly, he swirled it around. Exploring. Savoring.

I tried to slow down and match his rhythm, but I needed more way too quickly.

"Voron..." I whimpered, bucking my hips. "Please."

To my horror, he withdrew completely. His eyes glistened

wickedly as he looked at me from under the silvery strands hanging over his forehead.

"You want to come, little bird?"

"Yes. Don't stop. Please." I rose on my elbows, flashing a glare at him. "I swear, if you stop right now. I—"

He slowly slid a finger where his tongue had just been. "You, what? What will you do, my sweet little Sparrow?"

My inner muscles tingled and clenched around his finger as he slowly pumped it in and out of me. Too slowly, too gently for me at this point, and he knew it. His evil smirk told me he did it on purpose.

"You want to fuck me," I taunted. "Admit it. You're as hard as rock right now, Voron. You're dying to slam your dick inside me. But you're hating yourself for wanting me. And you're punishing me for not pushing you away. Is that it?"

His expression darkened as I spoke. The smirk disappeared. His brows shifted together, creasing his forehead. His mouth pressed into a hard line as he slipped two fingers in, pumping harder.

I wasn't going to let it go. "Admit it—"

His thumb pressed on my clit that was hot and swollen from the earlier caress of his mouth. The words stuck in my mouth. The phrase I was going to say fluttered out of my brain as the intense pleasure filled me.

I hated how easily he shut me up. How needy I was for his touch, surrendering instantly to the incredible sensations it caused. I hated letting him off the hook. But I loved, *loved* the orgasm he finally let me have.

Tossing my head back, I moaned and gasped as the intense pleasure rippled through me with bliss. My hips jerked, my breasts trembled with the aftershocks rocking my entire body.

"Just like that, my little bird," Voron murmured, milking the pleasure for me with his thumb and his finger. "Feel it all. Feel it for both of us."

There was no cruelty in his voice, just tenderness with a tendril of wistful sadness.

I lay spread over the window seat, my dress undone with my breasts spilling out, my skirt hiked up, my legs spread, and my inner muscles quivering, when he removed his hands from me and got up.

Silently, he walked to the exit from the library, stepping softly on the thick blue rug.

I couldn't let him leave. Not like that. Not again. I was sick and tired of watching his back as he left me time after time.

"Wait." I scrambled up from the window seat and rushed after him. "Please wait, Voron."

I caught up with him at the door.

"Don't go." I threw my arms around him from behind.

"Sparrow—" he growled with warning.

But I tightened my arms around his middle, pressing myself to him.

"Stay."

The side of my face pressed to his back below his shoulder blades. His heart thundered in my ear, loud and fast.

He was so much taller than me. Stronger. He could have easily freed himself from my embrace, but all he did was grip the door frame on each side of us.

"This is not a war, Voron. There are no battles. You and I are on the same side."

I rolled my head on his back, pressing my forehead to him. I so rarely got to hug him. It didn't even matter that he wouldn't look at me right now, wouldn't even turn around to face me.

I slid a hand down his front. Covered only by the thin silk of his shirt, the hard grid of his abs rippled and flexed under my touch. Reaching the waistband of his pants, I slipped just the tip of one finger under it.

"May I?" I half-whispered, bracing for his rejection.

His entire body trembled as he took in a long breath.

"Please, Voron," I begged, gently sliding my finger across his hard stomach under the waistband. "Please, let me."

He didn't say a word. The only sound was the creak of the door frame as he flexed his grip on it when I tugged on the lacing of his pants, loosening it enough to shove his pants down his hips a little.

Standing behind him, I couldn't see what I was doing, acting blindly. I slid a hand inside his pants and closed my eyes, letting my other senses guide me.

He strained toward my hand. Hot and hard, his erection practically sprang into my hand, eager and ready.

He hissed at the contact, jerking his hips away from me as if I'd burned him. The next moment, however, he was thrusting into my hand.

I prayed I was doing this right. Unlike with swimming or knitting, I couldn't tell with any confidence whether I'd done something like this before with any other man. But I'd never touched *Voron* this way. And that alone already made this unique and special.

He released a strangled groan. The sound could come either from pleasure or pain. With Voron, both appeared to blend often. The door frame cracked, the vines holding it creaked, whining at being dislodged. He jerked, thrusting frantically into my hand.

It didn't take long, just a few hard, desperate pumps, before the hot spurts of his release hit my skin.

I relaxed my hand a little, stroking along his entire length from the thick bulbous head down to the taut sack at the base of his shaft.

He trembled in my arms, his climax resonating through me. Pleasure spread warmly in my chest. I loved it, loved making him feel the ecstasy he'd given me before. Only unlike him, I wasn't going to run away. I was right there, hugging and stroking him down from his high.

I kissed along his spine through his shirt and murmured, "Was it good for you, darling?"

He seemed to have enjoyed it, but I felt a little insecure about my skills and needed some reassurance. Also, I just wanted to hear his voice. He stood with his back to me, and I longed to see his face.

From the corner of my eye, a shimmer caught my attention. I leaned back to see it better. A thin line of bright blue light appeared through the shirt on his back. I'd seen this before, back in Elaros.

I pressed a finger to the fabric over the light.

"Voron, are you feeling this?"

Reaching up, I slid the shirt off his shoulder. A wing design was etched into his skin in raised shimmering lines, like a glowing tattoo inked over scars.

"It's wings, Voron! They're glowing on your back. Are you getting wings?"

"It's nothing but a picture. A birthmark."

Voron unclenched his fingers from the ruined door frame and rolled back a shoulder, shrugging my hand off.

I gripped his arm, trying to turn him to me. "But it's lit. It shimmers with magic."

He barely turned his head, speaking over his shoulder.

"It shimmers with lust, not magic," he scoffed. "It's been happening lately when I'm aroused."

"But Voron—"

He whipped around, yanking his shirt back in place.

"Don't, Sparrow. It'll never be anything but empty hope."

A servant's hooves sounded in the distance down the hallway as we stood in the open doorway to the library.

Tucking himself in, Voron stumbled down the corridor. He didn't look back at me, not once.

Again, I was left staring at his back as he walked away. The silver-blue lights on his back formed a complete outline of folded wings. Then, they flickered and died under his shirt.

# Chapter Six

SPARROW

It took me a long time to fall asleep that night. I tossed and turned, kicking the sheets off, then pulling them back up to my ears.

The events of that day haunted me. The moment I closed my eyes, the images of Voron rose in my mind. The phantom sensations of his hard length in my hands and of his tongue between my legs sent shivers of pleasure through my body, but my mind remained troubled by it all.

I didn't regret not returning to the human world. I just wished I understood the fae world better. More than anything, I longed to understand the man who was quickly becoming the entire world to me.

It rained that night. A real deluge with a storm. But I felt too lazy to get up and close the window in my bedroom. Eventually, I drifted asleep to the splashing sound of raindrops hitting the windowsill.

A deafening explosion of thunder woke me up. Then, the door to my bedroom creaked open. Groggy with sleep, I peeled my eyes open just as Voron sneaked into my room and quietly closed the door behind him.

"Voron?" I rubbed my eyes, utterly confused. "What are you doing here?"

He climbed onto my bed as if it was his own but stayed on top of the sheet I used for cover. It was so hot, even one thin sheet felt too much.

"Why don't you lock your door?" He sounded grumpy, as if it was *my* fault that he ended up in my bed.

"Why don't you stay on the other side of it, whether it's locked or not?" I snapped.

"I wish I could."

Wrapping me in the top sheet, he rolled me to him, then tossed his arm and a leg over me as if I were his body pillow.

"What the—" I tried to protest against being swaddled like that and even managed to free my arms from the sheet.

"Shhh." He disarmed me with a gentle kiss in my hair. "Let me stay. Please. Just for tonight."

He inhaled deeply, tucking me into his chest. His body relaxed against mine, his breathing evened out, as if all he needed to find peace in life was to have me next to him.

"Did you have a bad dream or something?" I asked, with my nose pressed to his naked chest. All he was wearing was a pair of thin linen pants.

"Something like that..."

His breathing deepened. He seemed asleep before I even could come up with another question.

When I woke up the next morning, Voron was gone. His scent still lingered on my pillow, mingling with the fresh after-rain air from the outside. But he was no longer in my bed. If it wasn't for his scent and the dent in the pillow formed by his head, I could've believed his coming to my room last night was nothing but a dream.

"Voron went for a ride with Alcon," Brebie informed me at breakfast.

He'd just come home after a grueling ten-day horseback trip that by his own admission, he didn't enjoy. And he'd left again, already?

"A ride where?" I asked.

"Just around the estate." She twirled her hand in the air vaguely.

"When will they be back?"

"He wasn't sure. Probably after dinner, unless they decide to spend the night in the village. Oh." Her voice lifted like it always did before delivering something she considered good news. "They took the scarf you made to give it to the barber's kids. I told him to get you some more yarn, too."

"Thanks."

I couldn't help the feeling that Voron was running from me. He'd searched out my company on a stormy night, but he was going to all lengths to avoid facing me in the daylight. Something kept him coming to me, over and over. But he fought it every time.

Maybe he was right, and it *was* a war he was waging. Only I wasn't sure who or what his enemy was, because it certainly wasn't me. I'd told him we were on the same side.

He'd opened up to me yesterday, more than he'd ever done before. He'd told me about his childhood, including all the bitter, tragic parts of it.

I tried to imagine what it must've been like for him as a ten-year-old child to be abandoned by the entire kingdom. His mother was taken away from him, and no one else cared about him enough to stop the cruel king from dumping the innocent boy in a land he'd never been to before.

But every time, he survived. Against all odds.

Voron thought of his life as borrowed time, believing he was meant to die at the very beginning. But didn't everything he'd gone through mean his fate was to *live?* The birth didn't kill him. People failed to get rid of him. Not only did he survive, he thrived, finding power and success.

Many questions remained about Voron. But not all of them he could answer.

I had lunch on my own, then went for a walk and swam in the pond.

Voron and Alcon didn't return before dinner, and I ate on my own again as even Brebie happened to be occupied elsewhere that night.

After dinner, I went back to the library and tried to read a little, but my attention wavered. With my mind crowded with so many thoughts and questions, I found it difficult to focus. After reading the same paragraph five times and still not getting the meaning of what it said, I closed my book and left it on the window seat.

Too restless to knit, too, I aimlessly paced the library for a while. Pausing in front of the fireplace, I remembered what Voron told me about the book in the hidden room behind it.

Coming closer, I examined the panels on each side of the fireplace and found the outline of the door on the right. It wasn't locked. When I pushed on it, it gave in with a slight creak.

Remembering what Voron told me about the wards guarding the book, I didn't rush in. Keeping the door open just a crack, I peeked in cautiously, ready to jump back at the slightest threat of pain.

It was dark inside, with only a faint bluish-white glow filtering through. Nothing had hurt me yet, so I carefully opened the door just a little bit wider.

The walls of the windowless room behind the door were of solid black stone with no crystals in them. The space was illuminated by a single column of pale blue light that stretched from the floor to the ceiling right in the middle of the room.

Inside the light column, at my chest level, a massive book

hovered suspended by nothing. It was bound in leather of the same pale blue color as the ray of light that held it. Its corners were enclosed in silver, and its spine was set with gemstones.

There was no text anywhere, neither on the front nor on the spine. I was hoping the book would be open at least to the title page, but it was closed. Two ornate clasps of bejeweled silver held its yellowed pages together.

Crossing the threshold, I came a little closer to the book. The air was stale and permeated with scents of leather and old mortar. I slowly walked around the glowing column that looked like a beam of moonlight, except that there was no window here for the moon to peek in.

A single moth fluttered at the edge of the glow, its wings shimmered with the reflected light of the magic that protected the book.

"Shoo." I waved at it, worried that it would get scorched if it came any closer. The moth swerved to the side, evading my hand. Drawn by the light, however, it turned around and flew right in.

"Careful, dummy," I whispered, bracing for the poor insect to go up in blue flames or be ripped apart by lightning, or whatever other horrible things the magic wards were supposed to do to those violating their boundaries. But nothing happened.

The moth landed on one of the book's glistening silver corners, then flew up again, unstoppable in its search for the source of light.

"Hmm, it doesn't hurt you, then?" I tilted my head, watching the moth closely.

Maybe Voron was mistaken about the wards. Maybe they weren't as bad as he thought, or their magic had worn out with time. Did those things have an expiration date?

Carefully, ever so carefully, I extended a finger toward the light. If the magic wards were there, what would they feel like? A zap of electricity? A punch in the chest? I didn't remember personally experiencing either, but I knew both were unpleasant.

Biting my lip, I quickly poked through the glow with the very tip of my finger, then jumped back before any sensation came. I waited for the pain to register, but my finger felt fine. It didn't look scorched or bruised either.

How did the wards work exactly? I doubted their effect would cause a delayed reaction. That defeated the purpose of keeping the book safe. The way I understood it, they were supposed to prevent me from taking the book, not to punish me for it later.

Halting my breath, I plunged my hand into the light and yanked the book out. There was no resistance other than the weight of the book. It slipped out so easily, I slammed myself in the chest with it and staggered backwards, nearly falling on my butt. Other than the impact of the book's sharp, silver-tipped corners digging into my boobs, there was no pain, either.

I glanced at the book in my hands, then at the empty column of bluish light, expecting something horrible to happen any minute now.

But the walls didn't crumble, and the ceiling didn't collapse. Neither were there any giant stone balls rolling my way.

Moving carefully, just in case, I backed to the door slowly, then got out of the room and promptly closed the door in the panel.

The book proved heavy and even bigger than it looked when suspended in the light. Pressing it with both arms to my chest, I took it to my room, then closed the door firmly behind me.

My heart beat frantically. I hadn't planned on taking the book. Now that I'd taken it, would it look like I stole it?

I wished Voron was home, so I could tell him I had it. The easiest thing would be to bring the book back. But since I already had it, maybe I could at least look inside first?

I dropped the book on the low table by my unlit fireplace and sat in the armchair next to it.

It didn't feel right to learn Voron's family secrets behind his back. I really wished he were here with me.

But he wasn't. He was taking a trip around the countryside,

rather than spending any more time than was absolutely necessary under the same roof as me.

Reaching over, I unlocked the clasps, then tentatively lifted the front cover. The next page was blank, no title text, no introduction, nothing. I flipped it, finding nothing on the next page either. And the next one, and the next. The book of what seemed like hundreds and hundreds of pages was completely blank inside.

Leaving it open, I slumped in my chair.

"Is it a joke?"

It made no sense whatsoever.

Suddenly, a pale glow lifted from the yellowed pages. Thin tendrils of bluish light rose higher, curling above the book into letters.

"Recorded history of Elaros, the royal Sky Palace."

"Elaros? Isn't it supposed to be Vensari?" I muttered.

The light shifted, the silver-blue lines uncoiled from the shape of the letters and re-curled into a series of different images.

First, I saw a cloaked horseman approach a gate. He was holding something under his cloak. The images were so detailed, I quickly recognized Voron as the horseman and myself as the short, curvy shape in his arms. I was dressed in a long black shirt, a little too tight around my hips, considerably too long in the sleeves and overall. It was Voron's black shirt that he'd put on me when I was about to jump into the River of Mists.

The book was recreating the night when I first arrived in Vensari.

Alcon flew into the image.

"Brebie is here," he reported to Voron. "I brought her from Elaros, as you requested, my general."

Voron dismounted from his horse, taking me with him, and marched up to the front entrance of his family home.

Brebie met him in his bedroom, finishing putting sheets on the bed.

"Sparrow will stay here." Voron headed for the bed.

"Oh gods!" Brebie gasped at the sight of me. She promptly spread a dark blanket over the luxurious bedspread.

"I want a hag," he ordered, not laying me down. "Healers. Priests."

Brebie ran an assessing look over my body.

"She doesn't need a priest or a hag, my lord. She hasn't been cursed or bewitched. All she needs is a nice bath, some rest, and good food."

For once, Voron looked lost. Clutching me to his chest, he lingered by the bed.

"Put her down, my lord," Brebie instructed. "Let go of her. She'll be fine. She's more likely to suffocate in your arms, the way you're squeezing her."

He let her lead him to the side of the bed, then set me gently on the covers.

"I'm so sorry, little bird. It's all my fault. All of it," he said softly, dropping his head between his shoulders.

"Oh, stop it." Brebie waved a hand. "There is no point in blaming anyone. Let's just focus on making her feel better now. Come, help me undress her. I have to wash all that dungeon grime off the poor thing."

She fetched a large bowl of warm water from the bathroom. Together with Voron, they got me out of my clothes, then she rinsed my hair and expertly cleaned my body with a fluffy washcloth.

All that time, she also had to deal with Voron, who acted uncharacteristically unsettled. He paced around, raking his hands through his hair, or tried to help her but mostly just got in the way.

By the time a servant brought a tray with tea for me, Brebie had had enough of Voron and his "assistance."

"I'll settle Sparrow for the night, my lord. Why don't you retire to bed, too, now. I made the corner bedroom in the south wing ready for Sparrow. But since she's staying here, you can sleep there."

"I'm staying here." He kept pacing in front of the bed.

Too distracted by his thoughts, he almost bumped into Brebie on *her way to the bathroom to dump my bath water out. She shook her head with an annoyed eye roll.*

"Really. Sparrow will be fine on her own, and I'll check on her first thing in the morning. You should go get some rest."

"I'm staying here," he repeated stubbornly, then plopped into the chair next to the bed, the same chair where I found him when I woke up about a day and a half later.

"Suit yourself," Brebie blew out an exasperated breath.

"Can you get Alcon in here?" he asked as she opened the door. "I have to deal with the queen before she sends an army to search for me. No one can know Sparrow is here."

Voron had stayed up, worried about me and watching over me.

"It's all my fault." There had been so much regret in those words of his.

He felt guilty and responsible for me in some ways, but there was more than that in his voice. Whether he liked it or not, Voron had grown to care about me.

I reached for the image of him over the page. The silver light broke into shimmering dust under my fingers. It swirled around my hand before settling back into the open pages of the book.

The urge to turn the page for more images nagged at me, but I closed it and locked the clasps.

It was late into the night now. But more importantly, the main content of the records was about Voron and his family. It didn't feel right for me to snoop behind his back and learn things he might not even know himself. The right thing to do would be to let him know I had the book. Then maybe he would let me read it with him.

I got up from the chair and stretched. After unlacing my dress, I got out of my clothes, then changed into a long, light nightshirt.

The night was hot. The reprieve from the storm the night prior didn't last long. The dark clouds churned ominously in the sky, blocking the stars. The moon was but a pale patch of light barely visible behind them.

I used the bathroom and was brushing my hair, ready to go to bed when the approaching stomping of boots sounded in the corridor behind my door. I paused with the brush in my hand.

The door to my room suddenly swung open, and Voron barged in. My heart flipped from both excitement and worry.

"What's going on?" I dropped the hairbrush back on the vanity table. "Why are you here?"

My breath hitched at the sight of him. I hadn't heard him return, probably because I was in the bathroom when he arrived to Vensari.

Now, there he was, his riding cloak gone already. His boots were splattered with mud from the road. His black shirt undone on his chest that rose and fell with his rapid breathing.

He groaned, taking me in as I stood by the window wearing nothing but my transparent nightshirt. Closing the door, he leaned with his back against it.

"You really, really need to lock your door, Sparrow."

"Why?"

"To keep me out, if nothing else." He ran his hand through his hair that was in a worse disarray than ever.

He really looked like a man at war. At war with himself.

I shook my head.

"I'm not going to fight this battle for you, Voron. I like you. I enjoy being with you. I don't belong to anyone anymore but myself. And I want you to have me. But that's a decision you'll have to make on your own."

He peeled his back off from the door and stalked toward me.

"I already have."

Chapter Seven

SPARROW

Voron licked his lips on his way to me. He tugged his shirt out of the waistband of his pants, then ripped it off over his head.

I sucked in a breath as he took my face between his hands.

"Voron..." I searched his eyes. They were dark and filled with determination.

Lowering his head, he touched my lips with his. There was passion in his touch, almost bordering on desperation, but no hesitation. He no longer fought it, kissing me thoroughly and without haste.

My heart raced. My stomach fluttered with butterflies the size of crows. I splayed my hands on his chest. He was shirtless now, all mine to touch, and he didn't pull away.

With a moan against my mouth, he walked me backwards until my back hit a post of my bed.

"My Sparrow. All mine," he murmured, kissing my face, then my neck, and down along my collarbone. "For the entire night."

"Or longer," I added, threading my fingers through his hair.

He looked up at me, and I met his gaze with a smile. His

expression remained serious, however, as if he was on a mission, not simply about to get in bed with me. He didn't reply, just took me into his arms and laid me on the bed. He kissed the dip between my collarbones. Tenderly. So sweetly, my throat tightened.

He patiently unbuttoned the tiny silver buttons down the neckline of my nightshirt, then just ripped the flimsy material all the way down to my belly button.

"Hey, I liked this shirt," I exhaled breathily.

He shook his head with a lopsided smirk.

"It hid *this* from me." He threw the sides of my shirt open, exposing my naked body. His eyes flashed with heat. He cupped the underside of my breast. "Gods, Sparrow, do you have any idea how amazing you are?"

I just smiled in response. Voron always made me feel *amazing* about myself. When he looked at me like that, with eyes full of longing and hunger, I felt like the most desirable, the most beautiful woman in the world, no matter what anyone else said or what I might think when scrutinizing myself in the mirror.

Propped on an elbow above me, he gently massaged my breast, rolling the nipple under his thumb.

"I'll keep you awake all night, little bird. Please don't hold it against me."

"It depends." I gasped softly, his touch zapping through me with desire.

"On what?"

I shrugged a shoulder with a teasing grin. "On what you're planning to do with me all night."

"How about this?" He lowered his head and kissed the tip of my other breast. My nipple hardened between his lips. He sucked it into his mouth, grazing it with his teeth.

Heat surged through me, pressing with need between my thighs. I drew in a sharp breath and released it with a long moan as he continued to play with my breasts. He thrust his hips against my thigh, and I felt how impossibly hard he already was.

I reached down for the laces of his pants. "Let me take that thing out before it rips through your clothes."

"Sparrow, sweetheart, you have no idea how long I've been in this state."

He shifted up a little to allow me to untie the lacing.

"You want me so?" I teased, shoving his pants down his trim hips.

"Constantly," he moaned between the kisses on the side of my neck. "I don't remember the last time I fell asleep without pleasuring myself first. Because the moment I close my eyes, you're always there. I can't rest. I can't sleep. And now that I have you here, in my home, I can't even pretend I wish to stay away..."

He slipped a hand between my legs and growled softly at finding me soaking wet already.

"You want me, too, don't you, little bird? I've seen how you look at me. You can't hide your emotions to save your life. And lust is especially hard to hide. Believe me, I know." He caressed ever so gently between my folds, spreading my arousal. "Tell me you touch yourself while thinking about me?"

I hadn't, not yet. I'd resisted doing it so far because I knew whatever relief I'd get wouldn't be the same as him touching me.

"I wanted to, Voron. Many times. But I need your touch more than mine." I breathed out a moan as he pressed just a little harder. "Oh, yes... I want you. I've wanted you for so long. Since the day of that silly inspection you conducted of me."

He smirked smugly.

"I knew I heard some rather interesting sounds from you, then."

"Interesting?" I struggled to breathe under the swells of pleasure rolling through me from under his dexterous fingers.

"Your sweet whimpers and tiny moans, my little bird. They have been haunting me ever since that day. Let me hear them again."

He slipped a finger inside me, running it along my inner walls in circles. I arched my back, taking it deeper.

He chuckled at my eagerness. "Slow down, my sweet Sparrow. Let me make it last."

Taking his sweet time, he played my body, strumming every nerve with desire. I writhed under him as he kissed my breasts and sucked on my nipples while his deft fingers danced inside me.

Ripples of pleasure ran through me, but none of them was strong enough to bring on the release I craved.

Every now and then, he'd press his thumb where I needed him most, zapping me with ecstasy. But he'd ease the pressure quickly, letting me squirm in desperate need once again.

"Please, Voron, please..." I pressed my legs together, trapping his hand between them. Arching my back, I rubbed my thighs against each other, gyrating against his hand in desperation. But he stopped moving his fingers, depriving me of the little stimulation I had. "Oh, you're a mean, cruel man," I groaned, letting my legs drop to the sides and freeing his hand. "Do you always have to be in control?"

"When it comes to you, sweetheart, I've lost my control long ago," he growled. Taking his engorged length in his hand, he fitted himself between my legs. "I've lost my fucking mind."

He drove into me in one long, punishing thrust.

I mewled, shifting up the mattress to escape the pressure of his massive cock invading me. The stretch was intense, overpowering the tingling need for a moment.

"Is this what you want, little bird?" he gritted through his teeth.

I exhaled as my body adjusted and eased around his.

"Yes." I gripped his shoulders as he pulled back a little, only to push right back in again. "Oh, yes..."

I slid my hands down his back, then gripped the hard mounds of his butt cheeks. His muscles contracted under my palms as he thrust again. Slowly, so slowly. His arms shook.

"By all the fucking gods of Nerifir..." he cursed under his breath. "It's been so long, so fucking long... And you feel so good."

A shudder ran through his entire body, and he jerked out of me, shifting away. His head tossed back, his teeth bared, he pumped his length in his fist with a growl. Long, creamy spurts of his release shot out, hitting the sheet under us.

I couldn't tear my eyes from him kneeling at my spread legs, his strong beautiful body arched back, his massive erection pointing straight up, fisted in his hand.

The muscles in his arms rippled as he exhaled a shuddering breath. His shoulders slumped forward, and he peered at me apologetically between the hair that draped over his eyes.

"So much for me *making it last*," he said, his hard-on relaxing to a half-mast position.

I laughed softly, with only a slight hint of disappointment. He'd made me come before on many occasions. If we were to spend the rest of the night just cuddling in bed, I was all for it. Voron hadn't cuddled, at least not when he was fully awake. And I was looking forward to him holding me in his arms.

"Well, if *staying up* isn't happening..." I closed my legs and stretched my arms toward him. "Come lie down with me."

He leaned forward, sliding his hands up my hips.

"But I'm not finished with you yet."

Gripping my hips, he rolled me over on my belly, then helped me get up on all fours. He stretched on his back under me, fitting his head between my legs.

"Come closer, Sparrow." Pressing on my ass, he brought my core down to his mouth.

Desire surged through me anew as his warm, slick tongue swirled around my opening. His lips closed over my clit, sucking and nibbling. In seconds, he had me riding his face like a woman possessed.

"Oh, Voron... I..."

I was teetering on edge, my orgasm coming closer with no way to stop it now.

Suddenly, he slid from under me. His hand replaced his mouth, tormenting my hot, overstimulated clit. Rising on his knees, he drove into me from behind, rock-hard and ready once again.

"Come for me, Sparrow," he gritted between his teeth. "I want to feel you on my cock when you do."

With another hard press of his fingers, I came undone. My arms buckled, sending me face down into the pillows. My legs trembled with the most intense climax rolling through my body.

Voron roared above me, gripping my hips so firmly his fingers dug into my flesh. Pounding hard with abandon, he pumped his release into me.

The next moment, he let go.

"Fuck." Shoving away from me, he leaped from the bed.

My post-orgasmic glow vanished instantly. I turned around, sitting up. His release trickled out from me. Its fragrance reminded me of the scent in the air after a heavy rain in the fields, heady and fertile.

"Voron? What happened?"

He stood at the foot of the bed, breathtakingly naked. His pale skin shimmered softly, making him appear as if carved from moonstone. His expression was that of pure terror.

I'd never seen Voron so afraid before. Never. The terrified look in his eyes sent a cold shiver down my spine.

"Voron?" My voice came out weaker and higher than I'd intended. "What's going on?"

I shifted on my knees to the edge of the bed, getting closer to him.

"Don't!" He raised his hand between us, pushing on it as if trying to keep me away telepathically. "Don't come any closer."

He took a step sideways toward the door.

"Voron, you're scaring me," I pleaded.

Pain crossed his features.

"Oh Sparrow. My dear, sweet, wonderful Sparrow. I'm so sorry. I lost control. I broke my promise."

My heart plummeted into the hollow of my stomach.

"Voron, no... Please." I climbed out of bed, but he stopped me again.

"Don't come too close. I don't want to hurt you."

"I broke my promise."

His words echoed through my mind, their horrific meaning exploding through my brain. The blood-curdling howls of the cursed sounded in my ears.

Was that what he was going to become?

I searched his face for the signs of insanity claiming him. I scanned his body, looking for the clear patches, the signs of the impending death.

"What promise was it? How did you break it? When?"

He brought his hand to his face, looking confused.

"I don't feel any different."

"You don't look any different, either." I was afraid to hope. "How old was that promise? Maybe it has just...worn off?"

"Worn off?" He arched an eyebrow. The devastation on his face eased into amusement for a second.

"Yes. Expired." I waved a hand in the air. "Evaporated, like the wards on that book." I gestured at the table by the fireplace where the magical book of records lay in the shadows.

"What book?" He followed my gesture with his eyes.

"The one that keeps the records of your family life in Vensari. I only read one small part of it so far."

"You read it?" he echoed, looking flabbergasted. "And you brought it here?"

He marched to the table and reached for the book.

The air around the table exploded with a flash of bright white-blue light, throwing his arm back. With a cry of pain, Voron clutched his hand to his stomach and staggered back into the chair by the fireplace.

"Oh my God, Voron. Are you okay?" I rushed to him.

Dropping to my knees in front of his chair, I gently pried his hand from his torso. The tips of his fingers turned blue with bruising. Broken dark-blue lines ran up his hand to his wrist.

"Magic is eternal, little bird," he gritted through his teeth, wincing in pain. "And promises last a lifetime."

"It looks terrible." I stroked his palm gently. "What can I do to make it better?"

He flexed his fingers, balling his hand into a fist, then opening it again.

"It's better already."

The bruising receded, with the lines retreating from the wrist back to the fingertips.

I rubbed his hand, massaging it gently. "Are you going to be okay?"

"The wards are meant to teach a lesson, not to injure permanently." He chuckled, shaking his head. "Clearly, one lesson wasn't enough for me. I already went through this decades ago, and now I ended up sticking my hand right in again."

"Because I told you I brought it here."

I glanced back at the book.

The light from the magical explosion had dimmed but didn't disappear completely. The bluish glow shimmered over the book like a wide halo, and in the middle, the light formed into letters.

"No fae can touch me. No fae can read me.

The bloodline dies, my records end."

I turned back to Voron. He stared at the letters, too. His eyes narrowed with focus as understanding spread across his face, and I knew exactly what it meant.

"No *fae...*" he whispered, moving his gaze back to me.

I splayed my hand on the front cover of the book. No explosions followed. The letters dispersed into the air. The glow settled down, then disappeared as if absorbed by the leather of the binding.

"I'm not a fae."

Chapter Eight

VORON

This woman was in his dreams constantly. He knew her body better than his own by now. Because hers had been often on display in all those see-through clothes she wore in Elaros, and he just couldn't stop staring, salivating over each and every curve of hers.

He knew he'd never met anyone like her before, and he probably never would for as long as he lived. Yet it'd never crossed his mind to search his memories for the exact wording of that damn promise he'd given decades ago.

"That's right, my dear Sparrow. You're not a fae."

He cupped the side of her face, then slid his hand down her neck in a caress. He stroked her breast, enjoying the way her curves filled and overflowed his hand. Her skin was soft, her body subtle, but neither felt nor looked quite the same as those of his kind.

"You're so delightfully human, my little bird."

He caressed the swell of her stomach, savoring the delicate softness of her. Every touch made his unquenchable desire for her surge higher. With his arm around her waist, he brought her closer, fitting her between his open knees. His cock jerked, touching her belly as she was kneeling in front of him.

He pressed her against him, her body so willing and pliable in his hands. Yet he sensed some resistance in the way she propped her hands on his shoulders when he kissed her breast.

She took his head in her hands, forcing him to face her. He groaned inwardly, interrupting his kisses.

"How long does it take to become the cursed after a promise is broken?" she asked, her beautiful mind working on things he couldn't focus on with her naked body so close to his.

"Instantly." He reached for her lips with his mouth but managed to steal just a tiny peck before she pulled away.

"So, the fact that you're... well, still very much *you* must mean that your promise has not been broken."

"Right." He lifted her into his lap, making her straddle his thighs.

His cock bobbed at her entrance, eager to dive in.

"Does it have something to do with me being a human, too?" she chirped another question, so relentlessly curious. Only his mind remained clouded with lust, thick and steamy.

"Probably..." he murmured.

He lifted one breast in his hand, kissing the inside of it before moving to her other breast, both equally fascinating and utterly fantastic. All he could think about was getting inside her again. He wished to spend the rest of the night right there, inside her warm, slick softness.

She scrunched her nose in a most adorable way. "For someone who has been practically celibate for decades, you're way too horny all of a sudden."

He lifted his head with a grin, feeling drunk on her scent and the sensation of her body in his hands.

"You have no idea, sweetheart, no idea how hard it was to stay celibate since you came along."

She tilted her head, gazing at him with those eyes that held all the colors of a forest. "Had it been easier before I came along?"

The lustful fog cleared from his mind when he thought back to all those years he'd spent bound by the promises he'd given. The burden of this particular one weighed down on him, robbing him of joy like the dark shadows of Under. No matter how careful he was, he could never fully enjoy making love to a woman.

"I managed," he said briefly, unwilling to place any of his burden on her delicate shoulders.

A wrinkle appeared between her eyebrows. "Why did you do it to yourself? Why did you make all those promises?"

His cock throbbed impatiently, but he ignored it for the time being, thinking back to that day when the royal couple appeared here in Vensari. They had come under the pretense of personally congratulating him on his latest victory. But he knew they wanted to secure their arrangement with him in a much firmer way. The real problem was, as it turned out, that back then, he wished for that too.

Sparrow misunderstood the pause.

"You don't have to talk about it if you don't want to," she said. "But will you let me read the book? Will it be in there?"

He stretched his neck, running a hand through his hair. He had given the promise here, in Vensari, so it should be in the book since it recorded every event of any significance to his family.

"Let's read it," he agreed. "It'll be good for me to refresh my memory."

She made a move to get off his lap, but he hooked his arm around her middle, keeping her in place. He'd agreed to read the book, but not at the cost of parting with her now. He'd come here to spend the night, driven insane by the need for her body. And he wasn't nearly done with her yet.

Instead, he dragged their chair closer to the table with the book and shifted Sparrow to sit sideways on his lap, her hip pressing against his hard, long-suffering cock.

Sparrow lifted the front cover of the book.

"I saw the part when you brought me to Vensari," she said. "It's at the beginning though, for some reason."

"The records are kept from the back to the front," he explained. "The most recent events will be at the beginning. The later ones are at the end."

She flipped several pages at once. "How do you know if you never read it?"

"All house records are kept in a similar manner. I read the records of Elaros many times. The royal events are public."

"This one said it was a record of Elaros, too."

"Did it?" Surely, she was mistaken. The book belonged to Vensari.

"Maybe it's because the royal couple have been here?" She pointed at the pictures of King Tiane and Queen Pavline rising from the pages.

She jerked her hand away, avoiding any contact with their images. He couldn't blame her. One of those two wished to slice her open for his perverted pleasure. The other one sentenced her to death just to keep her people from learning her husband's darkest secret.

Sparrow grabbed the page to flip it over, but Voron stopped her.

"I believe that's it. Right here."

The image solidified. Memories of that day rose in his mind as the scene unfurled.

The king and the queen stood in the main hall of Vensari with Voron entering the picture.

"My king. My queen." He bowed to them both before leading them into the library where they could speak in private.

"Have you thought about our offer, Lord Voron?" The queen took the seat he offered by the lit fireplace.

"I have, and I don't believe it's necessary. I've already promised to obey the crown."

"Just like every other warrior has in the Royal Army." The king took a seat next to his wife, with Voron standing in front of them. "And if so, why do we have to hold you in higher regard than any of them?"

Voron's spine stiffened.

"Because no other warrior has done as much for the crown as I have. I won this war for you. Without me, you'd still be fighting. More wars are coming. High Lord Corneil has just passed away, and his son hasn't sworn his loyalty to you yet. I have reasons to believe he never will because he's plotting against you." He leaned forward, adding emphasis to his words. "You need me. You know that I'll lead your armies to victory in any war. I've proven it to you. There is no other High General, whether you give me the rank or not."

The queen leaned back in her chair, holding his stare firmly.

"You have to promise not to procreate, Lord Voron. That is the condition, the only condition at this point."

King Tiane had communicated it to him clearly enough before. Yet hearing it again made him cringe.

"Do you even realize what you're asking from me?"

"Perfectly," she assured him. "I also see perfectly clear how ambitious you are. No rank you've been given, no title you've held has satisfied you for long. How are we to know you wouldn't reach for the Sky Crown when there is nothing else above you and everything else is below you?"

"I've pledged you my loyalty," he resisted. "I can never go against you without breaking my promise."

"But your offspring can." The king frowned.

Voron laughed.

"What offspring? I'm not bonded. I don't even have a wife and don't plan on having one."

The queen's eyes narrowed at him intently. "But you fuck, a lot, from what we've heard."

"And you want to take it away from me?" How was he supposed to accept that?

She flicked her wrist dismissively. "There are other ways to receive sexual pleasure. Ways that don't result in procreation."

"Fuck them in the ass." King Tiane shrugged. "It's even better. Tighter."

The queen gave her spouse a disgusted look, then produced a scroll from the wide sleeve of her silver dress.

"Here." She handed it to Voron.

"What's this?"

"The promise. Read it as it is, word for word."

Voron opened the scroll. It contained but one sentence, clear and concise, with no way out.

"You're giving me no choice."

"Of course there is a choice," the queen objected. "You can go right back to where you came from. Stay here in Vensari and lead a quiet country life. Or even better, climb back into whatever hole you were down in the Below."

He glared at her, the muscles in his jaw moving. He swallowed hard, running his eyes along the words written in the scroll, then blew out a breath, shaking his head. "I'll never have a child."

The queen scoffed. "Since when is it important to you?"

"Many of the army tent whores aren't highborn," King Tiane dismissed. "You can't breed them, anyway."

Voron waved the scroll in front of the royals. "But this doesn't limit my promise only to highborn. You want me to give up sex with all fae, here or Below."

"Right." The queen nodded. "It's best to keep it simple. You promised to obey us, but we wished for this to be your choice, Voron. We're not going to order you."

But they could. They could give him a direct order, and because of the other promises he'd already given them, he would have no choice but to obey.

He moved his gaze to the window, as if he could find advice or encouragement out there in the clouds.

"What do you have to lose?" the queen urged.

"The future," he replied somberly.

"The future is a cruel master. We slave for it, missing out on what really matters—the present. The current day is where we are, the only thing we can enjoy. Embrace it, Voron. Seize it. Make it yours, and everything else will fall into place. You have *but only yourself to please. Get what you really want, High General."*

Her use of the title he coveted sent a rush of excitement through his chest.

The king stretched his legs, crossing them at his ankles. "It's such a small thing to give up. But think about everything you gain. You won't just get the title, you'll be my right-hand man in everything. My favorite. The richest, the most feared and powerful, with only me and the gods above you."

What Voron was giving up seemed but an abstract idea if compared with everything he stood to gain. As long as he was loyal, the king would elevate him above all others. The kingdom that had rejected him before would be at his feet now.

His skin prickled with anticipation. He could almost taste the power. It had a heady, addictive flavor.

He lifted the scroll and read, trying not to flinch at the way the sentence was worded.

"I promise not to spill my seed into the womb of any fae for as long as I live." He tossed the scroll back on the table. "There. No procreation. No offspring to threaten the crown."

The scroll fluttered over the marble surface, disturbed by the shimmer of magic. A light breeze came from nowhere, tousling Voron's hair, ruffling the feathers in the king's wings and billowing the light fabric of the queen's long sleeves—sealing Voron's promise for the rest of his life.

The images shimmered and dissipated. The glow trickled down to be absorbed by the pages. But the memories were now fresher than ever in his mind.

He remembered the buzz of anticipation. The power he'd wished for was so close, all he had to do was to reach out and grab it. All he had to give up was sex, and not even all of it, just one part of it.

Back then, he didn't realize how putting any restrictions on the activity largely led by instinct would forever inhibit any pleasure for him from then on. He hadn't been able to get lost in desire ever since. Even when his seed wasn't anywhere near a womb, he couldn't fully relax with a woman. The mere awareness of the promise stripped enjoyment of any form of sex from him.

At the end, he preferred celibacy to whatever scraps of intimacy he was allowed to have. Only when the need for the touch of a woman grew stronger than the need to breathe would he make use of a willing mouth or a skilled hand of one of the queen's ladies-in-waiting.

He exhaled, leaning back in the chair.

"You gave up any chance of ever having a family," Sparrow said softly. "It's not just sex, you essentially ended your bloodline with that promise. Willingly."

Turned out, that part bothered him the least.

"I didn't see much sense in perpetuating my father's bloodline, Sparrow."

She looked flabbergasted. "So, you gave up sex as revenge against your father?"

He winced. When she said it like that, it made the whole thing sound rather foolish.

"Not as much a revenge as I just didn't care about preserving the bloodline that I happened to belong to. The main reason for that promise wasn't taking revenge on anyone. It was to get me where it eventually did."

The frown remained on her face, that slight crease staying between her dark-brown eyebrows.

"What is your bloodline, Voron? Who was your father?"

He squirmed in the chair uncomfortably.

"I don't know. And that's exactly the point. My father wasn't there, either for me or my mother."

"Maybe he died before you were born?"

Irritation stirred in him. When he was little, he wished that were the case. That his father couldn't be with him because he was dead, not because he chose to ignore his son.

"Even if he died, he never was a good man to begin with. My mother refused to speak of him, dead or alive."

He rose to his feet. She squeaked in surprise as he took her with him, lifting her in his arms.

"I don't want to talk about him, Sparrow. Not on the night when I finally found such a delightful way out of this promise." He carried her to the bed—the only place where he wished to spend the rest of the night with her. "Now that I can fuck you any way I please, that's all I want to do." He placed her down. "Please tell me you'll let me."

Linking her hands over her head, she arched her back, stretching like a lustful little kitten in the silky sheets.

"Far be it from me to deny you, my lord." Now of all times, his little vixen decided to speak like a proper lady. And it went straight to his crotch with another shot of lust.

Rolling to her side, she rose on her elbow. "So, you came here tonight with the intention of having sex, right?"

"Wasn't it obvious?" He climbed onto the bed after her. "And I'm far from done yet."

With his hands on her knees, he opened her legs, dropping his head between them.

"Wait." She took his head in her hands, making him look up at her. "Before the book, though, you thought the promise applied to me, too. You didn't know it would be okay for you to make love to me in the way that... um, may lead to procreation."

"Right. It's been so long since I made that promise. 'No fae' or 'no one.' In my mind, they meant the same, and that's how I remembered it ever since."

It didn't even occur to him that she was different and the promise might not apply to her because of that. To him, Sparrow was his equal.

She rubbed his temples with her thumbs, smiling at him warmly.

"You knew you might die a horrible death, yet you still came here."

"For the entire night, sweetheart." He grinned.

Deep inside, he'd known it might not be much longer than

just one night. But he'd lost his fucking mind. He'd wanted her so much and for so long that at some point, trading his life for a single night with Sparrow had started to look acceptable.

Had his promise been worded differently—"no one" instead of "no fae"—he'd be going insane and feral right now and would've died within days.

By the look of her, she knew it too.

"Voron..." She closed her legs, sitting up. "Do you understand that one word, one single word, could've killed you? Literally. You were the one who taught me to always pay attention to the words."

He rolled to his side, propping his elbow onto the mattress and resting his head on his hand.

"I was hoping I'd be able to hold back." He smiled. "Stupid. I know. I had no idea how amazing you'd feel on my cock. So slick, and tight, and wonderful. There was no way I could hold back."

The ache in his groin became unbearable. He fisted his straining erection and gave it one tantalizingly slow pump. A growl vibrated deep inside his throat. He couldn't wait to be inside her again.

Leaning toward her, he kissed her thigh. The scent of her arousal reached him, making him groan with need.

"You came here to die." She touched him gently.

"I took precautions to protect you if the worst happened," he assured her, suddenly remembering that he'd placed Alcon outside her door. "Fuck. I completely forgot."

The poor man was staying awake for no good reason.

Voron climbed out of bed and went to the door.

"Alcon?" He cracked the door open and poked his head out. "It's all good here. Go to bed."

Alcon was sitting with his back to the wall, a sword leaning against his shoulder. He climbed to his feet.

"Are you sure, my lord?"

"Absolutely. Go get some sleep. Good night." He closed the

door. There was no time to chat. He had Sparrow, warm and naked, waiting for him in bed.

"Has he been there all this time?" she asked. Her face turned a lovely shade of pink as she must've remembered how loud he'd made her moan earlier that night.

He strolled back to the bed.

"Yes. For your protection. If you were in any danger, Alcon had my orders to come here and kill me."

He placed a knee on the mattress, and she reached for him, wrapping her arms around his neck.

"You were ready to die? Just for one night with me?"

"It's not that I planned to die. Of course, I hoped to live. It just somehow no longer mattered much if I didn't." He scooped her into his arms, kissing her lips, her cheeks, her neck as they both fell into the sheets. "I wanted you so fucking much," he growled against her skin. "I still do."

As he moved inside her just a few minutes later, both of them sweaty and moaning in bliss, a thought bounced in his mind.

"It'd be worth it."

Being with her was worth anything, even death.

"I feel like I could die, too," she whispered, meeting his thrusts. "Just for one moment like this with you."

Chapter Nine

SPARROW

I didn't get much sleep that night. Voron kept me awake, making me come too many times to count before we both finally collapsed into the sheets, sweaty and exhausted.

He held me as I fell asleep, his naked body pressed against mine, with no clothes, no sheets, and what felt like absolutely no distance between us.

Deeply sated, I slept with no dreams. Until his touch woke me up in the morning. Spooning me from behind, he was kissing my shoulder. His hand caressed my breast. His appetite for my body seemed endless. He acted like a starving man who finally got access to food and now couldn't stop himself.

"You are insatiable," I murmured, turning in his arms.

He hummed in agreement, his hands and mouth never leaving my body. It thrilled me to be wanted by him so much. I loved seeing him so infatuated. He seemed ready to forgo food and sleep in favor of making love to me.

I didn't exactly free him from his promise, but we managed to find a loophole that allowed him to be fully himself with me. And it happened through no effort on my part, simply because I was who I was—a human. For once, I felt utterly happy being a human among the fae.

Kissing my neck, he skimmed the curve of my hip, palmed my ample backside, circled the thickness of my thigh, bringing my leg over his hip. Every part of my body was substantial, solid, and real—human, like all of me. And he clearly enjoyed it immensely.

I stretched in his arms, basking in the glow of his attention. I still felt sore from having him inside me most of the night. He was rather big. Or maybe I was small? I had no memories to compare him to any other man ever being inside me.

The thick length of his was hard once again, nudging and prodding against my lower stomach. I ached between my thighs as he parted them.

"Voron," I stopped him. "Last night was...intense. I'll need time to recover."

He tore his mouth from my breast and studied my face.

"Did I fuck you too hard, my delicate little bird?"

I smiled, thinking of so many amazing things he'd done to me, both rough and gentle.

"It was wonderful. I love being ravaged," I assured him. "But..."

He grinned. "Too much of a good thing?"

"Your *thing* is huge, you know?"

He glanced down his front with a frown, assessing his length and girth.

"I suppose it is," he agreed. "Especially for someone so tender and fragile like you are." He didn't let go of me, however, sliding down my body instead. "Well, let me kiss you better, then." He eased his head between my legs.

His warm tongue slipped between my folds, stroking me soothingly. Pleasure twirled gently inside me with each languid glide of his tongue. He worked me slowly, taking his time, coaxing desire to rise and surge.

I shifted along his side, needing to touch him too. He

hummed in pleasure when I circled his hard length with my fingers.

I tugged at it, urging him closer. "I want to taste you, too."

He obliged. Rolling onto his back, he brought me over him and aligned my hips with his mouth again.

Taking him in my hand, I dragged my tongue along his impressive length. His scent was stronger here, the freshness of the rain mixed with the musk of a man. I wrapped my lips around the thick bulbous end, then slid my mouth down his shaft.

He moaned and hummed with approval. With his hands on my ass, he brought my hips lower, pressing his mouth to my most sensitive spot. My thighs trembled with a rush of pleasure. He lapped harder, sucking on my clit in between.

Desire spread through me, making it hard to focus on what my mouth was doing. All my awareness seemed to shift downward where Voron nibbled and sucked me into yet another orgasm. As it exploded through me, I squeezed my hand around him. He jerked in my fingers, joining me in climax. His release shot against my open mouth and coated my hand. I collapsed over him, riding the waves of pleasure.

When a shred of awareness finally returned to me, I rolled off him, afraid I might suffocate or crush him.

Laughing, he rose to his knees. "What a glorious way to start a day."

He gave me a delighted once-over, taking in my tangled hair, sweaty skin, and my face and hand splattered generously with the evidence of his pleasure.

"Look at you, my filthy little minx," he murmured, clearly enjoying the view.

All I could do was just smile in reply.

He scooped me up from the bed and carried me to the bathroom.

"Let's clean this mess up."

It was almost noon when Voron finally let me leave the bedroom. We had breakfast—or more like lunch, already—on my favorite patio off the library. The mood was relaxing, as neither of us was in a hurry.

We both were barefoot. I wore just a light dressing gown over my nightshirt. Voron had a pair of pants on and one of his frilly shirts that he never bothered to button up. I loved it just like that on him, with his wide, muscular chest on display.

"I always thought your eyes were gray," I said, taking a sip from my second cup of tea. "But they're vividly blue right now, just like the sky."

The stifling heat under the thick clouds had finally let go today. The light breeze coming from the gardens felt refreshing against my flushed skin. The clouds had parted enough to let a rare ray of sunshine through.

Voron glanced up at the sky, as if to verify its color. He then looked back at me, popping a grape from the fruit tray into his mouth.

"And your eyes are the color of the forest," he said.

I shook my head. "But they aren't green."

He reached over the table for my hand, but then pulled away, placing his hand by his plate instead. All through the breakfast this morning, he'd been trying to hold back somewhat, to give me some space, but it'd been a struggle for him to keep his hands off me. He seemed restless, shifting in his chair again.

"A forest is never just green," he replied. "It's also gray, and blue, and brown, and gold. And you have all of those colors in your eyes."

I felt flustered, my cheeks warming with pleasure from his words. I hadn't thought he'd gazed into my eyes enough to notice all that.

There was a new tenderness in his expression. Like he'd lost a layer in the thick walls he'd built around his heart, and now was trying to figure out how he felt about being that much more exposed.

"Sparrow," he said, putting down his teacup. "That book. Would you read it for me again please?"

In this case, "reading" was me simply turning the pages. But I didn't correct him.

"Sure."

He got up from his chair, ready to follow me, but I stopped him.

"Let's stay here. The weather is too nice to go inside. I'll get the book. You'll help Brebie clean up meanwhile."

"Clean up?" He glanced at the dishes on the table, looking confused.

"You do know how to do that, don't you?" I teased, leaving him alone with the dirty dishes.

When I came back carrying the heavy book, neither Voron nor Brebie were there. But the table was clean. I set the book down when Voron returned to the patio.

"The dishes have been cleared," he reported proudly.

"Well done," I laughed, lifting the heavy cover as he took his seat at the table. "Um..." A scandalous thought came to me. "Will last night be recorded here, now?"

He smirked, his gaze turning lascivious. "Why don't you take a look?"

"I'm not sure how I'd feel about you pounding into me doggy style being depicted in the magical light for centuries," I muttered under my breath, while leafing through the book to the very beginning.

Tossing his head back, he laughed loudly.

"*Doggy style?* How crass and so unladylike from you, my dear Sparrow." He gazed at me warmly. "I love it."

The scene of Voron rushing through the corridors appeared above the pages. He ripped his riding cloak off, tossing it aside, then clawed at the ties of his shirt as if his clothes were suffocating him, burning his skin.

"You really, really need to lock your door, Sparrow," the image of Voron rasped.

"You look pretty desperate here." I arched an eyebrow, tossing a teasing look his way.

He didn't deny it.

The scene ended with his *"I already have."* The words that had sent tingles down my arms both last night and now.

The light thinned and shifted after that. Then, the picture of us sleeping together appeared. I was lying on my back. My hair was a total disaster, but my face looked ridiculously happy, even in my sleep.

My right arm was under Voron's neck, his nose pressed to my shoulder. His arm was hugging me under my breasts, and his leg was tossed over my hips. No wonder I woke up all hot and sweaty, with him being plastered all over me like that in the night.

"This is so damn sweet," I heard him say.

I met his eyes across the table, catching a flash of vulnerability in them. He was worried about this, about the depths to which his need for me had grown. But there wasn't much I could say or do to alleviate his worries. All of this was new to me, too, and I had even less life experience to evaluate all these feelings between us. All I knew was that I wished for this to last. I wished to see where it would lead us.

"It's lovely," I agreed, looking at the peaceful picture of us sleeping together, the long curtains on the open window swaying in the breeze lightly. For as long as I lived, I vowed to remember this moment of utter peace and comfort the two of us had shared.

"Well," he cleared his throat, "no images of me 'pounding' into you have made it into the records after all."

"Thank goodness." I exhaled in relief. "It makes sense, I guess, to keep the house records PG-rated."

He arched an eyebrow at my mentioning the PG rating but didn't ask for a clarification as I started turning the pages again.

I moved toward the end of the book, closer to the earlier events. There was a gap in time in the records—probably when Voron had been in the Dakath Mountains, down in the Below—as just after a few flips, a picture of a young boy reading a book in a chair by a lit fireplace appeared.

"Is that you?" I asked, already knowing the answer.

So much about this boy seemed familiar. He had the same challenge in his eyes, the same stubborn set of the mouth like Voron did. Only the boy's hair was completely black. Not a single strand of it had turned silver yet.

He didn't answer my question. Sitting at the table across from me, Voron the man was staring at Voron the boy—so much like him, yet so different, too, separated by over a century and a half of suffering and experience.

Voron's lips moved as he looked at the scene unfolding from the book's pages.

"Mother," he said softly.

A tall, slender woman rushed into the room and shut the door behind her.

"Voron." She crouched in front of the boy. "They're coming for me..."

Her eyes wide with horror, she darted a glance at the window where large, winged shapes approached, obscuring the sky.

"Who?" The boy jumped from his seat.

The woman held both his hands in hers.

"Whatever happens, please remember I love you." The words rushed out of her in a hurried, fervent whisper. "I always loved you, from the moment I held you in my arms."

The winged figures outside soared closer. One of them kicked the smooth crystal out of the window.

The boy glared in that direction, but the woman kept holding his hands. She shook with trepidation and fear.

"Please, remember me." Her hands trembled as she yanked a ring off her finger and shoved it into her son's hand. "Whatever

they do to us, don't let it break you. You were saved for a reason. Remember that."

The royal guards rushed through the window at the same time as the door crashed open. Splinters of wood flew across the room.

Gripping his mother's hand, the boy looked lost and scared, but he tried to hide it. He stepped in front of his mother, shielding her from the guards who rushed them from both sides.

Some grabbed the woman and dragged her to the window. The rest yanked the boy from her grip, hauling him toward the door.

"Mother!" The boy who had tried so stoically to act like a man finally crumbled as the woman who'd cared for him since birth was torn away from him.

"Stay strong, Voron. I love you..." came from the window as they flew her out of the room and out of his life forever.

He bit a guard's hand and kicked another one, but the men were so much stronger than the boy. As the guards hauled him out of the room, another winged man landed on the low windowsill of the tall window.

Draping his ink-black wings over his shoulders, he stood in the window, watching as the guards took the little boy away. The man's long, silver-white beard blew in the gusts of the approaching storm. The black feathers of his wings rustled in the wind. A circlet of golden thorns graced his head. On the back of the circlet, the thorns were much longer. They rose up and branched out, like antlers.

"Who's that?" I tore my eyes from the book to look at Voron.

His hands balled into fists on the table, but his expression was calm. Only his eyes appeared a bit glossy. He blinked slowly, meeting my gaze, and I couldn't stand the suffering shining in his eyes. He never stopped mourning the loss of his mother. She didn't need to beg him to remember her. He never forgot.

"Voron..." I got off my seat and took a step his way.

He shoved his chair away from the table, then yanked me onto his lap. Drawing me close, he rested his chin on my shoulder.

I threaded my fingers through the hair over his temple.

"I'm so sorry, Voron."

He drew in a breath and nodded.

"Let's read more," he said, sounding somber but resolved.

"Are you sure?" I pressed the side of my face to his, hugging his neck. "I can read it alone, then tell you what happens."

He lifted his head from my shoulder. "No. I need to see it."

The image of the bearded man dissolved slowly.

"Who was it?" I asked again.

"King Herane, Tiane's father. I didn't know he was there. I didn't see him that day."

No wonder he didn't. The guards were already hauling him out of the room, kicking and screaming, by the time King Herane appeared.

Why was he there? What was so important about the young wingless boy and his mother that the king personally needed to see them gone?

"Let's see this from the very beginning, then, shall we?" I flipped the book to the very end, to the very first record.

It was supposed to be the records of Vensari, but it clearly appeared to be the chronicles of Voron's life. And as such, the book had to begin with his birth.

Sure enough, as I flipped the page, the image of a pregnant woman appeared. Her wings were open wide, moving strongly as she hovered high above the clouds. Only it wasn't Mulena, the woman who'd given Voron the ring before being dragged away by the guards. The woman Voron called his mother was there, too, however. She hovered in front and slightly to the side of the pregnant woman and was holding a long piece of silk draped over her arms.

At least two dozen other highborn flocked around them. Dressed in fine outfits and dripping with gold and gemstones, they soared around and chatted animatedly, adding excitement and commotion to the scene.

Behind the pregnant woman, King Herane loomed, his black wings shading her. She arched her back with a moan and threw her arms over her belly. She was clearly in labor.

"Whose birth is it?" I asked Voron.

His forehead creased in concentration.

"I'm not sure."

"Who is the pregnant lady?"

"King Herane's wife, the queen and Tiane's mother."

The queen's features pinched with tension. She groaned, then released a long, wailing scream.

The courtiers flew around even more agitatedly. Someone produced a stringed musical instrument and started playing it, the music drowning out the screams of labor.

The queen bent over, gripping her round belly with both arms.

A man in a long golden robe of a priest flew around her, reading from a scroll, "On this day, a great king will be born. The king, who will lead the Sky Kingdom to glory and prosperity. He will unite the High Lords, bring peace to our lands, and will make us whole. But only as long as he is whole himself. Hail to the king!" the man shouted, waving the scroll in his hands.

Somehow, in all this commotion through the cacophony of noises, the thin wail of a newborn was heard. It pierced the air fiercely, demanding attention.

A head with wet, dark hair appeared between the pearl-gray thighs of the queen.

The court rejoiced. Mulena eagerly opened her arms, stretching the cloth she held between them.

Then, the baby fell.

It separated from the queen, the umbilical cord miraculously snapping on its own.

The baby plummeted down, but only for a short distance. The woman Voron called his mother dove after the newborn and caught it into the cloth.

The music died instantly, as did the chatter and the laughter. The priest stopped shouting the words from the scroll.

The king's face darkened, as did the thick, heavy clouds gathering on the horizon.

Mulena pressed the baby to her chest, with a terrified expression on her face that turned as white as the cloth in her arms.

Then, among the utter shock and silence, the queen's weakened voice sounded. "It's not done yet."

She bent over once more, gripping her stomach with an ear-piercing scream.

The image paled and faded away. And when I quickly flipped the page, eager to see what happened next, the view of Vensari appeared instead.

A toddler with unruly black curls ran along the garden path in a bout of delighted giggles. Mulena, the same woman who'd caught the baby, opened her arms wide, catching the toddler as he ran to her.

"Look at you run, Voron!" She kissed his face. "Who needs wings when you can run free like a wind, my prince."

The moment the image faded, I flipped the page again, moving through the scenes of Voron growing up, of him playing, reading, laughing. There was a scene with him feeding turtles in the pond. Another one with him learning to ride a pony. And another, where a servant taught him how to use a sword.

In every scene, Mulena was there, watching over him, raising, and nurturing him.

Not once was Voron visited by his biological parents. But he was hugged, kissed, and cherished. He was loved, and he treated Mulena as his mother.

I flipped to the very first page, where the words of the title lit up again.

"Recorded History of Elaros, the Sky Palace."

Voron leaned back in his chair, staring past me into the sky.

"Do you think the queen had twins?" I asked tentatively, afraid to poke whatever wounds the book might have just opened inside him.

"Now I know she did," he said. "The records of what happened next that day are kept in Elaros, accessible to everyone. The queen gave birth to Tiane, crowned as the next Sky King."

I drew in a long breath, the enormity of this discovery crashing down on me full force.

"You are the king's twin brother."

He shook his head, settling his stare on me.

"No, my dear Sparrow. I was born first. I am the king."

Chapter Ten

SPARROW

I looked into Voron's eyes. During the time I'd known him, they'd been every shade between the darkest gray and the brightest blue. But they'd always been the color of the sky, changing with it but never straying from it.

"You're the true Sky King, Voron. You are the one who controls the weather. How did I not see it sooner?"

King Tiane had laughed and raged. He'd acted sweet and cruel. But the weather in this shadowless kingdom had stayed mostly somber and gloomy. It was because King Tiane had never possessed the power to control it. His moods had no bearings on the weather. Only Voron's did.

"The only time I saw sun in Elaros," I said, "was on the day you came back after making sure Magnus survived being shot by the king. Everyone thought the sun came out that morning because King Tiane finally got what he wanted with me. But it was all you. You were happy because Magnus got well."

He kissed my shoulder, holding me in his lap.

"I was also happy to see *you* again. For the first time in my life, I returned to the palace in a better mood than I'd left it. I was looking forward to our lesson, even as I knew I'd be spending the entire hour trying to tame my lust for you. My cock just wouldn't stay down whenever you came to my rooms."

"Does your *cock* have something to do with the heat we've had lately?" I teased, with my arms wrapped around his neck.

He placed a quick kiss on my lips. "You have no one to blame but yourself for the heat both outside and in my pants, sexy little minx that you are."

A spark of heat flashed in his eyes, but only briefly this time. With another peck on my mouth, he got up, gently shifting me from his lap onto the chair. Then he stood by the table, staring at the book with the title letters still glowing above the front page.

"Elaros," he read out loud. "This isn't the Vensari records after all. The book belongs to the Sky Palace."

"Then why is it here?"

"Because the royal family didn't want anyone to know the whole truth about King Tiane's birth. They found a way to extract the portion about me. No one can destroy the records, but they warded and buried it here, so no one would ever learn the truth."

"How could your own family do that to you?"

He frowned, running a hand through his hair.

"Frankly, I can't really blame them. What choice did they have? Either a wingless boy, who by all logic and tradition should've died if it weren't for one overly eager lady-in-waiting, or his brother born with perfect snow-white wings and a magnificent pair of antlers. 'Born wearing a crown,' they say about Tiane. 'He was *born* to rule.'" Voron spread his arms aside. "Which one would you choose to be the next Sky King, Sparrow?" He didn't wait for me to reply. "The answer would be clear to anyone. My parents took Tiane to the Sky Palace and raised him as the prince and future king. And I was sent to Vensari with Mulena."

He stepped back from the table and paced the patio.

"All my life, I believed I was the son of a queen's lady-in-waiting, a *disgraced* lady-in-waiting. It was a rather humble origin for someone making it all the way to Elaros."

"For all intents and purposes, Mulena was your mother," I pointed out.

"She was the only mother I knew. And I love her for that. Always will."

"Did you ever wonder who your father was?"

He stopped at the table again, propping his fists on it.

"As a child, I asked Mulena about him. But she told me never to speak of him again. She said he was not a part of my life and never would be. As I got older..." He inhaled deeply and released the air slowly. "I wondered if my mother might've been King Herane's lover at some point and I was his illegitimate son. It would've explained why my mother didn't want to talk about him or why he ordered me gone. Bastard children are often accepted and raised by the families, especially if there are no legitimate children. However, with Tiane already there, I suspected, King Herane saw me as a potential threat to the succession of his legitimate son."

"Do you think King Tiane and Queen Pavline know you are of the royal blood? Could that be one of the reasons why they didn't want you to reproduce?"

"Not likely." He shook his head. "If they knew who I am, they would've never bestowed the rank of the High General on me, allowed me to move to Elaros, or even to return to Sky Kingdom. If they knew, I'd be dead."

I sucked in a breath. "Do you think the king would've killed his own brother?"

"He wouldn't have flinched," he replied confidently. "That's why I've kept quiet about my own suspicions on where I came from and hid anything that might give Tiane a hint. For example, my magic is stronger than most, and I made sure to suppress it as much as I could. There are some things that only the king and I can do."

"Like taking people's memories?"

His gaze warmed as he slid it over my face. "Yes, little bird."

I remembered he'd said he'd never done it before taking mine.

"Have you ever noticed your connection with the weather?" I asked.

He tilted his head. "Don't *you* ever feel like you're connected with it?"

"Me?" I smiled incredulously.

"Yes. Don't you feel down on gloomy, cloudy days? Don't you find sunshine uplifting and light drizzle melancholy inducing?"

"I do. But that's not the same. The weather just impacts the way I feel sometimes."

"But that was exactly what I thought, too. I noticed the connection, but I believed the weather affected my moods, not the other way around."

"That'd be a more logical assumption," I agreed. "No one would think themselves a king just because they felt happy on a sunny day. So," I touched his fisted hand on the table. "What are we going to do now?"

His fist relaxed. Spreading his fingers under my touch, he laced them with mine.

"Now, you'll take care of the book, my darling human, since you're the only one who can touch it. And I will get Alcon in here, as well as the rest of my men."

"Can I stay for your meeting with them?"

"No, sweetheart. The less you know, the safer you will be. Once the word gets out about all of this," he tipped his chin at the book, "being close to me may make you a target. Why don't you run to your room now and get some rest?"

He kissed me quickly before ushering me from the patio.

An unpleasant feeling nagged at me from his dismissal, but I tried not to let it fester. What Voron had just learned about himself was mind-shattering and life-altering. His entire world had been turned upside down. Surely, it needed some time to settle in his brain.

Being "a great king" was a tough job, I imagined. But Voron had already been doing it, on his way to fulfilling the prophecy. He'd been the one to end the wars and bring peace to Sky Kingdom. The peace that might be threatened soon.

Voron had to prove to the world that the Sky Crown belonged to him. With the new instability on the horizon, he had his work cut out for him, and he hadn't even taken the throne yet. It was safe to say, there'd be a fight for that too.

I wished for him to take his rightful place with all my heart. But a tiny, selfish part of me already mourned our short but swelteringly hot exile here in Vensari.

The rest of the day I spent on my own. Voron locked himself in the library along with Alcon, Farion and a few more of his men who'd flown in.

At night, when I was already in bed, the door to my room opened quietly, and he slipped under the covers with me. Hugging me from behind, he kissed my hair.

"I'm sorry I was busy, little bird. Did you have a good day?"

"Mhm…" I turned to face him. "It was quiet and relaxing."

"So, you got some rest?"

"I did."

"Good." He kissed my face, drawing me closer. "Because I need to keep you awake just a little bit longer."

His hand found my breast inside my nightshirt. His thigh nudged my legs open.

I brushed his hair away from his face.

"Voron, what will happen now? Have you decided?"

He trailed kisses down the side of my neck. "Right now, my sweet, enthralling Sparrow, you'll tell me how you want me to make you come. Do you want my hand, my mouth, or my cock?"

All of the above. But I also wanted some answers.

"Will there be a war?" I asked. "It's not like Queen Pavline will give the crown to you willingly. Are you planning to fight her for it?"

He halted his kisses, burying his face between my neck and my shoulder.

"You're right. She won't," he said against my skin. "And yes, I'll have to make her."

"How?"

He leaned back, and I half-expected him to shut me out again. But he stroked my hair, searching my eyes in the moonlight that flooded the room through the open window.

"Are you scared, Sparrow?"

"Instability is always intimidating, isn't it? But I'm not scared. I trust you." After all, I'd stayed in this world with the promise to trust him.

"I'll keep you safe." He cupped my face.

I turned my head, placing a kiss on the inside of his palm. "How will you fight the queen?"

"I'll need an army. And for that, I'll need to get High Lords on my side. They aren't the easiest bunch to convince, but I can be very persuasive." He gave me a cocky smile.

"Will you have to leave Vensari, then?"

"We both will."

"Me, too?"

"Of course. You're the only one who can handle the book, and the book is our main proof of my claim to the throne. Will you come on the road with me, little bird?"

I smiled. "I'll come with you anywhere."

He rolled me to my back and slid his hand between my thighs.

"From now on, I want you everywhere with me. You're moving to my bedroom until we leave."

"To your bedroom? Again?" I asked breathlessly, desire quickly taking over my body.

He nodded before kissing along my jawline, his finger slipping inside me.

"You really shouldn't have left in the first place, sweetheart. It would've saved me the trouble of stomping through the corridors at night, looking for you."

My body arched toward his as he circled my clit with his finger. I moaned, and he jerked his hand away, then entered me swiftly, taking my breath away.

He exhaled into my hair. "This is where I belong, my sweet Sparrow. Inside you is the only place I want to be."

At that moment, I believed it was true.

Chapter Eleven

SPARROW

I folded a long undershirt and put it into a leather-bound trunk. This one would probably be trunk number a million and one of those Voron planned to take on the road with us. For someone who could live from only a saddlebag for weeks, if necessary, he insisted on bringing almost an entire household with us this time.

Part of it was to ensure my comfort, he'd said. But the main reason, I believed, was to demonstrate his status. He didn't want to knock on High Lords' doors, looking like a weary traveler asking for charity. He wished to travel in style and command respect.

Brebie had been busy packing, surrounded by every available servant she could find. And I was helping her, trying to be useful.

"Brebie, can I ask you something?" I started folding another garment, avoiding looking at her.

"Sure. What is it?"

"What do women do in this world to avoid getting pregnant?"

"Avoid it?" She paused with a string of beads she was packing dangling from her fingers. "Why would they avoid it?"

"I know pregnancies are rare among fae and almost always wanted. But what if it was not?"

She dropped the necklace into a jewelry box. "Sparrow. If it happens to you, I'm sure Voron will be happy. I always thought he'd make a great father."

I couldn't help a blush flooding my face. Voron and I hadn't announced our relationship to the world, but to those in Vensari, it must be pretty obvious. One didn't need to be as sharp and perceptive as Brebie to figure it out. Voron hauled me to his bedroom every night, like a dragon stealing a treasure. He'd ordered all my things moved to his bedroom, too, yesterday morning.

Since the night he'd first made love to me, Voron had been generous with his affection, even if other people were around. He didn't try to hide whenever he felt like hugging or kissing me.

But I hadn't spoken to Brebie about us before.

"It's just that they say humans are more fertile than fae, and right now, I simply don't think it'd be a good time."

She peered at me closely.

"Have you talked to Voron about it?"

"I will." I nodded. "But I just wanted to know if there is anything at all like that in Nerifir."

"Well, I don't personally know anyone who'd worry about that in Nerifir, but I've heard *yara* pearls prevent a woman from getting pregnant. The pearl would need to be placed inside you, you know?" She waved a hand in front of her pelvis area. "Where it can remain indefinitely."

"Where do I get a *yara* pearl?"

"They come from the Olathana Ocean. Sirens collect them from the shells to trade with orcs from another world of the River of Mists."

"What world?" I'd never heard of orcs before.

"It's outside of Nerifir, connected to us only by the River of

Mists, just like the human realm is. Voron read about it in the records somewhere. He reads a lot. When does he find the time?" She waved her hands before grabbing another thing to pack. "Apparently, orcs are just as fertile as humans. *Yara* pearls are in demand in their world. Which is a good thing. Who needs an orc overpopulation, really?" She shuddered.

"Is there a place here in Sky Kingdom where I could get that pearl?"

She tapped her chin with her finger. "I don't know. I haven't heard of one. You really should speak to Voron about all of this. If anyone was able to get it for you, it'd be him."

I didn't tell her that it'd been rather difficult to get a chance to talk to him lately. In the past two days, he hadn't even eaten with me once. He got out of bed before I woke and took all his meals in the library with his men. I didn't even know how many of his people were staying in Vensari. They were constantly coming and going, with boots stomping in the corridors and wings flapping outside the windows.

Throughout the day, I only saw Voron in passing here and there, when he would pull me to him in a hallway for a quick kiss or suddenly hug me from behind as I packed and he'd come into the room to get something.

At night, I went to bed alone. Sometime later, Voron would join me, tired but more hungry for my body than ever.

His appetite for me never ebbed. He was truly insatiable, making love to me with the desperation of the first time and as fervently as if every night was our last night together.

"Talk to him," Brebie urged. "You need to know what he thinks about either having a baby or not having one."

"I will."

She held up her hand to the ray of sunshine spilling from the window and smiled at the shadow it cast onto the bedspread.

"The weather has been so lovely lately. Kanbor must be glad to see the sun finally out."

Her fingers trembled slightly, and she squeezed her hand into a fist, moving it to her side. She missed her husband, even if she never said so out loud.

I knew I'd miss the peace and quiet of Voron's exile, but it had hurt many other people. With Voron on the royal throne, things would get better for all of them. Voron would fulfill his life's purpose. And Brebie would finally reunite with her husband.

We left Vensari three days later. I traveled in a comfy carriage while Voron rode horseback, alongside some of his men.

I had the carriage all to myself. I put my feet up onto the seat, leaned with my back against the padded side wall, and took out my knitting.

Sitting sideways like that allowed me to see directly out of the window. Every now and then, I would lift my eyes from my work to watch the green hills of Sky Kingdom roll by. After almost three months spent in this world, I'd seen relatively little of it. Whatever travel I'd done before had been out of necessity. This trip had a purpose, too, but I felt safe with Voron's escort. I could relax and enjoy the scenery.

We rode for a few hours before the carriage stopped and its door opened.

Voron poked his head in. "How are you doing so far?"

"Good, thank you." I lowered my half-finished scarf onto my lap. "And how have you been?"

He took my question as an invitation to climb in and shut the door behind him.

"Bored." He slapped his hand against the front of the carriage, giving the man driving it a sign to keep going.

A moment later, we were on our way again, with the carriage bouncing softly along the packed dirt road.

Voron lifted my feet from the seat and placed them on his lap, sitting down next to me.

"You're bored, so you came here, hoping I'll entertain you?" I smiled.

He rolled his head my way on the high, padded back of the seat. "Could you? Please?"

I laughed, rolling my eyes. "Why don't you just say you missed me?"

"That too," he confessed.

Slipping a hand up my leg and under my skirts, he leaned over for a kiss.

I met him halfway, eager to feel his lips on mine. Grabbing me around the middle, he drew me closer, but I shrank back, pulling the knitting needles with my work out from between us.

"Careful. You'll hurt yourself. These are sharp."

I tossed the whole thing—the needles, the scarf, and the ball of yarn—onto the seat across from us.

Voron narrowed his eyes at my long knitting needles.

"These are handy weapons for a lady."

"Right. To defend myself against the naughty men with wandering hands," I quipped, pressing my legs together to trap his hand between my thighs.

He leaned over me, making me sink backwards into the seat cushions.

"There'll be no other men, Sparrow. Only me," he said firmly. His serious expression no longer matched the light mood of our conversation.

Next, he untied the ribbon in front of my dress, freeing my breasts.

"But that's not the way of the Elaros Court, Voron. When you move back to the Sky Palace, will you change the rules and impose monogamy on them, too? The nobles won't like it."

He sat up, not releasing me from his arms. Hiking up my skirts, he made me straddle his lap, facing him.

"I don't care about the others. They're free to do as they please. But you are mine now. And always will be."

He claimed me so blatantly, a shiver tingled through me at his words.

"How about you, Voron? Will you be only mine, too?"

He arched an eyebrow. "You know I will."

Right. He had no choice. Sex with a fae carried a risk for him. But was that all there was between us? Just sex?

His gaze slid down my chest, stopping on my right breast.

"The image of another man's mouth on your body is haunting me." He kneaded my breast gently, rubbing his palm over my nipple, as if trying to erase every memory of King Tiane's touch from my skin.

"You gave me to him."

"I know. Which made it so much worse." He drew me to him, burying his face in the side of my neck. "I forced myself not to care. I kept repeating that you weren't mine. I believed I simply felt responsible for your wellbeing and wanted you to find something or someone to make you happy in this new world. But I always wished it were me who made you happy, Sparrow. You weren't meant to be mine, but I ended up taking you, anyway. Now, you belong to me and only me."

"I wish for no one else," I breathed out.

He kissed my neck down to my breast, then lifted it to suck the tip into his mouth. He raked his teeth over my skin, kissing and sucking so hard it almost hurt, erasing every sensation of the other man touching me before.

I sank my fingers into his unruly hair and kissed the top of his head. "I am happy to be with you, Voron."

The words and feelings he'd kept to himself in Elaros were pouring out of him now. "You seemed to be willing and content with him, Sparrow. I had no right to stand between the two of you. But I did. I kept Tiane away from you for as long as I could."

"You did? How?"

"By distracting him. I kept other women close to him, organized that hunting trip, hired entertainers... Anything to keep you out of his bedroom."

"It was you, then?" While I'd fretted about gaining and keeping the king's fickle attention, Voron had been sabotaging my efforts.

"It worked. But not for long. The moment I left Elaros to save Magnus, Tiane got you. And I didn't even learn about it until later the day after my return."

"I didn't give you a chance to learn anything. I barged into your room first thing in the morning, remember?"

He smiled, stroking the side of my face. "You were so eager to see me."

I didn't deny it. "I was. I missed you. The palace didn't feel the same without you."

With a hand behind my head, he moved me to him for a kiss.

"I can't share you, Sparrow," he whispered against my lips. "It'd kill me to see you with anyone else. Please, stay with me and me alone."

I rocked my hips, rubbing against the bulge in his pants. He eagerly shoved his hand between us, yanking at the laces of his pants to free his erection.

"There is no one else, Voron. Just you." I rose onto my knees as he aligned himself with my opening. Then I slowly slid down, taking him in.

He tossed his head back with a groan. "Gods... Sparrow, you feel so good."

I rode him slowly at first. Then as the desire burned brighter, demanding a release, I angled my hips, rubbing against him harder. He gripped my thighs, thrusting upwards to meet me.

Voron was the only one I wanted. But he never said those three little words I hoped to hear from him.

He didn't say them when I came, my inner muscles gripping him inside me. Not when he groaned my name about to pump his release into me. I jerked up that very moment, making him slide out of me. Reaching under my skirts, I finished him off with my hand.

"Why, Sparrow?" he asked. "Why did you do it?"

After decades of not being able to climax inside a woman, Voron loved being able to do that with me. But too many doubts and worries swarmed my mind to enjoy him like that with abandon.

I let go of him, searching for the best way to explain.

"Humans are more fertile than fae, they say. With everything that's going on... Have you thought about it, Voron? What would happen if I got pregnant?"

He'd given a promise depriving himself a chance to procreate. He'd made it clear he didn't want to continue his bloodline. But that was before he knew exactly what bloodline he belonged to and in what capacity.

Focus sharpened his features, banishing his relaxed, post-orgasmic expression.

"Every king needs an heir, I suppose." He sounded more concerned than enthusiastic about the prospect.

"You're not the king yet," I pointed out. "You'll have to fight to get the crown, then probably fight even more to keep it. A war is not a good time to have a baby."

He stroked my naked thigh under my skirts, but it felt more like an absentminded gesture than a caress.

I cleared my throat, making a decision. "Voron, how hard would it be for you to get a *yara* pearl?"

He shot me a glance. "How do you know about that?"

"I asked Brebie, and she told me. Is it possible to find one for me?"

Wincing, he shifted under me, but when I made a move to get off his lap, he gripped my waist tightly, keeping me where I was.

"It's not easy," he said. "But if that's what you want, I'll get it for you."

"Thank you."

He kissed my shoulder.

"Now, let's get you cleaned up." He opened the food basket on the seat across. It had a stack of napkins and a bottle of water packed on the top.

His movements remained sure and gentle, his expression calm. But something shifted in the air around us. Instead of being steamy-hot and simple, the atmosphere now felt cooler and tense.

After I was clean and our clothes straightened with all the ribbons and laces tied back in place, I sat next to him on the seat. He wrapped an arm around my shoulders, allowing me to lean into him.

"What are you making?" He pointed with his eyes at my knitting.

I was pleased with the way the royal blue and the steel gray looked together in the stripes of my unfinished scarf. It promised to turn out very well.

"It'll be a scarf once it's done. It's for those freezing storms when you're feeling grumpy," I teased, wishing to lighten his mood a little.

His expression warmed, the corners of his mouth lifting in a smile.

"Stay with me, Sparrow, and there'll be no storms."

"No storms sounds lovely. But how about the rain? Plants need rain every now and then, don't they?"

Hugging my shoulders, he rubbed my arm.

"Rain happens when the Sky King cries. I don't cry, little bird. Not unless I dream, which I have no control over."

True. Every single rainfall I could recall so far had happened at night.

I tilted my head back to see his face better. He was staring out of the window, his mind no longer with me.

"Do you have to get out there again?"

He nodded. "In a minute."

I took in his familiar features, including the deep wrinkle of worry between his eyebrows and the strands of hair draped over it. The hair that turned silver when the woman he loved as his mother was taken away from him and killed. When as a child, he was kicked out of his home and dropped into the strange land Below, left to die.

But he survived. He returned. He succeeded. And I had no doubt he would rule this kingdom soon. Nothing stopped Voron in getting what he wanted.

"Sky King," I said softly, brushing the strands away from his face.

He smiled, catching my hand and kissing my fingers.

The discovery of his origin had been truly mind-blowing, but it no longer shocked me. It was easy to envision a crown on Voron's head. He had enough determination to take what was his, and enough pride to wear it with confidence.

Chapter Twelve

SPARROW

The palace of the High Lord Cardinali was almost as grand and tall as the Sky Palace in Elaros. Its glistening turrets poked like iridescent icicles through the dark woods surrounding it. The facets of the crystal walls shone like diamonds in the sunlight—something I hardly got to see in Elaros, since the sunshine had been so rare back then.

Now, the white fluffy clouds moved along the blue skies above like signs of hope. The sun didn't have the full reign of the sky yet, but it had plenty of room to shine between the clouds.

Compared to the palace, the wide road leading to it didn't look nearly as grand or even well maintained. Thick tree roots and wide rocks in the dirt made my carriage jump and shake. The High Lord clearly didn't care much about maintaining the road. And why would he if everyone of any importance in his household had wings?

When we finally stopped at the door to the palace, I was glad to climb out of the carriage and feel the solid ground under my feet.

Voron dismounted, meeting me on the way to the entrance. A

group of people gathered by the door. Most of them were *snakanas* with some *ariens* and a few *taureans*. They bowed to us, looking uncertain.

A flock of highborn descended from above and landed in front of the servants. The man who acted as the leader of the flock stepped forward. He was shirtless, with golden designs painted over his face and his pale, hairless chest. His floor-length silver cape had a large collar of long bright feathers that fanned out around his neck, making it look as if his head rested on a giant platter.

"Is that the High Lord?" I asked Voron quietly.

"No. That's his current favorite, Barbet."

By the way Barbet held his head, however, one would think his station was far higher than simply a lord's favorite.

Voron marched straight to him.

"Greetings. We've come to speak with your High Lord." He sounded weary; the journey had been rather tiring for all of us.

Barbet hiked his chin up even higher, making me wonder if wearing that many giant feathers made his neck stiff and sore.

"High Lord Cardinali sent *me* to greet you. He doesn't like using the servants' entrance himself. Sadly, we don't have much choice in this case, do we? The main entrance is seven floors up, which clearly is too high for some."

His lips quivered either in a condescending smile or a grimace of distaste. It didn't matter which one. The insult was obvious in his words, as was the pompous look he gave Voron.

Indignation jolted through me like an electric shock. This was such a low blow, even for the arrogant prick that Barbet looked to be. Anger blinded me. I barely heard the swishing of Voron's sword being drawn as I took a step forward.

"Whoa." I squinted at Barbet, tilting my head. "You're way too full of yourself, my lord. Your ego is so bloated, you better hold on to something before you fly off like a balloon, without even having to use your precious wings."

Barbet jerked his head back, blinking at me as everyone

around us broke into laughter. Even the highborn who had come with him snorted and snickered.

He rotated his head back and forth, as if searching for help. His confusion was comical on its own, making the laughter intensify.

The High Lord's courtiers chuckled, some more furtively than others. The servants behind them guffawed to their hearts' content, holding their sides and slapping their thighs or the sides of their tails.

"Who the fuck is *she?*" Barbet shrieked, pointing at me with both hands.

"Lady Sparrow." Voron moved him aside with his sword. "Remember her name with gratitude. She's just saved your life. I would've skewered you like the dumb turkey that you are."

He strolled past Barbet. I stepped around the haughty courtier, too, and said to Voron with a sideways glance at Barbet, "There'd better be a reason for all that self-importance other than those flashy feathers. Though I doubt there is one."

Slapping Barbet's painted face would've felt wonderful. But seeing the look of humiliation in his eyes was almost as satisfying.

Voron shrugged. "Lord Cardinali changes his favorites more often than even Tiane did. He'll probably be replaced before we even leave here."

I noticed he'd stopped referring to his twin brother as "the king." Voron either already thought about himself as the monarch or was training his mind to think that way.

"Now," Voron addressed the crowd gathered behind Barbet. "Is there anyone here less chatty and more useful? You." He pointed with his sword at an *arien* man. "Take us to your High Lord."

High Lord Cardinali was a tall, slender man with long, crimson-red hair and skin just a shade lighter. He rubbed his chin in thought, staring at the tablecloth in front of him.

The dinner had ended. The entire household had been dismissed, leaving Voron and me one-on-one with the High Lord. Voron had told him who he was, and judging by the High Lord's expression, he remained skeptical.

"That sounds interesting, Lord Voron. Nice tale and such, but why have we never heard of your birthright before? Where are the eyewitnesses? There are usually crowds of nobles flocking around a royal birthing. Yet no one has said a word about your birth for almost two hundred years."

"Out of the people present that day, only two have survived," Voron replied.

The High Lord shook his head. "That's impossible."

"Not if they have deliberately been eradicated."

Scratching his chin, the High Lord mulled over Voron's words.

"Who are the surviving two?"

"The priest and the musician." Voron leaned back in his chair. "But I'm sure they have given so many promises to the royal family that they would perish the moment they even think about speaking the truth."

The High Lord frowned.

"That makes your claim rather problematic, don't you think?"

"No, I do not. Because I do have proof." He turned to me. "Sparrow, would you bring the book here, please?"

Since none of the servants could touch the book to take it to our rooms with the rest of our things, I'd brought it into the dining hall with me and left it on one of the narrow stands by the wall.

I carried it to the massive dining table covered with a delicate lace tablecloth and placed it in front of the High Lord.

Lifting his eyes at me, he said to Voron with a smirk, "You stole the king's pet and now you want his crown."

A snappy reply froze on my tongue. This wouldn't be the same as putting Barbet in his place. Angering a High Lord would have far worse consequences. Besides, Voron needed his help to go against the queen.

I kept quiet. Voron calmly folded his arms across his chest.

"*Lady* Sparrow," he said with emphasis, "is no one's pet. And the crown was never meant to be Tiane's." He nodded to me. "Show him."

I opened the book, quickly leafing through to the very end when it all began. I couldn't watch the scene of Voron's birth again. It was still fresh in my mind, including all the emotions it had caused in me the first time around. Instead, I watched the High Lord.

His eyebrows rose higher and higher in surprise as the scene of the royal birth unfolded in front of his eyes. Once it finished, his forehead furrowed in concentration. Now, he too became an eyewitness.

"That's impossible," he mumbled as I closed the book. "Fae don't birth multiples. Only animals deliver litters."

Voron's expression remained impenetrable, but his voice came out hard enough to cut steel when he replied, "There have been three deliveries of twins recorded in Sky Kingdom in the past millennium."

The High Lord shook his head. "Twins *and* a wingless child. Talk about being rare."

"Rare indeed." Voron smirked confidently and echoed the prophecy. "A great king was born that day. I am one of a kind."

By now, I knew him well enough to glimpse the vulnerability in his cockiness. He used his unbridled confidence as a shield against the judgment of those who thought him lacking. Whatever others deemed as his disadvantage, he displayed it as a unique quality that made him special, forcing people to appreciate it. And it worked.

The High Lord nodded slowly, giving Voron an appraising stare.

"So, you want to take the Sky Crown?"

Voron nodded. "It was meant to be mine all along."

The High Lord's coal-black eyes glimmered with calculation.

"With the current king as good as dead, now would be the best time to act. But the queen won't give up that easily."

"I know. She'll fight. That's why I'm here. I need an army."

The High Lord shifted uneasily.

"I pledged my loyalty to the Crown of the Sky Kingdom."

"Right." Voron rolled back his shoulders, placing his elbows on the armrests. "But the crown is on the head of an imposter—a nearly dead imposter, I should add. You'll be doing it a favor by returning it to its rightful owner."

High Lord Cardinali looked doubtful. "If I join you in your quest, I'll break my promise of loyalty."

"No, you won't. I gave the same promise you did. But the crown is currently on the wrong head." The High Lord stirred uneasily, clearly not ready to take such a risk. Voron lifted his hand in a pacifying gesture. "Either way, I'm not asking you to risk it, my lord. In fact, I would insist you keep your promise and fly to Elaros promptly to warn the queen. Leave your army here, under the command of your son, who is *not* bound by that promise. Isn't that what High Lord Bussard did right after his father passed away? He fought against me and the royal army in the last war."

The High Lord nodded with a knowing smile.

"He and the son of the High Lord of Elandor, as well as the son of the High Lady of Miraren, and —"

"And a few others," Voron finished for him. "They all have tried to fight me, and they all have lost. I always get what I want, my lord. It's best for you to be on the winning side from the beginning. Once the Sky Crown is finally on my head where it belongs, your support will not be forgotten."

"Hmm." The High Lord placed his elbows on the table and steepled his fingers, pondering Voron's words.

Voron didn't hurry him, idly straightening the lacy frills on the cuffs of his sleeves.

"You want the queen to know your plans?" the High Lord asked.

A sly smile ghosted across Voron's lips.

"No. Of course I don't want her to know them. That's why I didn't reveal any details to you. But I do want you to tell her and the entire royal court what you saw in the book. I want all of Elaros to know the true king is coming to claim his rightful place. And I want to give everyone a chance to decide whose side they want to be on."

"Well," the High Lord grunted, rising from his chair. "I shall rush to Elaros to inform the queen of the upcoming unrest, as my loyalty vow dictates. Meanwhile, I'm leaving you in the capable hands of my son, Lord Bruant."

As the lord left the room, and just before his son entered, Voron smiled at me and winked.

He did it. He got his way.

"Do you think it'll be possible to convince the rest of the High Lords like that, too?" I asked Voron once we finally were alone in our room, much later that night.

Not wasting a second, he'd already started working on the ribbons of my dress.

"Not all of them," he said. "Bussard and Caitore, for example, are firmly on the queen's side. She's playing them against each other, while keeping them both hopeful they'll become the next Sky King by marrying her. There are a few others that I may not sway. But we don't need them all, dear Sparrow. We just need enough to show the queen I have the power to take what's mine."

He wasn't the ten-year-old boy anymore, someone easily cast aside and forgotten. Voron had real victories behind his belt now. The highborn had seen him repeatedly prove his skills and knowledge in battles. He'd earned the respect of many. He had what it took to lead and govern. And now, he also had a legitimate claim to the throne. One had to be either delirious or stupid not to see that.

Voron slid my dress down, then took my shirt off over my head.

"Come here," he murmured, dragging me to him.

"You must be exhausted after the day we had." I helped him take his shirt off, too, as he lowered to his knees in front of me, kissing down my chest.

"I am." He grinned, glancing up at me. "That's why we need to do this fast before I fall asleep."

I laughed softly. "Will you stay awake long enough for me to have a bath? I really need one after that dusty road."

"Fine. But only if I can have it with you."

He pulled off his pants and boots, then scooped me up into his arms and headed to the bathroom door.

I wrapped my arms around his neck and pressed my nose to his neck, breathing him in. No matter how tiring our journey had been, as a fae, Voron always smelled fantastic. As a human, that made me long for a bath even more.

He sat me down next to the warm pool in the bathroom.

"You don't have to carry me everywhere." I smiled. "I can walk, you know?"

He cupped my face with his hands, staring into my eyes.

"And I can fight my own battles. But it was nice having you stand up to Barbet for me today. Thank you."

"I don't have much to fight with, just my words. But I'll never let anyone disrespect you like that," I said earnestly.

There was no smile on his face, no pretense or cockiness. His expression was raw and real. This was the true Voron, just the way he was. He knew he didn't need to hide from me any longer.

"My fierce little bird." He leaned his forehead against mine. "That's more than anyone has ever done for me in my adult life."

As he lowered me into the warm water, covering my body with his, I knew every word I'd said was true. I would fight for him, either with words or a sword if I had to. I would fight for this man to the end.

Chapter Thirteen

SPARROW

It wasn't always quick or simple, but one by one, Voron had convinced every single High Lord we visited in the next two weeks to join him. His mix of confidence, power, and detached charisma proved invincible.

As the time passed, he also grew more impatient. Almost everything was ready, and he longed for action. The energy burst from him. He was so close to what he wished for. There remained just one more palace left to visit.

"High Lord Pelargos," Voron said the name of the man we were about to see.

Like most of the trip, I traveled in the carriage, and Voron rode horseback. I leaned out of the open window, resting my folded arms on the frame, and he kept his horse close enough for us to talk.

Several of his men, including Alcon, soared above us, watching out for any signs of danger in the sky and below. Magnus flew nearby, ducking in and out of the trees on the side of the road to catch bugs and whatever else that bird deemed food.

"Does High Lord Pelargos have a son, too, who will lend you his support despite his father's vow of loyalty?" I asked.

"No. He has a daughter as far as I recall. But he has only recently taken over the throne of his father, the late High Lord. He hasn't given any promises to the crown yet. He is expected to show up at Elaros to do so. But I politely asked him to grant me an audience first."

He grinned, his eyes twinkling with amusement. This was a game he played well, and he clearly enjoyed it.

We arrived at the palace with enough time before dinner to wash up and get changed. When a servant came with the official invitation for dinner, I grabbed the book on the way out of our rooms.

"Ready?" Voron smiled at me. "This is the last time you have to carry this." He tipped his chin at the heavy volume in my arms.

"Just when I finally got used to schlepping it around," I quipped. "You should see my arm muscles."

He leaned down for a quick kiss just before the doors to the dining room opened.

"I'm looking forward to seeing your arm muscles tonight, as well as everything else you're hiding under that dress," he murmured in my ear only for me to hear.

My face flushed as I entered the room with him, pressing the book to my chest.

"Lord Voron!" A blond man rushed to greet us. Grabbing Voron's hand in both of his, he bowed. "It's an honor to welcome you to my family home."

"High Lord Pelargos." Voron inclined his head politely.

The High Lord promptly whisked Voron to the head of the table where he offered him a seat next to a richly dressed, beautiful woman.

"Do you remember my daughter? Lady Lark?" The High Lord asked.

"Of course." Voron bowed with a smile. "How could I ever forget?"

The lady smiled sweetly in response. "We hardly had a chance to talk the last time I saw you, my lord. I hope to remedy it tonight."

I put the book on a marble console by the wall. There was no need to guard it. No one could take it. Turning back to the table, I pondered where to sit now that Voron was making new friends. He twisted in his chair, searching the room.

"Sparrow. Come here." He gestured at the seat on his left as Lady Lark already occupied the one on his right.

Lady Lark gave me a brief nod as I came closer.

"Would you introduce us, please?" She touched Voron's sleeve to get his attention, then casually let her hand linger on his forearm for far longer than was necessary.

"Lady Sparrow," he introduced me. "A dear friend of mine."

A friend.

It was a huge step up from my previous official position as a royal pet. But with Voron, somehow it still didn't feel enough.

Was I too greedy to wish for more?

What did I really want? Voron proclaiming his undying love to me in front of all these important people? It was ridiculous.

And yet... I wouldn't mind hearing the words from him, both in public and in private.

"Nice to meet you, Lady Lark." I took my seat on Voron's left.

The lady was already chatting away with Voron, however, paying me no attention.

"How long has it been since I had the pleasure of seeing you last, my lord?" She tapped her full pink lips with the tip of her slim finger. "A few years back for sure, right after my fiftieth birthday, in Elaros."

Voron nodded noncommittally. "I believe you're right."

About twice my age, Lady Lark radiated youth and beauty. Her pale skin had a delicate blue shimmer, making her appear as if glowing with moonlight. Her flaxen blonde hair was braided and styled with gemstones and violet blossoms.

The semi-transparent material of her flowing white dress

allowed for a good view of her small, perky breasts with pink areolas and the hard, pearl-sized nipples. Despite the partial nudity, nothing about her could be called trashy or vulgar. She looked elegant, beautiful, and sensual—everything to make any woman jealous.

"Don't Lord Voron and Lady Lark look wonderful together?" a woman on my left cooed, leaning toward me.

I tore my gaze away from Lady Lark's nipples and sank it into my wineglass instead.

"Yes, yes, they do."

"You don't need to worry, dear." The woman kindly petted my hand. "My niece is a fair and kind woman. She treats all her servants well. One should welcome the opportunity to become a part of her household."

What on earth was she talking about?

"Just look at her," the woman gushed. "So regal. I always said Lark was born to be a queen."

A queen.

The nice lady on my left was already envisioning her niece as Voron's wife. He had succeeded in making the lords view him as the future king. And as such, the position of his wife was now coveted, too.

Lady Lark's aunt didn't need to sing praises for her niece. Anyone could see how smart and beautiful her niece was. How easily she could maintain a light but interesting conversation, engaging not just Voron but everyone around the table.

Her humor was so fine, more than one of her jokes went right over my head. But Voron laughed at all of them, and that was what mattered. She made him laugh.

The dinner seemed to drag on for an eternity. But like all things, good and bad, it finally came to an end.

The High Lord rose from his chair. "Lord Voron, would you join us in the drawing room? We have a few things to discuss."

"With pleasure." Voron got up, his movements closely shadowed by Lady Lark, who promptly lined up on his right, ready to escort him to the drawing room.

I hurried to get the book, then followed them to the open double doors on the side of the dining room.

After everyone entered, the guards at the door blocked my way in.

"The High Lord doesn't need to see the book," one of them said.

"He doesn't?" I blinked, confused.

"The High Lord knows what it contains. He's heard enough people talk about it."

"Well, but I..." Rising on my tiptoes, I craned my neck, trying to catch Voron's attention over the guard's shoulder.

Voron wasn't looking in my direction, however. His head inclined gracefully, he listened to Lady Lark saying something into his ear. She gestured animatedly with one hand, the other was hooked into his arm as she pressed herself into his side.

"You're free to leave, my lady," the guard said, spelling it out for me as I lingered by the doors.

"Um... Can I just speak to Voron for a moment? I meant Lord Voron? He has to know where I am, in case he needs me later."

What if he didn't need me anymore? Ever?

The book had done its job. There were now enough witnesses to confirm Voron's birthright. People had accepted him as the rightful king. What he needed now was an army, which I couldn't give him, anyway.

He no longer needed me.

The doors to the drawing room were shut, and the guards crossed their spears in front of them, sealing any possibility for me to enter.

Pressing the book to my chest, I tried to ignore the emptiness forming inside me and the burning of the tears welling in my eyes. I turned away, hiding my face from the guards. There was nothing left for me to do but to retreat with dignity. Holding my head up high, I exited into the hallway.

Trying to remember the way back to our rooms, I turned left, then walked down the narrow staircase.

Like in any other palace we'd visited, the stairs here were used primarily by servants. The highborn moved between the floors by simply flying from one open patio to another. There wasn't even the inner staircase like the grand stairs in Elaros.

I turned into a narrow, dimly lit corridor and went down the stairs when a dark, winged shadow crossed the floor. Rough, strong hands grabbed my shoulders from behind, then jerked to my neck.

"Wha..." I only managed to gasp before the hands closed over my throat.

The hard grip blocked my airway. The person clearly intended to kill me.

Panic speared me.

Horror blanked my vision as I struggled to breathe.

Gripping the book in my hands, I swung it up and whacked my assailant over his head. My mind was already floating into darkness, and the blow wasn't hard. I barely tapped him. But the book did the rest.

A ball of light exploded. My would-be-killer groaned in pain, letting go of my neck. The invisible force of the magic wards knocked him down to the ground. Like everyone else in this kingdom, my attacker was a fae and couldn't touch the book without the consequences.

Pressing my weapon to my chest, against my racing heart, I ran back to the stairs. Someone was jogging down them, however. The sound of a sword sliding out of the sheath made me pause.

"Voron?" I called out in hope.

I wished it was him. He was the one whose arms I needed so much to feel around me right now.

Of course, it could also be another attacker, coming to finish me off. I raised the book over my head, getting ready to hit again.

"Lady Sparrow?" Alcon rushed down with the rustling of his wings that he used to practically glide over the stairs. "Are you all right?"

"Alcon." I leaned with my back against the wall, relief banishing the tension of fear from me. "Someone has just attacked me. There." I pointed down the corridor.

Alcon dashed in that direction, chasing the retreating footsteps. He returned quickly, however.

"Did he get away?" I asked.

Alcon nodded. "Whoever he is, he knows this palace better than I do. I don't want to leave you alone now. Come, my lady. I'll escort you to your bedroom."

He didn't put his sword away, holding it ready as he led me down the corridor and into the rooms that were given to Voron and me.

"I'll stay close until Lord Voron returns," Alcon assured me.

"When will he be back, you think?"

He shifted to another foot. "Probably not for a while. A lot of details need to be worked out."

The details that I wasn't allowed to know or be a part of.

I nodded, doing my best to look unaffected.

"If it's going to take him that long, why don't you come and sit inside, then? There is a couch in the front sitting room. You may as well be comfortable while you're watching over me."

"As you wish, my lady."

With Alcon in the sitting room, I took my time in the bathroom, getting ready for the night. I took a bath, washed and brushed my hair, cleaned my teeth and my face, all the while keeping an ear on every sound outside the bedroom door.

When Voron still hadn't returned, I climbed under the covers and closed my eyes. My throat hurt. I'd probably have bruises tomorrow from the rough grip of the stranger trying to kill me. Chills ran down my back. I rubbed my neck, trying to chase away the memory of the ruthless fingers crushing my windpipe.

I didn't think I would sleep that night, but the exhaustion of the travels took its toll. Eventually, I drifted asleep. The dip of the mattress from someone climbing into the bed with me woke me with a start.

"Who's here?" I jumped up, wide awake.

"Shhh. It's me." Voron wrapped an arm around me from behind, settling me back under the covers.

"Oh." I relaxed with my back pressed to his hard, warm chest. "What time is it?"

"Late. So late, it's almost early again. How are you? Alcon said you were attacked? Did you see who it was?"

"I didn't see his face." I rubbed my eyes, trying to think through the lingering fog of sleep. "It was a man. That's all I know. Maybe he just was after the book?"

"Maybe." He didn't sound convinced. "I'll get to the bottom of it and will serve the attacker's fucking head to you on a silver platter, even if it's the last thing I do."

I snorted a laugh. "The last thing I need is a dead head on a plate." His outrage was genuine. But it masked fear in his voice. The fear for me. "I promise to be more careful next time. I'll try not to walk anywhere on my own."

He nodded. "From now on, Alcon will go everywhere with you when I'm not around. For your protection."

How often would it happen, I wondered, that Voron wouldn't be around. The more I thought about him as the king, the harder it was to envision myself at his side.

"How was your night?" I asked, unsure if I even wanted to hear the answer.

He kissed my shoulder. "Good. Very productive."

Lady Lark's name was on the very tip of my tongue, but I didn't want to say it out loud.

"They didn't let me into the drawing room," I said instead.

"Mm-hmm," he hummed against my skin, kissing along my shoulder toward my neck. "It was best for you to stay away this time. Especially now when they're sending assassins after you. But I will make sure you're never alone."

He slid his hand into the neckline of my nightshirt, quickly finding my breast. His erection, already hard like a rock, pressed to my behind.

"Voron." I gently but firmly retrieved his hand from my nightshirt. "I'm really tired. Can we just sleep, please?"

He stilled. This was the only time since the day he'd first touched me that I refused him.

Was he shocked? Hurt? Angry?

Probably all of that, to some degree. But he didn't show it.

"Sure. Let's sleep. Good night." He sounded perfectly composed, so freakishly good at hiding his emotions, even from me.

I didn't intend to hurt him. This wasn't some misplaced revenge on my part. But something inside me had fractured, at least for tonight. I couldn't simply get lost in his touch like I had so easily done before.

With a sigh, I closed my eyes, wishing he would still hold me. But he didn't. Rolling to the other side of the bed, he left me alone.

Chapter Fourteen

SPARROW

The Sky Palace looked very different to me this time.

The crystals shone brighter than before. The sky-touching height of it was as impressive as ever. But there was a sinister energy in that building to me now. The last time I left here, I had barely escaped with my life. And here I was, coming back to this cursed place, hoping that this time, it'd be different.

Swarms of royal guards flying around the palace in protective formations brought a wasps' nest to mind, which only intensified the heavy feeling inside me. Flocks of Voron's men and allies surrounded the palace. He rode ahead. At a full gallop on horseback, he was able to keep up with his men who flew.

Soon, I lost him from sight. The shimmering crystal walls seemed to swallow him. My carriage dragged along the road way too slow.

We entered through the castle gates and stopped. Alcon made a wide circle around the carriage before landing at my window.

"Stay inside, my lady." He sounded tense. His sword drawn, he scanned the skies above.

A battle was raging over our heads. Instead of the clouds, people and wings obstructed the sun this morning. Clanking of weapons, cries of pain, and swishing of wings filled the air.

With a thud, a body dropped from the sky onto the road. Blood splattered the pavement stones. I watched in horror as a twister of speckled brown feathers settled around the dead guard, his wings of the same color twisted and broken under him.

I clutched the book of records to my chest, the book that started it all. Actually, *I* started all this bloodshed by finding and reading the damn book.

Voron ran from around the palace. He caught sight of me in the window of the carriage and rushed to me.

Dressed in armor, with a silver-tone breastplate, bejeweled pauldrons, and wide arm bracers, he looked both magnificent and fierce. His sleeve was slashed, the arm underneath scratched. Blood was dripping from the sword in his hand. His eyes glistened, his cheeks flushed.

"Kiss me for good luck." He gripped the back of my neck, pulling me to him for a hot, messy kiss.

His fervent excitement seeped into me. I rooted for him with all my heart. I wished for him to succeed.

"Go, Voron. Get what you want," I urged when he broke the kiss.

He flashed me a grin, taking off toward the palace doors. At least a dozen guards homed in on him from above. But once Voron had crossed the threshold into the palace, they were forced to land and fold their wings to follow him. Inside the first few floors of the palace with the low ceilings and narrow stairs of the servants' quarters, wings gave the guards no advantage over Voron. He knew it, choosing to climb the stairs to get up to the royal chambers.

With my focus on the palace doors, I didn't see the guard sneaking around my carriage until it was too late. He yanked my door open.

"And what do we have here?" he sneered, reaching inside the carriage for me.

Struck by horror, I gulped in air.

"How about a very important book?" I blurted out. "Here, take it!"

I shoved it into his outstretched hands. The explosion of light blinded me. But I didn't feel the impact that tossed the fae to the ground. Howling in pain, he rolled on the cobblestones.

Like an angel of vengeance, Alcon descended from the sky, his sword pointing downwards. He speared the guard, pinning him to the ground, then gestured to me.

"Time to go, my lady. You're needed."

Still shaking with adrenaline, I climbed out of the carriage, pressing the book to my chest. Alcon eyed it suspiciously.

"Um..." He rubbed the back of his neck. "I'll have to fly you up there."

"Right." I shifted the book to my side, holding it under my arm. "Just make sure not to touch it, and we'll be fine."

Alcon stepped around me gingerly, as if walking on shards of crystal. Holding me with one arm around my shoulders and another one under my knees, he lifted me up and pressed my book-free side to his chest.

"All right." He hit the air with his large, brown-gray wings, taking us up.

I held my book out, ready to zap anyone who dared getting in the way. But Alcon masterfully maneuvered through the battle in the sky, avoiding a collision. He landed on the patio outside of the king's rooms and quickly ushered me inside.

Not much had changed in the royal bedroom. The layout and the furniture remained the same—all stark white and glistening gold.

The king lay in his bed behind the light curtains that gently billowed in the breeze. Voron and his men faced a group of courtiers and priests of the various gods of the Sky Kingdom.

I recognized some of the courtiers. All were armed, their

weapons lowered at the moment. Tension hung heavily in the room. No one was fighting, but a battle threatened to break out any minute, ending the stand-off.

"Show them, Sparrow," Voron ordered.

I didn't need to ask what he meant. Placing the book on the stand at the foot of the royal bed, the very same stand where King Tiane had put my empty glass after tricking me into drinking the *camyte*, I opened it to the last page. The scene of Voron's birth started playing, and I averted my eyes. I'd heard it played many times over by now, but I'd only seen it once. And once had been enough.

My gaze traveled to the king instead. Through the gaps in the swaying curtains, I saw his chest move with his breathing. He appeared to be sleeping peacefully if it weren't for the dagger sticking out of his chest.

My stomach tightened with knots at the memories of the night I'd stabbed him.

Why hadn't the queen pulled the dagger out and set his spirit free? It was safe to assume there were no sentimental feelings holding her back. Queen Pavline had clearly moved on already, searching for a new husband.

Then the circlet of golden thorns over the king's brow caught my attention, and the answer came to me. The queen didn't dare take the crown off. That piece of jewelry held too much power to risk removing it. Tiane was the one of the current royal bloodline, not Pavline. And Tiane wasn't the only one of the ruling bloodline left.

Now, I understood why Voron wished for the queen to know early on who he was, why he allowed High Lord Cardinali to warn her weeks ago. He wanted her to know she could not start a new dynasty as long as the current one still existed. It gave him time to gain the support of the High Lords, while the queen spent weeks plagued by indecision, scared to remove the crown from Tiane. Voron controlled the weather, but as long as Tiane wasn't dead, the power of the crown remained with Tiane.

"You see, ladies and gentlemen," Voron said as the sounds and sights of the scene faded back into the book's pages. "I'm not the usurper here. I simply come to claim what's mine."

The people in the room remained still, stunned by the proof they'd just seen. In their silence, Voron sauntered to the bed and ripped open the curtains between him and his twin brother.

The two looked nothing alike. Voron was pale and dark-haired. Tiane had tan skin with hair so blond, it looked almost white with silvery shine. Only the color of Tiane's eyes was the same as Voron's on a sunny day. But Tiane's eyes were now closed, never to open again.

"This should've been done long ago," Voron said softly, reaching for the handle of the dagger.

His fingers hovered over the handle. I waited, expecting him to grab and pull it out. But he fisted his hand, pulling away.

A confused murmur ran through the small crowd behind us. Two kings in one kingdom were one too many. The world seemed suspended in anticipation, unable to move on. It needed a solution.

Voron stared at the face of the man who had usurped his power and taken his place. But I believed that was not what Voron was thinking about right now. Maybe he saw the twin brother he never got to grow up with, the last of his real family he was never allowed to be a part of. Maybe he wondered if things could be better between them under different circum-stances.

Whatever it was, I realized that if Voron ended his brother's life, it would haunt him forever.

I saw past the gorgeous blond locks and the innocent serenity of Tiane's face on the pillow. I thought back to when his eyes were open and there was nothing but cruelty in them. I remembered when he held that very same dagger at my chest, slicing my skin open for his entertainment. I remembered the fear that racked me and how it thrilled him. I recalled the helplessness, terror, and desperation I felt just before I stabbed him. I'd been ready to die that night. And I would have died, had it not been for the other-worldly magic in the weapon I used.

A wave of resentment and determination washed over me. I stepped forward, approaching the bed from the opposite side.

"Allow me." I grabbed the handle of the dagger and yanked it out in one firm movement.

My hand didn't shake, not even when I tossed the dagger back on the bed, a rusty smear of blood staining the pristine white coverlet.

"Sparrow." Voron gazed at me from across the bed, looking shocked but relieved.

I turned to face the courtiers and the priests.

"You have one king, now," I said, my voice ringing high with the emotion I refused to display in any other way. "Voron is the one true Sky King."

I finished what I had started. I killed a man. I didn't regret it. It had to be done. But I mourned the last shred of my innocence that disappeared with my becoming a murderer.

The doors to the room burst open and royal guards rushed in, followed by the infuriated Queen Pavline.

"How dare you?" She glared at Voron and his men, then at the courtiers, who promptly retreated to the walls. "How dare you disturb the peace—"

Her eyes widened in horror as she spotted the dagger on top of the covers.

"What have you done?" she wailed, wringing her hands.

"He deserved it all and more for what he's done to others," Voron replied calmly.

The queen shook with hatred.

"You should've stayed down in the Below," she snarled. "King Herane took care of you for us. He thought you dead and never warned us about the vulture that you are. Now look what you've done! You murdered your own brother."

"He didn't," I said. "I killed your husband. I believe you know why."

"You?" The queen turned her head to face me, her movements ominously slow. "You were meant to be a solution. But you, dirty little rat, you ruined everything!"

Shimmering green-and-purple wings snapped open from the queen's back. She leaped over the king's bed to me. Swiping the dagger off the bed, she lunged at me with it.

The air sang with the swish of a blade cutting through it.

The queen staggered back with a gurgling noise trapped in her throat, Voron's sword piercing her chest. Red sparks of Nerifir iron flashed along his blade, poisoning the queen's blood.

Voron yanked his sword out, and the queen fell backwards, across the dead body of her husband spread out on the bed.

"Sparrow." Voron rushed to me. "Are you hurt?"

He grabbed my shoulders, scanning my face.

I swallowed hard, staring at the dagger on the floor. If it wasn't for Voron and his quick sword, that thing would've been in me right now. I'd be joining Tiane in whatever hell he'd departed to. But there was not a scratch on me at all.

"You saved me," I exhaled, barely able to move my lips from the horror still gripping me. "I'm fine."

Cupping the back of my head with his free hand, he pulled me into his chest. "Thank gods."

"You saved my life," I repeated into his hard breast plate.

He kissed my hair. "A small repayment for everything you've done for me, little bird."

With one arm around my shoulders, he wiped his sword on the bedspread before sheathing it in its usual place on his back. He then leaned over and ripped the golden circlet from Tiane's head.

It was not the same crown that King Herane wore in the book. Tiane had it modified to fit under his antlers. He'd removed the tallest spikes and had an opening cut on the back.

Instead of putting it on his head, Voron lifted it high in his hand.

"The Sky Crown is mine."

The courtiers in the room got down on one knee, followed by the guards and Voron's men.

"Long live the king!" Their voices blended into one.

I bowed my head, too, sinking into a deep curtsy. "Long live the king."

There was no place for any confusion or uncertainty anymore. The Sky Kingdom had the one true king.

Chapter Fifteen

SPARROW

The next afternoon, Alcon knocked on the door to Voron's former living room that was now mine. The new king gave me his entire suite.

"Lady Dove and Lady Libelle are here to see you, Lady Sparrow," Alcon announced.

I was glad to hear their names, glad to have company because even though I stayed in Voron's rooms now, Voron wasn't here. I spent the last night alone with Alcon, Farion, Raine, and Zinfir, some of Voron's most trusted men, who took turns in the sitting room as my personal guards.

"Thank you, Alcon."

"Should I get Alacine to bring you tea?" he asked, giving me a pointed look. My bodyguard was far more versed in palace etiquette than I could ever hope to be. He knew I should serve some refreshments when receiving highborn visitors.

"Sure. Thanks."

With a bow, Alcon left, leaving the door open.

"Sparrow!" Dove rushed in. "Oh, Mother Goddess of Beauty, just look at this suite!" She danced through the spacious living room, her arms outstretched. "These are the nicest rooms after the royal chambers."

The space was nice. It was just right for Voron when he was the second most powerful man in the kingdom. Now, however, he preferred different accommodations.

The joint funeral for Tiane and Pavline was held last night, barely hours after their deaths. Voron made sure they received a lavish send-off, appropriate to their station as the royal family. As per tradition, their bodies were laid atop the tallest tower of Elaros.

The entire court had gathered around the tower. I was there, too. Invisible patches appeared on the skin and in the hair of the royal couple as the air claimed their physical forms. I was told there would be nothing left of their bodies soon. As for their souls, they'd be judged in the afterlife. I hoped the judgment was fair, but my personal dealings with these two people were now done. Finally free of them, I held no grudge against their memories.

"It's so nice to see you again, Dove." I hugged her and might have held her a little longer than was appropriate or necessary. "Thank you. Thank you for everything."

She giggled, petting my shoulder, then passed me to Libelle for a hug.

"Look how well it all worked out." Libelle smiled, enclosing me into an embrace. "We have a new king, and you're still the royal favorite."

"And these rooms!" Dove gushed. "They are such a step up from your old little bedroom. King Voron clearly holds you in much higher regard than King Tiane ever did."

"*King Voron*. It still sounds so bizarre to my ear." I gestured for them to take their seats at the table that Alacine had set for tea.

"We'll all get used to it soon enough." Dove sat down, promptly followed by Libelle. "The coronation is tomorrow. It'll be easier to think of him as the king when the Sky Crown is on his head. One thing is for sure now, you're not going to any menagerie, Sparrow."

Libelle nodded, picking up her teacup. "They say the new king is even more besotted with you than the previous one was."

"What's your secret?" Dove giggled.

Besotted.

The word scraped my hearing. It echoed what people used to say about King Tiane's feelings for me.

I didn't want anyone to be obsessed or *besotted* with me. When it came to Voron, I just wished for something gentle and warm. Something real, more enduring than infatuation and far longer lasting.

"Her secret is that she is human," Libelle answered Dove. "It's easier to catch a man's eye when one is so unique. She's truly one of a kind."

"Yes, but she didn't just catch his eye. Voron, I mean *King* Voron, is smitten. Did you know that he told High Lord Pelargos that he's not interested in marriage?"

Libelle shrugged. "Maybe he just doesn't fancy the High Lord's daughter Lady Lark. Which makes sense, she is such a snooty stuck-up."

"He said that?" The prospect of Voron getting married made me sick to my stomach. "He said he's not interested in her?"

"Something like that. Yes." Dove fluffed her curls by running her fingers through them. "But Pelargos won't give up. Every High Lord with an unmarried daughter, sister, or niece is extremely excited. It's not often that an opportunity to marry into the royal family presents itself. My father sent me a message with the snow owl this morning. He's offering the king my hand in marriage, too." She laughed. "Imagine that!"

I did not want to imagine Voron marrying anyone at all, least of all, someone I considered my friend. I swallowed hard against the tightness in my throat. "Will Voron *have* to get married?"

Libelle lifted a pastry from the tray. It was a snowberry tart, my favorite. Only right now, I couldn't even think about food. My stomach felt too tight to squeeze even a single berry in.

"Sooner or later, he will have to choose a bride," Libelle said. "The date hasn't been established yet, but the Council won't allow the king to remain unmarried for too long."

"Why not?" I asked.

"Because the stability in the kingdom depends on the continuation of the royal bloodline. The king has to get married, with his queen hopefully giving him an heir soon thereafter."

"Every king needs an heir," Voron had said.

And now, I was no longer the only woman who could give him a child. His coronation was tomorrow. The Crown of the Sky Kingdom would be formally put upon his head. And with it, all the promises made to the crown will become the promises to him. He can finally release himself from all of them. He'd be free to procreate with any fae of his choosing.

Dove noticed my crestfallen expression.

"Oh, don't worry, Sparrow. The king likes you. I'm sure he will keep you as his favorite. The queen will be there only to sit at his side for all the boring official functions. But you'll have his bed."

"You'll be at all the after-dinner parties," Libelle chimed in. "You'll have all the fun."

"He'll only have to visit her chambers once in a while until they have an heir."

The thought of Voron having sex with another woman, no matter how infrequently, made my chest tighten, depriving me of breath. I felt physically sick. I couldn't even look at the food on the table, afraid I'd throw up.

The image of Lady Lark's hand on Voron's arm wouldn't leave me, making me want to scream. What would I do, knowing that he was spending a night with her or anyone else?

"What is it, Sparrow?" Dove set down her teacup, staring at me with a shocked expression.

Libelle blinked. "Poor thing, she looks white like marble, which, with her complexion, isn't ideal."

"You're in love with him!" Dove gasped.

Libelle coughed, choking on her tea. "What? You love Voron?"

"*King* Voron," Dove corrected her mechanically. Her throat bobbed with a swallow. "Sparrow, sweetie, I won't marry him, no matter what my father tells me. All right?"

"Thanks." I shut my eyes and dropped my head into my hand, my elbow propped onto the table.

I loved Voron?

When did it happen?

How?

I distinctly remembered giving a resolution to hate him from the very beginning. He had approved of that, too.

But then...

Was it sex? The sex with Voron was insanely good. Physically, I'd always wanted him, even when I knew it was best to hate him.

Oh, but there was so much more between us than just sex. I'd gotten to know him well, and I felt like he was the only one who truly knew me.

I admired Voron's strength, endurance, and determination. It was hard not to love those qualities in him. But I also knew all about his faults, weaknesses, and vulnerabilities. And what was worse, I loved all of them too.

"I'm so screwed," I groaned.

I'd hoped so badly to hear the three little words from him, first. Then, I could've loved him back with abandon, without any reservations or the fear of getting hurt.

Instead, I fell for him first.

Now what? What if he didn't care about me as much as I cared about him?

"It's not so bad," Dove chirped optimistically.

I lifted my head, looking at them both for help, or advice, or something. Anything.

"What future can we have?" I asked. "It's not like he would ever marry me, right? Not while he's a king. And I'm... My status here is barely a step above a pet."

So many fine ladies from noble fae families were vying for his attention. I brought nothing to the table—no title, no wealth, and no connections. I had nothing. Even my name was the one he gave me.

"What does *he* think about it?" Libelle asked.

I knew Voron cared about me. I felt it in his every kiss, every word, and every gesture. But was it enough?

"He said there would be no other man for me but him." I remembered.

"That's good." Dove nodded encouragingly.

Libelle looked less optimistic, however. "It's common for a favorite to belong only to her lord if the lord doesn't like sharing."

"He said that I would be the only woman for him, too. It was after he already knew he was the rightful king but before he took the crown."

Before he faced the pressure of the lords to marry. Tomorrow, he'd be released from all his promises and will be able to have any woman in the kingdom. Would that change his feelings for me? Or his plans for us?

"Well." Libelle bit her lip, tugging at a strand of her long dark hair in concentration. "Maybe that's where you should start, then? Talk to him again."

"Should I tell him I love him?"

Dove nodded in enthusiastic support of that idea.

"Would that really change anything?" I asked because no matter what I did or said to Voron, he'd still be the king, and I... well, I'd still be me, the "unique" human with nothing to her name, not even the name itself.

Dove shrugged, taking another pastry off the tray. "What's the worst that can happen? What do you have to lose?"

I didn't have much, but I could lose it all.

Chapter Sixteen

SPARROW

That night, I stood on the terrace where Voron had taught me to play the game War of Kings. Back then, it seemed so important for me to learn it in order to entertain the king and gain his favor. It had proven useless for that, but I genuinely grew to like the game and I treasured the memories of our lessons.

They brought me closer to Voron and gave me a chance to get to know him better. He'd been hiding behind his even expression, calm voice, and layers of clothes. It'd been a thrill to peel all of that off him, finding the man he was inside.

I loved everything I discovered about him. All his parts, whole and broken, fit so well with mine. And maybe because I had no past of my own, I took his so close to heart.

Watching the night sky, I tried to gauge the mood he might be in right now. It wasn't completely overcast. The wind wasn't strong but steady. It shepherded the clouds of all shapes and sizes above, making the stars blink and disappear behind them.

Worries, big and small, must be clouding the new king's mind. I wished he would come to me with all his worries, that he would find reprieve in my body from the hassles of the day like he'd so often done before. I knew that getting lost in his touch would ease my worries too.

I also hoped our connection was stronger than just physical.

Now that I'd figured out how I felt about him, I wished I could tell him. He had to know. And if he felt the same about me, maybe we could figure out how to carve out a life for the two of us together amid all the duties and responsibilities of his new position.

But Voron wasn't here. Once again, I was spending the night alone.

I never got the chance to see him during the day, either. Voron had sent me a message through Alcon. He was staying in the royal chambers. Alcon had explained that Voron had ordered a number of changes to the royal rooms. The construction was going on, and the noise was such that Voron feared it would disturb me.

In addition, he'd been holding meetings day and night. He'd been seeing the Council members as well as the army officials. There was a lot to catch up on for him after his absence from Elaros. I was sure he was impatient to make changes to the court, too.

Meanwhile, I had plenty of time to plan what I was going to tell him when I finally saw him again.

I t was hard not to get excited the morning of the coronation. The entire palace was abuzz. I'd heard it normally took months of preparations to organize an event like that. But Voron wanted things done fast. He was the one true king, and he refused to wait to be officially proclaimed as such.

Courtiers, servants, and the Council did the impossible, getting ready for the ceremony in just a couple of days.

Every level of the palace twinkled with light. Artfully arranged formations of crystals had been placed throughout, in addition to the illumination coming from the crystals in the walls.

The official ceremony was taking place in the Throne Room, located on the very top level of one of the biggest towers.

"Am I invited?" I asked Alcon, just to confirm.

Brebie had already sourced an outfit for me: a pale blue gown stitched with golden moths above the silver wisps of fog along the hem. But I never got a word from Voron about any of it.

"You don't need an official invitation to attend, my lady," Alcon replied. "You are the king's personal guest."

Alcon looked dashing when he came to pick me up just a few hours later, wearing a silver-gray jacquard coat with a golden sash.

The skirts of my dress were light and semi-transparent, but the bodice was solid and fitted. It was laced with a silk ribbon in the front, in the style that I'd grown to prefer to any other. I felt beautiful, wearing it paired with elegant, blue slippers with silver bows.

My hair was braided on the sides and lifted into rosettes but left to fall free in the back. The only jewelry I had was Voron's necklace of dried berries with the witch's stone pendant. But that was all I wanted, anyway.

"Ready to go, my lady?" Alcon offered me his arm.

I threaded my hand into the crook of his elbow with a smile. "Lead the way, my lord."

We ascended the grand moving staircase. I remembered Voron taking me up here the first time. So much had happened since. We'd grown so much closer, yet somehow, I felt further away from him than ever.

The Throne Room on the very top of the Elaros Palace was filled with people. The highborn nobles congregated close to the wide platform with the royal throne on it between the four columns of twisted vines. The servants kept closer to the walls and the exit.

Alcon led me through the crowd toward the platform. The closer we got, the louder the whispers grew around me. The courtiers turned to look at me. Those who knew me from before explained to the newly arrived who I was.

"The former mistress…"

"The new favorite…"

Yes, I was both, depending on which king they were talking about, the last or the present one.

"She's a human. So different…"

"So delightfully plain. Short and chubby, like a baby owl…"

"Is it because of her that the king refuses to marry?"

"No, it can't be. She's just a pet…"

I tugged on Alcon's arm about halfway through the room. "Let's stop here, please."

I couldn't move any further through all these whispers and scrutinizing looks.

"As you wish." He stopped, remaining at my side.

Musicians soared under the high ceiling of the interwoven vines. Music filled the air.

The High Priest moved over to the platform, flanked by several priests and priestesses, each representing a different god or goddess of the many deities of the Sky Kingdom. Their robes shone in the multi-colored glow of the crystals, the light material flowing down their bodies like liquid gold. Long *snakana* tails slithered from under the hem of several robes. They climbed up the first step of the platform and formed a line, shoulder to shoulder, facing the entrance.

A group of guards carried in the Sky Crown on a silver cushion. It'd been altered slightly. Voron didn't make it any higher than it was, keeping it a simple circlet of golden thorns that intertwined together like Elaros's vines. But he had made it a full circle now. There was no longer an opening at the back to accommodate the antlers of the former king.

The crowd parted like the sea as Voron entered. And I forgot how to breathe.

He was dressed in a dark-blue knee-length coat with a silver sash tied below his waist. Raven-black feathers decorated his wide shoulders and the high collar of the coat. For once, he didn't have his sword, but a bejeweled sheath with a dagger was attached to the decorated belt that lay over his wide sash. His long, royal-blue cape glowed with silver constellations. It trailed behind him along the entire room, billowing in his wake like a night sky.

As he reached the throne dais, he bowed to the High Priest who held the Sky Crown in his outstretched hands.

Yanking at the cape to make it flutter aside and pool around the throne platform, Voron turned to face the court. His eyes roamed over the crowd as the High Priest recited all the blessings that supposedly came with the crown he was about to bestow on the new king.

Finally, the High Priest placed the crown on Voron's head, atop his unruly hair.

"Long live the king!" the entire court shouted as the music surged higher.

Voron's eyes sparked with triumph. He got what he wanted. A long time ago, the kingdom had discarded him, tossing him aside to die in oblivion. Now, they crowned him as their king, to rule them all.

My chest was full of pride for him, my heart soared. His gaze found me in the crowd, and his expression softened. A corner of his mouth twitched up slightly. It looked far from a smile, but I knew him well by now to recognize it as such.

The king smiled, looking at me. He'd played a long and complicated game for decades, and he had won. Now, he clearly wished to share this profound moment of his victory with me.

Our eyes connected across the sea of people. I smiled back at him, happy for him. The world fell away. Only the two of us appeared to remain in this enormous room, connected by the long stare of mutual understanding.

But the court was watching. They saw that at the moment of his greatest triumph, surrounded by a crowd of the finest courtiers and the highest nobility of the highborn, the king chose to turn to his lowly human "pet."

When the time came for the High Lords to pledge their loyalty to the new monarch, High Lord Pelargos stepped forward.

"Power and magic to the king." He bowed his head but did not go down on one knee as the etiquette demanded. "My family and I have fought for you. We helped you get what's rightfully yours, asking for nothing in return."

That was a lie. I'd heard all the families of the High Lords who supported Voron in his quest for the crown had already been handsomely rewarded with land, jewels, and titles. But they clearly wished for more.

Voron's eyebrows moved closer, forming a crease of displeasure between them. A king could not rule without obtaining the promises of loyalty from the High Lords. That was the law. But it was more than that.

There were currently thirteen High Lords in the Sky Kingdom. Two of them, Caitore and Bussard, weren't present. They left Elaros the moment Queen Pavline fell. Each of the two lords had believed himself to be the next king. They had very good reasons to feel cheated out of their chance for the crown now and might plot a revenge against Voron. He needed to ensure the continuous support of the remaining High Lords. But I knew it must pain him to be pressured into any new concessions.

High Lord Pelargos spoke politely, but there was a clear menace in his words.

"Elaros was built by sky fae and for sky fae. It's no place for humans."

Realization speared me with a jolt. He was talking about me. Why? I had no chance to cross him. We'd hardly even spoken.

Voron's eyes narrowed into slits as everyone in the Throne Room, every single person, it seemed, turned to face me.

"Send your pet away, my king," the High Lord demanded. "Keep her in the menagerie where she belongs. Or gift her to someone worth your favor."

I couldn't believe my ears.

What had I done to the High Lord for him to hate me?

But it wasn't about what I'd done or said. The High Lord clearly found my mere existence undesirable.

An approving murmur rolled through the crowd. Just like the High Lord, they didn't necessarily hate me, just wanted me out of the way. Some might like the idea of the king "regifting" me, possibly hoping to get me for themselves, the "rare pet" that I was. Others might have connected Voron's reluctance to marry with my presence in his life.

One way or another, the entire court seemed to be in strong support of the High Lord's demand. I saw not a single friendly face in the crowd.

"Lady Sparrow is not a pet!" Voron's voice rose, reducing the murmurs to a faint buzzing. "She's an ally. Her support was instrumental in my ascending to the throne. Because of her you got the rightful king at last."

A sly smile curved the lips of High Lord Pelargos. "Then reward her. Gift her an estate of her own and let her live in peace away from Elaros."

That didn't sound so bad. If the nobles wished for me to leave the palace, I would, as long as it didn't mean giving up Voron as well.

Voron's frown didn't ease, however. Dark shadows drew over his face. The other High Lords moved closer to the dais with Lady Lark among them. Lifting elegantly the hem of her blush-pink gown, she stepped forward.

"It is a small favor to ask for, Your Majesty," she murmured. "Let's honor the tradition and keep the Sky Palace for sky fae only. After everything that we've done for you, it'd be but a tiny price for our ongoing loyalty. Isn't it so, Councilor?"

She smiled sweetly at the Head of the Council standing nearby.

"That is a tradition." The councilor nodded. "There is not a word about humans ever living among us as equals. There is no law that states they have any right to occupy Elaros. She shouldn't be here."

"Rewrite the laws!" the high voice of Dove pierced the air. "Sparrow has been a part of our court for months."

"And no harm has come from it!" Libelle chimed in. Lord Faisan, her fated mate and husband, quickly yanked at her arm, shoving her behind his back and out of sight.

But my heart fluttered in gratitude. Whatever was about to happen, I wasn't entirely alone against the High Lords and the court.

High Lord Pelargos lowered his head, giving me a glare from under his brow. Another man, High Lord Cardinali, crossed his arms over his chest with his son, Lord Bruant, standing next to him with a similarly threatening expression on his face.

"Get rid of the human or lose our support." High Lord Cardinali's voice was cold and sharp like a dagger and his words pierced my heart like a blade.

I'd now been in the Sky Kingdom for almost three months. This had been a challenging, even life-threatening time. I'd met most of the High Lords present. They saw my contribution to the king's campaign for the crown. They witnessed his gratitude and affection for me. Yet they still refused to see me as anything else but a royal plaything. They never accepted me as a person. It seemed they never would.

Voron raised his head, as if having made a decision. The Crown of Sky Kingdom sparkled with gold and magic in his raven-black locks.

"Lady Sparrow was brought into this world against her will," he spoke loudly, for everyone in the Throne Room to hear. "She was a part of the deal made between a king and a goddess and couldn't go back home, even as she always wished to do so. That deal has now been honored, all promises fulfilled, and I can finally grant her wish. Lady Sparrow," he addressed me without meeting my eyes. "You are hereby allowed to return to the human realm."

"What..." I could barely whisper in disbelief.

What was he talking about? He knew I'd decided not to return to my world. He was the one who had asked me to stay.

Of course that all happened weeks ago, before he became the Sky King.

"This is our reward for her service to the crown," he continued, looking in my general direction but still without eye contact.

Lady Lark sank into a curtsy with a serene smile on her beautiful face. "Your Majesty is benevolent and just."

Others nodded approvingly.

I froze, unable to move or to tear my eyes away from the king. This must be a mistake, some ploy on his part. He couldn't possibly mean it.

But Voron gestured to Alcon. "Get everything ready for Sparrow's departure tomorrow—"

"No," High Lord Pelargos interjected. "Today. Right now. My people will make sure she's gone, as per Your Majesty's order."

I gasped, shaking. The royal guards moved my way, flanked by the people of High Lord Pelargos. I backed away from them, trying to hide in the crowd. But the crowd parted, shrinking back, as if I carried the plague.

There was no support from anyone. Even Dove and Libelle had been pulled away from me. Alcon was gone, too.

"No, please..."

The guards grabbed me, dragging me to the exit.

"Voron!" I screamed in desperation.

He couldn't just let them take me. Not like this. Not without even saying goodbye.

However, he had already turned away from me and ascended the stairs to the royal throne—the place where he belonged.

"I did as you wished," he said calmly to High Lord Pelargos. "I need your promise of loyalty. Now."

Chapter Seventeen

SPARROW

I screamed as they dragged me out of the Throne Room. I kicked and fought them as they carried me to the nearest balcony. Two guards grabbed my shoulders as another one held my ankles. Their wings open, they leaped off the balcony.

Air rushed by me. Panic filled me, blinding me. I kicked and struggled against their grip.

"Get off me!"

"I can't hold her. She's like a fucking wildcat," the guard gripping my legs complained.

"Get her down," another one ordered.

Jerkily from the struggle, we all descended to the plaza in front of the main entrance to the palace. The royal guard, who appeared to be their leader, landed in front of me.

"Hold still, human," he ordered sternly. "Or my men will drop you to your death."

I yanked my arm out of their grip, but someone immediately got hold of it again.

"Then do it!" I yelled. "Drop me. Kill me. But I'm not going back."

The leader tilted his head, giving me a curious look.

"You'd rather die than go home where you belong?"

I shook my head vehemently. "I don't belong there. Not anymore. Chances are, I won't even land in the time period I used to live in. And if I do, I have no memories of my life there. I don't remember my own family if I ever had one. Taking me to the River of Mists would be the same as murder. You may as well kill me now."

The guard looked hesitant, and for a moment, I hoped he might listen.

"Please." I gripped his hand. "Let me speak to the king. There has been a mistake."

All I needed was to ask Voron one simple question. Did he really wish me gone? He wouldn't even need to say anything. One look into his eyes, and I would know the truth. Despite all his experience, he wouldn't be able to hide his feelings about something as enormous as this.

Six new guards descended from above. Instead of the silver-gray uniforms of the Elaros guards, they wore tan-and-white ones, in the colors of High Lord Pelargos' household.

"We have an order." Their leader stepped forward. "King Voron generously granted your wish. Are you ungratefully refusing it?"

"I just need to speak to him. Please. To thank him for his *generosity*." I tried not to sound sarcastic but failed.

The guard's stern expression didn't change.

"The king gave an order. And we're here to make sure it's executed properly."

Someone led a horse to us.

A royal guard grabbed my waist. "If you won't let us fly you, you'll have to ride." He heaved me up and into the saddle. "This way, if you fall and crack your head open, it won't be through our doing."

I gripped the horn of the saddle with both hands as the guard kept the horse's reins. He flew slightly ahead of me, leading the horse at a brisk pace. The rest of the guards followed, both those of the king and of the High Lord.

As we passed through the gate and headed down the windy road toward the Cloud River, I held on tight to stay on the horse. Hills covered in grass and low shrubs flanked the road. If I jumped off the saddle and ran, it'd be hard to get away. They'd easily spot me from the air.

Hope refused to die in my heart. And I waited.

All the way to the forest, I waited for the sound of horse's hooves behind us. I kept looking back over my shoulder, searching the road for a horseman and scanning the sky for the crow, the horseman's loyal companion.

Everything inside me rejected the idea of Voron giving me up so easily. I knew how much the Sky Crown meant to him. I knew it better than anyone else in the kingdom did. And I refused to believe he would abandon me for it. And still I waited for him to come for me.

Once we entered the forest, however, my hope withered. Fear took over, wrecking me with worry.

I couldn't go back. I decided the last time I came to this bridge that my life was now here, in Sky Kingdom. And now, there was even more to that decision than before. An invisible but unbreakable thread stretched between Voron and me. I refused to believe in his betrayal, and I couldn't leave this world just like this, without even a single word of goodbye between us.

As the trees closed in on us from both sides and their thick canopies obstructed the sky from view, the leader of the guards softly landed on the path in front of the horse. The rest of the guards walked behind us. There wasn't much space left on either side of the horse for any of them to walk next to me.

Choosing a spot where the tree trunks were especially close to each other and the shrubs were tall enough to hide me, I jumped off the saddle and ran.

"Hey!" the guards yelled behind me.

But I didn't stop. Crashing through the underbrush, I dashed between the trees, running deeper and deeper into the forest.

I had no plan, very little sense of direction, and only one goal —to get away from them. I wasn't going to give up without trying.

I ran as fast as my legs and my lungs would let me, away from the shouts and stomping of the guards behind me. I ran until the trees ended unexpectedly, and I found myself in a clearing.

"Got you," came from the sky. Then, the leader of the High Lord's guards dropped on top of me. "What a hellcat you are, feisty little human. Kings may love taming you, but I've got no fucking time for your mischief."

I kicked and clawed at him as he crushed me to the ground. He hooked his arm around my throat from behind, and I bit into it. Sadly, my teeth weren't sharp enough to pierce through the fabric of his uniform.

"Hush!" he snapped, landing a punch to the side of my head.

The blow rang like a bell inside my skull. Momentarily disoriented, I let go of his arm, allowing him to haul me up and fly back toward the road.

"That's better," he murmured approvingly. "I have my orders to get rid of you. And I'll do it one way or another. Do you want to arrive in your world with a bloodied face and broken ribs? Because that's what will happen if you try to run again. Do you hear me?"

I groaned something, my head feeling fuzzy and my vision blurry. He took my groan for a sign of confirmation of my cooperation.

"Good," he said. "Here we are."

He placed me with both feet on the road again, and I had to grip his arm for balance as my head cleared slowly.

Just a step to my left, the road turned into cobblestones. We were at the bridge across the Cloud River that merged with the pink fog of the River of Mists in the very middle.

It was overcast, with dark storm clouds gathering along the

horizon. The wind increased, bending the tops of the trees, their branches rustling and creaking ominously. Oddly, the wind did nothing to disperse the thick fog rising from the river and shrouding the bridge.

"Let's go." The leader grabbed my arm, forcing me up the bridge and into the clouds rolling over it.

The rest of the guards followed us to make sure the royal order was fulfilled.

Halfway across the Cloud River, the leader stopped.

"Climb up," he ordered, nudging me toward the railing. "Or I will drop you in and hope you'll make it."

"Please, don't push me in." I climbed onto the thick stone parapet that served as the railing of the bridge.

"I won't," he relented. "But only if you jump yourself. And promptly. Do you see the pink mist far below?"

Standing tall on the parapet, I peered down into the thick fog.

Was it the River of Mists shimmering far below? Or was it the shimmer of the tears gathering in my eyes?

Voron sent me here with nothing this time. I had no money, no food or jewels. All I had was the gown I was wearing, and even that wouldn't fit into any time period on Earth. How far would I make it there, even if I managed to cross the treacherous River of Mists unharmed?

But worse of all was the burning pain in my chest—the agony of betrayal. My heart fractured, and I desperately tried to keep it together, hoping for a miracle I already knew was not going to happen.

Voron wasn't coming for me.

"Ready?" The leader poked me in my calf with a finger. "We don't have all day."

I jerked in panic, glancing back. The fog grew so thick, I couldn't see any of the guards anymore, not even the leader, only his hand and some of his arm sticking out from the haze.

"Just step back, okay?" I pleaded, regaining my balance. "Give me a minute."

I closed my eyes and drew in a long breath.

What difference would it make if I jumped into the thin wisp of the River of Mists or missed it and ended up falling through to the Below?

The second outcome might even be better. Death would possibly be faster. Maybe I should take a step to the left and miss the pink mist on purpose?

"Jump!" the leader snapped.

A rough hand shoved into my back.

I screamed, losing my balance.

Another hand grabbed my ankle, yanking me down.

My feet slipped off the railing.

And I fell...

The stones of the bridge rushed by me. Then suddenly, the bridge was above me, right over my head. And it wasn't moving. Patches of images emerged and disappeared back into the thick, gray clouds.

An arm held me around my middle. A hand closed over my mouth, and a strange raspy voice sounded in my ear, "Shut up, now. They need to think you're gone."

With the stranger's hand over my mouth, I couldn't scream, but after those words, I stopped even trying. My eyes open wide, I peered through the fog, gathering my bearings.

Someone was holding me from behind. Their speckled brown wings moved to keep us both in the air, right under the bridge.

"Good," the person said. "Keep quiet."

The voice sounded so dry and cracking, it was impossible to tell whether it belonged to a man or a woman.

"Did she jump?" a guard on the bridge above us asked.

"Looks like it," the leader of the High Lord's people replied.

"Looks like it?" the royal guard mocked. "Did you or did you not see her jump?"

"Yes. I did," the other man snarled. "She's gone, alright? It's not like she could fly away."

"I guess."

Their voices sounded a little closer, like both men were leaning over the railing, searching through the clouds for me.

"I'll take my men. We'll check, just to make sure," one of them finally said.

"Just stay away from the pink stuff. You don't want to be sucked into that. The human world is a nasty place, I've heard."

The person holding me hissed into my ear, "We need to get out of here. Keep quiet."

We flew under the bridge, away from the guards. And when we reached the riverbank, I realized it was the opposite side of the Cloud River, the one I hadn't been on before. The forest appeared thicker and darker here. The road was overgrown with weeds, less traveled.

"Run." My rescuer tugged me by my arm, urging me to move.

The person was small for a sky fae. The hand that gripped mine was thin with long, bony fingers and a mesh of see-through lines—the sign of aging in sky fae. It must be a woman. An old one. Hunching over made her look even shorter.

She ran fast, however. I could barely keep up as she ducked under the tree branches and weaved through the underbrush.

"Who are you?" I panted, rapidly running out of breath at the pace she'd set. But I had to know where she was taking me. What fate was I running to now?

"I'm Sova," she said, not slowing down. "My wagon is just down this path, behind the purple pine tree. We'll be safe th—"

She jerked suddenly. Letting go of my arm, she rotated on her heel. Her back came into view, with a long arrow sticking out of it. The end of the arrow was still trembling from the impact of the shot.

"Got one!" a male voice announced triumphantly from the forest on the side of the path.

Shocked to the core, I didn't even think about jumping behind the nearest tree trunk to hide.

Another arrow sang through the air. It hit Sova in the chest this time. Then a man trudged out from behind the trees—an *arien*, judging by his curved horns. He tossed a confused glance at me. Belatedly, I stepped behind a tree, but his attention was now fully focused on Sova.

"What the..." The man appeared terrified. "Fuck..."

Blue sparks ran up both arrows, merging into a bright ball of light above the woman's head.

"No!" The *arien* pivoted on his hooves as the ball surged his way.

The blow of light hit the man in the back. A clear wound opened, perfectly round like a porthole on a ship. Transparent lines spread like sun rays from around the wound. With a silent explosion, the man was torn apart into pieces. They shimmered like fireworks before dissipating into the air.

Nothing was left of the man but his clothes by the time Sova's body even hit the ground.

A crushing sound of more hooves running this way sent me into a mad dash in the opposite direction.

"What did you get?" a curious voice came from the distance.

Then another one yelled with alarm, "Oh, by all the gods of Nerifir! The poor bugger killed a hag."

"It must be a mistake. He couldn't be that stupid..."

I didn't hear the rest. Mistake or not, if they killed the old woman, they could very well kill me, too. I darted down the path, almost running into a huge purple pine up ahead.

"My wagon is just down this path, behind the purple pine tree," the woman's words rang through my head. *"We'll be safe..."*

Safe.

I hadn't felt safe for a while now. The concept was too enticing not to whirl around the tree. There was nothing behind it, however, just empty space. Disappointment seized me. Either the woman had lied or this was the wrong tree. I flattened my back against the wide pine tree trunk, catching my breath. My lungs burned from running. My feet hurt in my thin slippers.

The *arien* men's confused voices sounded from a distance behind me. Then, the far more terrifying sounds came—the questioning, commanding voice of the leader of the High Lord's guards.

They must be searching for me.

The wide tree trunk hid me from view, but I couldn't stay here. If they searched the area, sooner or later, they would find me.

I had to keep running.

With a deep, bracing breath, I pushed away from the pine tree and ran right, off the path and deeper into the woods.

There was nothing but trees and shrubs ahead of me. Yet I only made two steps before I slammed into something so hard, the impact sent me backwards and down to the ground.

"Did you hear that?" a guard's voice came from down the path.

They were close!

Panic sent me up to my feet. I had to run.

But where?

Something was in my way, hard and solid. Only I couldn't see it, even as my body was still sore from running into it at full speed.

Stretching my arms in front of me, I moved forward slowly. My palms flattened against a hard surface, but I still couldn't see anything, using my hands to guide me. Taking a step to the right, I tripped over something closer to the ground. My hand slid down and landed on something shaped like a handle, a metal one.

I pressed on it, and it gave. The motion was that of a door opening. Though I saw neither the door nor where it was opening into.

"This way, I think." The guard's voice was so close, the fine hairs on the back of my neck stood up as if I already could feel his breath behind me.

Frantically patting with my hands, I found the door opening and the step just above the ground, then climbed in. I felt for the handle on the inside of the invisible door and closed it a moment before two guards rounded the purple pine.

Hugging my knees, I stared at the guards in horror. I could see them clearly. Surely, they could see me, too. I was sitting on something invisible that held me off the ground. But the door and the entire structure it belonged to were as clear as air.

Yet the guards didn't make eye contact with me. They didn't even look in my direction, moving along the path.

"I'm telling you, the human fell. The lieutenant saw her jump off the bridge. We can't toss her into the same river twice, anyway. What are we still doing here?" one of the guards complained.

"Wasting our time," the other one agreed. "That's what happens when you get two leaders on the same mission. Each of them is now trying to prove his cock is bigger."

I released a breath as they moved on. Somehow—I couldn't even begin to explain how—but they didn't see me. The thing I was in was completely invisible, but it must have made me invisible, too.

"We'll be safe," the old woman had said, talking about her wagon.

That was where I must be, then, in her wagon that turned out to be the best hiding spot ever.

Fear receded a little, leaving my body weak and drained. My legs shook, and my hands trembled. Hugging my knees to my chest, I lay down on my side.

Safe was such a temporary state. But right now, I felt safe enough to close my eyes and allow my body to relax just a bit.

Voron's guards and the men of the High Lord were searching for me out there. I had to stay quiet to make them believe the order of their new king had been fulfilled.

How could you, Voron?

I'd given you my trust, and you broke it. Shattered it to pieces, along with my heart.

My chest tightened, making it too painful to even draw a breath. A hot tear rolled from under my closed eyelid.

"How could you, Voron?" I whispered, letting the pain take me. "What have you done?"

Chapter Eighteen

SPARROW

A knock jolted me out of the daze. I felt so groggy, it took me a while to even realize that the knock was on the invisible door of the invisible wagon inside which I was hiding.

It was dark around me. The sky above had turned that muddy gray color it took at early sunrise when it was densely overcast with thick, dark clouds.

Was it morning already?

Had I fallen asleep?

A headache pounded inside my skull. My face felt hot and puffy, and my eyes sore, as if I cried all through the night. But somehow, after all that crying, I must've managed to fall asleep.

A dark figure stood in front of the invisible door. Hunched over and shrouded in a dark-gray cloak head to toe, it looked exactly like the old woman who had snatched me off the bridge.

But I'd seen her being shot and killed just a little while ago.

Did she come back to life?

Or was it her ghost?

Both prospects were equally disturbing. Especially, since she'd never told me what she wanted with me in the first place. Why did she steal me from the guards?

Apprehension creeped up my spine with chills, jolting me completely awake now. Moving as quietly as possible, I crawled backwards, away from the door.

The woman knocked once more.

"Sova? Are you here?"

It couldn't be the same woman, then. I distinctly remembered her introducing herself by that name.

Her ghost wouldn't come here looking for her like that, would it?

She shoved against the door, pushing it open. Breath stuck in my throat as she poked her head in and spotted me.

"And who the fuck are you?" She scowled at me.

Frozen in fear and, frankly, not expecting an ancient fae to have a filthy mouth like that, I just blinked at her in silence.

"Where is Sova?" she demanded, crossing her scrawny arms over her narrow chest.

I kept staring at her. How was I to explain anything to anyone when I myself had no clue what the hell had been happening? My brain had been working way too hard as it was, just trying to think a few moments ahead to keep me alive.

"She... she was killed. Yesterday," I finally managed to squeeze out through my dry throat.

The old woman moved in menacingly.

"Did you kill her?"

"What? No!" I crab-walked backwards, away from her, until my shoulder hit a hard corner of something invisible inside the wagon. "I've never hurt any—" The words stuck in my throat.

I could never honestly claim again that I'd never hurt anyone. King Tiane was dead because of me. I didn't kill Sova, but I *was* a murderer.

"Who did it, then?" The newcomer demanded. "How? Where?"

"An *arien* man. Over there, down the path. He shot her with arrows."

"Hmm," she hummed. Suspicion was etched on her wrinkled face riddled with thin transparent lines.

Rummaging through a canvas satchel hanging on her side, she pulled out a small ball of wool and unwound the end of the string from it.

"You'll show me where."

Flicking her wrist, she propelled the end of the string my way. It snapped around my forearm, winding tightly around it.

"What is this?" I sat up, shaking my wrist, but the string fit snugly and securely around it, not coming off.

"Show me where you saw Sova last," the old woman ordered, tossing the ball out onto the path.

The string yanked at my wrist with so much power, I fell forward, face first.

The old crone chuckled. "You better keep up, girl. Or it'll drag you through the mud and rocks out there."

I scrambled to my feet, almost falling out from the invisible wagon, and stumbled after the ball that rolled down the path.

It had rained last night. My dressy slippers were quickly soaked with mud. The train of my gown dragged through the wet grass and puddles. But I couldn't stop even to lift my skirts properly. The ball kept rolling along, bouncing over the puddles and pulling at my wrist insistently. I had to rush to keep up with it.

"Here!" I yelled when we reached the place where Sova was shot. Or at least I thought this was the place. I only managed a glance at the area as the ball kept dragging me up the path and toward the bridge over the Cloud River in the distance.

I was out of breath. Surprisingly, the old woman had no trouble keeping up with the punishing pace of the ball.

"Stop." She snapped her fingers again.

The tension around my wrist eased. The wool thread slacked as the ball halted in the middle of the path. The woman bent over to swipe the ball from the ground. The thread untied itself from around my wrist, and she wound it onto the ball again then put it back into her satchel.

"*Where* exactly?" She gazed at me with piercing dark-brown eyes. Their color was rich and vivid, and the expression in them focused. Her body might look old, but her mind remained sharp. It would do me good not to underestimate this woman.

"It happened here." I took a few steps back and waved a hand around me. "In this general area."

"Can you try to be a bit more specific, lady?"

From her, the word "lady" came out more like an insult than an honorific.

"All right." I turned around, reconstructing the events of yesterday in my mind. "We were running this way, from the bridge."

"Why were you running?"

"Royal guards were in the area," I replied, keeping it as vague as possible.

Vague wasn't good for her, however.

"Why?" She folded her arms over her chest. "Why were the guards around, and why were you running from them?"

"It doesn't matter," I snapped. I had no idea who this person was. I had no reason nor obligation to be honest with her. "You wanted to know how your friend died, so I'm telling you how. An *arien* man shot her with two arrows from a longbow from behind those trees over there. After that, the arrows exploded with light and killed him too."

It looked incredibly strange when it happened. Now that I said it out loud, it sounded outright crazy. But the woman nodded, her expression contemplative.

"Was the man alone?"

"He was. At the beginning. I think he didn't mean to kill her. He screamed something like 'Got it!' or 'Got one!' Then looked very confused when he saw what he'd done."

"What an idiot," the woman muttered under her breath. It

was unclear whether she was insulting me again or the shooter this time.

She reached into her satchel once again, producing a long crystal mounted onto a pewter stick. The crystal glowed faintly. When she flicked her wrist, however, it burst to life with bright blue light.

Bending over, she held the crystal low to the ground while moving around in circles.

I kept talking. Maybe if she replied, I'd learn more about what the heck was happening here.

"More men came out after," I said. "But I ran at that point. They didn't see me. They said Sova was a hag. Are you a hag, too?"

She tossed me an incredulous glance. "What do I look like to you?"

"I'm not sure," I said tentatively, afraid to offend her with an assumption. She looked jumpy and snappy, not the way I'd imagine an old wise woman would be. But she definitely had some interesting magic at her disposal. The last thing I wanted was for her to use that magic against me. "I've never spoken to a hag before."

King Tiane had one in Elaros. Queen Pavline had her inspect me. But the queen remained in the room the whole time. And I'd been lying on the bed with my face up. The royal hag had never even looked at me above the waistline and never said a word in my presence.

"Weird." The woman shrugged. "Well, my name is Sauria, and I'm a hag, just like Sova was. Now stay where you are. I need to make sure you're not lying."

She shone the light of the crystal onto the ground. Bending over it, she moved toward the spot where the *arien* man had stood. Moving in circles, she stepped carefully over patches of grass, studying something on the ground. The clothes of Sova and the *arien* man were now gone. Either the man's friends had picked them up or the royal guards had.

"Poor bugger," Sauria said softly.

"That's what his friends said when they found what was left of him. The guy literally exploded, you know."

"I know." She nodded confidently. "The protection spell ended him. We all have one. Everyone knows it's impossible to kill an experienced hag without being killed, too."

I hadn't known that, but I kept it to myself, not wanting to distract her or divert her focus to me.

"They said it was a mistake," I said instead.

"Looks like it was." She nodded, now circling over the area where Sova had fallen. "No one in their right mind would just come and shoot a hag in the open." She bent lower and picked up a small object from the ground—an arrowhead. "A hunter's arrow." She sniffed it. "Laced with *ebon* weed for a quick and painless kill." She tossed the arrowhead into the bushes. "Poor Sova. One of the most powerful women I've ever known died because some hot-headed idiot mistook her for a boar. He must've caught her unaware?"

"He did. We didn't notice him until it was too late." Her genuine grief subdued my mood, too. "I'm sorry about the loss of your friend. Is that what Sova was to you?"

She nodded, staring at the ground, her frail shoulders dropped.

"She was many things to me. A friend, a teacher, my mentor. The question is..." She lifted her head, pinning me with her brown inquisitive eyes. "What was she to you? Who are you?"

I took a step back, retreating under a tree. Were the shadows here thick enough to hide what I was?

No such luck. Her eyes narrowed as she poked her crystal torch into my bare arm.

"Oh, by the fucking wings of Death! You're the human, aren't you? The one they now think they've tossed back into the River of Mists?"

So much for hiding. My very appearance betrayed me again.

"Please, don't tell anyone."

"Why not? You don't want to go back to your world?"

"No."

"Hmm." A calculating expression flashed in her eyes as she filed that piece of information away, possibly to use it against me later. If so, she miscalculated. There was nothing she could take from me. All had been taken already. I had nothing but the muddy slippers and the ruined dress I was wearing.

Raising the crystal in her hand, Sauria came closer, peering at me with her dark eyes.

"So, you're Sparrow," she said, examining my face, then my exposed arms. "The human pet of kings." She reached to touch my face, and I shrank back from her. "Hold still," she ordered. "I need to know what exactly I'm dealing with here. It's not every day I meet your kind."

"What do you want with me?"

She stepped closer until my back hit a tree trunk, blocking my retreat.

"That's what I'm trying to figure out." She pinched my cheek, then poked my shoulder. "What are you good for? What do you think Sova wanted you for?"

"To sell me," I exhaled with a bitter laugh, then bit my tongue belatedly. There was no need to give her any ideas.

"Right. You'd fetch a good price." She poked the side of my breast with her finger. I swatted it away, but she immediately prodded with her other hand against my stomach. "Not in your condition, though."

"Yeah, take me through a car wash first," I quipped. "And slap a new coat of paint on me before you put me on the market."

She ignored me, poking at me some more, despite my protests.

I tried to figure out the best way to get out of here. Sauria looked old and frail, but judging by her energetic performance on our dash from the wagon, it wouldn't be easy to run away from her.

"So." She seemed contemplative. Or calculating again? "You've been with both our late king and the new one, right?"

"That's really none of your business," I bit out, taking a step aside to evade her intrusive touch that had turned borderline inappropriate by that point.

"It kind of is, since I'm the one stuck with you now. Which one of our kings is the father of your baby?"

"What?" The old woman must've lost her mind. "What baby? I don't have a baby."

"But you will have one. In about eight months from now, I'd say. Give or take a few days."

My knees trembled. If it wasn't for the tree behind me, I'd surely tumble.

"Are you insane? I'm not... No." I crushed my skirts in my sweaty hands as the world around me turned to a blur. "It can't be."

Sauria tilted her head, giving me an unimpressed look.

"Why not? Did you have sex?"

I nodded, unable to say a word. My throat was too tight to speak. Bile was rising up from my stomach. If I spoke, I feared I'd puke.

"Well, there you go," she said, spreading her arms wide. "If you fuck, you can reasonably expect to get pregnant. Has no one told you that?"

I nodded again, staring straight in front of me. My knees finally gave in, and I sank to the ground with my back against the tree. I closed my eyes and pressed an arm across my stomach.

Now what?

The question bounced in my mind like a ping-pong ball, non-stop and without an answer.

"Are you all right?" Sauria's voice sounded on my level in front of me.

I slowly opened my eyes, finding her staring at me just a step away as she crouched in front of me.

"So, I take it you didn't know you're with child?"

I shook my head and cleared my throat.

"It can't be..." I mumbled. "I have no...symptoms. Signs, you know?"

I hadn't felt any different. I'd felt no more nausea than normal. What other signs should be there? I couldn't remember, but I was sure I hadn't had any of them. I hadn't even missed my period yet. At least, I didn't think I missed it. It should be coming soon, like any minute now.

"Not everyone has the *signs* this early," Sauria pointed out. "Or is it different for humans?"

"I don't know." I scraped a hand down my face.

God, I was an idiot. I should've checked somehow. I should've known before. But was it even possible to find out such things this early, without the hag's magic?

"It must be a mistake..." I exhaled, trembling.

"Ha! No such luck, lady. I know what I know. And I'm never wrong about this matter. So, who's the father?" Sauria insisted. "The late king, the new king, or someone else?"

She wouldn't rest without my answer.

"Someone else..." I echoed.

I had no idea what to do, but I knew it was best not to disclose that I was going to have a royal baby. An heir to the throne...

I was going to have a baby.

Another bout of nausea hit me, and I gripped my throat, fighting it.

"How do you know I'm pregnant?" I desperately clung to the hope that she was mistaken. "You didn't do any tests. Anyone can say shit. It doesn't mean it's true."

She raised a silver eyebrow at my swearing, then giggled like a little girl.

"A lady you are not," she stated.

"Never pretended to be one." I leaned with my head back against the tree. "Are you absolutely positive about this?" I dipped my gaze to my belly.

She scoffed at my skepticism.

"A part of what I do for a living is telling women when they're pregnant. We're not like gargoyles, you know. Sky fae don't feel they're with child right away. Some don't know it until they start showing." She gave me a penetrating look, taking in my messed-up state. "I guess humans can't feel it, either."

I just sighed heavily in response. My brain refused to function properly.

"What am I to do now?"

"Right." Her gaze warmed with compassion. "The king wants you gone."

"He does." I halted my breath, waiting for the stab of pain through my heart to subside a little before drawing some air back into my lungs.

"Crossing the River of Mists always carries a risk. Even more so in your condition," she weighed out my options out loud. "Do you want to return to the human realm?"

"No. Not really... I'm not sure." Did it matter where I went, at this point?

"Can you go back to your lover? The one who got you pregnant? Will he stand up to the king for you to keep you here?"

I blew out a humorless laugh. "He certainly will not."

"Is he that loyal to the king?"

"More than loyal. He thinks and feels very much the same."

I didn't know this woman. There was absolutely no reason for me to talk to her or be honest with her. But right now, I was just grateful to have someone with me at all.

This new turn in my circumstances changed everything. I couldn't run. I couldn't be alone. I needed help, any help I could get.

"Maybe he'd change his mind if he knew about the baby?" Sauria's voice sounded hopeful. "Children are rare and precious. Wouldn't he want to have a continuation of his bloodline?"

"Every king needs an heir," Voron had said.

Before that, he'd also said he didn't care about the continuation of his bloodline. Would all this baby be to him—an heir?

How would he feel about my news? What would he do?

Voron had sent me away not because he wanted to do it. I believed he cared about me and would have kept me in Elaros if he could. But he gave me up under the pressure from the Council and the nobles. That was what really mattered—he gave me up.

The king did what the court told him to do, and the court didn't want me around. Would me being pregnant change that? I believe it would make matters worse.

I pressed my arms to my middle. Setting aside my emotions, I tried to think about the future objectively.

Now that Voron was free of his promises, he could procreate to his heart's content with the most noble women of the kingdom. He was free to marry and to continue his bloodline. He might have a legitimate heir in the future. In which case, an illegitimate older child would be a roadblock on the smooth path of succession. That certainly would be how the royal court would view it.

My personal feelings didn't matter here. I wasn't safe in Elaros. Just like my future baby wouldn't be. They had tried to kill me once already, back at the palace of the High Lord Pelargos. If I showed up now, with a real threat to their plans for the throne in my womb, they certainly wouldn't allow me to stay alive for long.

Voron wouldn't protect me. He'd already made his choice. Between me and the crown, he'd chosen the crown.

My instincts told me to run away from the Sky Palace, not toward it.

"I can't go back to Elaros. It's not safe for me there."

Sauria sat on her butt and placed her elbows on her knees.

"That's quite a situation you got yourself into, girl. And now, you're dragging me into it, too."

"I'm not dragging anyone with me. You don't have to help me—"

She tilted her head. "Do you have anyone else?"

"No," I confessed.

She pursed her lips. "See? I'm the only one, then. And I can't really leave you here on your own. If a wild beast doesn't eat you, someone else may find you. Someone far less agreeable than I am." She scratched her chin. "Maybe you should go back to the human world after all? It would be so much easier for everyone here if you did."

It would be easier, wouldn't it? No one would have to worry about me anymore. Not Sauria, either. But the more I thought about it, the less I wished to leave Sky Kingdom. For one very simple reason if for nothing else.

"If I go back, there is a good chance I'd die. And I prefer to live."

Despite everything that happened to me, I wasn't ready to give up. Now, less than ever. I didn't want to die.

"Fuck." Sauria sighed. "I wish I'd lost my ability to care when I became a hag. It's grown smaller, but didn't completely disappear, sadly. It's so inconvenient at times. Besides, I swore to protect those I treat, and pregnant women are my patients. Well, let's see what we can do with you, now."

She rose to her feet and shook the grass and twigs out of her dark gray cloak.

"All right. Follow me. Do as I say, and nobody will get hurt."

I nodded, getting up, too.

Her words didn't reassure me, though. It seemed that every time I turned around, someone did end up getting hurt.

Chapter Nineteen

SPARROW

"Poor Sova," Sauria sighed when we returned to the invisible wagon. "Such a meaningless death."

She shook her head, splayed her hand on the door I couldn't see, and murmured something quietly. The air under her hand wavered and appeared to solidify. Colors leaked out, spreading like ink through water and molding into shapes of painted boards. A door handle appeared. Then two windows materialized on each side of the door with a step below it.

Soon, the entire wagon became visible. Its boards were painted in a cheerful sunny yellow, with garlands of vines and flowers around the windows and along the door frame.

My heart squeezed in a new grip of sadness for the woman who used to live here. She must've been a nice person because only someone nice could own such an adorable wagon.

Sauria entered, gesturing for me to follow her in.

"We'll need to get it out of here, the sooner the better," she explained. "It's not safe to leave it here. But I want to make sure things are in order and ready to be moved first."

She roamed around the wagon, opening and closing the

cupboards and arranging dishes and other things in some only-known-to-her order.

Inside, the wagon was just as colorful as on the outside. Bright pinks and purples were added to the yellow color on the walls and cabinet doors. A flowery tapestry separated a section from the main area. The tapestry was lifted aside and tied up with a green-and-yellow cord, revealing a neatly made bed behind it.

The wall with the door was lined with shelves floor to ceiling. It housed a collection of jars, glass boxes, and metal cages with odd things in them. There was a thick blue worm in one jar, with a gorgeous plumage on its flat head. A cage held a live snail with the high shell on its back shaped like an upturned bunch of grapes and long purple tentacles undulating from under it. In a jar filled with liquid, a fetus of a three-headed piglet floated.

I averted my eyes, afraid to study other contents too closely.

"What do you think Sova wanted with me? Why did she rescue me?"

Sauria shrugged a bony shoulder.

"I wouldn't call it a rescue. She just took you, didn't she?"

True. Sova had snatched me from the bridge railing, just before I was about to jump, possibly to my death. It felt like a rescue to me. But it could very well be a kidnapping, too.

"Do you think she wanted to sell me?"

"Well, she didn't know you're pregnant."

Pregnant.

My hand splayed over my belly. I felt nothing different about my body. Could Sauria be wrong, after all? The news she had sprung on me felt so surreal.

Sauria examined the jars on the shelves, making sure each of them was attached with a cord to the wall, so it wouldn't move or break while the wagon was moving.

"Your pregnancy would certainly make selling you more diffi-cult," she explained matter-of-factly. "There are laws against selling or buying fae in Sky Kingdom. And a child of a human and a fae is always a fae. What would the potential buyer do with the baby once it's born? By law, the fae baby can't be anyone's property. Besides, everyone knows you came from Elaros. So, the father of your baby is likely a highborn. Probably a member of the royal court." She paused, giving me an expectant look, but I kept quiet. Eventually, she continued, "What if the father decided to claim the child one day? No buyer would want to deal with that. It promises nothing but aggravation with a lot of potential problems. To tell you the truth, however, I don't think Sova's plan was to sell you. Money or riches mean little to us."

"Why would she take me, then?"

She ran her gaze over the display wall.

"Sova liked collecting odd things. Maybe she just wanted to add you to her collection? It's not every day that one meets a human in the Sky Kingdom, or anywhere else in Nerifir for that matter."

I followed her gaze with mine, trying not to think about what all those things were inside the jars. Some of them looked really creepy, taking away from the charm of the wagon's cheerful interior.

"I'm a bit too big to fit on a shelf," I pointed out.

"Oh, there are ways to make things smaller if necessary." She touched the jar with the blue worm. "This one, for example, is a giant serpent from the Wetlands of Lorsan. He used to be as long as the tallest tree in this forest. But she fit him in here, see?" She showed off the jar with pride.

I took another step away from the wall. My butt hit a round metal stove, blocking any further retreat.

"Do you have a collection like that, too, Sauria?" I asked carefully.

"Me? No." She shook her head. "I have neither time nor patience to collect stuff. I still have a lot of spells to learn."

She did another dash around the wagon, making sure everything was properly tacked, tied, and put away.

Once again, I noted the energy with which Sauria moved. She lacked that measured deliberate confidence that often came with an advanced age. Instead, she made plenty of unnecessary gestures and steps. She bent and crouched lower than was necessary. She climbed up on a chair to check on top of the cabinets, then hopped off it with the ease of a monkey.

"How old are you, Sauria?"

She stopped in her tracks, leveling me with a glare.

"That is a very inappropriate question for a hag." She sulked. "We don't reveal our age. We always are as old as we look."

"I'm sorry if I offended you. I didn't mean it."

"I'm not that easy to offend, girl," she scoffed, looking every bit offended. "Come. Time to get moving."

Lifting the hem of her cloak, she climbed out of the wagon.

The wind had picked up. The treetops groaned and bent under its onslaught. Dark clouds rushed across the sky like shadows of doom.

"We need to get out of here," Sauria muttered under her breath, her delicate features scrunched into a frown of concern.

Stuffing two gnarly fingers into her mouth, she whistled so loudly, I jumped and slapped my hands over my ears. The thudding of hooves hitting the ground and the crushing of the branches deep in the forest made me freeze with trepidation.

"Who is it?" I asked. "Whom did you call?"

Two deer ran out from behind the trees.

"What do you think?" Sauria cut me a glance. "Someone needs to pull the wagon. Unless you want to do it yourself?"

I shook my head, which made her cackle. She dug a couple of carrots from her seemingly bottomless satchel and fed them to the deer.

"Come, my beauties," she cooed, putting harnesses on them. Once done, she turned to me. "Keep them on the path. It gets wider after a while. Hopefully, the storm holds off for a bit."

"Me? You're kidding, right? You want me to drive the wagon?"

She tilted her head, giving me a mocking look.

"Would you rather fly?"

Two wings sprang open on her back. They had no feathers. Instead, soft-looking suede stretched between long thin spikes similar to the wings of a bat.

"So? Where are *your* wings, human girl?" She laughed at her not-so-funny joke.

I rolled my eyes at her, not even dignifying that with an answer, and turned to the two animals.

"How do I even steer wild deer?" At least, the pair appeared docile, peacefully chewing on the underbrush.

Sauria flapped her wings, lifting off the ground.

"Just like horses," she yelled, fighting the wind. "You've ridden a horse, haven't you?"

"Yeah... Kind of." I wasn't that great on horseback, either.

"Come on," she urged, hovering over the path. "We've stayed here for way too long already. We need to leave."

With a long, heavy sigh, I climbed into the small seat in the front of the wagon and gripped the reins.

"Well, you heard the lady." I jerked the reins, slapping the deer's backs slightly. "Let's go."

The animals lifted their heads, casting cautious glances of their large brown eyes at me.

Sauria dipped toward them and smacked their rumps with both hands. "Let's go, my beauties!"

The deer jerked forward, spooked by her flapping wings, then took off between the trees.

"Wait!" I yelled, pulling on the reins while trying hard not to fall from the seat. "That way!"

I jerked the right rein, steering them toward the path. Somehow, they listened. They galloped at a neck-breaking speed, but at least they ran in the right direction.

Sauria's gleeful cackle came from above. "Way to go, girl. You got it!"

"You're lucky I have my hands full," I muttered, my focus glued to the running deer. "I swear I'll toss something at you the first chance I get."

After dashing through the forest like a maniac in a painted wagon pulled by two speeding deer, I made it to the road running between wide open fields. The deer calmed somewhat, slowing a little.

The storm grew stronger. Feral winds tore from every direction, howling and groaning between the crops in the fields. The sky turned as dark as night.

Tired from fighting the storm to stay airborne, Sauria descended from above and landed on the bench seat next to me. She clapped her hands, and the harness on the deer glowed brightly, illuminating the way.

"Are you having fun?" she asked, her eyes twinkling with excitement.

"Fuck you," I snapped, catching my breath and collecting my wits after the terrifying ride.

She laughed heartily. "Hey, you lived!"

"No thanks to you."

"And you gained a new skill." She tipped her chin at the deer trotting ahead at a much more manageable pace. "Now, if anyone ever asks you if you've ever done it, you'll say you have."

"Great. One thing off my bucket list that I don't even have. Yay," I quipped, feigning enthusiasm. "Where are we going, anyway?"

Mirth melted off Sauria's wrinkled face. She glanced around cautiously.

"You know what..." She pulled out of her satchel a long, gray cloak identical to the one she was wearing. "Put this on. And pull the hood up, too, just in case. You don't want to stand out."

Handing her the reins, I quickly wrapped the cloak around myself and pulled the hood over my head, hiding my hair. The cloak was thin, but warm, which proved handy in this miserable weather.

"Are you taking me to the place where the hags live?" I asked.

She snorted a laugh. "You mean like a Hag Court or a Hag Palace?"

I shrugged, sensing it was best not to reply to that unless I wished to be made fun of again.

"We don't all live together," she explained. "We aren't ants or the Royal Court of Elaros, you know?" She chuckled.

"Where do you live, then?"

"Everywhere." She made a sweeping gesture with her arm, encompassing the fields around us and another forest far in the distance. "I have a wagon, like Sova. I also have a hut. And when I go to the summits of my Council, I stay in a cave."

"You don't have a court or a palace, but you have a Council?"

"Right. A Council and a Coven." She gave me a sideways glance. "Anyway. I have many places, but none is suitable for a human woman void of magic and her future baby."

I bit my lip, gripping the reins tighter. Soon enough, I might be responsible for another person, and I had no idea how to support us.

"There must be something for me to do in this kingdom, other than being someone's pet," I said bitterly. "I'm not useless. I can work. I may not do things as perfectly as fae with their *calling*, but I can learn to do something well enough to earn a living. Just point me in the right direction, please. I know very little about life out here."

Sauria fell silent, sitting uncharacteristically still for a few moments.

"Well, the only thing I can think of is..." She squinted in concentration. "I have a friend... No," she stopped herself, "not a friend. One simply can't be friends with this guy, no more than one can befriend a tree stump. He's my neighbor, of sorts. My hut is in the woods next to his farm. That's where we're going."

"Will he give me a job?" Hope twitched in me.

Sauria made a face. "He doesn't really employ anyone. The man is as strong as a bull and does everything himself. But his farm is an ideal place for you, I think. It's far away from any town. Bavius is a loner. He never has any visitors. No one will find you there."

That, indeed, sounded ideal for my situation.

As a dark, low-set building came into view up ahead, however, anxiety gnawed at me.

"Are you sure he won't mind?"

Sauria shrugged, not looking very optimistic. "We'll see."

"What's his name again?"

"Bavius. He's a *taurean*. He lives alone, doesn't talk much, and always looks grumpy. But he hasn't hurt anyone. Not that I know of, anyway."

That wasn't very reassuring. But what choice did I have?

It was almost noon by the time our wagon rolled into the packed dirt yard of Bavius's farmhouse. The place looked simple but neat. The front porch was swept clean of fallen leaves and pine needles, with a woven grass rug laid by the front door.

"This is about the time when he comes home for lunch." Sauria climbed down from the wagon's seat. "Keep your hood on. Let me talk to him first."

Noon would be the time when most courtiers took their breakfast back in Elaros. Bavius must be an early riser, which probably should be expected from a farmer.

Sauria knocked on the door, then shoved it open.

"Hey, Bavius!" she called inside. "Can we come in? I'd like to talk."

She barged right in, gesturing for me to follow.

After a small front room that had no windows and held various crates and barrels lined up along the walls, we entered a much larger one. A rock fireplace stood in the middle. It was wide but not very tall. There appeared to be a sleeping space on top of the fireplace behind the chimney, with a fluffy comforter draped over it and a curtain hanging from the ceiling.

A massive *taurean* man stood in a fighting position by a large wooden table in front of a window to the left. Dressed in a linen tunic and a pair of dark pants, he held a huge club in his hands. Long metal spikes studded the wide end of the club. His horns tilting our way menacingly, he presented a rather terrifying picture.

I stepped back tentatively, getting ready to bolt.

"Sauria. It's you." The man's bovine mouth curved in displeasure, but he set his weapon down behind the bench.

By the look of the clay bowl steaming with something very appetizing and a thick slab of bread next to it on the table, it could be assumed we'd interrupted his meal. And for that, we almost got our heads smashed in by his giant mace.

Sauria either didn't realize the danger we'd barely escaped or just didn't care about it, as she casually sauntered toward the man.

"Hey, neighbor. It's been a while."

"Has it?" Bavius grunted, taking his place on the bench at the table and turning his back to her. He hadn't even spared a glance in my direction.

Sauria was absolutely right when she said he didn't speak much.

He picked up a carved wooden spoon that could easily work as a ladle anywhere else and dipped it into his bowl. Another whiff of mouth-watering aroma wafted to me from his dish. I folded both arms across my belly, afraid my stomach would make a needy, hungry noise. I hadn't eaten for so long, I could eat a bucketful of whatever he was having.

Uninvited, Sauria slid onto the bench across from Bavius. "I have a proposition for you."

"Not interested." He kept eating, without looking at her or me.

She remained undeterred. "I'd love you to house a friend of mine for a little while."

He put his spoon down, clearly stunned by her audacity.

"Why the fuck would I do that?"

She leaned back against the wall and folded her arms across her chest. "Out of the goodness of your heart?" He scoffed, and she continued, "And also because she would help you around here, like cleaning the house and stuff—"

"*She?*" Finally, he turned my way, only to glare at me with scorn. "I don't need a female in here."

"I'd say you most definitely do." Sauria wrinkled her nose, darting a glance around.

Just like the rest of Bavius's property, the house was fairly clean, but that was mostly because it hardly had anything to get dirty. There were no rugs on the floors, no furniture other than the table and the two benches. Nothing to dust. Not even a table-cloth to wash.

"No." He picked up his spoon again.

"She's pregnant," Sauria added casually.

"What?" He turned to look at me again. "Not a hag, then?" His stare traveled down to my feet, which weren't a pair of hooves or a *snakana* tail. "A highborn! What the fuck, Sauria? Why would I want a pregnant highborn in my house? She's not my problem. Where is the lord who knocked her up?"

I shifted from foot to foot, growing increasingly uncomfortable. It had been a bad idea to come here and ask this complete stranger to interrupt his peaceful existence for my sake.

"Sauria, I should go," I said softly.

"But where will you go, girl?"

That was a very good question, the one I had no answer for.

She turned to Bavius, gesturing animatedly. "She got kicked out of her home. She has no one to help her and nowhere to go."

He shrugged his wide shoulders. "*You* keep her, then."

"I can't have her in my hut. There's barely enough space for one person. Besides, she has no magic. When I'm not around, she won't even be able to turn the lights on or keep it warm."

"Why does she have no magic?" he thundered, his brow furrowing with menace. "Who is she?"

Sauria pursed her lips, realizing she'd said more than she should have. I appreciated her talking for me, but if I were to stay under the same roof with this man, I would have to build a rapport with him on my own. I had to be honest.

I took a step closer to the table and pulled my hood off.

"Greetings, Bavius. My name is Sparrow."

"The human!" Tossing the spoon on the table, he jumped to his hooves. "The royal pet. What the fuck, Sauria? Why did you bring her here? What were you thinking? Who's the father of her baby? The king? One of the High Lords? Does she even know who the father is? Or did she just fuck them all, the way they do in Elaros?"

For someone who didn't talk much, he sure said a lot just now.

I hated to be the cause of anyone's distress, but could he wait a little before forming his lame opinion about me? He knew me for all of two seconds and already thought the worst of me.

"Well, I'm sorry, but—" I started.

He rubbed his forehead, stomping around the room agitatedly. "The next thing you know, this place will be swarming with all those snooty highborn coming from Elaros in search of her."

"No one will come for me," I said firmly. "Aside from you and Sauria, no one even knows I'm still in Nerifir."

"Sova stole her from under their noses," Sauria explained. "As far as Elaros Court is concerned, Sparrow has gone back to the human realm. She's as good as dead to them."

"So, she was sentenced to leave, but she didn't? You want me to break the law for her?"

"There is no law involving humans. None," Sauria argued. "No one knows Sparrow is in Nerifir. She's content to keep it that way. She just needs a quiet place to hide until we figure out what else is out there for her and her child. I'll stick around, too." She slapped the table resolutely. "For as long as she lives here, you can have my services for free."

"For free?" He squinted at her, looking intrigued.

"Yes. Next time you sprain an ankle or any of your mares need help with foaling, I won't charge you anything, not even a favor."

He folded his burly arms across his broad chest, chewing on his thick bottom lip.

"I want a dog, too."

Sauria's mouth dropped open. "What?"

"A huge, vicious dog that barks at everyone who enters my property. So that the next time you come anywhere near my house, the dog would warn me in time to lock the doors."

She rolled her eyes. "Yeah, no. I'm not getting you a dog. It'd be doing a disservice to the poor animal. But I'll tell you what, you can choose whatever you want from Sova's collection. She doesn't need it anymore, but you can sell it on the market and buy yourself another horse."

He stared out the window, pondering her offer.

"Can she cook?"

I understood he was talking about me, even as he wasn't looking in my direction.

"I can make a meringue," I said.

He frowned. "What the fuck is *that?*"

"I mean I can bake," I clarified.

I'd learned how to make the meringue, I could figure out how to bake cookies and bread if I had to. Hopefully, Bavius wouldn't demand the refined perfection of the royal meals from me.

"Give her your mother's recipes," Sauria said. "She'll learn."

He rubbed the back of his neck, then stomped to the fireplace and grabbed two more bowls from a shelf on the side. After filling them with the stew from the giant cauldron bubbling on the fire, he brought the bowls to the table.

"Eat." He shoved one toward Sauria. He then gestured for me to join them at the table. "Once we're done, you'll do the dishes."

I didn't wait for him to ask me twice. Holding my skirts up, I sat down on the bench next to Sauria, then took a spoon from Bavius.

"Thank you," I said to him, then turned to her. "Thank you, too, Sauria."

"Pff. Don't thank me." She waved me off. "Pregnant women are a hag's livelihood. We're meant to protect them."

Bavius said nothing.

I eagerly dug into the steaming, fragrant stew. It looked and tasted nothing like the dainty little portions of airy food back in Elaros. And that was how I wished it to be.

Whatever lay ahead of me, I wanted no reminders of the Sky Palace or the man who ruled in it now.

Chapter Twenty

SIX MONTHS LATER

SPARROW

A deafening clap of thunder startled me awake. The roof over my small room in the back of Bavius's home was pelted with sleet and hail. High winds shook his sturdy house to its foundation.

We made sure to shutter all windows before going to bed every night. Which was necessary, as a rare night passed without a storm, even now, in the dead of winter.

Lightning slashed the shutters into splinters of blinding light, cutting through the gaps in the wood. A vicious thunderstorm raged out there. Against all my best intentions and firm resolutions, my thoughts flocked to the royal palace, to the man who must be turning and tossing in the silks of his bed right now.

What tortured him so almost every night?

Back in Vensari, a night rain would always end with Voron's arms around me. I used to be the one to soothe his storms and terrors.

Now, he was alone. Without me, it didn't look like the mighty ruler of the Sky Kingdom had found anyone or anything capable of bringing him peace. Compassion swelled in my heart, filling it with tenderness.

Through the day, I did my best to keep the embers of resentment for Voron glowing inside me. He had sent me away. He'd made his choice. He had no one to blame but himself for whatever turmoil plagued him now.

But at night, I was too tired to hate him.

Another explosion of thunder sent a shudder through my body, and I allowed the memories of his arms around me to slip in.

"Stay with me, Sparrow, and there'll be no storms," he'd said to me once.

I imagined snatching him from his sweaty, crumpled sheets and out of his lavish royal chamber and bringing him here, into my narrow single bed with a squeaky frame and hard mattress. Because despite everything, I believed he'd be much happier here with me than anywhere else in the world.

"Come to me, Voron," echoed through my mind. *"And there will be no more storms."*

The phantom caress of his hand on my breast sent warm tingles down my body. I remembered how he loved spooning me from behind, clinging to me like I was his one true anchor in the eye of the storm. He loved my body with so much passion and devotion, I knew no one would ever look at me the way he did.

The ache for him spread torturously from my chest down to my core. My inner muscles spasmed deliciously, tingling with need. I slipped my hand between my thighs, imagining his mouth there instead.

His tongue instead of my finger stroked my clit, sending a surge of desire through me. His hand instead of my own kneaded my breast. His thumb flicked my nipple, making it pebble at once.

His name fluttered from my lips.

"Voron..."

As my eyes closed, his face appeared so clear, as if he were indeed here. His stormy gray eyes darkened with lust, their glimmer shaded by the silver-and-black strands hanging over his forehead.

"Come for me, little bird," his voice sounded in my mind, setting off the explosion of pleasure through me.

The storm thundered again. Energy zapped through my body, rippling inside me with the ecstasy of orgasm.

"I love you, Voron." I whispered into the night the words I would never say in the light of day.

I pressed my face into my tear-stained pillow, hugging my belly that had swelled round and big with his child. I loved Voron, and there was nothing I could do about it. Love couldn't be controlled. It had come to me uninvited. And now, it wouldn't leave, no matter how much I wished for it to go.

The thunder rolled once more, but far in the distance this time. The winds had died down, and the relentless pelting of hail had gradually stopped.

The Sky King had finally found some peace. At least for tonight.

TWO MONTHS LATER

Carrying a thick slab of smoked ham in my apron, I climbed out from the cold cellar and shut the trap door behind me, then went to the main room of the house. The cauldron with our dinner was already simmering in the hearth. The stew should be ready by the time Bavius returned from the fields that night.

Winter was at its end. Snow was still lying in patches all over the fields. But Bavius was already anxious about this year's crops. Every morning, he'd go out to clear the debris the storms had left behind or to dig new traps for the boars and other wild beasts that might threaten the plants he wouldn't seed for a month or two yet.

Bavius used to set a cauldron of stew first thing in the morning before he left the house, then eat it for both lunch and dinner. Since I'd been living with him, I made him a ham sandwich for lunch and put the stew on the fire at around midday. That way, it tasted the best by dinner time.

Pressing the ham to my chest, I waddled to the table. A cramp low in my belly made me pause to catch my breath. My middle had widened so much by now, I had to tie my apron right under my breasts. I slowly breathed through the pain, waiting for it to subside.

It'd been happening for a few days now. My term was up. The baby would be arriving any day now. But I still had no idea how I felt about it.

Some days were better than others. I would rub the spots where the little feet kicked me from the inside, smiling. A wave of indescribable tenderness would take over me, making me want to cry, overcome with love for the little being I'd never even met yet.

Other days, I'd cry for different reasons. Uncertainty racked me with worry. What kind of life would I be able to give my child? How long could we keep hiding? And how could I protect us from whatever lay ahead?

Life on the farm flowed slowly, as if suspended in a bubble. There was little joy in endless, monotonous chores. Bavius worked all day, every day, and I got no breaks or holidays, either, earning my keep. But there was also no immediate danger. And I wished to keep it that way.

Back at the table, I cut a thick slice from the ham, then buttered two slabs of the bread I'd made that morning. I covered one slice with a layer of roasted vegetables and placed the ham on top of it. After assembling the sandwich, I didn't bother cutting it in half, wrapping the entire thing in a clean kitchen towel.

Bavius liked everything large and "substantial" as he said. He got annoyed with little, delicate things that required any kind of finesse to handle. Understandably so, since everything about that man was also huge, from his giant hands with thick fingers that tended to break small things, to his wide mouth that could gobble up an entire loaf of bread in three bites.

I packed his sandwich along with a couple of apples and a clay jug of water into a basket, then put my cloak on. The farm was so remote, I hadn't seen anyone other than Bavius and Sauria for the eight months I'd been here, but one could never be too careful. Out in the open fields, I always made sure to wear a cloak with its hood up.

Before I came along, Bavius would come home for lunch. Now, he preferred to work through the day, having me bring lunch to him.

The weather was hideous. Wind tore at my cloak the moment I stepped past the fence and out of the yard. Dark clouds hung low, heavy with rain that would undoubtedly spill overnight.

"Always in a pissy mood, aren't you?" I muttered under my breath.

In a world where the king's moods controlled the weather, there was no escaping reminders of him. Voron was on my mind constantly. With Bavius working out of the house year-round and Sauria leaving the area often for whatever hag business she had to attend to, I was left alone often, one on one with my thoughts. And my thoughts always returned to Voron, no matter what I did.

I hated it. Hated that I kept talking to him in my mind. Hated that he was the star of all my sweaty fantasies whenever I touched myself. And most of all, I hated that even after everything that had happened, I still couldn't truly hate him. As I stared into the clouds, I couldn't stop wondering how he was doing.

From the news that Bavius brought occasionally from his rare trips to the town market, I knew that the High Lords' campaign against Voron had never really ended. Some highborn still refused to be ruled by the wingless king. The rest of the kingdom wasn't happy either, worn out by the brutal storms during his reign and blaming him for the bad weather.

Voron had put an end to some unrests, but new ones would

flare up often. Claiming the Sky Crown might be his biggest and greatest achievement in life. Only judging by the dark, ominous clouds in the sky, it didn't bring him much happiness.

A part of me felt vindicated in a way. He'd sacrificed *us* and everything we could've been together to this ambition of his, and it had failed to bring him any satisfaction or give the kingdom even a ray of sunshine.

The other part of me—the far gentler part I could never silence whenever Voron was concerned—was sad for him and wished he'd be happy, even if without me.

My boots sinking into the wet fertile dirt, I crossed a field, then turned toward the one where Bavius was working that day. With the heavy basket dangling over my left arm, I held my cloak closed against the wind with the right hand.

The wind grew stronger, tearing at my skirts. The clouds thickened, making the midday look like evening.

A painful cramp stabbed like a prolonged punch into my insides. I tripped, bending over. A gust of wind slammed against me, nearly knocking me over. Anger flared in my chest.

"Fuck you, Voron!" I screamed through the pain into the approaching storm. "*You* did this to me."

I dropped the basket, holding my sides with both hands. Spreading my feet wider, I braced against the wind and the pain. The need to have someone at my side at that moment was so strong, loneliness hurt more than any physical pain ever could.

"You should be here, Voron," I whispered.

My knees shook, and I gave in. I sank between the icy patches of snow in the moist soil of the field.

"You should be here, dammit. With me!" I cried.

Hot tears streamed down my cheeks. The wind smeared them over my skin, tossing my hair into my face. Bent over with another swell of pain rolling through my abdomen, I was scared and more alone than ever.

Heavy drops of water suddenly hit the dirt around me. Some

landed on my skirt, quickly absorbed by the coarse material of the dress I wore. The pattering of the drops grew faster and faster.

My tears halted as I stared at the water hitting the ground all around me. I held out my hand, letting the drops chill my skin.

It rained. Heavily. In the middle of the day. This was the only daytime rain I'd ever witnessed in the Sky Kingdom. And I knew exactly what it meant.

The king was crying.

He was crying during the day, not in his nightmares at night.

"Cry, Voron," I whispered, cruelly. "Cry, my king. May you feel at least a fraction of the pain you've caused me."

I tried to hold on to that unkind thought to prolong the spark of resentment and anger, but it went out quickly.

The only thing that remained was an all-consuming longing.

Sauria found me drenched and curled into myself under the torrential rain. She called Bavius from the other end of the field, and he carried me back to the house.

I paced inside the tiny bedroom behind the main room with the fireplace. Bavius used to store here some of the spare furniture and his family's mementos going back many generations. After he'd agreed to my moving in, we'd cleaned this room out, by taking most of the things over to the barn and leaving only a narrow cot for me to sleep on, a dresser for the few things I now had, and a rocking chair in the corner.

A couple of weeks ago, Bavius had also brought in an old, carved-wood baby crib. I didn't ask where he got it from, but I suspected it used to be his, centuries ago. It looked so ancient, it might've also rocked his father and his father's father, when they were babies.

During the long winter nights, I'd knitted a few blankets,

some tiny sweaters, and hats. Sauria had sourced a length of soft swaddling material that we had cut into baby blankets.

All was ready for the baby to arrive. Whether I'd caught up emotionally with that fact or not didn't matter anymore. This baby was coming.

Another torturously long spasm gripped my belly, depriving me of breath. With a groan, I bent over the cot, propping my hands into the stiff mattress, and waited until the pain eased enough to allow me to draw some air back into my lungs.

"Fuck you, Voron." Bounced around my brain.

The rocking chair squeaked with Sauria sitting in it. She gave it a push with her foot against the floor.

"Do you love him?" she asked.

That was a random question, but I knew exactly whom she was talking about.

"No," I lied, hoping it would be true one day.

"But did you love him?"

"No," I said, lying a little less this time.

My feelings for Voron weren't love at first sight. There had been a time when I didn't love him, or at least didn't know that I loved him.

With one leg bent under her, she pushed herself in the rocking chair with the other.

"Are you ever going to tell him?"

The creaking of the old chair was getting on my nerves, but it was not nearly as annoying as the questions she was bombarding me with.

Bending my elbows, I rested my forearms on the cot, then pressed my forehead into my hand, riding another brutal swell of pain. They seem to roll one on top of each other now, with hardly any break for me in between.

Sauria had given me some tea earlier. It warmed my insides, relieving the pain, but not enough.

"Do you have more of that tea?" I exhaled the moment the cramp rolled downwards.

"You can't have any more." She got off the chair and massaged my lower back through my undershirt. "But you're doing great, Sparrow. Tell me about your life in the palace. What were the royal parties like?"

I didn't want to talk about Elaros. It'd be impossible to do without talking about Voron, and I was in enough pain already.

"No." I shook my head. "How about you tell me how you became a hag instead? How old were you when it happened?"

She kept rubbing my back, her slim, quick fingers loosening the knots of pain out of my muscles.

"It didn't happen overnight," she said. "It takes a while to become a hag, and I'm still learning. But I always knew my magic was stronger than that of anyone else in our town."

"You did?" I stiffened, racked by yet another contraction. Focusing on Sauria's dry, rustling voice made this one easier to bear, though.

"Yes," she said. "My parents knew it, too. My father served in the army of a High Lord. I'm not going to tell you which one. Because it doesn't matter, he's dead now."

I panted through more pain and tension. "Who's dead, your dad or the High Lord?"

"Both, actually. They happened to be on the wrong side during one of the wars of King Tiane. The king won, and my father was killed, along with the High Lord he served."

That must have been one of the wars that Voron had won for King Tiane. And now, my thoughts flew back to that man, like a flock of homing pigeons going home.

"How about your mother?" I asked quickly, keeping the conversation on topic.

"She's well and alive."

"She is?" Somehow, I'd assumed both Sauria's parents would be long dead by now.

"Yes. She lives in the High Lord's palace with the court of his successor. I visit her sometimes."

"Did your parents want you to become a hag?"

She shrugged. "It didn't matter what they wanted. No one can force you to take the hag's vow or to stop you from taking it. But they didn't stand in my way, for which I am grateful. I was ten when I asked to learn more about hags and their magic. At nineteen, I was allowed to attend the convent."

"To pray and stuff?" I could only speak in short sentences now.

"To pray? Ha!" She prodded my belly, checking the baby's position. "No. That's not what hags' convents are for. We're not priestesses. We serve people, not gods."

"What did you do in your convent, then?"

"For three years, I had to subject myself to every possible kind of debauchery out there, to be fully informed of what I was giving up by taking the hag's vow."

"Debauchery? Like what?"

"Like every kind of sex." She laughed. "I enjoyed it well enough. Sex is fun, especially for those whose magic is too weak to do anything better in life. But it wasn't difficult for me to give it up. It's been six years since I've taken my vow, and I haven't missed having someone rutting into me. I'm sure I never will." She curled her lips in disgust. "The hold of magic is so much more enticing and satisfying. And the more you have of it, the stronger it pulls you in."

I gripped her hand, parting my legs wider and rocking on my knees. The pressure inside me felt as if my entire lower body was expanding like a balloon.

"You were nineteen?" The pressure eased just a little, and I took a few short, shallow breaths. "Three years in the convent. Six as a hag. Sauria, you aren't even thirty yet, are you? We're about the same age."

I exhaled a strangled laugh at the shock on her wrinkly face.

"Fuck, Sparrow. How did you even figure it out in your state?"

I had no idea how. But our conversation distracted me from fear and trepidation before each new wall of pain crashed into me.

Focusing on something else helped me get my mind off the agony, too.

The pressure grew too strong, however, impossible to ignore now.

"Sauria... I have to..." I gripped her thin, scrawny hand so hard it was a miracle I didn't crush it.

"Push, Sparrow." She patted my back soothingly with her other hand as I bent over the cot again. "Push, my brave human girl."

He was born just a few minutes later.

"I got him." Sauria chuckled, retrieving the being I'd just brought into the world. "Such an impatient little boy."

"A *boy?*" That one word, followed by a high-pitched wail from a person who hadn't been there before, made it all real at once. "There was a baby boy in there?"

It was so stupid to ask after carrying that baby inside me for months. But only when I actually saw him did the enormity of it all finally hit me full force.

I gave birth to a baby. I produced an entirely new person right now.

The immediate physical relief was euphoric. But I couldn't focus on the sensation of my body. My mind, my heart, and my entire being were pulled to the wiggling, screaming little thing in Sauria's hands.

I could barely wait until she had cleaned him off a little with a cloth and the warm water that Bavius had just brought in.

"Congratulations," Bavius boomed, giving me a smile, then helped me climb onto the cot properly and covered my legs with a blanket.

Sauria bent over, handing me the baby.

My baby.

"And there he is," she cooed.

He stopped screaming when I put him to my chest. His eyes were closed so tightly, only the very tips of his dark eyelashes peeked out. Wet wisps of black hair plastered his little head.

"He's perfect," I choked out, too overwhelmed to even breathe properly. "Hi, sweetheart. I'm your mommy."

I stroked his wet hair and traced the delicate shell of his ear. He squirmed in my arms, poking with his face at my chest.

"He needs to feed," Sauria stated expertly.

With a grunt, Bavius grabbed the bucket with dirty rags and water and stomped out of the room. I untied the laces of my shirt, and Sauria guided my little son to latch to my breast.

"Do I even have any milk yet?" I was worried.

But she waved at me reassuringly. "Let him work on it."

He seemed to like snuggling to me, looking content. I caught his tiny fist, and he promptly curled his hand around my finger, gripping it tightly.

The peace that descended upon me in that minute was indescribable. The emotion was so enormous, I wished to share it with the entire world.

"Damn you, Voron," a bitter thought wormed into my brain. *"You should've been here. Even if you hated me, even if you couldn't stand me and wished me dead, you should have at least talked to me instead of kicking me out. Now, you missed the birth of your son. Nothing would ever give this back to you."*

The baby squirmed again. I leaned back into the pillows, laying him on top of me, his belly to my chest. The skin on his back rippled, suddenly glowing blue.

"What's going on?" I shot a worried look at Sauria.

She smiled contently. "Just watch."

The blue light shimmered and thickened, growing darker. Then, two small black wings emerged from the back of my baby. The feathers were so dark, they glistened with purple and blue.

"Wow..." I gently stroked the edge of a wing, the silky feathers trembling slightly under my finger.

Sauria nodded. "He's a highborn. There's no doubt about that. What are you going to name him?"

"I don't know."

I didn't have a name prepared. It just hadn't felt real to me all this time, not until I saw his little face. I couldn't name someone I'd never met. And now, no name seemed good enough for this perfect little being.

My son.

I pulled a blanket higher to cover us both, careful not to ruffle his little wings too much. He stretched them out, then folded them neatly against his back but didn't hide them. I wondered if he even knew what he was doing or if the movement of his wings was mostly instinctual, like gripping my finger.

"Aww," Sauria cooed. "He really is the cutest, and you know I've helped deliver quite a few babies in my life."

I didn't care about other babies. I just knew mine was the best, and I couldn't take my eyes off him.

"Hey, how about the name Aithen?" Sauria suggested. "Like the God of Death? He has black wings, too, just like him."

"What?" I bristled. "Why would I name my baby after death?"

She rolled her eyes. "Not death, but the God of Death."

"Isn't it the same thing?"

"Of course not. God Aithen doesn't kill people. They die from the hand of an enemy, from an accident, or from old age. The God of Death just comes to take them into the afterlife, so that they don't have to make that trip alone."

"That's nice of him," I mumbled, a little less revolted.

"Isn't it?" Sauria nodded enthusiastically. "In fact, he's the most merciful god of all of them, if you ask me. Most of the others are a rather spiteful, cranky bunch of egomaniacs."

"Aithen," I tested the sound of the name, then looked back at the sleeping baby in my arms. "I'll think about it. It may grow on me still."

"Good." Sauria got up to take care of the afterbirth wrapped in rags. "Oh, and by the way," she narrowed her eyes at me from the doorway, "if you ever tell anyone my real age, I'll turn you into a six-legged frog and lock you in a jar to add to Sova's collection.

Even the fact that you gave birth to the cutest boy in the kingdom won't stop me. Do you hear me?"

I smiled at the fake menace in her voice.

"Sauria, I promise, your secret is safe with me. If anyone asks, I'll tell them you're so old, the God of Death has already shaved and put on his best cologne, getting ready to meet you."

She left the room giggling, very much like the woman in her twenties that she was.

Chapter Twenty-One
EIGHT MONTHS LATER

SPARROW

"And one more?" I smiled, lifting a spoon filled with mashed potatoes and squash.

"Ma, ma, ma." Aithen bounced in the highchair we had found among the many things stored in Bavius's barn.

"That's right, my boy. I'm your mama." Sometimes, he would say two of those syllables close enough for it to sound like one word.

He eagerly opened his mouth for me to feed him at the same time as he grabbed for the spoon, too.

"Nope, my boy." I maneuvered the spoon around his little grabbing hands and into his mouth. "*You* eat the peas, *I'll* feed you the mushy stuff. That's the deal."

With his chubby little fingers, he rolled the cooked peas inside the shallow wooden bowl I'd served them in. I'd let him eat his entire breakfast on his own for him to squish, mush, and taste it all. But mornings were busy; I couldn't afford to lose a second on cleaning the mess he'd make.

Bavius stomped into the house. He was still shirtless after his morning visit to the small log bathhouse outside.

"Are my cakes ready?" he boomed, looking as grumpy as ever.

"The dough is ready." With both my hands full, I gestured with my elbow at the large bowl with the rising dough by the fireplace. "I'll fry them up in a second."

"Why don't you do it *now*? Let the lad eat on his own."

"All right."

With Aithen occupied by chasing the peas in his bowl, I put the mash and the spoon out of his reach and wiped my hands on my apron.

Bavius didn't even look at the baby. He rarely noticed him—or me, for that matter—unless he needed to have something done. We lived together but tried to stay out of each other's way, like planets in space, each moving along their own orbit.

It was easier to accomplish before Aithen was born. I'd worked hard, learning to do as many chores as I could to justify my living under Bavius's roof. I cooked and cleaned, mended his clothes, and helped him in the fields whenever he needed me to.

He wasn't a bad landlord, but he never let me forget he was a reluctant one. He had managed just fine without me, and he would do just as fine if I chose to leave the farm tomorrow. In fact, he'd be relieved if I left.

After Aithen was born, the demanding little creature that he was, he'd taken most of my attention and became my main focus in life. It just couldn't be any other way. I'd drop everything to tend to his needs. I no longer went out to the fields because I couldn't leave Aithen alone in the house. And even the house chores often had to wait, which irritated Bavius.

"It won't take me long." I grabbed a cast-iron frying pan and put it on the stove next to the fireplace.

By the time Bavius got dressed and poured himself a mug of coffee, I already had the first batch of his morning cakes stuffed with mushrooms and onions sizzling on the pan.

"Ma-Ma-Ma-Ma." Aithen clearly got bored with his peas. His wings materialized behind his shoulders. Thankfully, he hadn't figured out yet how to free them from the frame of the highchair.

"Almost done, my baby." I slapped the cakes onto a plate and rushed to the table.

Aithen bounced on his bum impatiently. With a slap of his hand, his bowl flew off the table. It crashed, spewing the leftover peas all over the floor.

Bavius made a face, wincing in displeasure. I shoved the plate with his breakfast his way along the table, then bent over quickly, grabbing the empty bowl from the floor. As I straightened out, I noticed his eyes focused on my backside. His gaze then rode upwards to my chest as I grabbed a broom and swept the peas from the floor. My spine stiffened with unease. As soon as I was done, I quickly retreated to the fireplace again.

During the entire sixteen months that I'd spent on the farm, I hadn't seen Bavius with a woman. He seemed to prefer taking care of his needs on his own.

He slept on the mattress laid on top of the massive rectangular fireplace in the main room of the house. His sleeping place was separated from the rest of the house only by a curtain. On a rare stormless night, I sometimes could hear him through the door to my bedroom because he didn't care to stay quiet when he pleasured himself. It never lasted long, ended with a satisfied grunt, and was almost immediately followed by his loud snoring as he'd fall asleep right after.

Since when did he start stealing glances at my body?

It certainly wasn't a direction I was willing to go with him. I was grateful to Bavius for housing us, but I had no other feelings for him.

Maybe it really was time for me to leave here?

I'd gained quite a few useful skills by now. There must be a way for me to use them to earn a living. Except that the moment I'd set my foot into any town, I'd be recognized. The word would go out, and the guards would come for me.

There was so much I had to lose now. I glanced at Aithen, who started fussing, clearly growing bored and tired from sitting in the chair.

Bavius finished his breakfast promptly and wiped his large mouth with the back of his hand.

"I better go. The potatoes won't dig themselves out." He headed for the door, leaving the dirty dishes on the table.

With him out of the room, it became easier to breathe. His presence always made me nervous, like I'd done something wrong and upset him. He always seemed annoyed by one thing or another.

I rubbed my chest. The left side had been giving me trouble ever since Aithen was born. The top part of my breast ached. And in the past few days, the skin there turned hot and red. I should probably show it to Sauria the next time I saw her. Maybe she could give me an ointment for it or something.

Aithen finally lost his patience completely. Bouncing in the chair, he screeched and smacked with both hands against the table.

"Okay, okay." I hurried to him. "Let's get you out of that chair already."

As I lifted him out, he stopped fussing and started pulling on my hair instead.

Bavius's deep voice unexpectedly came from the outside. Who was he talking to?

"Do you think Sauria came for a visit?" I asked Aithen with a smile.

Sauria popped in whenever she could. She had been a huge help, too. I didn't think I'd manage without her.

Aithen cooed, stuffing a loose strand of my hair into his mouth.

"You like Sauria, don't you?" I retrieved my hair from him and propped him on my hip, then leaned to the window to look out.

Sauria wasn't there. Instead, Bavius was talking to a man—a highborn man dressed in fine clothes that even the wind and dust of travels couldn't make any less dashing.

I recognized his gray-brown wings.

Alcon!

Panic shot through me like a bullet. I shrank away from the window and leaned with my back against the wall. My heart thundered so hard, I feared they would hear it through the wall.

What if they came into the house?

Pressing Aithen to my chest, I rushed to my room and shut the door behind me.

Would this door hold them?

Would they try to force their way in?

And why on earth did Alcon even come here?

Any possible reason I could think of for his visit had to do with me. No one ever visited Bavius's farm. He had no family left. He made no friends and had no neighbors other than Sauria.

Aithen squirmed in my arms, demanding I set him down. The boundless energy of this child urged him to start on his usual morning rounds of crawling all around the house.

"Not yet, baby." I kissed his soft, silky hair. Just as ink black as on the day he was born, his tresses had grown longer since. They curled adorably around his ears and on the back of his head.

I inhaled his sweet familiar scent, cuddling him to my chest. "Shhh."

All seemed quiet out in the main room. But from here, I couldn't hear or look out into the front yard.

Did Alcon leave?

The door between the front room and the main room opened and Bavius's heavy hooves thudded on the wooden floors. A set of footsteps accompanied them, sending me with my back into a corner.

I looked around in desperation, searching for a way out. Did I have enough time to get out through the window? Would it be enough to stay hidden? Or did Alcon know I was here and would keep searching and chasing me?

What would happen if he found me? If they wanted to finish what they had started and throw me into the River of Mists, what would happen to my baby boy?

I pressed Aithen to me so tightly, it was a miracle he didn't start crying yet.

The door to my room was flung open, and I froze.

"Here she is," Sauria announced cheerfully.

Had I not been so terrified, I would've realized earlier that her light footsteps weren't loud enough for Alcon. Sauria came in the house with Bavius. Alcon wasn't there.

The relief was so strong, my legs felt too weak to hold me. If it wasn't for the wall behind me, I would have dropped to the floor.

Bavius continued to stomp in the main room, pacing back and forth.

"Fuck!" He rubbed his horns. "Fuck."

"What's going on?" I struggled to hold Aithen, who grew even more determined to make it down.

"You're having guests for lunch." Sauria rolled her eyes in Bavius's direction. "Though he makes it look like the farm is coming under siege."

"But isn't it?" Bavius bellowed. "I didn't invite them here."

Coming out into the main room, I set Aithen down, and he crawled right back toward the table to pick up from the floor the same peas he didn't want to eat from the bowl earlier. I thought I'd swept them all, but he managed to find a few under the table.

"Who *they?*" I rushed to grab a broom and a dustpan, then raced my son to sweep up the remaining peas.

"The royal court." Sauria made her eyes big to emphasize the importance of the visit.

My heart dropped into my stomach. "Why?"

"Exactly! Why?" Bavius boomed. "I didn't call them here. I have work to do. This is *my* house. They can fuck right off! A bunch of lazy asses with nothing better to do."

"The royal court?" The dustpan trembled in my hand, nearly spilling the peas I'd swept onto it.

"Yes!" Sauria sounded thrilled. "The councilor was leaving just when I landed in the yard."

"What councilor?"

"Councilor Alcon." She squinted at me. "You must know him from your time back in Elaros?

Bavius stopped, leveling me with a stare.

"No." I shook my head quickly. "I don't know him."

Technically, it wasn't a lie. Back when I lived in Elaros, Alcon was the Head of The Royal Guard. I never knew him as a councilor. That must be a huge step up for him, but it made perfect sense. Alcon was sharp and even-tempered, with a proven track record of loyalty to Voron. It was no surprise that the new king had elevated his position and put him on the Royal Council.

"Well, anyway," Sauria continued. "Apparently, the royal court is traveling by horses. They need a place to stop for a rest and have some food. They chose Bavius's farm because, as you know, there is nothing else around here."

"That fucking wingless king," Bavius spat through his teeth. "His brooding moods are going to cost me crops next year again. Not a ray of sunshine for sixteen months. Nothing but storms, hail, and flooding. And now, he's coming here with all his high-born mob in tow, expecting me to feed them all?"

My stomach spasmed with a jolt through my chest. "The king is coming here, too?"

Sauria threw her hands up in the air, facing Bavius.

"Who is to talk about brooding here? If anything, you and the king are so much the same in that department that you may be brothers."

"Except that *my* moods don't affect the livelihood of people," he grumped.

"They very much do affect those who are close to you." She propped her hands on her hips, standing up to the man three times her size. "It's not the king's fault he has no wings and can't travel as fast as other highborn. This is actually to your own bene-fit, you dummy. The king is not afraid to get the road dirt on his boots and see the life in the kingdom from the ground, not just from the sky. He's been doing a lot of good for the ordinary people, you know. Besides, Councilor Alcon said the king will reward you for your trouble."

Bavius huffed air through flaring nostrils, his tail lashing against his boots.

"I don't need his reward. I just need him to leave me alone."

For once, I was entirely on his side.

"Do they have to come here? Is there any way to decline it?" I moved my gaze from him to her, desperately hoping for a way out of this.

Sauria regarded me with curiosity.

"You don't want them here, either?"

"No." I averted my eyes from her penetrating look. "Not really. What are we even going to feed them? I can't cook the food they're used to eating in the palace."

"Fuck that!" Bavius stomped his hoof, making the whole house shake. "If they want to eat in my house, they have to eat what we do. I'm not here to please them."

"I'd rather not feed them at all." I said softly. "Can't they go elsewhere?"

Sauria's look turned sympathetic. "You know there is nothing else close enough, Sparrow. You can't possibly turn down the Sky King without risking some very unpleasant consequences."

I clasped my hands in front of me.

"Fuck it," Bavius still fumed, but he seemed to have cooled off a little.

I felt sorry for him. He was very much a man of habit. This morning, he woke up with the intention of digging potatoes in his field all day. Now, the plans had changed on him drastically. He wasn't the one to switch gears quickly or easily.

With time, however, the change had a chance to settle in his mind somewhat. He'd still be brooding and complaining for the rest of the day and beyond. But his behavior was already changing from rebellious to resigned.

"They'll eat the goddamn stew," he grumped.

"Do you have enough?" Sauria asked. "How many of them are going to be here? Thirteen?"

Her voice sounded as if coming from a distance. I could hardly focus on what they were saying, stunned by the fact that Voron would be here. In just a few hours, I'd get to see him.

But I couldn't let him see me.

"You'll need at least one more table here," Sauria said. "Do you have one in the barn?"

"Right. I'll get it." Bavius stomped out of the house to get the table.

I pivoted to Sauria. "I can't do this."

"What do you mean?"

"I can't let them see me. I'm not supposed to be in Nerifir, remember? As far as the rest of the Sky Kingdom is concerned, I'm gone. And I need to keep it that way. If they see me—"

She tilted her head. "Do you think the king is still angry with you? After all this time? Maybe you could use this opportunity and ask for his mercy?"

"His mercy?" I scoffed, not holding back a derisive laugh. "Trust me, he has nothing to be angry with me about. *I*, on the other hand..." I shook my head, grinding my teeth. This was not the time to discuss any of this. "What's important right now is that if they see me up close, they'll know who I am. And I can't risk it."

She looked skeptical. "Well, I wouldn't count on Bavius to pull this off, completely on his own."

"Sauria." I gripped her hand. "Can you do this, please?"

"Me?" She chuckled. "You know I don't cook. At least nothing that regular people would eat. I can barely boil an egg. Unless it's a curse or a potion, I'm useless."

"I'll cook," I begged. "I'll make more stew, bake more bread and some pies, and whatever else Bavius wants me to make. But please, I can't serve it to them. I can't let them see me or Aithen."

Her eyes followed my gaze to the baby, who found the spoon

he'd tossed to the floor earlier that morning and now was gleefully chewing on it with the only two teeth he had so far.

"I'll fly him to my hut," she offered. "Pack his lunch, I'll feed him there."

I shook my head, desperate. "I have to hide, too."

"You don't have time to walk to my place. You have a bunch of food to cook for a lot of hungry highborn, remember? I can't be here instead of you, either. No one knows your kitchen better than you do. I'll break something or dump a bowl of stew on the king's head, which would get Bavius in trouble."

The way my hands shook, I'd dump or spill things myself. Fear vibrated through me so strong, my entire body was shaking.

"I can't let them see me," I kept repeating.

"Then don't."

I stared at her, confused.

She rummaged through the pockets of her cloak, muttering under her breath, "Let me see. I should have some spotted ragweed in here somewhere. It has many uses, I don't leave the house without having some on me."

"What are you doing?"

She produced a small bundle of long dried grass with round bumps along each blade.

"Give me something of yours that you have worn against your skin for a while," Sauria demanded.

My hand went straight to Voron's necklace around my neck. It had long lost every trace of his scent, saturating with mine instead. I hadn't taken it off ever since King Tiane had made me do it that one time.

"What for?" I asked, not willing to part with it now or ever.

"I'll glamor you to look like someone else." She chewed on her bottom lip, considering my options. "Like a *taurean* woman. You'll pose as Bavius's wife."

"His wife?" I winced.

The idea made me rather uncomfortable. But it made sense

for a woman living on a remote farm with a man to be his wife. It'd be the simplest explanation of my presence here.

Sauria nodded. "Aithen and I will spend the day in my hut, meanwhile. Right, little guy? You'll help me collect some swirly-cup mushrooms under the birches, won't you?"

My son giggled when she addressed him. Dropping the spoon, he flapped his wings, rising off the floor and up to my chest level.

"Careful, baby!" I plucked him from the air and pressed him to my chest.

This ability of his made me nervous. I feared he'd bump into things or forget to move his wings and fall. Flying was one of the things I couldn't teach him. I couldn't watch over him up there and dreaded that inevitable day when my fae baby boy would fly higher than I could reach.

He wiggled in my arms, restless and on the move. I smoothed his wings gently, until he hid them again, then settled him back on the floor to crawl.

"So, do you have something on you that I can glamor?" Sauria prompted.

I slid Voron's necklace off over my head and handed it to her, feeling almost naked without its familiar weight over my chest.

"Are you sure it'll work?" I asked.

She nodded, plucking one long blade of grass from her bundle. She then threaded the dry blade between the beads of the necklace, whispering something under her breath. With her thumbs coated in the powder from the crushed bumps of the spotted ragweed, she pressed over my eyebrows then rubbed along my nose and the jawline. She then crouched down and smeared circles around my ankles and finally pressed a hand to my back-side, all the while mumbling something softly.

"Hey!" I arched my back, jerking my butt away from her hand. "What's that for?"

"For the tail." She smirked, putting the necklace back around my neck. "You're going to have a tail now, human girl."

The moment the necklace touched my skin again, I felt it. I

felt the tail growing out from the end of my spine, just above my butt crack. The weight of horns pressed above my temples. My face felt much bigger than it ever was, the nose and lips wide and protruding. I flapped my ears and stomped a hoof.

"Oh my God…" I was a *taurean* now.

I slapped a hand over my mouth, expecting to feel the bovine jaw. But it encountered my regular human mouth, instead. The sensation under my palm didn't match what I felt with my face. I brushed a hand over my ass, not finding the tail either. Yet when I looked down, I saw a long brown tail swaying behind me, its tip furnished with a thick tassel of fur.

"The touch can't be tricked as easily as the eye," Sauria explained. "Don't let the visitors touch you, and you'll do just fine."

I made a slow turn, testing the sensation of having hooves instead of feet. "This is so weird."

"I'll let you wear the glamor now, so you get used to it by the time the guests arrive."

"You want me to cook like this? I don't think I can."

"Of course you can. Your hands aren't affected at all. And by the time the royal court arrives, you'll stop tripping over your hooves and learn to be mindful of your tail. It wouldn't do for you to stick it into the fire or something like that when they're here."

Bavius walked in at that moment.

"Can you hold the door while I carry in the table—" He stopped in his tracks, sliding a gaze up my body all the way to my face.

The russet skin on his cheeks warmed with a blush. His wide tongue lapped at his lips as he stared at me with hooded eyes.

"Don't get too excited, Bavius," Sauria chuckled, holding the door open for him to carry in the table he'd left in the front room. "This is just for today. The glamor will wear off by dinnertime." She turned to me. "Or earlier, if you take off that necklace."

SPARROW

Sauria stayed a little longer to help Bavius and me get ready for the royal lunch. We had the two tables set with clean tablecloths and every spare dish we could find in the house and in storage in the barn. The long benches on each side of the tables provided enough sitting for the people coming over.

The heavy tables, plain linen tablecloths, and roughly hewn benches were so unlike anything the royal courtiers were used to in Elaros. But if they wanted a palace experience, they should have stayed in the palace. I decided not to fret over what they might think about the way we lived here.

My cooking had improved greatly, but it couldn't be compared to the fantastic creations of the royal head chef. As a result, I didn't even attempt making molded jelly or air-light souf-flé. Instead, I tripled my stew recipe and baked dozens of pumper-nickel bread rolls. I also roasted a yellow squash and red beets with oil and garlic. Bavius brought some ham and a head of pickled cabbage from the cellar. I sliced both the ham and the cabbage and arranged them on two platters as side dishes.

For dessert, I grabbed a jar of snowberry preserve, planning to bake pies with it, then paused. I'd eaten snowberries in Elaros. Voron knew I liked them. He always made sure to serve snowberry tarts with tea when I came to his rooms to learn how to play War of Kings.

Memories threatened to rush me. I put the jar back on the shelf in the cellar, then grabbed an apronful of apples and a basket of fresh cranberries instead. There would be no memories of Elaros. I couldn't allow myself to think about Vensari either if I wished to make it through this lunch without falling apart.

By the time the trotting of horses' hooves sounded in the front yard, the food was ready. The farmhouse was filled with appetizing smells of cooking and baking, and I was ladling the stew into an earthenware serving bowl.

"Fucking freeloaders are here," Bavius cursed, but straightened his tunic under his belt and stomped outside to greet the guests.

I set the stew bowl onto the table, then took off my apron that was stained with cranberries and dusted with flour and put it away.

Waiting by the fireplace, I crushed the skirt of my simple dress in my sweaty hands, wishing I could just hide in the cellar until everyone left.

What would be the worst that could happen if I hid?

Bavius would be pissed. He'd probably accidentally—or not so accidentally—spill the ale into the king's lap, then lose his temper and get himself arrested. But even that no longer seemed so terrible compared to me having to face the royal court once again.

I'd done so well hiding from both the world and my past. But now, the door burst open, and my past rushed right in.

Four elegant court ladies dressed in pastel-colored cloaks trimmed with snow-white fur fluttered in, chatting.

"Oh, it smells wonderful in here!"

"Such a neat, quaint cottage in the fields!"

"It's so warm in here, too, thank goodness. I'm freezing."

They took their cloaks off, looking around for a place to put them.

I cleared my throat and stepped forward. "Welcome."

"Oh, hi there," all four said in unison.

"You must be the mistress of the house," one of them clarified as the rest smiled at me pleasantly.

I didn't recognize either of the four. These women weren't at Elaros during my time there. That fact allowed me to breathe a little easier.

"Yes. Welcome to my home," I said. "I'll take your cloaks." I opened my arms, and they piled their fine garments into them, giving their thank-yous in sing-song voices.

I smiled back, refusing to ponder if any of them had shared the king's bed. It was none of my business. Not anymore.

The men came in next, flanked by Bavius and led by the Sky King.

I retreated to the fireplace again, hiding my face behind the fragrant pile of ladies' cloaks in my arms. But the moment the king entered, I saw no one else. As if I'd spent the past year and four months in a desert, I drank in every familiar feature of his.

He looked just like on the day I first met him. Black cloak. The ornate handle of his sword was visible over his shoulder. The same unruly hair had possibly a little more silver in the front, now. The severe expression, usual for the former High General, was still there under the circlet of golden thorns of the Sky Crown.

This was every bit the cold and bitter Voron I knew from Elaros. With not a single trace of the smiling, sensual Voron I'd gotten to know in Vensari.

Bavius stomped to me. "I'll take these." He grabbed the ladies' cloaks out of my arms, looking every bit as uncomfortable as I felt.

Praying that Sauria's glamor worked, I smiled and bowed my head to the newcomers.

"Welcome, Your Majesty," I said in a voice altered by both the glamor and my nerves. "Gentlemen." I reached for their cloaks, avoiding every chance for eye contact with the king.

He and Alcon were the only two I recognized from the former Elaros Court. Most of the men in his party were the High Lords who supported Voron in his claim to the throne. A few were new faces to me.

It appeared Voron had surrounded himself with different people than those preferred by his late brother. It was a change for the better, I decided, returning the simple greetings and friendly smiles of the new courtiers.

Voron placed his cloak on top of the others, and I couldn't help but steal a lungful of his scent. Turning around to take the cloaks to my bedroom where Bavius had already piled the first batch on my narrow bed, I furtively pressed my face to the soft velvet of the royal cloak. It smelled cool and fresh, like the air after a storm, and so painfully familiar, my heart squeezed, skipping a beat. I felt lightheaded, having to grab onto the door frame for support on my way out of my bedroom.

"Please, dear guests," I said, with an exaggerated energy in my voice. "Lunch is served."

The sooner they ate, the faster they'd leave, and the sooner I could go back to my life of trying to forget Voron while raising our child who looked so much like him. The resemblance between the two was uncanny. I was glad Sauria had whisked Aithen away. If anyone saw him next to Voron, they'd know the two were closely related.

And then where would we be?

The king's order for my deportation still stood. And even if it didn't, how could I ever forgive the man who had cast me aside so easily? More importantly, how could I ever trust him again?

I had so much more to protect now than I'd ever had before. What would happen to Aithen if the world knew about his existence? My son was a prince by birth. An *illegitimate* heir to the throne. And I was Aithen's only protection against anyone wishing to use him in their political game.

That said, I wasn't going to deny Aithen his birthright. Sooner or later, I'd have to tell him the whole truth about his father. But I'd do it when he was old enough to understand and able to protect himself from the dangerous intrigues of the highborn. I would not allow anything bad to happen to my baby. He would not have to go through what his father had gone through as a child.

My thoughts, as worrying as they were, kept my mind occupied, allowing me to focus on getting the dessert ready at the stove, instead of stealing glances at the man sitting at the head of the table.

Maybe when they had left, I would look back at today as just a dream. A momentary blast from the past that came and went, leaving no consequence.

Bavius brought a jug of ale from the cellar.

"You pour it." He pressed it into my hands.

I didn't want to go anywhere near the table, but forcing Bavius to refill the guests' steins in the crammed dining area would most likely end in disaster. He barely fit behind the table even when there were just the four of us with Sauria coming over for dinner on occasion.

"All right." I took the jug from him and inhaled a bracing breath, as if about to jump off a cliff. "I'll do it."

I approached the table, my leather shoes looking and thudding like hooves against the wooden floor.

"Would you like more ale?" I asked the lady closest to me with a smile, my lips feeling full and long on my elongated bovine face.

"Oh no, thank you," the lady declined with a sweet smile in response. "I'm happy with my water."

"I would love some, please." Another woman moved her stein closer to me. "This stew is amazing," she gushed as I refilled her stein. "What meat is it?"

"Wild boar." I glanced at Bavius, who was fidgeting by the fireplace, looking like he'd rather be anywhere else but in his own house right now. "My husband traps them in the woods around our fields. Stops them from destroying the crops."

"You are an amazing cook," one of the men at the table

complimented. "It's not easy to prepare wild meat in the way that would make it so tasty and tender."

"Thank you. I used an old family recipe."

I made my way around the entire table, stopping next to Voron at last. By etiquette, I was supposed to serve the king first, but it'd taken me this long to work up the nerve to finally approach him.

"Ale?" I silently begged he'd refuse and send me on my merry way.

But he lifted his stein to me. "Yes, please."

I leaned around his shoulder, mindful not to touch him in any way. But I couldn't avoid his scent invading my nostrils.

My gaze traveled up his shoulder to his neck, to that spot just above his collar. I knew exactly how his skin would feel there if I pressed my nose to it. I knew the scent of him would be stronger there—warmer. I knew the ends of his hair would tickle the side of my face, forcing me to close my eyes and smile.

I knew I would enjoy every moment of that if only I dared come this close to him ever again.

"Is something wrong?" He glanced up at me.

Our eyes met for just a fraction of a moment before I blinked and quickly moved my gaze away.

Voron.

He wasn't the king back when I first met him or when I fell in love with him. But that was the reason I *had* to think of him as the king now. As someone unapproachable and unattainable. A stranger.

"Nothing is wrong, Your Majesty." I focused on pouring the ale into his stein without spilling, then promptly retreated away from the table.

I felt his gaze follow me all the way back to the fireplace. The skin on my back tingled under my dress. The fine hairs on my nape stood on end.

"Can you serve the dessert when they're done, please?" I

tossed to Bavius over my shoulder, rushing to the door. "It's just the pies on those plates. I'll be right back."

I didn't look back to see how he took my request and whether he was complying. I needed to put a physical wall between Voron and myself. I had to clear my lungs from his scent and my head from the fantasies about him.

I had to get away for a few seconds.

Running through the door, I stomped out onto the patio, then leaned against the wall next to the door frame, catching my breath.

My heart was pounding. My head was spinning. I was falling apart and the only thing that could keep all my pieces together was having his arms around me. The arms of the man who had caused it all.

The door to the house suddenly opened, and a man walked out. He stopped at the end of the patio, looking out into the yard.

Even from the back, I recognized him immediately.

"Is something wrong, Your Majesty?" I echoed the question he'd asked me earlier.

He jerked his head my way, spotted me in the shadows by the wall, and gave me the same answer I'd given him. "No. Nothing is wrong."

We both lied so well.

I remained by the wall, wondering if he would notice if I slipped back into the house behind him. I'd come out here to get away from him. His presence now negated my efforts.

He was looking out into the yard again, his back turned to me —a dark silhouette against the gray sky. I peeled myself from the wall, making a tiny move to sneak back inside.

"It's peaceful here," he said with a deep breath in.

His voice halted me in my tracks.

"Yes," I replied. "Very quiet."

"How long have you been here?"

"Just under a year and a half. Give or take."

He turned to face me again. "What's your name?"

The only name I had was the one he gave me. I couldn't tell it to him without blowing my cover.

"Sauria," I blurted out the first name that came to mind.

He nodded slowly. Thoughts appeared to cloud his mind.

"Are you happy, Sauria?"

"Yes."

There simply was no other one-syllable answer I could give him that wouldn't potentially invite more questions.

A smile ghosted his lips, that barely-there smile that one had to look very closely to spot or, like me, one had to know and love this man so much, they would *feel* his moods shifting.

Voron was wistful, melancholic, sad. He was calm. But he wasn't happy. He hadn't been since he'd lost me. I was sure I'd been the last person to hear him laugh. The Sky Crown failed to replace me, no matter what he might've told himself.

He looked down and adjusted the black lace of his cuff. The familiar gesture robbed me of breath. My eyes burned with unshed tears. So, so many tears I'd kept inside me. How was I supposed to go through life without him when he was the one who made me feel alive?

"Thank you for having us," he said in that formal, detached voice he'd used with the courtiers back at King Tiane's court. "Sorry for the rather sudden intrusion." He slipped a large sapphire ring off a finger on his hand that had a few more rings now than he used to wear before. Though, the little silver band of Mulena still glistened on his pinky, irreplaceable. "Your husband will be rewarded. But please accept this as my personal thank you to you as well."

I didn't move from my spot by the wall.

"It's not necessary. We didn't do much. Hospitality is an old tradition to be honored. It's our pleasure to welcome you here."

He inclined his head with a polite half-smile. "The ring won't buy you happiness, dear Sauria, but you don't need any. You are one of the very few people I've met to admit they are happy. Take it, if simply as a token of my appreciation. I insist."

I shuffled forward and held my hand under his for him to drop the ring into my palm. I couldn't let him touch me, no matter how much I longed to feel him again.

Curling my fingers around the heavy ring that still held the warmth of his body, I lingered. I realized I couldn't leave him without hearing from him the answer to this one question.

"Why aren't you happy, Your Majesty? What do you need for happiness?"

"There is nothing I need, dear." He gave me a puzzling smile that waned before taking hold. "Nothing from *this* world."

My heart ached for him. I used to make him happy, and I had loved doing it. I'd lived for it.

Maybe I could do it again?

All I had to do was to step forward, wrap my arms around him, and tell him my name.

My fingers trembled. My entire body shook with nerves, need, and longing. I wished to be in his arms. I craved his touch more than anything in my life right now...

Once again, the door to the house opened.

"Your Majesty?" Alcon exited out onto the patio.

He gave me a curious look. I smiled and curtsied in reply.

Never before had I been so grateful to see Alcon. His interruption brought me back to my senses and possibly saved my life. Aithen's life, too. I couldn't afford to take any risks. How could I be so reckless and forget even for a second what was at stake here?

With my head down, I stepped back into the house where I was safe, where my baby had been growing in peace, undisturbed by the perils of wealth and power. The only thing I could do was to make sure it remained that way.

Chapter Twenty-Three

VORON

"Is everything all right?" Alcon inquired.

"Why wouldn't it be?" Voron shrugged. "I'm having a conversation with our hostess." He flicked his wrist toward the *taurean* woman, but she was already going through the door, back into the house.

Regret pinched his heart as he watched her leave. There was something in her large brown eyes that made him want to keep talking. He felt he could tell her his entire life story and, somehow, she'd be able to make it all better. As if the random stranger from a secluded farm could ease the pain of his past.

The pain was of his own making now. And it was his to bear for as long as he lived.

He rubbed his chest. The spot over his heart had been red and burning for months—a small inconvenience compared to the endless agony racking his soul.

"Time to get going," he told Alcon. "Please settle the account with the farmer and catch up."

He headed for the horses tied at the water trough by the fence.

Magnus sprang from the saddle of the royal horse. Voron jumped in as the bird took off.

Restlessness buzzed through his muscles, urging him to move. Sorrow wrapped around him, swaddling him like an old, thick blanket, familiar but suffocating—inescapable, even after all these weeks on the road.

He looked forward to the exhaustion the long ride would bring. Maybe he'd tire himself enough to get some sleep tonight? He'd pay a king's ransom for just one night of restful, dreamless sleep.

Alcon caught up with him on the road, gliding on his outstretched wings just above him.

"Your cloak, Your Majesty?"

He jerked his head, spurring his horse into a gallop. "I don't need it."

His skin felt flushed. His body burned, welcoming the cold of the autumn wind pummeling him at full speed.

The hooves of his guards' horses hit the cold mud of the road behind him. Three of them had caught up on horseback to keep a close eye on him, allowing Alcon to soar higher. The man was on the Royal Council now, yet he still viewed watching over Voron as his duty.

The rest of his royal escort joined Alcon in the sky. Voron had personally picked every one of the people who came with him on this trip. He'd invited the lords he respected and their wives, whose company he enjoyed. This trip was supposed to be useful and refreshing.

Useful, it had been. The Sky Kingdom had been ruled by winged highborn, historically leaving many needs of those who couldn't fly unmet.

Over the past several weeks, he'd traveled the holdings of three High Lords, identifying the problems that could be fixed to make the lives of those without wings easier. Now, there would be new bridges built, old roads fixed, and some unpassable swamps drained—all at the expense of the crown.

Tiane had left the royal treasury nearly completely drained, but Voron had been replenishing it steadily. Unlike his predecessor, he had no desire for lavish parties and had been extinguishing every flare of rebellion ruthlessly before it had a chance to grow into a lengthy, costly war. The expenses of the crown were lower than they had ever been. And now, he wished to put that treasure to good use.

The work was rewarding. Some of the High Lords remained suspicious. A few even expressed a strong dislike for the crown "meddling" in the infrastructure of their lands. But the majority of the general population loved the improvements. Their gratitude made it all worthwhile.

The trip had proven extremely useful. But it didn't bring him the peace he'd craved. He didn't feel refreshed and didn't look forward to returning to the grand Palace of Elaros.

He'd made some good changes to his court and the Royal Council, but the danger to his crown had not been fully eliminated yet.

High Lord Bussard evaded pledging loyalty to the new king by never returning to Elaros. He was rumored to be hiding in the Below. Unfortunately, Voron's people had failed to find him either above or below the clouds so far. It was safe to assume the High Lord was biding his time, watching Voron's every move from a distance like a vulture and waiting patiently for the best moment to strike.

Voron had to remain vigilant. But he was also tired. Both his soul and his body needed rest that he would never get in the bustling court life of the Sky Palace. He was tempted to swerve off the road and spend a few days elsewhere.

Maybe another day in a quaint farmhouse here in the sleepy countryside on this bank of the Cloud River would do him good? In a place similar to the one they had just left, with simple food and a soft-spoken hostess who made him feel like burying his face in her chest and crying openly until the tears washed every burning ember of pain out of his heart.

But the Silk Festival was taking place in Elaros in a few days. It only happened every ten years and, historically, the king never missed it. The Council had already informed him his presence was expected.

People traveled from the furthest parts of the kingdom, some by air, but many by bumpy dirt roads, tossed and jolted in rickety wagons or stuck in the saddle for days, just to see their king. They expected him to be there. Many were bringing presents for him. He couldn't let his people down by not showing up.

There was no place where he could hide from his pain, anyway. Vensari used to be his safe haven, his one true escape. He used to go there to take a break from Tiane's phony court.

But Vensari had lost its calming effect long ago, turning into a place of torture instead. It had been saturated with the memories of *her*.

Everywhere he looked, he saw Sparrow. She'd be knitting on the window seat in the library, sunbathing on a lily pad in the pond, or strolling in the shade of the treed alleys. She'd smile, her eyes filled with tenderness so warm, no one else could ever match it. So real, he could almost taste her. But she'd disappear the moment he'd try to touch her.

Leaving him. *Always* leaving him.

On a rare night when he found some sleep, he dreamed of her. She kissed him and made love to him in his dreams, only to leave him again in the morning.

He lived for those dreams and he dreaded them. Because he knew he was destined to lose her the moment the dream ended. A most exquisite kind of torture that threatened to plague him until the day he died.

There was no escaping it. But he held on to it, treasuring his torment. Because that was all he had left of her—his memories and the dreams. He'd traded his sanity for both. Gladly.

Chapter Twenty-Four

SPARROW

I couldn't watch him leave. But I *felt* it, anyway.

Even as I escaped back into the house and made myself busy by cleaning the dishes, I felt my heart being wrenched out of my chest all over again.

I thought I'd been doing well in having my broken heart mended. But it hadn't healed at all. It'd been patched up and held together by a thread, temporarily numbing the pain. The wonderful things like my little boy's hugs and giggles would pour a balm over the wound, preventing it from festering. But it didn't heal. It never would.

All Voron had to do to rip my chest open all over again and tear my heart into a million pieces was to simply show up. And then...leave again.

The void in my chest grew bigger the farther he rode away from me. All I wanted was to crawl into a hole somewhere and cry until I had no more tears left or until the pain would end me. But there were dishes to do and a kitchen to clean. Sauria would bring Aithen back soon.

I couldn't fall apart. Not now, not ever. Life left me no time for meltdowns, and in a way, I was grateful for that.

Bavius stomped around. Instead of calming down now that the uninvited visitors had left and the quiet in this house had been restored, he looked even more agitated than before.

I took the tablecloth off the spare table and tossed it into a bucket to wash later.

"You can take the table back to the barn," I said to Bavius.

Maybe having something to do would help him calm down? He'd missed a day of working in the fields during the harvest season. For someone who thrived on a routine, such a big deviation must be unsettling and irritating.

He grunted in agreement. But instead of taking the table and carrying it out, he propped his hands onto it and dropped his head between his bulky shoulders. The events of the day had clearly upset his slow, measured way of life. He hadn't asked for any of it to happen, but he had gone along and saw it through.

Moved by sympathy, I came closer and placed a hand on his shoulder.

"It's okay, Bavius. The table can stay where it is for now. Here." I took Voron's sapphire ring from my pocket and put it on the table in front of him. "Add this to the payment for today's lunch."

He turned his big head my way.

"Where did you get it?"

"The king gave it to me."

"Why?"

I shrugged. "He was in a generous mood."

"Generous?" He scoffed. "Why wouldn't he *generously* cheer the fuck up and let the sun shine next spring? So that we can keep feeding his useless court and ourselves?"

"That's not how it works." I shook my head. "Fake smiles won't affect the weather. And true happiness... Well, it doesn't come easily in his case."

"How do you know?" He pushed away from the table.

I cast my eyes down, afraid he might see in them more than I was willing to disclose.

"Just a guess."

His stare lingered on me. I could almost feel it probing my face and my body as he breathed deeply.

"Sparrow." He touched my arm, then moved his large, calloused hand up to my shoulder.

I looked up at him, confused, but from the way his eyes roamed over my face, I remembered he was still seeing a *taurean* woman in front of him.

He stepped closer, placing his other hand on my other shoulder.

"We've known each other for a long time, now," he said in his deep, rumbling voice that was amplified by the elongated shape of his nose and mouth. "I'm used to having you around. I hope you like it here, too."

He paused, giving me a chance to reply. But I kept quiet, trying to figure out where he was going with this.

His hands moved down my back, then gripped my ass.

"Bavius?" I jerked out of his embrace, but he held me firmly.

His gaze heated. His wide nostrils flared with a powerful puff of air.

"Marry me, Sparrow."

"What? Really?"

He pushed me against the table.

"Can't you see how much sense it makes? We're already living together. There'd be hardly any changes at all."

I could see how a minimal distraction to his routine would appeal to someone like Bavius.

"You have no status at all right now," he continued. "Once we're married, you'll be my wife. You'll have a place you can call your own, for life. I'll protect you for as long as I live, which will be longer than you do. I've just started my fourth century. I have many years ahead of me still. You and your child will never have to worry about anything. I'll take care of both of you."

He pulled me closer, caging me in his burly arms and allowing me to rest my head on his wide chest. He smelled of ale and freshly churned soil—real tangible scents, grounded in the stable lifestyle he led.

I knew it would never work between us. But a part of me—a lonely, exhausted part—wished it would.

Life with Bavius would be steady and reliable, just like the man he was. Maybe if we were married, Bavius would warm up to Aithen, too? My baby would get a father figure in his life.

There was no love between Bavius and me, and there never would be. But I wasn't searching for love. I'd had that—a crazy, passionate, all-consuming love that made my heart soar with achy tenderness and my body melt with intense desire. That love had nearly cost me my life.

Now, what I needed the most was peace of mind and stability. Bavius could give that to me.

But what would he get from me in return? He wasn't Voron. I didn't know how to make Bavius happy. I didn't have what he needed.

He rubbed my lower back, the spot in the middle just above my butt. The spot where the tail would be if I had one. But all I had was an illusion.

I leaned back, awkwardly shifting out of his arms.

"Bavius, it's not me you're attracted to. It's this." I reached behind my neck and opened Voron's necklace. Taking it off, I placed it on the table.

The sensation of the tail and the horns disappeared instantly, along with the feeling of the differently shaped face.

The heat in his eyes cooled somewhat, but he didn't let go of me completely. His stare slipped from my face down to my chest.

"I can get used to it," he said. "Eventually, your face won't bother me."

It was honest but hardly romantic.

I shook my head. "You deserve better than the mere convenience the marriage with me would bring you. Because that's the only thing I can give you as a wife."

"But that's all I look for in a wife, Sparrow—the convenience of the familiar, tried, and true. Our marriage will change nothing. Our kids will be *taureans*, too, because a child of a human and a fae is always a fae."

Kids.

Bavius saw children in our future. Of course, as his wife, I'd have to have sex with him. Unlike him, I wasn't repulsed by his face, but I felt no attraction to him either. My heart remained with Voron, whether either of us wished for it or not.

Could I ever learn to have sex for the physical aspect alone, when I already knew what making love felt like when two souls connected?

My chest ached again. I winced, rubbing the left side through my dress.

"It'll never work between us, Bavius."

"Why not?" He lowered his head stubbornly.

"For one, I'm not a *taurean*. I believe that's the wife you really want."

He stared at my hand rubbing my chest.

"Is that the true reason you're refusing me?" His eyes narrowed. "Or is there someone else?"

He hooked a finger into my neckline and easily tore the sturdy fabric down the middle.

"Bavius!" I caught the ends of the bodice of my dress, trying to pull them together to cover my breasts.

He'd never acted like this before. Yet I didn't believe he would hurt me. I felt more shocked than scared.

He easily fought my hands away, yanking the fabric aside to expose my left breast.

"Just as I thought," he said bitterly.

The skin on my breast was red and felt hot as if inflamed. Raised welts I'd never seen there before appeared, as if someone carved the intertwined letters V and S into my flesh. The lines were broken, forcing the eye to compensate by imagining the connections. But the letters were readable.

I sucked in a breath with a gasp. "What is this?"

Palming my breast in his giant hand, Bavius rubbed his thumb over the letter V.

"Is this for Voron? The king is the father of your child, isn't he? The lad looks just like him, too."

"Oh God..."

My legs suddenly felt like cotton. I propped my butt against the table for support. I didn't even care that Bavius was practically fondling me. I didn't have the presence of mind to demand he stop. My head was spinning. The images of golden letters T and P painted on Queen Pavline's chest flashed before my eyes.

"The mating mark," people had said.

Hers was painted and carefully re-applied before every party and official function.

Mine...

Mine was carved into my skin, deep and permanent, without my knowing or drawing even a drop of blood.

"What does it mean?" I breathed out, afraid to hear the answer.

Bavius flexed his fingers, painfully squeezing my breast before releasing it.

"It means that you're a liar," he snapped, pushing away from me.

The accusation was cruel and unfair. It felt like a slap in my face.

"I haven't lied to you," I protested. "I just never told you who Aithen's father was."

"Well, you should have," he fumed. "You are his fucking bonded mate! You should've told me, Sparrow. I needed to know that before getting involved."

"The mark is new."

"But the baby isn't."

"Would it have changed anything if I told you that Voron is his father? Would you have let me stay here if you knew?"

"Probably not," he admitted.

"I see."

He stomped around the room, his tail lashing around his legs agitatedly.

"Do you realize what you got yourself into, Sparrow? What you got *me* into? Your boy is a prince by birthright. He's the only heir to the throne this kingdom has right now. Sooner or later, someone will come for him. Either the king or his enemies, I don't know who. But I don't want to be a part of it in any way. I want to have nothing to do with Elaros and its power struggles." His voice boomed like thunder in the confined space of the house. "Nothing!" He slammed the tabletop with his hand.

I drew my head into my shoulders, faced with his temper.

"Do you want Aithen and me to leave?" I asked quietly.

We had nowhere to go. But we couldn't stay here any longer against the will of the owner of the house.

Bavius knew that, too.

"Fuck!" he roared, shoving at the table so hard it tipped and crashed to its side. "Fuck!" He stormed past me and out of the door.

I slammed a hand over my mouth to stop a sob. Then I tried to straighten the table, but it was way too heavy and cumbersome for me to handle it alone. Leaving the table where it was, I paced the floor between it and the stove.

Thoughts buzzed like a swarm of angry wasps in my head. In the past few minutes, I'd lost a place to live and gained...a bonded mate.

A mate?

I stared down at my breast. The letters V and S were unmistakable, even if the lines were still unevenly carved, deeper in some places and shallower in others. Inside the deepest parts, gold glistened. Thorns and flowers were also visible around the letters, forming a beautiful rosette.

Human love transcended magic and could form a bond. Only it made no sense.

Why now? When Voron and I weren't even together and

never would be.

How was I supposed to live with this? The mark claimed me as his woman more effectively than a wedding ring would. Yet he thought me gone. The whole world thought I was long gone, never to return.

"This is insane," I groaned, rubbing both hands over my face. "Just crazy."

But I had much more pressing concerns to address. I'd just lost a roof over my head. Where would I take my son now? How would I keep us both alive?

I felt terrible about the way this conversation with Bavius went. He was angry, and I searched for my part in that.

Maybe I shouldn't have kept the secret from him for this long? Maybe if I told him sooner, on a calmer day, without his nerves being already frazzled by the unwanted visitors, he'd be a little more understanding?

Either way, I needed to talk to him. If he really wished us gone, maybe I could at least negotiate a few more days to buy me time to figure out where to go? Maybe I could find another isolated place somewhere, where people wouldn't care who I was and where my baby came from.

I ran to my bedroom to change out of the dress Bavius had torn, then grabbed a cloak from a hook by the door and stepped outside into the biting wind.

Shutting the door behind me, I hurried across the yard and along the path that led out into the fields.

The hooves of Bavius and the many generations of his ancestors before him had formed and maintained this path. He used it daily, and I assumed that was the way he'd taken off. In his irritated state, his hooves would take him down the worn and familiar path, as his mind would be clouded by anger.

It was early evening, and the thickly overcast sky helped the darkness to set in sooner. Only the angry red glow of the sunset remained on the far horizon over the endless open fields on my left. On the right, the dark woods creeped close to the path.

Bavius's deep voice boomed from up ahead in the distance. He was talking to someone. Yelling at them.

"You missed him. The king has left. Now, get the fuck off my land!"

He was furious. Probably still fuming from our conversation, but also with the added anger at whoever he was talking to.

I followed the bend in the path around the trees on my right.

Up ahead, Bavius faced two highborn men with their wings out. I couldn't see their faces in the thickening darkness, but they both wore the uniforms of the royal guards.

Why would they be looking for Voron? How did they not know his whereabouts if they served him?

Both guards had weapons ready. One held a sleek crossbow. The other had a curved knife in each hand.

I slowed my steps, keeping to the shadows from the forest.

"When did the king leave?" The one with the crossbow demanded.

"Not soon enough," Bavius snapped. "Now, get the fuck out of here before I lift you on my horns."

His hands fisted at his sides, he stomped his hooves menacingly, digging grooves in the dirt of the path.

The two men looked at each other.

"We may still catch him on the way to Elaros?" one suggested.

The other one shook his head. "It's hard to get close to him when he's on the road. His personal guards are vicious and incorruptible."

Bavius loudly puffed the air out of his nostrils, lowering his head.

"I said get off my land!" he boomed.

The guards raised their weapons.

"Bavius, no!" I tried to stop him in vain.

With a deafening roar, he charged, aiming his horns at them. A crossbow bolt hit him in the chest. His tunic turned dark around it, soaking up the blood from the wound.

The bolt didn't stop him. The pain only seemed to enrage

him. He slammed into the guard, sending him to the ground. Spinning on his hoof, he tossed the second guard aside with a jerk of his massive head.

"Fuck." The first guard released another bolt.

It embedded into Bavius's shoulder but still failed to slow him down. He stomped over to the man lying on the ground, training his horns to pin him to the path.

The man whimpered. A furious *taurean* presented a terrifying sight, his large nostrils flaring, his eyes glaring from under his heavy brows. His long, curved horns promised a gory, painful death.

The second guard flew up, higher than Bavius could reach him. He dropped from the sky, jamming both of his daggers into Bavius's thick neck. The blades sparked with the red of Nerifir iron. Blood rushed out in two dark crimson streams.

Bavius staggered on his hooves, then crashed onto the field, between the neat rows he'd made and tended to all his life.

I froze, paralyzed by horror and disbelief. Nothing could fell Bavius. He was the picture of strength and health, permanent like the land he worked. Yet there he lay, fallen in the field, drenched in his own blood.

"Well..." His killer wiped his daggers, panting for breath. "That was unplanned."

"Just as well. He saw our faces." The other one scrambled to his feet, his hands still visibly shaking. "With the king dead, he would've talked."

The king?

Dead?

I slammed both hands over my mouth in shock.

"I think I heard someone here." One of the guards turned around.

I forced my feet to move, stepping back into the shadows. But it was too late.

They had spotted me.

Chapter Twenty-Five

SPARROW

Both guards flew into the air, heading toward me.

Panic speared through me like an arrow. I had no chance against them in the open, so I bolted into the dark woods.

I crashed through the underbrush and ducked under the low-hanging tree branches. The sound of the branches breaking and twigs cracking behind me meant the guards had landed and now pursued me on foot, too. They must've seen that flying over the tall trees was useless. It was impossible to see me under the canopies in the dusk.

As a result, they lost the advantage of flight over me. But even on foot, they were faster. The sound of their footfalls grew closer by the second.

I couldn't outrun them. I had to do something else. And fast.

Taking a sharp turn to the left, I took the direction parallel to the path around the field. A clearing was just behind the next several trees. The guards wouldn't see it yet, but I knew it was there. I'd helped Bavius gather branches to put them in that very spot.

Pumping my arms harder, I forced my legs to move faster. My life depended on this. Aithen's life, too.

My lungs burned, fighting for every breath. My feet hurt, sliding in the wet, old leaves that covered the ground. But I pushed on. The moment I passed the last tree before the clearing, I held my breath and jumped.

I landed short. My foot shoved through the branches covering the hole in the ground. But I threw my body forward, crashing chest-first onto the solid ground on the very edge of the concealed pit.

The guards weren't as lucky. Not anticipating the trap, the first one ran right into it. The dry branches cracked, giving in under his weight. The old leaves that Bavius and I had used to cover up the branches over the deep hole in the ground flew up and were caught by the wind, twirling over the clearing.

The first of my pursuers screamed, falling through. His screams turned into a gurgling noise as the sharp vertical spikes embedded into the bottom of the pit pierced through his chest and lungs.

His fall gave a warning to the second guard, though. He snapped his wings open just in time. Frantically beating the air with them, he rose over the trap pit. I crawled backwards, away from the pit, but the guard saw me, aiming the crossbow at my chest.

My insides turned to ice, as if life had already been drained from my body.

A shadow dropped from the sky. Quick and silent. Her leathery wings opened softly just before Sauria shoved her feet into the man's back with force. The unexpected blow stole his balance. He lurched forward, crashing down into the pit.

Sauria landed softly next to me, looking unperturbed by the gurgling screams of the dying fae in the pit. She cradled Aithen in her arms.

"Now, girl." She looked at me sternly. "What did you get yourself into this time?"

It all had happened so fast, I felt dizzy sitting up. My body was shaking. Even with the immediate danger now gone, relief was slow to come.

"Give him to me." I stretched my arms out for my son.

She handed me the baby. I grabbed him greedily and pressed him to my chest, kissing his soft dark curls.

"Ma. Ma. Ma," Aithen chanted, promptly getting hold of a strand of my hair.

I said a quick prayer to all the gods I knew for getting a chance to hold him again, both of us safe and sound.

"Sauria, I can't believe you just killed a man while holding my baby in your arms." My voice came out dry and raspy. My chest still burned with every breath I gasped for.

Sauria shoved her hood off, then propped her hands onto her hips.

"And I don't believe I got here just in time to kill him for you," she retorted. "What the fuck did you do to get them to hunt you? I left you to feed the king and his people, not to make them chase you through the woods."

"I doubt these were the king's people." I shook my head. "Their uniforms are fake. They're just a disguise to allow them to get closer to the king and fool those in charge of his security."

Sauria stepped to the edge of the trap pit and glanced down at the two men skewered by the wooden spikes.

"Who are they then?"

I sighed. "Assassins, I believe. I overheard them talking about the king's death."

She looked around the pit, clicking her tongue appreciatively. "Bavius did a good job on his traps. He used the *ebon* weed on the spikes. Once the vital organs are pierced, there is no escaping death, be it an animal or a fae."

"Or a human," I added in my head.

A shudder ran down my body at the thought of how narrowly I'd escaped the fate of the guards.

"Where is he, by the way?" Sauria turned to me. "Where's Bavius?"

I closed my eyes, taking a deep breath before I could say the words out loud, "Bavius is dead."

"What?" Her face fell. "No way. Nothing can take down that boar. He's meant to live forever. Everyone knows that." Her chin trembled, despite her upbeat tone of voice.

Holding Aithen to me, I climbed to my feet.

"I'm so sorry, Sauria. But Bavius is gone." I tipped my head in the direction of the pit. "They killed him."

She threw another look at the guards, filled with real hatred this time.

Turning Aithen away from the pit, I glanced inside quickly. Both men were completely still now. The sharp, bloodied spikes poked through their chests, stomachs, and thighs, as well as the wings of the one who'd had them open.

The web of transparent lines already spread over their skin wherever it was exposed, crisscrossing their hands and faces. The gruesome scene reminded me of King Tiane's Garden of the Cursed. Except that the guards had a quick death. Soaking the wood in the juice of *ebon* weed had been an act of mercy on Bavius's part. He ended up showing more kindness to the wild animals he trapped than King Tiane did to his people.

"We'll need to cover it up again," I said.

The bodies of the guards would eventually disappear, joining the air of the forest. But their clothes would remain. Anyone could see them from the air when flying, especially if they were looking for them.

Sauria nodded. "Let's do it right now. Then, you'll show me where they got Bavius."

"Do you want some tea?" Sauria asked when I exited my room after having put Aithen to bed.

"Tea would be nice." I nodded.

I left the door open to keep an eye on Aithen. All windows in the house were closed and shuttered, all curtains drawn together. The door was locked. I couldn't shake the feeling that someone might come looking for the men we'd killed, seeking to avenge their death.

Sauria poured a fragrant herbal tea into a cup, then shoved it to me along the table. It was the same table that Bavius had tipped over. Sauria must've straightened it while I was with Aithen. As a fae, she was much stronger than me, despite her frail appearance.

I'd left the table on its side for Bavius to pick it up later. Only now, he was dead. Neither of us knew when he'd stormed out of here that it'd be his last time in his house.

I dropped my head between my shoulders.

"It's all my fault."

Sauria took a sip of her tea. "What are you talking about?"

I'd taken her to the place where Bavius was killed. I'd told her how it happened. She'd touched the bolt sticking out from his shoulder. It glistened with red.

"Nerifir iron," she'd whispered. "It's fatal. Sorry, Bavius. You were a good neighbor, even if I often said otherwise."

I wanted to move him into the house, but she wouldn't let me.

"Let him be," she'd said, brushing a tear off her wrinkly cheek. "His life began in these fields and ran its course here. Let the fields keep him, now."

Like all sky fae, *taurean* bodies were absorbed by air after death. Bavius's flesh had already turned invisible in many places. Soon, he would fully become a part of the winds over the land that always held his heart and his soul.

I tried to find consolation in the thought that he died where he loved to be, but it didn't ease the guilt gnawing at me.

"Had I not forced Bavius to let me live here, none of it would've happened. He'd still be alive."

Sauria smoothed her silver hair pulled back into a neat bun. "First of all, you didn't force him to take you in. I did. Second, King Voron didn't come here because of you. He came for food, plain and simple. And third, those assholes showed up here, searching for the king not for you. You sure aren't responsible for Bavius's temper, either. The man always was as stubborn as a bull and severely lacked social skills. Maybe if he handled those men with a little more caution, he'd still be alive. We'll never know now. One thing is clear—his death was tragic, but it was not your fault."

Sauria didn't know it all, however.

"Bavius wanted to marry me," I said.

She choked on her tea, coughing to catch her breath.

"He *what?*"

"He...suggested we get married. He said it'd be easier that way."

She studied me over the rim of her teacup.

"What did you say? Did you consider it?"

"Sauria, you know I couldn't marry him. It'd never work on many levels. Besides, I'm kind of not exactly available, right? Or whatever this thing means." They said a picture was worth a thousand words. So, I just loosened the laces at my neckline and shoved the material of my dress aside, exposing the top of my left breast. "Here. This appeared today."

She slammed her cup onto the table so hard, her tea splashed out.

"I swear on my fucking cauldron, which is the most precious thing I own, that this is a mating mark!" She reached to rub along the lines. "It's not painted on, either."

"No." I sighed. "It's not."

She stopped rubbing my skin and squinted at me.

"Should I ask who the letter V stands for? Or should I just take the most obvious guess?"

Evading her piercing stare, I admitted, "It is the king. He's Aithen's father, too."

She didn't look surprised. Not even a little bit.

"Did you know?" I asked.

She shrugged. "There have been rumors."

"What rumors?"

"That High General Voron hid you from Queen Pavline when she'd ordered your execution. That you helped him acquire the crown. That as a reward, he got rid of you in order to keep that crown." She pursed her lips.

"It's uncanny how true all those rumors are," I muttered, sinking my gaze into my tea.

"And of course," she continued, "anyone who'd seen Aithen would know who his father is."

"Is the resemblance that obvious?"

She nodded firmly. "Your son is a spitting image of King Voron. Just much cuter and with wings."

I glanced at the open door to the room where my baby was sleeping, peacefully unaware of any danger. He trusted me to keep him safe.

"What do I do now?" I covered up my chest and tightened the laces again. But my skin burned hot, feeling like the mark could glow through my dress. "Is there a way to get rid of it?"

"Ha!" Sauria blinked at me incredulously. "So many people pray all their lives for the bond to find them. And you want to get rid of it?"

"They pray for a soulmate, someone to spend their life with. But I'm now tied to a man who wants nothing to do with me."

Her lips curled into a wicked smile.

"Well, if there are more people who want King Voron dead, you may be a free woman soon."

Her words slammed like a punch to my gut, knocking the air out of me.

"I don't want him dead," I gasped.

"Why not?" She arched an eyebrow, either questioning or teasing, I couldn't tell.

"I just don't." I couldn't even elaborate on such a possibility. The idea of Voron dying terrified me even more than the thought of my own death. "But you have a point. Those two couldn't be the only people who wanted him gone. If there is anything I've learned about the royal court, it's that highborn rarely execute their darkest plans on their own. They hire people to do it for them. The men we killed weren't the masterminds of the assassination. Someone else was. Someone who is still out there and most likely will try again."

Sauria chuckled. "All they'd have to do for it to work next time is to hire someone who'd show up on time. Those two must have thought the king would party here all night, like his predecessor would."

The blood chilled in my veins at the thought of what would've happened if they arrived earlier or if Voron stayed later. What if they shot him while he was talking to me on the porch? He'd been a perfect target then, standing outside, with not a single guard to protect him.

"The king needs to know that someone is after him," I determined.

"Are you going to be the one to tell him? Because the Silk Festival is coming up. Which will give you a great opportunity to sneak into the palace."

"Me?"

"Who else? You know the Sky Palace better than anyone else around here, including myself. Or do you want to hire someone to *execute your darkest plans*?" she tersely paraphrased my words from earlier.

I ignored her mocking.

"What is this festival for? There wasn't one during my time in Elaros."

"No. It only takes place once in a decade. Everyone who is

involved in silk production is invited. People bring gifts for the king."

"What kind of gifts?"

"Usually things like lengths of silk, pretty garments, and *firrian* beetles. He rewards them with diamonds and gems. Some get royal favors as a payment. There will also be feasts with dancing and drinking all over the city, if you're into that kind of thing."

"But I don't have any silk or *firrian* beetles. How will I get into the palace? And even if I make it in somehow, there is a chance someone will recognize me."

"Not if I glamor you again."

A glamor could work. I wouldn't even need to speak with Voron himself. I could just tell what I knew to Alcon. He'd recognize me as the *taurean* woman and Bavius's wife. It would add credibility to my story. I can tell him everything as it was, without hardly changing anything.

"As for the gift," Sauria continued. "Bring the king something from Sova's collection. That serpent from Lorsan would do great as a novelty gift worth royal attention. It'd be much better off in the royal menagerie than in my hut, anyway. I'm tired of catching flies and crickets to feed it. Its body has been shrunk but, I swear, its appetite very much stayed the same."

It could work. It all fell into place so well. My stomach tightened. I might be going to Elaros soon.

"How would I get there?" I asked. "I don't fly."

"Use Sova's wagon. It's been sitting without a purpose for over a year now. It'd do it good to be put to use again."

"It'll take hours to ride to Elaros. Hours to get back here. I won't make it in one day. I can't possibly leave Aithen for that long."

"Why not?" She waved me off. "You don't nurse him anymore. He's great with solids. Just pack some food for him. I'll take him to my hut. He likes it there. I'll put an invisibility spell on it, like Sova did with her wagon. No one will find us even if they try."

I'd never been away from Aithen overnight. Before today, we rarely parted at all.

"I've never left him for that long. I don't think I can." I shook my head, nervously turning the cup on the table in circles.

Sauria casually leaned her elbow on the table.

"You know what? It's just as well. Leave the king to his fate, just like he left you to yours when he ordered you tossed into the River of Mists. If he's killed, he'll only get what he deserves. Payback, *Your Majesty.*" She spat the last two words out like a curse with a wicked glint in her dark eyes.

What would this world be without Voron?

He hadn't been a part of my life for sixteen months now, and I'd survived. But I always knew he was out there, living the life of a king. Whether I wished for it or not, the thoughts of him were my constant companion to the point that he'd become a part of me now.

Without him, I feared, the emptiness in my chest would grow big enough to consume me. I couldn't let Voron die, no matter what he'd done to me.

Drawing a lungful of air, I exhaled, "I'll do it. I'll go to Elaros. I have to warn him."

A smug smile rearranged the wrinkles on the hag's face.

"Well, there you go. Glad I made it easier for you to figure it all out, girl. But just so you know, that's the only decision you can make, anyway. You don't have a choice in this matter. You're mated now," she replied to my questioning stare. "You and the king share a magical bond. From now on, you will live as long as he does, be it centuries or just a few days. If one of you dies, the other will quickly follow. Bonded mates can't survive each other's death for long. And if both of you die, where would that leave Aithen?"

I looked back at the open door to the room where my son was

sleeping. He was the most important person in my life now, and he needed me.

"I don't have a choice," I echoed Sauria's words. "I've no one to blame but myself for that. It's human love that creates the bond. I doomed myself the very moment I fell in love with a man who doesn't care about me."

Sauria looked at me somberly.

"A bond is not a river, Sparrow. It doesn't flow in one direction. It's more like a bridge between two souls. You started building it on your side by falling in love with the man. But he has to love you back for the bridge to be complete."

"Voron doesn't love me." I exhaled a painful laugh. "He gave me up, remember?"

"That doesn't mean he hasn't regretted it every day since."

"What do you need for happiness?" I'd asked him the last time we spoke, out here on the porch.

"Nothing from this world." He'd said.

I was the one who made him happy, and he knew it. But he didn't know I was still here, in *this world.*

"That doesn't change anything," I muttered defiantly. "He broke my trust. He broke my heart. He—"

Sauria rose from her seat with a pat on my shoulder.

"All I'm saying, girl, is don't be surprised by what you may find in Elaros. Make sure you're ready."

Chapter Twenty-Six

SPARROW

The old wagon bounced and creaked, rolling over the cobblestones of the main road in the City of Elaros. I hadn't made it far past the gate, however, before the royal guards requested I leave the wagon and head to the palace on foot—or on hoof as was my case, since I was wearing the glamor of the *taurean* woman once again.

This time, however, Sauria layered the spells, making me look like a hag of *taurean* origin. The illusion was uncanny. I was wearing one of her gray cloaks over my simple dress of a farmer's wife. Transparent lines of aging crawled up my hands between the wrinkles. The ones on my hooves were so wide, I could see the paving stones through them as I walked.

Traveling as a hag had immense advantages. The guards spoke to me with respect. People stepped out of my way and nodded politely. No one questioned my being here. I just hoped no one would ask me for a spell or a potion.

I left the wagon behind a tavern and paid two bags of potatoes to the owner of the establishment to look after the horses.

Neither I nor Sauria had any actual money for this journey.

But everything went as a payment in Sky Kingdom. Farm produce seemed to be especially in demand this year, as judging by the king's current moods, there wouldn't be much sun next spring, either, which meant another poor harvest for most crops.

Just like Bavius, some people on the streets of Elaros complained about that, blaming the king. Others, however, were quick to point out all the current projects happening both in the city and out in the country. Roads were paved. New bridges had been built. And many other improvements had been done to benefit all people of the kingdom at the crown's expense.

Two *arien* men argued passionately in front of a jewelry store on the main street. One of them told the other about a fence erected around the pasture lands in his hometown. The new fence apparently protected the livestock from wolf attacks in that area, and the king fully paid for it.

"Say what you want about King Voron," the man spoke loudly enough for everyone on the street to hear. "But we saw no sun with the old king, either. The crops have been shit for decades. The folks back home live on white cranberries and wild mushrooms—the only things that still grow well in this fucking weather. But King Tiane built no fences for anyone. All he did was fight and party."

I shouldn't care whatsoever, but it warmed my heart to hear this man defending Voron so fervently. Many appeared to agree with him, too, nodding their heads and murmuring approvingly.

"King Voron has no wings," a *snakana* woman said. "He knows what we need down here because he walks on the same streets we use and travels the same roads we do."

"Sure, it'd be nice to have some variety of the crop with better weather," a *taurean* man added. "But my tomatoes did well enough for the past few years. It sure was handy to use the new bridge built by the king to get them to the market faster this fall."

After leaving behind the small crowd gathered by the jewelry store, I stopped by a food cart and traded a jar of snowberry jam for a couple of fried pies stuffed with rabbit meat and onions for lunch, then headed to the palace.

Not much had changed in Elaros in the past year and a half. Fae generally disliked big changes. But the city had freshened up for the festival. Multi-colored lengths of semi-transparent silk hung over the streets and decorated the buildings. They billowed in the wind like sails and floated like wisps of rainbows, creating a festive mood despite the gloomy weather.

My disguise as a hag was wearing off. Sauria planned for it to last only until I made it to the palace.

Shortly after I entered through the doors of the palace, I looked like an ordinary *taurean* woman again, with hooves, horns, and a tail, but no wrinkles or transparent flesh. I needed Alcon to recognize me as Bavius's wife, whom he'd seen at the farm. He'd be more inclined to hear me out that way, I believed, than if I showed up disguised as a complete stranger.

"Can I see Councilor Alcon?" I asked one of the palace guards who directed the crowd up the stairs toward the Throne Room where the king was holding audience today.

"Is he expecting you?"

"No, but I have something very important to tell him. He'll—"

"Are you here to see the king or the councilor?" the guard snapped, looking down at me.

I immediately missed my hag glamor and the automatic respect it commanded. I also wouldn't mind if it came with the ability to turn this guy into a six-legged frog.

"I would prefer the councilor but—"

"Step out of the line, then. These people are here to see the king."

"But how can I see Councilor Alcon? Where can I find him?" I insisted, not moving out of my spot.

The guard gave me an exasperated look.

"The councilor is occupied in the Throne Room with the

king. You'll have to request an audience to see him, which isn't going to happen today, obviously."

"Obviously," I repeated, watching as more people arrived in throngs.

"All right, woman." The guard waved at me impatiently. "If you don't want to see the king—"

"I do." I moved up the stairs along with the other palace visitors. "I do want to see the king."

If that was the only option I had, I'd use it. I might be able to get Alcon's attention in the Throne Room. But if not, I'd have to face Voron again. He should recognize me as Bavius's wife, too. As additional proof, I had his sapphire ring in the satchel over my shoulder.

I'd just tell him about what happened on the farm after he'd left, then be on my way back to my baby son. I started missing Aithen right after I'd kissed him goodbye and even before my wagon left the yard of Bavius's farm.

A few floors up, another guard stopped me.

"What are you bringing for King Voron? Do you have a gift for him?"

Most of those around me held armfuls of silk, both pure white and hand-painted with beautiful designs. Some carried mesh cages with *firrian* beetles. That was the tradition. The gifts would be exchanged for jewels and favors, which didn't really make them gifts, but it wasn't a real trade, either, as the king usually gave more than the items were worth.

"Yes. I do have a gift." I reached into my satchel and produced the jar with the blue fancy worm that, according to Sauria, was not a worm but a shrunken serpent.

The guard made a face, shrinking away from me. "What the fuck is this?"

"A giant serpent from the Lorsan Wetlands in the Below," I announced proudly and glanced down at the "worm" that was swimming peacefully in a vial of water inside the jar. "He's been shrunk. A little."

"Why would the king want *that?*" The guard curled his lip as the people around me snickered.

"To feed it to his pet crow!" a wise ass cracked a joke, to the delight of the crowd that hooted and laughed. Those ahead of us craned their necks, trying to see what the fun was all about.

I stomped my hoof, not letting the jokes and giggles get to me.

"You have no clue, people, because *you* don't own a menagerie. If you did, you would want my worm, too. This is the only giant serpent of this size in the entire Sky Kingdom and, possibly, in the whole of Nerifir."

The guard looked at the jar with a newfound appreciation.

"Well, go on then." He waved for me to move along.

The crowd calmed, too, ogling my tiny, giant serpent with interest.

I carried the jar up staircase after staircase and finally up the moving steps. I remembered riding these steps for the first time with Voron, long before either of us knew what we would become for each other.

Despite my best efforts, my heart beat faster. Pressing the jar with the serpent to my chest, I finally reached the Throne Room. Apprehension prickled down my arms. My throat felt dry. I slapped my tail against my leg under my cloak to make sure the glamor was still on, then inhaled deeply.

Moving behind the long line of people, I entered the room and headed toward the throne. My chest ached, and I wasn't sure whether it was the mating mark or my heart or both. I kept my eyes down, drawing air in and out in small, carefully measured breaths. I could do this. I'd spoken to Voron just fine before, wearing the exact same disguise as I was now. Of course, I'd also nearly fallen to his feet then, almost revealing to him who I was.

I had to muster more control this time.

Voron sat on his throne, wearing a long, light-gray coat and a snow-white cape painted with faint rainbow swirls along the edge. The cape cascaded down the stairs of the throne dais, draping over it like feather-light spring clouds.

The golden spikes of his crown glistened and sparkled brighter than the crystals in the walls around us. But his expression under the crown remained as dark as ever.

The ceiling of the room was wide open, with the vines framing the gray sky above. The chilly wind reached inside, but there were so many people packed into the enormous Throne Room, I didn't feel the cold.

I kept staring at the king, unable to tear my eyes off him as the line in front of me grew shorter.

"What do you have there?" a courtier in charge of the royal presents asked the *taurean* man right in front of me, yanking my mind away from Voron.

The *taurean* had reached the throne dais. He stretched out his arms with a length of silk draped over them. The fabric was so fine it looked like a spider web with sparkling dewdrops clinging to it.

"A veil, my lord. My daughter embroidered it with the crystalized raindrops she had collected in the forest around our farm."

"Nice." The courtier carefully lifted the end of the veil and passed it to a guard by the throne, who then held it up for Voron to touch and admire.

"It's beautiful." Voron inclined his head. "Your daughter's hands weave magic."

The *taurean's* wide mouth spread in a pleased smile. "Thank you, Your Majesty. May the gods favor you with light and happiness."

"What do you want for your gift? Gems or a favor?"

"Gems."

The gorgeous silk veil was put away promptly. The treasurer poured the gems into the *taurean's* large hand, and the man was on his way.

My turn was next.

"Here." I handed the courtier the jar with the serpent. Remembering the earlier skepticism of the people in line, I explained not waiting for his questions, "It's a giant serpent from the Wetlands of—"

The courtier snorted a laugh, interrupting me. "It doesn't look that *giant*, good woman."

My nerves must have gotten the best of me. Because instead of defending my tiny serpent once again, I laughed with a shrug.

"He doesn't, does he? He must be a grower, not a shower."

The courtier burst out laughing. The guard on the stairs of the dais snickered into his sleeve, torn between laughing out loud and showing some respect to the king who was sitting so close.

I darted a glance up at Voron, realizing he'd heard me, too.

He smiled, the crease between his eyebrows smoothing out. My chest filled with sunshine. I knew I could make him happy, but when was the last time I truly felt happy myself? The answer was simple—when I was with him.

I drew in a shuddering breath, gathering my resolve.

"Give her some gems, Lord Pica," Voron said to the treasurer. "Both for the gift and for the joke."

I didn't need the gems. I had to talk to him.

"Um... A favor, please." I lifted my hand to get his attention. But his gaze followed the jar that the courtier was putting away with other gifts.

The king's eyes narrowed as he stared at the worm, looking as if he'd seen it before.

"Where did you get that serpent, good woman?" He turned to me.

The question caught me off guard.

"Oh, um...it belonged to a hag I knew."

The king rose from his throne. Pinning me in place with his stare, he descended the steps of the dais.

Alarm jolted me. I felt naked under his gaze, stripped of my disguise and my defenses. Desperately searching for a diversion, I rummaged through my satchel and yanked his sapphire ring out.

"We've met before, Your Majesty," I said, showing the ring on my outstretched hand.

"I believe we have," he echoed.

Ignoring the ring, he moved closer. His cape unwound from

around the dais, billowing at his back like a giant wing in the breeze.

Flustered, I took a step back, but there was nowhere to retreat with the long line of attendees pushing from behind.

Alcon appeared at the king's side. He darted a cautious look around the crowd surrounding us, then leaned to the king's ear.

"Your Majesty, you should be up on the throne," he said softly but firmly.

Voron ignored him, staring at me intently. His proximity trapped me. I drew in his scent, letting it permeate all my senses, and took in the sight of him, committing to memory every detail to keep for the rest of my life without him.

I struggled to remember what I came here for. My chest ached, and I rubbed over the mark, even though rubbing never made the pain any less.

Voron's gaze dipped to my hand, then leaped back to my face.

"Instead of the gems," I croaked, "I wish to request a favor... A word with you, my king. A minute of your time."

"Just a minute?" He slid his hands up my arms.

I shrank back from his touch, but it proved inescapable. There was nowhere to run in the crowd. There was no running from him.

"Yes," I breathed out. "A minute..."

He cupped my face, my human face beyond the glamor. His fingers trembled at the contact with my skin. Recognition sliced through his expression, like a slash of a blade.

"Will you take a lifetime instead?"

He slid a hand down my neck and hooked a finger under my necklace—*his* necklace that he'd given me so long ago. He yanked at it, tearing it from my neck.

The glamor was gone, and Voron saw me the way I was— exposed, undisguised, unguarded.

Shock was momentarily replaced by relief on his face. Tenderness softened his stare—that special kind of tenderness he only had when he looked at me, no one else.

Pain crossed his gaze next, an emotion so strong, it crumbled his handsome features with agony.

"Sparrow," he groaned.

Suddenly, he sank to his knees. The mighty king had fallen at my feet. Gripping my cloak, he crushed me to him, as if he wished to absorb me with every cell of his being and every fiber of his soul.

"My Sparrow," he murmured, pressing his face to my chest.

I closed my eyes, drawing in a shaky breath, and savored every sensation of him. The silky glide of his hair between my fingers as I cradled his head in my hands. The firm grip of his arms that caged me in the way that told me he'd never let me go. His warm breathing seeped through my clothes as he whispered something —a prayer, I realized.

Voron prayed to the merciful God of Death, thanking him for returning me to him.

The crowded Throne Room seemed to disappear. The entire world ceased to exist. I saw, felt, and heard no one but him.

My soul melted with his, the way it was meant to be.

A sapphire-blue glow surrounded Voron, overpowering the daylight or the shimmer of the crystals in the room. The light filtered through his white cape on his back, arching out like a silver-blue rainbow. The arch split in two, unfurling like sails from his shoulder blades.

The blue light solidified, turning black and taking the shape of two great wings. They spread over the stairs of the throne dais, their glossy feathers so black they shimmered with indigo.

I halted my breath in awe as Voron spread them out. Strong and beautiful, the wings loomed over the room.

With me by his side, Voron was finally whole. Complete. The king had been fulfilled. And so was the prophecy.

Chapter Twenty-Seven

SPARROW

Voron had earned the crown and won his rightful place in the kingdom without any wings. He didn't need them to succeed. But here they were—his reward.

The room stilled in awe at the miracle happening right in front of their eyes. Thousands of people fell silent as one.

Voron lifted his head, looking up at me with a smile so bright, it lit up the entire room, the entire kingdom, too, as the clouds above parted.

In the complete stillness, a thud sounded. Voron's body jerked against mine. His smile dimmed.

Worry lanced through my heart.

"Voron?" I cupped his face. A menacing golden glow crackled around my fingers touching his skin. "What's happening?"

A black crossbow bolt pierced his left wing to the throne dais behind him. The foreign golden-yellow magic of the World of Under sizzled and popped around it, spreading over the ink-black feathers.

"The king was shot!" someone shouted.

"No. Voron, please," I begged, tears burning my eyes.

He struggled to his feet, staggering back a step. His head lolled to the side, and his eyes closed.

"No!" I held on to him as if I could hold his soul as easily as I could hold on to his body.

The vines of the throne shifted and moved, unraveling. They curled around him like snakes, growing and multiplying.

"Voron, stay! Please stay with me."

I grabbed for his hands and his clothes, trying to pull him back to me. But the vines were relentless. They spiraled all around him, then yanked him back, molding him into the throne. Wrapping tightly around him, they hid everything. Not a shred of his clothes could be seen, not a feather of his new, magnificent wings, not a glimmer of his skin.

The king was gone. Only a wide pillar of interwoven vines remained where his throne used to stand.

"Voron!" I flung myself at it, clawing at the vines.

The room erupted in the screams of terror and anguish.

"Lady Sparrow." Alcon placed his hands on my shoulders, gently moving me away from the throne pillar. "We need to get you out of here."

"No!" I batted his hands away, but he grabbed my shoulders again.

"Come." He wrapped his arm around my middle. His wings beat the air, lifting us both up.

"Let me go!" I fought him, not afraid to fall. There were worse things in life, I'd learned, far greater plummets than this could ever be. "I have to be with him."

The guards ushered people out of the room. Those who had no wings rushed the doors. The highborn took to the air, leaving through the open ceiling.

"The palace is unprotected." Alcon held me tighter, taking me higher. "You're in danger here."

He whisked me around the palace and toward another tall tower. Flying through the open window of the wide patio, he brought me into the royal bedroom.

It took me a moment to recognize it. The round skylight was still in the middle of the ceiling, but everything else had changed.

Most of the glistening gold trimmings were gone. The white, round cloud bed was replaced with a square one with four posts of spiraling vines that merged with the ceiling up above.

Covered with a royal-blue spread richly embroidered with gold and silver, the bed was edged with a fringe of tiny crystals that cascaded down to the floor like a wall of rain.

Alcon deposited me in front of the bed.

"Stay here, my lady. It's the safest room in the palace. It's thoroughly warded, both doors and windows. Only the king's trusted men can enter here."

Magnus greeted me with a caw from a branch mounted into a dark marble stand by the entrance to one of the sitting rooms. A silver chain dangled from the ring around the bird's ankle. He was chained to his perch.

Voron clearly didn't want his beloved pet to follow him to the Throne Room today. Because he didn't feel it was safe. He'd been ready for malice to arrive from both inside and outside of the palace. Yet the danger still found him.

I couldn't rest. I couldn't even stand still. My heart thundered wildly. The mark on my skin throbbed, urging me to go back to the Throne Room. To Voron.

I went for the door, but Alcon blocked my way.

"Alcon, please, I need to go," I begged. "You don't understand. I need to be with him."

His brow furrowed. He didn't budge.

"I do understand, my lady. More than you know. I was here while you were gone. Do you know how many times I had to lock the king in this very room to stop him from riding to the Cloud River?"

"Voron wanted to go there? Why?"

"To hurl himself into the River of Mists because he deliriously believed he'd have a chance to find you. He preferred that one in a million chance rather than live in the world without you."

I stepped back, searching for support. My hand found the bedpost, and I leaned my shoulder against it, wrapping my hand around the cluster of warm, living vines.

Their life pulsed under my fingers. My skin tingled with power I never knew before. But there was something familiar in the gentle touch reaching for me. It felt comforting, and I reached behind me, splaying my second hand on the vines too.

"I didn't let Voron bring any harm to himself," Alcon continued. "And I won't let you hurt yourself either, my lady. Let Farion do his job in the Throne Room. He's the High General now. His people will find whoever shot the crossbow at the king. Meanwhile, it's best for you to stay here, because I fear the attack on the king was just the first step."

"The first step of what?" My voice trembled with worry.

"Of taking over Elaros. If they are to attack us, without the king, we can't even secure the palace. All patios are open, as are many roofs and windows. We'll have to send the court down to the lower floors to barricade in with the servants and hope that the palace guards can hold off the attack until more of the royal armies arrive." He inhaled deeply, looking somber. "With the king now gone—"

I shook my head, stopping him. "He isn't gone."

Almost everyone in the palace had seen what happened to the king. But I didn't think anyone knew what I sensed—Voron was alive. I felt his presence through the *liliala* vines of the palace. His magic ran through them like blood through veins. I closed my eyes, reaching for it with my mind.

Deeper and deeper the magic ran, and I was able to follow it from the tallest turrets down to their very roots. In my mind, I saw the entire system of the vines, running through every room and every floor of the palace.

The Throne Room was in the heart of it. And in the middle, Voron's heart beat steadily.

"The king is alive, Alcon. He's just...trapped."

The councilor nodded, not looking much relieved.

"The magic of the World of Under is holding him," he muttered under his breath.

The sinister magic had turned King Tiane into a living, breathing corpse. Was that Voron's fate, too?

Horror chilled me.

"I won't let it happen," I whispered, barely able to move my lips from dread. "I'll find a way to bring him back."

Queen Pavline spent weeks trying to reunite King Tiane's body with his spirit. She'd had help from the most powerful hags and every priest and priestess in the kingdom. And still, she failed.

But Pavline didn't feel for Tiane what I felt for Voron. For me, Voron was irreplaceable, and giving up was not an option.

Deep concern was etched on the councilor's face.

"I must leave you, my lady. You will be safe here."

Safe. Until the palace comes under attack, then all of us would be in peril.

I grabbed his hand. "Take me to the Throne Room, Alcon."

His brow furrowed deeper with worry. "My lady, it's not—"

"Please. Just for a few minutes. I need to try something. I may be able to make it safer for all of us."

The Throne Room looked eerily deserted. It was so strange to see it empty when just a little while ago, it was so crowded with people.

The wind tossed a few old leaves around the marble floor littered with things people had dropped in a hurry to get out. Torn off buttons, dropped handkerchiefs, and even a few gems had been left behind by those rushing to leave the room where their king was shot in front of their eyes.

"We shouldn't be here, Lady Sparrow," Alcon warned, scanning the sky through the open ceiling.

"Just a minute, Alcon. Please."

My necklace glistened in a pile of litter by the throne platform where Voron had dropped it. I picked it up and adjusted the clasp that had been bent. Once I put it back around my neck, the chaotic twister of emotions inside my chest slowed down.

Things had been happening at a breakneck speed, leaving me no time to process anything. I needed to focus on one thing at a time to make sense of it all.

"One thing at a time," I whispered, looking up at the dais.

A single wide pillar of intertwined *liliala* vines rose from the center. It had absorbed both the throne and the king. Ascending the stairs of the dais, I splayed my hands on the vines' warm, uneven surface. I pressed my forehead to them and listened.

The pillar pulsed with magic from both Voron and the bolt embedded in his wing. I focused on Elaros magic, ignoring the foreign power from the World of Under.

This time, I paid attention only to the Throne Room, to this wide pillar that rose to the open ceiling, and to the vines that ran all along the walls.

"Move," I commanded, willing the magic to go in one direction—up.

And the vines shifted.

With my eyes closed, I didn't see them move, but I heard the soft cracking as their branches extended. They grew thicker, taller, unraveling the woven pattern around the opening in the ceiling, then reaching across toward each other, and bridging the open space above. Their ends intertwined and knitted together, sealing the opening. Closing off the sky.

From one end of the room to the other, the vines crisscrossed and interwove with each other until not a speck of the gray skies could be seen through them.

I didn't stop there. Emboldened by my newly found power, I reached further, beyond the Throne Room, and all the way down to the roots of the vines that were buried deep in the ground under the palace. From there, I went up. Floor by floor, room by room, I made the vines straighten and grow, weaving their pattern over the windows, doors, and balconies. It was a slow process for me. Maybe Voron would've done it faster. But Elaros didn't have Voron right now. All it had was me.

Sealing the palace slowly had its advantage. It gave people who wanted to leave a chance to get out, and those who wished to hide inside, a chance to get in.

I moved the vines, grew, twisted, and bent them, until the entire palace, with all its floors and towers was enclosed into a safe, dark cocoon of magical vines.

The only vines I couldn't move were those around the royal throne. They kept Voron away from me.

My fingers trembled on the pillar. My muscles ached. I bent my knees, sliding down to the floor, then sat with my back leaning against the throne pillar.

Alcon gaped at me from the bottom step of the dais.

"How did you do that?" he gasped, his mouth hanging open.

My throat was too dry to answer. I didn't have enough strength left to even think about forming words. Instead I untied my cloak, then lowered my dress off my shoulder, exposing the top of my breast.

The mark had grown more prominent by now. The letters V and S glowed brightly surrounded by an intricate design of twisted thorns and golden flowers. Over both letters, a golden crown shone.

Alcon's eyes flared with shock.

"A mating mark. A human is a vessel for fae magic. You bonded with the king." He bowed his head, sinking down to one knee. "My queen."

I was no royalty. I wore no crown and wasn't married to the king. But through our bond, I could use Voron's magic, including the magic of the crown that controlled the Palace of Elaros.

Now, as soon as Farion captured the assassin, everyone inside the palace would be safe.

Chapter Twenty-Eight

SPARROW

Alcon escorted me back to the royal chambers.

"I actually came to Elaros, hoping to speak with you," I said when we were safely back inside.

"Me? Not Voron?" He looked surprised.

"No." I smiled awkwardly. "I didn't come here for some closure with him or something. I need to tell you what happened at the farm after you left."

"What happened?"

"Two men came looking for the king. They killed Bavius, the farmer." I swallowed against a tightness in my throat. Bavius deserved to live for centuries, quietly working in his fields and hurting no one. Instead, he was murdered so brutally. "They wore royal guard uniforms and spoke about the king being dead."

I told him the details and answered whatever questions he had. Before he left to speak to Farion, he said, "The Council is in session, Lady Sparrow. I strongly advise you to join them."

"Me?"

My first reaction was to refuse. What insight could I possibly give to the fae who'd been around for hundreds of years and surely knew better than me how to govern a kingdom in crisis?

"You are the king's bonded," Alcon insisted. "The only one who can use Elaros' magic."

I didn't hold any official position at the court, but through my bond with Voron, I had power, nevertheless.

"The Council needs to know," he said.

"All right. I'll go."

He gave me a critical once-over, taking in my dusty cloak and messy hair. I'd had no chance to wash or change after the long hours of traveling to Elaros City.

"I'll arrange for new clothes for you, befitting your station," he said before leaving the room.

While waiting for the clothes, I had a quick bath in the royal bathing pool. By the time I was done, a knock came on the door, then Brebie marched in.

"Sparrow... Sweetie." She paused at the door, pressing the pile of shimmering fabrics in her arms to her chest. "Alcon told me, but I still can't believe my eyes."

I smiled widely at the sight of her familiar face.

"Brebie. You have no idea how nice it is to see you again." I took a step her way.

With a strangled sob, she dropped the fancy dress and rushed to hug me.

"We thought you were dead," she mumbled into my shoulder. "Voron hasn't been the same ever since."

I very well could've been dead if it wasn't for Sova. But I didn't tell Brebie that. She seemed too emotional already, tears glistening on her long, blonde eyelashes.

She sniffled, releasing me from her arms.

"Well, let's get you dressed, honey. If you want the Council to listen to you, you'll need to look the part."

She quickly put me into the gown of purple velvet so dark, it almost looked black. The top skirt was of sheer silver that made the dress shimmer like a starry sky on a cloudless night.

Brebie dried and styled my hair into a sweeping up-do and pinned a single precious barrette shaped like a crescent moon on the back of my head.

Once it was done, I stared at the elegant lady looking back at me from the mirror. The goal of my outfit was no longer to help me entice or seduce anyone but to convey status and power. I couldn't say I didn't like the change.

Alcon arrived to escort me to the council meeting room and gave me an approving look.

"You are magnificent, Your Majesty."

"Don't call me that." I shook my head.

He met my words with a confident smirk. "But that's what you are. I wish I'd known about your mark sooner. It'd explain a lot of the king's behavior of late. I just never expected to see Voron in love."

Despite everything, I still couldn't believe that was the case. Voron never said he loved me, not once, not even when he was making love to me, his mind lost to lust and pleasure. How could sending me away have changed that?

We entered the council meeting room. Tall-backed armchairs lined the walls, but as comfy as they looked, no one was sitting in them. The councilors congregated in the middle of the room, passionately discussing the situation we all faced.

The discussion immediately ceased when Alcon and I entered.

"What is *she* doing here?" A woman snapped impatiently.

The others stared at me with various degrees of curiosity and annoyance.

"Councilor Alcon, care to explain?" a man demanded with poorly disguised suspicion.

I couldn't blame him. I was responsible for the death of the previous Sky King. And now, the new king had been shot the moment I showed up. At this point, even if they didn't blame the assassination attempt on me, they surely believed me to be a bad omen.

"Lady Sparrow is King Voron's bonded mate," Alcon

dropped this piece of info with a gleeful smile, clearly enjoying the shock springing to the councilors' faces at his words.

"It's impossible," someone gasped.

"She's a human," another one pointed out. "It's not so simple with them."

Alcon tipped his head my way. "Show them, my lady."

I nodded and slid the priceless fabric of my gown down my shoulder, then lowered my neckline to expose the mark for the fourth time in just two days. Queen Pavline's breast-revealing dresses made perfect sense now. Leaving the mark on display all the time seemed rather practical to me at this point.

"Is it really there?" the councilors whispered among themselves. "It couldn't be, though. How?"

They elbowed each other out of the way to take a better look at the golden mark gracing my skin. A man reached out to touch the letters on my breast, and I slapped his hand away. Honestly, I had to set boundaries here.

"It's real, okay. See?" I rubbed over the lines with a finger to prove the mark was permanent. "It's not painted on."

"Lady Sparrow is the king's bonded mate," Alcon repeated loudly. "And as such, she wields the magic of Elaros. She's the one who secured the palace against attack."

Their expressions turned a little friendlier now. I adjusted my dress back in place as they all watched me in silence. I felt I should say something, to let them know I had no plans to encroach on their authority.

"Ladies and gentlemen, please forgive me for the interruption of your meeting. I'm not here to tell you how to do your job. Just because I love your king doesn't mean I know how to run the kingdom or even the palace. But in King Voron's absence, I do have control over the magic of Elaros. If you need me to use it, please let me know."

They shifted, talking quietly among themselves.

A woman councilor cast a sideways glance at me. "As the king's bonded mate, she should be able to tell if he was still alive."

"I can," I said quickly, touching the mark through my dress. "I can sense him."

The councilors turned to me again.

"What's happening with King Voron?" one of them asked.

"He's trapped. The vines hold him, and I can't move them."

The woman nodded, looking contemplative. "Just as King Tiane had been. The same magic was used on King Voron. It's essentially the same as death."

A murmur ran through the group of councilors. "So, does the kingdom have a king or not?"

"We have to be ready to name a successor," someone said. "No need to prolong it."

The man closest to me scratched his head. "It won't be an easy task. The king has no heir."

The king had an heir—our son.

Only I couldn't throw Aithen to the wolves like that. He was out there, protected only by a young hag. His best defense was the world's complete ignorance about his existence. Once that information became public, it'd be out of my control. I feared for his safety.

"Don't name the successor yet. Please," I implored the Council. "Don't add another contestant for the crown to the pile. Let's just focus on protecting the castle from any possible attack and find out who the assassin was."

The man frowned. "But that's what the potential attackers would be counting on—the confusion and lack of leadership in the palace."

"There is no lack of leadership," I argued. "The palace is secured and protected by the High General." I glanced at Alcon for confirmation, and he nodded briefly. "See? High General Farion and you, the Royal Council, have it in your capable hands. Let's just make sure everyone here has a place to sleep and food to eat. I want to help, too. Alcon," I turned to the councilor I knew and trusted the most, "tell me what I can do."

He cupped my elbow. "Allow me to take you back to the safety of the royal chambers for now, my lady."

I glanced over my shoulder at the councilors. They bowed their heads, as if I indeed was their queen. I nodded to them as Alcon led me out of the room and up the stairs back to the royal rooms.

"There is something I'll have to ask you to do, my lady," Alcon said, lowering his voice when we were inside Voron's bedroom. "You have access to the king's magic now. Use it to search this place, please."

"The bedroom?"

"The entire palace. See what the vines might be hiding." He glanced at Magnus, who was preening his feathers on his perch. "If you need me, send the crow. He'll find me faster than the guards."

With the palace secured, it was safe for Magnus to roam free inside it.

Alcon left. I blew out a breath and slowly turned around the room, taking in every detail in the position of the vines.

I'd been here just twice during the reign of King Tiane. Back then, I'd had other concerns than to focus on layout and decor. Now, I couldn't tell with certainty exactly what had changed. If anything of value or interest had been hidden here, surely Voron would have found it already during the renovations. He'd moved the vines. The workers would have rearranged the wall panels and removed the old furniture. Could they have missed something?

I walked around the bedroom, looking for anything that would catch my eye. I paused by the shelf that hid the door to the stairs and into Tiane's "torture chamber." That room would be a perfect hiding place for all things sinister.

Memories of that night assaulted me. The echo of the fear and helplessness I felt then hollowed my chest, stilling my heart. I didn't want to go into that room to relive more of that. But I had to do it. For Voron. And for everyone who was currently hiding in Elaros, unable to go on with their lives.

Bracing my feet on the floor, as if the memories cowering in that room would rush me with enough power to knock me off my feet, I pushed on the bookshelf. It slid open, revealing a solid marble wall behind it.

Gone were the entrance and the staircase. The wall wouldn't budge, no matter how hard I tried to push against it or slide it aside.

Voron had gotten rid of that room. The tightness pressing on my chest since that night eased.

I slapped a hand against the wall and laughed softly. "Good riddance."

The room no longer existed. The man who tortured me in there had been long dead, unable to hurt me or anyone else ever again.

I shifted the bookshelf back in place and continued with my search. Contrary to what Alcon hoped for, touching the vines didn't give me much. Inanimate objects with no magic left no trace in the web of the vines for me to see.

Scanning the walls carefully, I tried to envision the way things were back when King Tiane was alive. I remembered he'd taken the box with the dagger from a chest by the wall.

The chest was now gone, with nothing else being put in its stead. I crouched by the wall, examining the white vines and the marble panels studded with light crystals.

The crystals shone brighter when I touched them. I jerked my hand away, then pressed my finger to one of them again, wishing for its glow to dim. It worked. The crystal dulled under my touch.

I was no fae, but some of Voron's light magic was now mine to use. Making the light brighter, I splayed my hand on the vines and willed them to shift with the intention of seeing inside the wall.

A leather pouch dropped onto the floor, released by the vines that had hidden it.

Hope pulsed in my chest. My hands shook with impatience as I untied the golden cord. Inside lay a tightly wound scroll. I opened it, running my eyes down the black ink of the letter written in the fae language I now spoke and read.

"Sire, I'm pleased to deliver on your royal wish," the letter read. *"I have descended into the world of shadows and traded with the creatures void of joy to obtain this wondrous weapon for you. My dreams will forever be marred with the memories of this journey, and my spirit will remain tainted by the deal I have made. I trust all of that will be worth your happiness and your favor in my regard. By granting me a position on your Council, you will forever gain in me the most fervent servant to Your Majesty."*

Another long paragraph of flattery mixed with requests for favors followed. After that, came the instructions on how to use "the weapon."

"Score the human's skin lightly and make sure the cuts heal fully before you inflict too many more. If the blade perforates her skin and penetrates the muscle, her mind will leave her, only her body will remain. It'll move, obedient like a doll to all your orders, as she will no longer be able to think on her own."

It was *me* the letter was talking about. The sender knew exactly what King Tiane wanted the dagger for.

The former king had "scored" my skin "lightly," allowing me to keep my mind. But I had no doubts it had just been the beginning of the long, sick game he had planned. His ultimate goal had been to turn me into the mindless moving doll, to do with me as he pleased without me being able to think or to speak for myself.

Fear chilled me at the thought of what could've happened had I not fought back that night. My instinct was to toss this scroll and the leather pouch it'd been kept in into the fire, but I forced myself to keep reading.

"If the dagger penetrates deep enough to pierce a vital organ, her spirit will leave her body, making her unable to move. However, for as long as the blade remains in her flesh, her body will be free of decay and therefore still usable for Your Majesty's pleasure."

Bile rose in my throat in a ball of disgust. How so matter-of-factly the sender was discussing my mindless, motionless body being "used" by the king.

"And finally, to let the human expire, you will have to remove the dagger from her body completely. Her spirit will then be released, and her body will rot, the way humans do after death. Apparently, human body decomposition is foul and exceedingly unpleasant to witness. I highly recommend you get rid of her at that point."

That would have been my future. Had I not stabbed King Tiane that night, I would've remained his plaything—consciously and otherwise—for him to use me until there was nothing left of me but a rotting corpse.

A shudder rocked my body. A tyrant never acted alone. He was surrounded by a flock of enablers who helped him do the most horrific things.

Who was this person who supplied the dagger?

There was no seal and no signature on the scroll. Whoever wrote and sent this letter clearly wished to remain anonymous in case the scroll fell into the hands of anyone else but King Tiane. I wondered if the king had granted them all their wishes. If so, there was a chance the person was still on the Royal Council. They'd be inside the palace right now—a predator in the place everyone thought was safe.

I rolled the scroll and shoved it into the pouch, climbing to my feet.

"Magnus!" I called the bird, waking him from his nap on his perch. "Come, buddy. I have a job for you."

I unclipped the silver chain from his anklet, and he followed me to the door of the suite. I opened it for him.

"Go find Alcon. Bring him here. I have something he should see."

Chapter Twenty-Nine

SPARROW

As Alcon read the scroll, his expression darkened.

"Why do you think the late king kept this?" I asked.

He frowned, his eyes narrowing. "Maybe he wanted to have the instructions on hand. Or maybe he kept it as evidence against the person who wrote it."

"Do you know who wrote it? Is this person still on the Council?"

"I hope not." He put the scroll back into the pouch. "Voron replaced quite a few members of the Council put there by King Tiane. He didn't trust any of them. Some were dangerous, but many were just lazy, not showing up for sessions in decades. However, we have to be careful. I'll talk to Farion. We can trace the favors mentioned in this letter to the person who received them."

"Should I come with you?"

"If you wish. But it may be best for you to stay here, my lady. At least until more of the royal army arrive to defend the palace. A *taurean* who came to Elaros for the festival says he saw a large force assembling just beyond the hills. I fear an attack is imminent. I'll inform you about what's going on as soon as we know more."

Alcon was gone, and I was left in the king's rooms alone, in the company of only my troubled thoughts.

Sauria was expecting me back at the farmhouse tomorrow. Yet here I was, trapped in the palace. For how long?

I'd left enough bread and cooked grains and vegetables for Aithen to last for a week. Sauria could also add some fresh berries and dried fruit to that. I desperately hoped I wouldn't be forced to stay away from him for much longer. But with a war looming over the kingdom, who could tell what the future held for all of us?

My heart swelled with worry and longing for my baby boy. I'd die to protect him. Only how could I keep him safe if I wasn't even with him? The best thing I could do for his safety was to keep his very existence secret from everyone.

Concern for both my child and his father tormented me. I restlessly paced the luxurious royal rooms, needing to do something.

The words of the letter from the scroll kept echoing through my mind. Sadly, they didn't explain what to do to reverse the effects of the magic from the World of Under. I was no closer to bringing Voron back than before finding the scroll. The protective *liliala* vines wouldn't release him to me. All I could do was pray he was not a motionless body without a spirit already.

I gripped a vine in the wall closest to me just to feel his presence in the magic of the palace. It pulsed in it, stronger than ever, giving me strength too. With it, I could think, instead of dissolving into a puddle of grief and tears.

If the scroll remained in the wall even after the renovation, what other secrets might these rooms hold?

After the bedroom, I inspected the spacious bathroom with the marble bathing pool filled by cascading fountains, then the several sitting rooms, each seemed to have a different purpose ranging from work to relaxation.

One room had been converted into Voron's reading space, with scrolls littering a wide table and books filling the tall shelves that lined every wall.

Voron would be the first person I would go to for answers. Intelligent and well-read, he seemed to know everything. Sadly, he wasn't here, and I had to figure out how to get him back.

His reading room held all the familiar signs of Voron. A warm, cozy blanket lay on the chair by the fire, because the weather was cold and gloomy without me by his side. A map of the area on the other side of the Cloud River, with all the ongoing improvement projects marked, was spread on the massive desk, because he was passionate about all of them, making the lives of his people easier. A midnight-blue satin robe was draped over the chair by the desk, because he must have left it here that morning when the servants had arrived to dress him for the festival ceremony today.

It was chilly in the royal rooms, but I didn't feel like calling someone to start a fire for me. Instead, I draped Voron's robe around my shoulders, his scent tugging at my heart with the feeling of loss.

I sat in his chair, gliding my fingers over the intricate carvings on the armrests. He'd sat right here just this morning. What was he doing? Going over the map? Reading?

I opened one of the compartments on the side of the desk, then another one, and the next. Clean quills filled the first, with a stack of writing paper lying in another, along with some clean and used scrolls in the third.

The fourth compartment wouldn't open, however. It wasn't locked, but there was a resistance of magic holding it closed when I tried to pull at the thick silver handle.

Closing my eyes, I willed it to move just like I had done with the vines. The small door shifted a little, giving in bit by bit until I opened it completely, revealing a thick, leather-bound journal inside.

Its cover bore no title and no adornments. The leather was

stained and discolored, and when I took it out, it became clear some pages had been bent, wrinkled, or torn. It looked like a practice notebook of a messy school child, not something that belonged to the monarch of a mighty kingdom. Still, this was the only item he kept locked in his desk.

The writing inside looked just as messy. The letters often ran too large, running off the page, or too small, making the words look squished together. Many pages were stained. The ink ran, smudged.

"Where are you, Sparrow?" The question took up the entire first page, like a title. And there was no answer.

I turned the page, running my eyes over the uneven lines.

"I need to write this down before the grief crushes my skull and destroys me... Will it purge the pain, too, once the words are out of my head and on the paper? I doubt it. But what choice do I have?"

The letters were written in broken, jerky lines that didn't convey the steady confidence Voron usually displayed in public, but I recognized his handwriting. He had written these words, every single one of them.

"Wherever you are, I have to be." The next page read.

I drew in a shaky breath. We were in the same world, in the same palace. So close, but still torn away from each other.

"How dare you fly away from me, little bird? How could you leave me? You own me. My mind, my heart, my body... My very spirit belongs to you and only you."

The words grew angry at times, forming into what seemed to be essentially one long letter to me that Voron wrote over the course of the past months.

"What are you doing to me? I know you're alive. I can feel you, but I can't get to you. You're in a place I can't reach. Do you know what fucking torture that is? I can't even die to be with you."

He was furious with *me* for something *he* had done to both of us. His letter was the result of pain and passion, without any logic at all.

"I hate you, Sparrow. I hate you for the torture you're putting

me through. For the numb days and the restless nights. For the yearning that's tearing me apart. For knowing that it would never get better. I hate you with more passion than I've ever hated anyone. And I love you, more fervently than I have ever loved, than I ever knew was possible."

He'd never told me he loved me. His feelings for me might've been different back when we were together. Did being away from me make him realize we belonged together?

I stroked the page. So much hurt and longing had been poured out on it.

But I felt hurt, too.

And angry.

"You did this, Voron. You did this to yourself." He must have known that, too. And maybe that made him hurt even worse. But it didn't make me feel any less angry. "You did this to both of us."

I slammed the open journal onto the desk, leaping to my feet. Tortured by regret for all the time we'd lost, I paced the room, letting the anger bubble and boil inside me.

He sent me away. *He* ordered me to be thrown into the River of Mists. *He* gave in to the demands of the court. In that one moment, he chose the crown over me. And maybe he'd regretted it right after. But the harm had been done. He broke my trust.

I pressed my forehead to a vine in the wall, needing to feel the comfort of him even as he was the source of my anger.

"Fuck you, Voron!" I slammed a hand into the wall panel. "Fuck you for what you've done to us. You have no one to blame for that but yourself."

The vine pulsed warmly. Voron's magic reached for me, touching my skin, dipping into my very soul.

"You own me." His words echoed in my ears, as if he'd said them, not written them. *"My mind, my heart, my body... My very spirit belongs to you and only you."*

Voron was mine.

The mark on my chest throbbed in affirmation.

He belonged to me, just like I belonged to him. And neither

the protective magic of Elaros nor the malicious sorcery of the World of Under would keep him away from me.

"Give him back," I ordered to the vines, willing them to move.

But they didn't budge. I felt the magic flow and ebb, but I didn't have enough power to direct it. I had no magic of my own to force it to move as I wished.

This palace, however, was filled to the brim with magic I needed. Everyone from the top councilors to the last kitchen helper wielded it here. They were fae, born with magic. And I was a human. *A vessel,* as Alcon had put it.

A vessel. One that needed more power to hold.

I pushed away from the wall. It was late. The clock over the fireplace showed the time was just past three o'clock in the morning. The palace must be asleep. But I was not afraid to wake them. All of them, if needed.

The door to the king's chambers was open, and I marched out into the corridor, then down the stairs to the floor with Voron's old suite. It was one of the best suites in the palace. I figured whoever lived here now must be important enough to occupy it.

I banged on the door with both fists until it opened and the sleepy face of a guard appeared in the gap.

"What's happening? Councilor Alcon is asleep."

Alcon. He was exactly the man I needed.

"Wake him up."

The guard made a face, looking at me like I was a pile of cow dung he'd stepped into.

"I need to talk to him. Urgently." I waved both hands at him impatiently, then added a little softer, "Please."

"It better be fucking important," he grumped.

"It is," I assured him. "It's a matter of life and death. King Voron's life and death."

Chapter Thirty

SPARROW

Alcon was fully dressed. Despite his guard's complaints, I didn't believe the councilor had been asleep when I came to his rooms. There were enough things to keep him awake.

"The palace is coming under attack," Alcon warned me. "Lord Vautour was the one who procured the bolt and the dagger from the World of Under. He did acquire a seat on the Royal Council for his service to King Tiane, but Voron expelled him shortly after his coronation. It looks like the lord has been holding a grudge against the king ever since."

"It took him a long time to act out on it," I said.

Alcon rubbed his neck. He looked exhausted, but I doubted he could sleep now, even if he tried. I couldn't think about sleeping myself, either. Every fiber of my being vibrated with anxious energy that wouldn't let me stand still.

"Vautour is one of the minor lords," Alcon explained. "He has no power to go against the king on his own. But he's found an ally in High Lord Bussard, who is apparently back from the Below."

"Is Bussard the one who is attacking us now?"

Alcon nodded. "He'd collected an army, enough to take the palace. And without the king..." He sighed. "The warriors of the royal army love and respect Voron deeply. They would fight and die for him. But if he is dead already, whom do we ask them to fight for?"

"He isn't dead." I shook my head. "Voron is alive."

Alcon placed a hand on my shoulder. "Lady Sparrow, as the king's bonded mate, if there is anything you can think of to bring him back, tell me how I can help. Elaros needs its king now more than ever."

He didn't have to beg me. I needed Voron more than anyone.

"Can you wake up people most loyal to Voron, please? Those who want him back as much as you do."

He gave me a penetrating look. "What are you planning to do?"

"Whatever it takes, Alcon. Everything possible and beyond."

The courtiers gathered in the Throne Room. Yawning and in various stages of undress, they blinked at me and rubbed their eyes. I spotted Libelle in the crowd. She was next to her bonded mate, holding his hand. Dove was there too, beaming at me while combing her fingers through her curls messy from sleep. Every one of Voron's men was there, too, including the High General Farion.

Alcon leaned toward me. "What do you want us to do, Lady Sparrow?"

I heaved a long breath and addressed the court, "Thank you, everyone, for coming here. I want you to help me bring our king back."

A murmur rolled through the crowd, confused but hopeful, as I ascended the dais.

"Please, work," I quietly prayed to the capricious sky fae magic that seemed to have a mind of its own.

Placing both hands on the vines, I leaned my forehead against them. Voron was trapped inside, and this was the closest I could get to him. But it wasn't right. His place was with me. For better or for worse, with all his faults and mine, we belonged together.

He was mine. I owned him. And I wanted him back.

"Give him back to me," I whispered, reaching deep into the magic of Elaros that held Voron prisoner.

It let me touch it, but I had no strength to do anything more.

"Help me." I reached a hand to Alcon.

He took it without hesitation, and I felt a rush of his magic connecting to that of Voron's through me.

"More," I demanded.

He stretched his other hand out toward the crowd gathered in the room. "Anyone else?"

Dove ran up the stairs and took his hand, stretching hers out to Libelle.

The power grew inside me, making my head spin. I pressed my side to the pillar, hugging it with one arm. The chain of people holding my other hand got longer, as the entire court was now linking hands, lending me their magic.

I might be just a vessel, but I was a limitless one. Ravenously gathering every tendril of their powers, I channeled them through to the man I wished to free so desperately.

"More," I kept saying again and again as more fae joined us.

The wondrous torrent grew stronger inside me. The vines trembled, resisting my push. But the deadly power of the crossbow bolt poisoned the light of sky magic. Even if I freed Voron, what parts of him would I get? Was his mindless body all that was left of him?

"I need all of you," I pleaded with him as if he could hear me. "Every single part of you belongs to me, Voron. Your spirit, too. Come back to me. Whole."

Farion was the last in the chain of people linking hands. He splayed his palm on the pillar, closing the circle.

Magic rushed through me, heating my body and making my skin tingle. The mark on my chest burned, shining brightly through the dark fabric of my dress. My very soul appeared to meld, merging with the vines of the pillar. My love found Voron inside it and curled around him, shielding him from the rest of the world.

"Mine," I exhaled.

The worry was extinguished. The restless anxiety plaguing me receded. We were together again. And when we were together, nothing could harm us.

The vines loosened and fell apart. Unraveling from around him, they crawled back, taking the shape of the royal throne once again.

Voron was in my arms, lying with his back on the throne. His new wings stretched over the armrests and draped down the dais.

With a loud clunk, the crossbow bolt fell out of his wing and rolled down the stairs for Alcon to grab it.

"Voron!" I took his face between my hands.

Did I kill him by freeing him?

"Are you trying to wring my neck, little vixen?" He sounded a little groggy, his eyelids lifting slowly. But he was here, all of him. A smile broke through his weariness, like a ray of sunshine through the clouds.

"You're here," I exhaled, shifting just a little. But his arms promptly flexed around me, pulling me to him.

"Stay." He buried his face between my neck and my shoulder. "You were always meant to be mine."

I melted into his embrace. My soul had found home. For once, my heart could rest, and I didn't want to move.

"I don't know how you're here, little bird. But even if you're just a dream, please don't leave me. I'd rather have an illusion of you than nothing at all."

"No illusion, Voron. I'm all here, in spirit and flesh." I took his hand and slapped it on the wide curve of my hip. "See? There is nothing wraith-like about this, is there?"

He gripped my hips through my dress, then moved his hands up, squeezing my sides, my arms, my shoulders, proving by touch that his eyes did not deceive him.

"It is really you. You came back to me. All of you." He smiled in wonder, skimming his thumb along my bottom lip. "Your smart mouth, too."

Sitting up on the throne, he made me straddle his thighs. I sank my hands into his hair as he kissed me.

He gripped my head in his hands, searching my eyes intently. "You're not going anywhere ever again, do you hear me? You can't leave. Please, Sparrow. Stay, share my life with me, love me. I can't breathe without your love. I can't be myself without you."

I brushed the silver strands out of his face. There were more of them now; his entire front was white.

"You're not an easy man to love, Voron. But I can't stop loving you. God knows I've tried."

My muscles trembled from the released strain. The world appeared to spin around us. But it all came to a standstill the moment his lips touched mine again. For months, I believed I'd never kiss him again. For so long, I thought my memories and my longing would be all I'd have for the rest of my life.

Kissing him now still felt like a dream. My heart overflowed with happiness so bright it seemed to flood the room with light like sunshine. I parted my lips, letting his tongue invade my mouth. He gripped me tighter, holding me to him.

I wished to lose myself in him completely. But Alcon cleared his throat next to us, bursting our bubble.

"It's good to have you back, Your Majesty."

His voice brought me back to reality. The entire royal court was watching us. I pulled back from Voron. But he followed me with two more kisses, lighter and quicker than the one before. Then he pressed me to his chest, looking at the court over my shoulder as he rose to his feet with me in his arms.

He set me down next to him, keeping his right arm around my shoulders. My mark pulsed with golden-blue light through the fabric of my dress.

"Let them see it, my love." He slid my dress down my shoulder, exposing the mark. "Let them all see what you are to me."

The courtiers gasped in wonder. Dove squeaked, bouncing on her heels. Libelle clapped, smiling. As the shock settled, the room erupted into congratulations and cheers. The magic bond that tied the king and me ended the speculations and rivalry, bringing stability to the court.

"Sparrow is my queen," Voron announced in a voice so powerful it reached across the entire room, reverberating between the marble walls. "The only queen I'll ever have."

Holding his head high, he moved his gaze over the crowd, as if challenging anyone to disagree. No one did. Especially after I'd just brought their king back from near death.

Instead, they bowed to me. Men got down on one knee and ladies sank into curtsies.

"Long live the queen!" rolled through the crowd.

It had been a rocky, winding road that brought me here, but I finally found where I belonged.

A crashing noise slammed into the tower from outside. The rumble shook the palace to the roots of the *liliala* vines.

Alcon paled. "They're here."

Farion stepped forward, quickly briefing the king on the defense measures taken. Voron nodded in concentration.

Another explosion shuddered through the palace.

"What is it?" I leaned closer into Voron.

"Magic and cannons make for an explosive combination," he replied softly, then addressed the room, "Farion and the Council will stay here. The rest of you will go down to the lower floors for safety. And you..." he said softly, turning to me. "Sparrow." He brushed the side of my face with the back of his fingers, as if needing to touch me to make sure I was still here. As if holding me to him wasn't enough to convince him I was not just a vision after all. "I'm equally terrified of both keeping you with me despite the danger or letting you out of my sight until the threat is gone."

He looked torn.

I understood his hesitation perfectly. Now that he was finally here, the last thing I wished was to let him go again. Especially, since there were cannons and deadly magic involved.

But if there was anyone capable of bringing order to Elaros, it was Voron. He'd won wars before. He had inspired people to follow him to victory even before he got his wings or wore the Sky Crown.

I wasn't a warrior. I had no wings and no weapon I could use. I'd only be in the way if I stayed with him—a distraction, or even worse, a liability.

"I won't go far." I promised, squeezing his hand. "I'll stay out of sight and out of the way, but I'll be close."

Dove fluttered to us.

"Allow me, Your Majesty. I'll take care of your bonded one." She took my other hand, squeezing it with barely concealed excitement.

I was thrilled to see her again, returning her smile.

"You can trust Dove," I assured Voron, who looked hesitant. "She's helped me before."

"Swear you'll keep my Sparrow safe for me," Voron demanded.

Dove jerked up a slim white eyebrow.

"The things the bond does to people," she muttered, then curtsied to Voron, speaking louder, "Of course, Your Majesty. I promise to keep Sparrow with me in your absence, protect her with my life, and deliver her safely into your own hands when I deem it safe to do so."

He nodded as the swirl of magic swished around us, raising the old leaves from the floor of the Throne Room and sealing Dove's promise.

Pulling me into him once more, he gave me one last kiss. "Stay safe."

"You, too," I pleaded as Dove tugged me out of the room, following the rest of the courtiers. With the return of the king, the court was buzzing with new hope and energy.

Just outside of the Throne Room, Dove suddenly grabbed me into a hug. I was sure she held back her fae strength, but it still felt like my bones were cracking in her embrace.

"I didn't think I'd ever see you again." She sniffled. Now that we were alone, she let her emotions show. "We thought you were dead. Where have you been?"

"It's a long story." I waved her off, rubbing at my eyes discreetly. Her warm greeting touched me, bringing tears to my eyes. "I promise I'll tell you everything one day, just not right now." The noise of battle was too close. The hostile magic hissed just beyond the palace walls. Voron would be going out there soon. "What's going to happen now? What do you know about High Lord Bussard?"

She curled her lips, wrinkling her nose.

"Not much, just that he's incredibly spiteful. He once had an argument with my father about who killed a boar during the hunt. My father won the argument, but High Lord Bussard hasn't spoken to him since." She gave me a long look. "Are you all right?"

I caught myself pacing the floor and stopped, releasing a breath. "Sorry, I'm just..."

"Worried?" She nodded in understanding. "Come." She tugged at my hand. "I'll take you to a spot where you can watch him safely."

The moment Voron had gone out of my sight, the invisible string that connected my heart to his stretched too thinly, spiking my anxiety.

"You bonded couples can be insufferable. I've learned that with Libelle," Dove lamented, dragging me through a door into a different tower of the palace, then up a narrow winding staircase. "Normally, I'd fly," she chatted. "But it's best to stay inside for now."

"When do you think it will be over?"

"The battle? Soon enough. King Voron has fended off many attacks on the palace already, defending his crown. He'll deal with this one, too."

I latched onto her words with hope, wishing to believe them with all my heart.

"High Lord Bussard thought he was clever to assassinate the king before the attack," she said to me over her shoulder, ascending the stairs. "One thing he hadn't accounted for was you being here to bring your sweetheart back to life. And look at you, little human. You are the queen now." She gave me a quick curtsy on the top landing and teased, "Your Majesty."

"Stop it." I shook my head with a smile. "I'm not."

"But that's what the king said—you are his queen. I thought I would never forgive him for what he did to you. He found and publicly executed the man who tried to assassinate you in the palace of High Lord Pelargos, but it didn't help the way I felt. I tried to leave Elaros, but my father wouldn't let me, even though I told him I would never marry the king. Not that the king wished to marry, anyway. He turned away every single bride presented to him."

"What happened to Lady Lark?"

"Oh, she was the first one to leave, after her father fell out of favor with the king. Losing all hope of ever becoming the queen, she married that stuck-up Lord Bruant. Which makes them a perfect pair, if you ask me. They can just sit in their palace now and argue for hours about what's the most elegant way to fold a napkin."

I snorted a laugh, shaking my head.

"Clearly, the king waited for *you*," Dove chatted, dragging me along. "He wanted no one else. When he fell to his knees at your feet, in front of the entire court... Oh." She fanned herself. "I forgave him for everything at once in that moment."

I wished my feelings were as clear on that, too. But it wasn't so easy. My love for Voron helped me forgive him. I might feel mad and rage at him in anger, but I did forgive any wrong he'd done to me.

I loved him. I forgave him. But I wasn't sure I could fully trust him again. Trust was more fragile than even the heart. Repairing it would take time. I had yet to figure out how to trust Voron with my most precious secret—our son.

Dove studied my face for a second. "What's the matter? Is something wrong, Sparrow?"

I couldn't discuss this with her. Not yet.

I shook my head. "Nothing is wrong. Tell me," I asked, scrambling to change the topic. "How did that lord do? The one you had tied to your bed? Remember the night you helped me escape?"

A dreamy smile lit up her face.

"Oh, Lord Colomb. Why? If you think he suspected anything, you don't need to worry. He waited patiently for me to return and never asked any questions. He's such a sweetheart."

"Oh, I'm not worried. I'm just—"

"Ooh. Are you curious?" She shot me an excited glance.

"Curious about what?" I couldn't quite focus, trying to keep up with her brisk pace up yet another staircase.

"Bedroom games are fun," she gushed. "There are so many exciting toys. You know what, I'll send you some new ones I have. They're waiting to be used."

What was she talking about?

But I had no chance to clarify.

Dove grabbed my arm, drawing me behind a tall pillar on the side of a high window in the tower. "All right. We're here. Can you move the vines a little?"

I touched the tight weave of the vines that concealed the

window, ordering them to move with my mind. They obeyed instantly, shifting aside to create a wide opening.

Dove yanked me back behind the pillar.

"Stay out of sight. We don't want the king to lose his fated one when he's just got her back. Besides, I gave him a promise I'd prefer not to break." She tilted her head in the direction of the window. "Look, but very carefully."

Out in the gray pre-sunrise sky, a battle raged. I'd seen an attack on Elaros Palace once before, back when Voron had taken the crown. That day, I watched it from the ground. Now, it was taking place right in front of me, and it was even more gruesome and terrifying.

The fighting was happening everywhere, from above to below us. The air was filled with groans of pain and anguished cries of people dying. Feathers of every color churned in the air, stirred by the wings of the highborn.

Voron stood on top of the highest tower of the palace, quite a distance away from us. His wings were hidden. Unused to his miraculous new acquisition, he led the battle the way he'd always done before—on foot.

Guards and warriors flew to and from him with information and orders. In between directing his forces against the enemy, he fended off the attacks of the brave few who dared charge at him directly.

As I watched, a man plummeted toward him from above, a spear directed downwards, aiming to kill. Without opening his wings, Voron leaped aside, slicing the man's head off with his sword.

I slapped my hand over my mouth. It all happened so fast, I gasped and it was over. The head rolled across the tower platform before dropping from it. The man's torso crashed at Voron's feet. He wiped his blade on the dead man's clothes, then stepped over it, returning his focus to the battle.

"He's good, isn't he?" Dove's eyes sparkled with excitement, as if this was a sport, and Voron had just shot the ball into the net, not cut a man's head off, risking losing his own in the same manner.

I pressed my hands to my chest, trying to calm my racing heart.

"God, I wish it was over already."

My stomach lurched as two other men barreled full speed at Voron from two different directions. He evaded the attack of one and met the other one with his sword thrust forward. Blood gushed out, coating the blade anew, as Voron stabbed his attacker through the chest.

"Not long now," Dove assured me casually. "Look, they already got Lord Vautour." She pointed at the approaching group of highborn dressed in the uniforms of the royal army.

They carried a man under his arms and dropped him at Voron's feet. As the lord's wings fluttered and shook, I realized they had been clipped. The longest feathers on their tips had been slashed off. Even with his wings out, Lord Vautour could no longer fly. He couldn't get away.

This was the man who wrote the letter to King Tiane with the detailed instructions about my torture and death, the man who sourced the crossbow bolt that had nearly taken Voron out of this world. As pathetic as Lord Vautour looked right now, I couldn't bring myself to feel sorry for him.

He crawled backwards, away from Voron, but the king stalked after him. His sword pointed down, painting a line of red on the white marble platform with the blood sluicing from the blade.

Voron said but one word, "Traitor."

It was both the charge and the verdict. Raising his weapon, the king delivered the punishment next. His sword went through the chest of Lord Vautour, piercing his heart. The red sparks of Nerifir iron danced along the dark blade, startlingly bright in the pale light of the early morning.

"It's so pretty," Dove said unexpectedly.

I tore my stare from the traitor, whose dead body was now

lifted on a spear for everyone to see until the winds would take every last trace of it.

"What is pretty, Dove?"

There was nothing to admire in the death reigning out there. Even as the battle had already been won, the fighting was still ongoing. Once ignited, the violence wasn't easy to put out. Some of Bussard's people were fleeing, but the warriors of Voron's army were close on their heels, catching them or shooting them with arrows out of the sky.

"There." Dove swept with her arm toward the east.

The sun was rising from behind the horizon. The clouds pulled back for the first time in so many months. The light of the new day shone like a golden jewel in the bright azure sky.

Dove smiled, basking in the sunlight like a kitten. "I don't remember the last time I saw the sun so clearly."

My gaze drifted to the man who had the power to part the clouds. Voron surveyed the battlefield in the sky, rotating slowly. Like the arm of the compass always pointing north, he ended up facing me. Our eyes met.

"Come." Dove grabbed me around my waist. "I'll take you to him and be done with my promise."

Her stunning wings opened, and she hopped from the window, taking me to the tower with the king.

Dropping his sword, Voron stretched his arms toward me, then plucked me from Dove's embrace.

"What are you doing here?" He frowned with concern but held me tightly. "It's not safe."

"But it is. You did it, my king." Dove flashed him a grin, dipping into a brief curtsy. "We came to congratulate Your Majesty on yet another victory."

"Where is High Lord Bussard?" I asked.

"Killed in battle," Voron replied, stroking my arm.

It clearly was a victory. The royal army took a wide circle above the castle, waving their weapons and bellowing in triumph.

Voron looked up, his eyes lit up.

"Go," I urged. "Fly with them, Voron. You earned it."

He glanced at me in wonder, as if it didn't even occur to him to join his men in the victory lap around the palace.

Tentatively, he slid his wings out, unfurling them from his back. He moved them once, twice, gaining strength before lifting into the air. Instead of joining his men above us, however, he circled the tower in flight as I turned on the platform to follow him with my gaze, my hands pressed together, my heart beating with pride.

He could fly!

My wingless crow was wingless no more.

With every move of his wings, his confidence soared. A smile curved his lips. With a cheeky flash in his eyes, he zoomed into a spiral toward me.

"You're coming with me." He snatched me from the tower.

I cried out in shock, then threw my arms around his neck.

"You promised to trust me," he said. "Remember? By the bridge over the Cloud River?"

I did. But that was before he broke my trust by ordering me tossed into that very river...

I shook my head, chasing away the doubts.

This was Voron's day, his victory. Today, he'd avenged his injuries and mine. And I wished to celebrate it with him.

I tilted back my head, turning my face to the gentle caress of the breeze.

"I love it." I laughed. "I love flying way too much for someone who has no wings—"

"But you do," he said softly. "My wings are yours, little bird. I couldn't have had them without you."

His great, black wings beat the air steadily, lifting us higher. The men cheered as we joined them in their victory flight above the palace. The rising sun pierced through their wings with the light of a new day.

Voron was happy.

And that made my heart lighter, too.

Chapter Thirty-One

For the rest of the morning, Voron wouldn't let me out of his sight, keeping some form of physical contact with me, too, whenever possible, either by holding my hand, touching my leg with his, or simply dragging me into his side in a hug.

Together, we went through the palace as Voron organized the court life back to order. I enjoyed watching him being in charge and got a chance to learn first-hand how he ran the place. I also got to talk with many courtiers of Voron's inner circle, including those who had accompanied him during his visit to Bavius's farmhouse.

I loved the changes Voron had brought to Elaros. I believed Aithen and I could be happy here. Still, I didn't tell Voron about our son. The invisible cabin in the woods felt safer for my baby to be at than the royal palace.

At midday meal, Voron sat me next to him, on his right hand side—the place reserved for spouses and closest allies. I got a chair, placed very close to Voron's. For once, I wasn't sitting in the king's lap, being hand fed like a pet. I got my own plate for every course, too, like every fae at the table.

After lunch, we joined the Royal Council in the meeting room where a seat was reserved for me, also on the king's right.

The councilors brought the king up to date on everything that had happened while he'd been trapped in the vines.

I listened carefully while trying to figure out where I fit into this part of Voron's life. No one questioned my place next to the king. Though uncrowned and unmarried, I was treated as the queen already. Such was the power of the magical bond between us. It gave me all the rights a marriage would and more. But I wished for my position to be more than just honorary, I wanted to be useful as well.

Listening to the councilors, I found the projects Voron was funding out in the country endearing. I'd spent many months on the farm, unable to visit the town. But through Bavius, I'd seen the challenges farmers faced. I knew what the life of a farmer was like, and I wished to improve it in any way possible.

For once, I saw a true purpose for me in the future. Being Voron's mate came with exciting opportunities to apply myself in other ways, in addition to being his mate and Aithen's mother.

When someone started talking about the politics of High Lords and reciting some financials, I found my attention slipping. It'd been a very intense couple of days. I'd stayed up through the night and had powered through the day, fueled mostly by adrenaline and the intense need to be close to Voron. But the exhaustion had caught up with me.

No matter how hard I tried to stay alert through the speech of the councilor delivering long strings of numbers in a monotonous voice, my eyelids kept drooping. I hid a small yawn behind my hand, but Voron noticed my struggle.

He called for the session to pause and took me out of the room.

"You're tired," he stated. "Come, I'll take you to bed." He swept me off my feet and into his arms.

"I can walk," I protested, even as my body already curled against his broad chest and my tired muscles melted into his warmth.

He gave me a self-assured grin. "Why walk if we can fly?"

He pushed off the open window, diving into the open sky beyond. The fresh autumn air lapped at my skin and combed through my hair as Voron took me up to the tower with the royal rooms.

He landed gracefully onto the same terrace that Dove had taken me from in my escape from King Tiane. The memory didn't affect me as much as it once did. I didn't even have so much as a pinch in my chest this time. All of that was in the distant past now, unable to hurt me ever again.

Voron kissed me, walking me backwards into the room.

"As much as I wish to be selfish and keep you at my side," he murmured against my lips, "I also want you well-rested."

"And why is that?" I smiled.

"Because I will keep you awake at night."

Kissing my mouth, my face, my neck, he kept walking me backwards until my back pressed to one of the bed posts. He groaned, tearing his mouth away from mine and gripped the post above my head.

"I have to go," he growled. "Fuck this crown for taking me away from you."

I scanned his face. Was it just a figure of speech on his part? Or did he really mean it?

"Would you give it up?" I challenged. "Would you leave the throne to be with me?"

His dark eyebrows jumped up in shock. "You don't want to be the queen?"

"What if I didn't? Would you leave with me?"

The string of questions exchanged between us grew longer, and with it, the tension stretched like a rubber band threatening to snap.

He drew in a breath, straightening his back. His gaze ran

around the room behind me, as if assessing everything he'd have to give up.

"All right." He met my eyes again with a smile. He took the priceless Sky Crown off his head and casually tossed it onto the stand at the foot of the bed. "Let's go."

"Where?"

"Wherever you wish. Vensari? That farmhouse? Anywhere you'll feel at home, dear Sparrow." He took my hand in his, heading to the doors of the patio, his wings spread wide.

I tugged at his hand, stopping him in his mad dash out.

"Just like that, Voron? Would you really leave it all behind for me?"

He tilted his head. "For *us*, Sparrow. There is no you or me anymore, just us. And yes, I will do everything for us to stay together. Including giving up this." He tipped his chin at the crown glistening on the stand behind us.

I searched his eyes, and for once there was no regret in them. He really meant it. He'd go anywhere with me.

"I feel at home when I'm with you, wherever that may be." I stepped back to pick up the golden circlet of the Sky Crown. "I'll never ask you to give up everything you've worked so hard for." I placed the crown back on his head where it belonged.

"Was it a test, then?" A corner of his mouth lifted in a half-smile as he squinted at me. "Did you just test me, little bird?"

"I had to know." I nodded.

"And now you do." He took my chin in his fingers, lifting my face to his. "I was separated from you for long enough to know with certainty that without you, nothing in this world has meaning. Please believe me, nothing is more important to me than you."

I rose to my tiptoes, placing a kiss on his lips. He gripped my waist, taking the kiss deeper, longer.

"Now, off to bed with you," he panted, tearing his mouth away from mine. "Lest I stay, keeping you awake for the rest of the day and all through the night."

I missed him the moment he left, but my heart felt even lighter now. The bed called to me with its puffy pillows and warm covers. The room was warded, making me feel safe. I touched the vines of the bed posts, willing the windows to close, and the crystal panels noiselessly swung together, following my will.

Too tired to look for a nightgown, I stripped off my clothes and climbed into the comfiest bed I'd ever slept in. After that, I passed out into a deep, dreamless sleep.

My awareness returned slowly. With my eyes closed, I burrowed deeper into the warm comfy blankets, not ready to face reality yet. Then I remembered, the reality was more pleasant than any dream could be. I had Voron back.

A knock sounded on the door.

"Shit," Voron cursed softly next to me. Then the mattress moved slightly as he left the bed.

I opened my eyes, poking my head out from under the covers. Voron's tall frame, clad in a silk, dark-blue robe, came into view by the door.

"I said *do not disturb us*," he hissed in a voice that would undoubtedly be shouting if he wasn't worried about waking me.

"I'm so sorry, Your Majesty," a male voice replied meekly, barely audible. "Lady Dove sent this..."

"It's all right," I said cheerfully. "I'm awake. You can bring in whatever she sent."

Voron pivoted around to face me.

"Sorry. Did we wake you up?"

The skylight above displayed the clear, dark sky outside. It was night already.

"I've slept enough," I smiled, running a hand over my face.

Two guards carried in a large wooden trunk and set it down heavily.

"Wow!" I eyed the trunk. "This is all from Dove?"

She'd promised to send a few things, some "toys" if I remembered correctly. But it appeared like she'd packed an entire shop in there, including the employees.

Voron closed the doors behind the guards. Wrapping the top sheet around my breasts, I climbed out of bed.

"What the hell did she send?" I muttered, coming closer.

Voron caught me in his arms. "Come here, now that you're up."

I leaned against him as he ran his hands up my body. His fingers traced my curves through the silk of the sheet, as if recalling the paths of the familiar landscape.

"I missed you..." he whispered, burying his face in my hair. "You have no idea, little bird, how much I missed you."

"I know." I pressed my nose to his chest in the narrow opening of his robe. "I read your journal."

He groaned, "You found it?"

I nodded. "It was addressed to me, so I read it."

His fingers stilled at my shoulders, digging into my skin. "There are a lot of very angry words in that book. They were not meant to hurt you."

"I understand. They're a reflection of the pain you were feeling." Reading his journal didn't hurt me as much as it made me angry.

He drew me into him, nearly crushing me against his hard chest. "I would've jumped into the River of Mists if I knew I'd find you there. Fuck, I was ready to jump just to end the agony."

I couldn't bring myself to feel angry at him again. Right now, I simply wished to revel in his closeness, something I hadn't thought I would ever get to experience again. I slid my hands into his robe, gliding my palms over his warm skin and the familiar relief of his muscles underneath.

"I'm here now," I breathed out.

"And I still can't believe it's not a dream." With his hand under my chin, he ran his thumb over my bottom lip. His other hand gripped my backside, yanking me so close, his rock-hard erection dug into my belly through the thin material of his loose sleeping pants. "I want to know everything—where you've been, how you lived, who was with you, what kept you away from me all this time. But first, I really need to be inside you, Sparrow, more than anything." His voice came hoarse and deep. "Only I'm afraid if I do, I'll end up fucking you until neither of us can draw another breath."

"What a way to go that would be." I kissed his chest, then glanced at the trunk behind him. "Maybe Dove has something to help you out?"

"Dove?" He looked confused. "Like what?"

"Let me see."

I slipped out of his arms and flung the heavy lid of the trunk open, revealing velvet-lined trays with items that looked both pretty and ghastly. It appeared as if Dove had robbed a medieval torture chamber, then wrapped all the metal in silk, fur, and velvet and tied it with ribbons.

"Oh." Voron peeked over my shoulder. "Did you ask for these?" he sounded curious, still somewhat confused, but not shocked or appalled. I assumed he might know what all these things were for.

"Not exactly, but..." Two pairs of handcuffs lined with white rabbit fur caught my attention. I grabbed them from their velvet nests in the tray. "These may help."

Voron squinted at me suspiciously, taking a step back. Though, his erection remained as hard as ever, pushing against the fine silk of his pants that could not contain it.

I arched an eyebrow, spinning a pair of handcuffs around my finger. "Are you running, Your Majesty? Already?"

"Sparrow. What are you planning to do?"

Putting my hands behind my back, I hid the handcuffs out of sight and smiled sweetly. "First, I'd like you to remove your clothes."

"No. You're first. In fact," he stalked toward me with a predatory smirk, "I'll take that sheet off you myself."

"Nope." I leaped back, then jumped onto the bed. "Tonight, *you're* the one taking orders, my king."

I climbed all the way to the headboard, holding the handcuffs and the sheet to my chest, then turned around to face him.

"Take off your clothes, Your Majesty," I demanded sternly.

Standing at the foot of the bed, he slowly lifted a hand to his shoulder.

"Hurry up." I twirled the handcuffs in the air again. "Or I'll tell you to dance while you're stripping, too."

He groaned with a long breath out, but slid the robe off his right shoulder, then shrugged it off his left.

I sucked in a breath at the sight of the golden mark over his heart.

"You have one, too?"

Of course he did. Like Sauria had said, the magic bond wasn't a stream but a bridge, with both people loving each other. But seeing it there took my breath away just the same.

Voron's mark was nearly identical to mine with one small difference. The letter S came before V. I needed to touch it, to press my lips to it. To feel the raised letters and the crown above them, to trace the frame of thorns and flowers.

"I earned it," he said firmly. "Just like you earned yours." His eyes glinted with heat and mischief. "I showed you mine, now show me yours." His gaze fixed on the sheet over my breasts.

I shook my head, tipping my chin at his pants. "Your clothes are still on. Take them off, now. Or you will have to dance for me, too."

He held my gaze as his hands drifted up to the laces at his waistband.

"You want a dance, little minx?" He swayed his hips side to side. His tall, muscular body moved gracefully as he hummed a light tune.

I had no idea that Voron could dance. I'd never seen him joining in at King Tiane's parties. I wondered what else he'd hidden from me? What other talents were waiting for me to discover?

His eyes trapped mine, however, making me lose my train of thought. He yanked at the laces, opening his pants. Not taking his eyes off mine, he let his pants fall to the floor. With his hands on his hips, he took a wide stance, putting himself on display for me.

"Happy?" He tilted his head, his eyebrow hiked up in question.

I raked my gaze over his body, drinking in every familiar feature, from his powerful thighs, to his trim hips, to his broad shoulders and that amused smile of his as he watched me ogling him.

Next, my eyes homed in on his erection that was pointing straight up, like an exclamation sign, demanding attention. I licked my lips, my inner muscles clenching with the memories of him inside me. Oh, how empty I had felt without him.

I licked my lips and curled a finger at him. "Come here, my king."

Bracing a knee into the mattress, he crawled to me on all fours, prowling like a predator, his eyes never leaving mine.

I drew my knees up to my chest, getting ready. He pounced on me, and I rolled aside, slipping away.

"Sparrow." His groan was a mix of frustration and bitter desperation.

"Let's try this," I murmured, quickly snapping a handcuff around his wrist.

He paused, staring at it in shock. I made the vines of his bedpost move closer before snapping the second cuff of the first pair around them. He reached for me with his other hand, but I fastened it to the opposite bed post with the second pair of handcuffs.

He threw his head back against the headboard with an exasperated groan. "Please explain how I'm supposed to touch you now?"

"That's the point, Voron." I leaned in, kissing the tip of his nose. "*I'll* be the one touching *you*."

His eyes flashed with need from under his silver strands in the front.

"Then what are you waiting for?" He rolled his shoulders back and spread his legs wide, exposing his body to me in invitation.

I bit my lip, shifting a little closer on my knees. Sitting over him, I splayed my hand over the mating mark on his left pec.

"When did you get this?"

"The day before the Silk Festival. The day before you came back."

I traced the letter S, the first letter of the name he gave me— my only name. And now, it was etched into his skin forever.

"It took you that long to fall in love with me."

He shook his head. "It took me that long to *recognize* what I was feeling for you. To stop fighting it. To accept it for what it was. To understand I was destined to be alone for the rest of my life, merely a half of a person, separated from my other half by the River of Mists."

Tragically, he realized he loved me when he thought I was gone for good. At least, I'd always known we were still in the same world.

"Oh, Voron." I leaned closer to him.

He jerked up suddenly and caught with his teeth the end of the sheet wrapped around me. Falling back against the headboard, he yanked the sheet from me.

"Voron!"

I grabbed for the sheet but, frankly, I didn't feel like covering up. The warm tingles rushed up and down my skin from his attention. The sensation was way too pleasant to stop it.

He eyed me with the same hunger I'd looked at him.

"Gods, you are a sight to see, Sparrow." He licked his lips, his throat bobbing with a swallow. "I need to touch you, sweetheart. Please."

He inched closer, but the handcuffs stopped him.

"Patience, my darling." I ran my hands down his chest, then over the tight squares of his abs. His muscles rippled under my palms. His hard-on bobbed, practically leaping into my hand when I reached for it.

He released a long breath as I wrapped my fingers around his hard length.

"By the wings of the merciful God of Death," he exhaled under his breath. "I didn't even dare to dream about having your hands on me again."

I trailed my fingers up his hard cock. It was as beautiful as I remembered, as if sculpted by a skilled hand of a master.

A bitter thought slithered into my mind. None of this would have happened had Voron gotten his way when he'd ordered me gone. I would've been worlds away from him right now.

The more I thought about that, the hotter the blood bubbled in my veins, the harder I squeezed him, making him hiss. The higher the old anger rose.

I loved Voron. Passionately, desperately. I'd walk through fire for him and fight his demons for him. I would annihilate anyone who dared hurt him.

Yet I wished him hurt.

I wanted him to feel the pain of rejection. The helplessness I felt when he cast me off without even a word of goodbye. The anguish that followed for months after.

I wanted him to feel the loneliness of carrying our child without having the man I loved at my side. Of giving birth to the baby without his father being there or even knowing about him. I wished he knew my fear of losing the roof over our heads. The constant, heart-wrenching worry about not being able to provide for my baby or to give him the life he deserved.

My touch became rougher. I gripped his length in my hands, digging my fingers into his tender, silky skin.

Yet he moaned in bliss, thrusting his hips into my hands. He tossed his head back. My name fluttered from his lips like a prayer.

His mouth slackened, his beautiful features tensing as his climax neared.

I wished I could join him in pleasure. It used to be so easy for me to do before.

Before he betrayed me.

Taking my hands off him, I sat back on my haunches. I left him needing, wanting me, his cock engorged and weeping with just a single drop of seed glistening on its tip. I didn't let the rest release.

"Sparrow, please," he groaned, thrusting his hips up in search of my hands or my mouth. In search of my mercy. But I wouldn't grant him any.

"How does it feel, Voron? To be denied something you wish for so badly it hurts?" Because it must hurt, judging by the state of his dripping, straining dick.

Yet when he slowly opened his eyes and found mine, his expression was calm.

"I learned what it feels like long ago, sweetheart." His voice remained gentle. "You know that, too. You've read how I felt when you weren't with me. You know I lost everything without you, from my sleep to my sanity."

I inhaled a shaky breath. Everything inside me reached out to him. I wished to hold him, to comfort him, to erase his pain.

Only it was *he* who had caused the pain in the first place.

"Guilt racked me," he confessed. "I should have never let you out of my sight."

"Exactly. You shouldn't have," I echoed, bitterly.

"I should have married you that very day and proclaimed you my queen."

Would that have been the solution I wished for?

I shook my head with a sigh. His position on the throne was so unstable back then. The many attacks against him that followed proved it.

"Chances were we both would've been killed if you did that," I admitted reluctantly.

He fisted his hands in the handcuffs. "When they told me Sova was dead and you were gone, I thought the world ended. And for me, it did. I didn't really live since that day. I breathed, ate, talked, functioned, but I did not *live*."

"Wait..." My mind latched onto something he'd just said. "Who told you her name was Sova?"

"I knew her well. I met Sova a long time ago. She found me on a battlefield once when I'd been shot and stabbed too many times to follow the army as they retreated. She healed my wounds and let me recover in her wagon where I saw that giant serpent of Lorsan that you brought as a festival gift for me." He smiled. "She was the one who brought Magnus back to life, too. I owed her for so many favors already, but I asked her for one more—"

"You!" I gasped, my body shaking at the realization. "You sent her to the bridge that day?"

"She didn't tell you?" He watched me intently as if wishing to pierce my mind to search through my thoughts. "You didn't know?"

I scraped both hands down my face, releasing a long, tortured groan.

"She had no chance to tell me anything. We hadn't even made it to her wagon when..."

He shifted higher up the headboard, sitting up.

"Sparrow, please tell me you didn't think all this time that I *intended* to get rid of you."

I stared at him through a film of tears welling in my eyes.

"But that was exactly what I thought..." I whispered.

"Fuck." He rotated his wrist, breaking the fuzzy manacle.

"There must be a key somewhere," I mumbled through a sob, but he already snapped the second one off, too.

"Come here, little bird."

And I did. I shamelessly came to him for comfort that I'd just denied to him myself. I fell against his chest, letting him wrap his arms around me. Relief flooded my veins with lightness. It purged the shadows from my heart. And I cried.

He stroked my back, kissed my hair, and murmured sweet words of comfort that felt like drops of lifegiving water falling on the dry desert floor.

"I may not have fully realized what you were to me back then, Sparrow. But I knew from the moment I saw you that you and I have to be in the same world. With you, I laughed for the first time in decades. Without you, there was nothing but blizzards and storms. I couldn't part from you. I never intended for you to leave, but I had to make the lords believe that I did. Your life was in danger. They had tried to kill you once, and I knew no matter how far away I'd hide you, they would try again if they knew you were in Nerifir."

They had tried to kill him, too. Life had been volatile in Elaros, and my presence would not have helped the situation.

"God... Voron," I sobbed. "I'm so sorry." I was sorry for the time we had lost. We would never get those months back, but it didn't happen because of him. "There was no betrayal. Just a mistake."

He cupped my face.

"Sweetheart, your trust is my most precious gift. I would never break it. Even before I realized how desperately in love I am with you, I knew I couldn't be without you. There wasn't much time to plan that day. I had to decide quickly. I knew Sova had the skill, experience, and enough magic to snatch you from the guards and to trick them into believing you gone. While the High Lords pledged their loyalty to me in the Throne Room, I sent Alcon and Magnus to Sova with the plea to take you. She was supposed to keep you for a day or two. The Sky Palace was a wasps' nest back then, buzzing with danger. I planned to bring you back to Vensari and hide you until it was safe for me to return you to court in Elaros."

"It was a solid plan," I agreed.

"Except that when they told me Sova was dead, killed in some foolish hunting accident, I thought it happened before she had a chance to take you. No one saw you. The guards swore you fell..." A shudder ran through his body, and he pressed me to him again.

I felt his anguish, his loneliness, and his pain. But there was no more darkness of betrayal festering inside me.

"I'm so sorry, Voron. Sorry, I doubted you for so long."

I kissed his chest, tracing with my lips the first letter of my name etched in his skin.

"There was no betrayal, Sparrow. Yet I failed you. I should've had a better plan. I could've stood up to the court and kept you with me. I—"

I pressed a finger to his lips, trying to stop the hurricane of guilt that clearly threatened to overtake him.

"It was an accident, my love," I told him. "Neither of us could've predicted or prevented it." His erection pressed against my hip. I straddled his thighs, getting closer. "All we can do now is to keep on living." I kissed the column of his throat when it bobbed with a swallow.

He gripped my hips as I slid my core along his hard length. Nothing held my lust back now. The desire for him burned unimpeded, consuming me.

The tip of his engorged cock probed at my entrance. Yet he held my hips tightly, his forehead pressed to my shoulder. His arms shook.

"Sparrow, is this what you want?"

I rocked my pelvis against him. The ridge of his erection brushed by my core, blinding me with a flash of need.

"Voron..." His name rolled off my tongue like an illicit plea, followed by a needy whimper. "It's what we both want. And there is nothing and no one to stop us."

Maybe he could resist me. Maybe he should've tortured me the way I'd tortured him. But he granted me the mercy I'd denied him. Raising his hips, he slid inside me, filling the emptiness in me.

I exhaled, relaxing into him. Every part of me merged with the corresponding part of him, perfectly linked and aligned.

"I need you," he croaked.

Cradling my head in one hand, he cupped my backside with the other, rolling us over. His body covered mine. His groans turned feral as he pounded into me. Each thrust felt as if it was his last one. Desperate. Punishing. Brutal. And I took it all, begging for more.

I needed it to be just like this, wild and real, Voron proving to both of us that this wasn't a dream. We were together. And this is how it was going to stay.

He roared, tossing his head back. The moment the spasms of his release subsided, he slid down my body. Gripping my thighs, he lapped at my heated core. He found my clit with his tongue. I fisted the sheets, my body braced for pleasure.

Orgasm washed over me, rocking my hips against his mouth. Gripping his hair between my fingers, I rode his tongue as he licked and teased every last shudder of ecstasy out of me.

"Sparrow," he murmured, kissing up my body. "My sweet, precious, brave little bird. My love. My life." He punctuated every endearment with a kiss placed higher and higher up my body.

I caught the latest kiss on my mouth.

"I want you," he begged against my lips.

"Again?" I giggled at his eagerness.

"I never stopped."

Grabbing my hips, he flipped me onto my stomach and entered me from behind. He leaned over my back. His hands found my breasts, playing with my nipples. New sparks of desire shimmered through me, and Voron moaned, resonating with my pleasure.

With an arm around my middle, he straightened, lifting me with him. My back pressed to his chest, I gripped the vines of the bed posts, standing on my knees as he pounded into me from behind.

"By gods..." he panted. "What are you doing to me, Sparrow?"

The torture in his voice brought to mind the words in his

journal. Only there was a relief for our longing now. He dropped his hand, fingering my most sensitive spot. A charge of pleasure surged through my lower belly. I rocked against his hand, and he rubbed harder, matching the rhythm of his thrusts into me.

The vines curled and branched in my hands. They spread chaotically in every direction, turning Voron's neat luxurious bed into an overgrown nest of wilderness. At that moment, it suited him, for he roared like a wild beast, pumping his orgasm into me. I bent over, coming on his hand and around his cock. My inner muscles spasmed, milking his climax with mine. The pleasant, potent scent of his release mixed with the smell of our heated bodies.

Spent, I would've crashed down onto the mattress, but Voron caught me, gently lowering me into the sheets with him.

He curled around me, holding me from behind. His one arm was wrapped around my middle, the other slipped between my breasts, the tips of his fingers tracing the lines of my mating mark.

Peace descended upon me, one I'd never felt before. Everything was as it should be, and I felt whole. I didn't miss the parts of my past I no longer remembered and felt no regrets about those that I did. Instead, I looked forward to the future.

He kissed my shoulder. "I've sourced the *yara* pearl as you asked, remember? Only it came after you were gone. Do you still want to use it?"

Well, it was way too late for that, wasn't it?

With a long breath in, I turned in his arms, needing to see his face.

He smiled lazily, brushing a strand of my hair from my forehead. "A part of me is afraid of falling asleep now. I fear you'd disappear again if I do."

I cupped his nape. "I'm not going anywhere. I'm here to stay. But I have something to tell you." I kept my eyes on his, determined not to miss a single change in them. "When I left Elaros, I was pregnant. I have a son now. *We* have a son."

Chapter Thirty-Two

VORON

One moment, he was floating in a warm and hazy afterglow, his woman wrapped in his arms where she belonged, his mind flirting with sleep that promised to be the best sleep of his life.

The next minute, the haze, the warmth, and the afterglow were blown away, blasted to shreds by four little words—*we have a son.*

He scrambled up to a sitting position. Sparrow got up, too, sitting on her knees in front of him.

"Voron?" She ducked her head, searching for his eyes. "Say something. Anything?" she pleaded.

He couldn't, even if he tried. His throat was blocked. He could barely breathe.

A son...

She had a baby?

While he mourned her, raging like a caged animal, consumed by grief. She carried their child, gave birth to him, cared for him... Alone.

How?

Did she have any help?

How did she survive?

These questions had always been on his mind. But until now, every moment with her had consumed him. She came back to him. It left no room to dwell on the time she was away.

A lot had happened while they were apart, it seemed. Much more than he could've ever imagined.

"Where is he?" he finally managed to squeeze out.

She drew another long breath and released it, hesitating. Did she still not trust him? Believing he was the cause of their separation must have left a scar.

He reached for her, and she let him stroke her arms.

"He's safe," she assured him.

"Where? He should be here. With us."

He knew nothing about being a father but, apparently, he was one now. He'd have to figure it out, somehow. Maybe he could start by being the exact opposite of what his own father was? And for that, he needed to be there for his son. Now.

Sparrow fidgeted with a corner of the sheet. "Do you think Elaros is a safe place for a baby?"

He couldn't blame her for her doubts. This place had been a real wasps' nest, filled with traitors waiting for the slightest misstep to strike.

"Can a baby be safe in a place where his father nearly lost his life?" she asked softly.

"A few months ago, I wouldn't be so sure," he admitted. "But there have been many changes, my dearest Sparrow. The court is loyal to me. I've expelled the fake, pretentious opportunists both from the court and the Council. What happened this morning was the retaliation of the last two of them. Both are now dead. High Lord Bussard was shot and killed with an arrow during the battle this morning, and I personally executed Lord Vautour."

"I know. I saw it."

"Elaros is safer than it has ever been. I'll protect you both. No matter what, we all need to be together."

Still, she hesitated, biting her lip.

"Tell me, Voron, what does having a son mean to you?"

He paused in thought. Most of his life, a child of his own had been a rather abstract idea to him, an heir to the bloodline he didn't care about extending. But now that his son was real, he realized it wasn't about any bloodline or legacy. The need to protect someone he'd never met burned strongly already.

He feared he wouldn't be able to put what he felt into words yet, though.

"I don't know, Sparrow," he admitted. "I've never had a son before. Fuck, I didn't even have a father to speak of. I have no idea how to be a parent, but I want to do my best."

"That's all any of us can do." She smiled. "No one is born to be a perfect parent. All I want you to do is try. Aithen is a sweet little boy. He means the world to me, and I hope you'll fall in love with him, too."

"You named him Aithen?" How many times had he said that name, praying to the God of Death to help his beloved find her way back to him?

She bit her lip. "Do you like it?"

"I don't think I'd come up with a better name myself for the heir to the kingdom."

The smile slipped off her face.

"Do you think you'll ever see him as something more than just your heir?"

"Of course I will." He grinned, his confidence returning along with a new excitement. "But, sweetheart, this is my first child ever, and I haven't even seen him yet. Come."

He jumped off the bed. A shiver rippled down his back as he willed his wings out. The sensation was so new, it made him aware of the movement of every feather. Yet it also felt natural, as if he'd always had wings. They had always been a part of him, it seemed, but lay dormant inside his body until Sparrow came along and turned his entire world upside down by helping him find himself.

"Where are you going?" She scrambled from the bed after him.

He tugged her toward the window.

"Let's go get our baby, Sparrow. Let's bring him home."

"Wait, you crazy man!" She laughed. "First, you're not going anywhere without your pants on."

She glanced down his body, sending a rush of heat to his groin. Maybe putting on some pants was a good idea before he dragged her back to bed for the rest of the night.

"And second," she pointed at the dark, starry night outside the window. "It's late. Aithen is sleeping. Trust me, you don't want to wake him like that. He'd be cranky and miserable for the rest of the day."

"Is he at the farmhouse where you were?"

She nodded. "Close to it."

She was right. It would've taken them the rest of the night and the next morning to travel that far by horse, but his new wings would take them there well before sunrise.

He paused, taking in the warm glow that lit her lovely face when she talked about their child.

"How old is Aithen?"

"Eight months. He isn't walking yet, but his crawling speed is impressive. And he has wings."

"He does?" He grinned.

"They're black, just like yours. He's been learning how to use them, and it's daunting."

"Is he afraid?"

"No!" She laughed again. "But I am. I'm worried sick that he would fly too high for me to catch him."

He drew her into his chest.

"I'll catch him. I'll teach him. We'll fly together." Now that he had wings, he could do it all.

A king fulfilled.

The prophecy had always referred to him, not to Tiane. But

the few people who knew the truth, including his own parents, did everything they could to deceive everyone else.

"Aithen is safe, darling," Sparrow assured him. "We'll get him first thing in the morning. You should get some rest before you fly us there."

She led him back to bed. After they climbed in, he drew the blankets over both of them, then listened to her soft breathing as she drifted off to sleep.

He lay awake for a while. But it wasn't the desperate insomnia of before. With Sparrow curled against his chest, the night was peaceful. He lay on his back, watching the stars blinking in the skylight above. It occurred to him that this was the only time he'd ever seen stars through that opening. Normally, they would be hidden behind the clouds, dark and gloomy, like his thoughts.

But tonight, his mind was clear.

Worries never truly left him, always lingering at least on the fringes of his awareness. But he felt optimistic that he could deal with them.

He had more people to worry about now. He had a bonded mate and a son. A family. The concept was new but exciting. He used to believe that his heart was so hardened and dry, love would never find its way inside.

But when Sparrow was gone, his heart broke. Love fluttered inside it and made a nest. And now, it was there to stay.

He drew the cover higher over Sparrow's bare shoulders, keeping her warm.

His Sparrow.

His to love.

Here to keep him sane.

His to protect.

"I love you," he whispered softly, closing his eyes.

W hen the bright light of the late morning sun warmed his face through the skylight, he felt rested and refreshed.

"Morning, sleepyhead." Sparrow smiled, sitting in bed next to him.

A tray with empty breakfast dishes was in her lap. His robe was draped over her shoulders, concealing her delectable curves.

"Breakfast, Your Majesty?" She gestured at the second tray standing on the side table.

This wasn't a dream. Sparrow really was here. Never again would he have to wake up alone, sweating and gasping after a nightmare that stole his rest.

"Later," he croaked, shifting the tray from her lap to replace it with his head and arms.

"Aren't you hungry?" She raked her fingers through his hair.

Turning in her lap, he wrapped his arms around her hips and drew her closer, then pressed his face to her belly.

"Hungry. But not for food." He shoved the ends of the robe apart, kissing her skin underneath. "I want you."

She shrugged out of the robe, exposing her body to him. Some of it was so familiar, he could draw each line and curve by memory. But there were subtle new lines and new curves that came from their son growing inside her. He kissed them now, learning and memorizing them, too.

"I love you," he said as he laid her down on the covers and slowly slid inside her.

She moaned in response, her eyes glazed with pleasure. He filled both hands with her breasts, trapping the nipples between his fingers. It was an exquisite pleasure to watch her writhe with desire as he thrust inside her, chasing her climax and his.

She unraveled under him, coming on his cock so hard, he had to cradle her head to protect her from hitting it against the headboard. He let go, too, the ecstasy blinding him.

Even after they both collapsed into the sheets, spent and utterly satiated, he couldn't let go of her. He kept stroking her stomach, kissing her shoulder, nuzzling that spot on the side of her neck where her scent was especially sweet.

"I love you," he said again, craving to hear it back from her.

But she just smiled, gazing up at the skylight.

He kissed the glowing mating mark on her breast, then slid down, unable to resist a caress on her nipple.

"You know, when people tell you they love you, it's customary to reply in a similar fashion." Did he sound too needy? Too desperate? When it came to her, he felt both.

She giggled softly, turning her head toward him. "Isn't this proof enough?" She circled the letter V on her skin.

"I want to hear it, too, dear Sparrow. Every day."

Taking his face in her hands, she pulled him closer.

"I love you, Voron," she said softly, leaning her forehead against his. "I love you with all my heart."

The words warmed his chest, spreading like a balm over all his wounds inside.

"My sweet, little bird," he murmured, climbing over her, his cock hard with need all over again. "We're never leaving this bed, are we?"

"But we have to." She laughed. "It's time to pick up our son."

"Ready?" Sparrow glanced up at him, her beloved face peeking out from the white fur trim of her cloak hood like from a snow cloud.

They came to a clearing, hidden so deep in the woods, he would never have found it without her. His son was inside the invisible cabin here. And Voron was about to meet him for the very first time.

How does one prepare for something like that?

"As ready as could be," he replied.

The door flew open before Sparrow could knock. A hag

appeared on the threshold, draped in a gray cloak with the hood drawn low over her face that was ridden with signs of aging.

"There you are," she said to Sparrow in lieu of greeting, but there was no heat in her words, despite a fist propped on her hip. "I was beginning to wonder what kept you so long. But now I see." She leveled him with a stare and smirked. "The father dearest."

A shiver ran over his wings under her glare, shaking out the twigs and pine needles from his feathers.

"Hi Sauria." Sparrow gave her friend a hug. "Sorry for the delay."

"Looks like you've been busy with some important things out there." The hag eyed his wings. "*A king is whole,*" she quoted the prophecy. "I'd bet my precious cauldron this had everything to do with you, girl."

"In a way." Sparrow smiled proudly, moving her gaze from her friend to Voron, then back again. He withdrew his wings into his body, a rush of magic spreading along his skin from the gesture.

"Thank you for taking care of my child and my woman." He bowed deeply to the woman who'd kept the most precious people in his life safe in his absence.

"Aww, he has manners," the hag cooed, pouting her lips in an almost childish expression. "So, you finally wish to claim what's yours?"

"Yes. I do."

"Where is Aithen?" Sparrow asked.

The hag pointed with her thumb back over her shoulder. "Having a snack. The wild blueberries are giving him a hard time, though, rolling away from his little fingers." There was warmth and familiarity in her voice when she talked about his child. While he, his father, was a complete stranger to his own flesh and blood.

He had so much to catch up on. And he wished to wait no longer.

"I want to see him," he croaked.

The hag turned to Sparrow for permission, and his mate granted it with a small nod.

"I'll get him." The hag slid a measuring glance down his frame. "I'm afraid there is not enough room inside my cabin for those long legs and wide shoulders of yours."

He shifted awkwardly from foot to foot, suddenly feeling out of place in his own kingdom.

Sparrow dashed into the cabin after Sauria and emerged a few seconds later, holding a baby boy in her arms.

"Look who is here, Aithen," she murmured, placing a kiss in the nest of the black curls on the baby's head.

The boy sucked on his berry juice covered finger, paying him little attention. But Voron stared at him, struck by the emotions unfurling through his chest. There was awe at seeing his flesh and blood—*his son*. And regret for all the time they'd lost. Fear of failure, but also hope for a future together.

"Aithen," he tested the sound of his baby's name on his tongue.

Sparrow looked so natural and comfortable in her role as a mother, when Voron felt like an imposter in the role of a parent.

"Do you want to hold him?" she offered.

"Can I?" He reached for the boy tentatively.

The baby eyed him suspiciously as he took him from his mother, but didn't cry.

"Greetings." Voron settled his son on his forearm, holding him with his other hand. The thick knitted sweater the boy was wearing felt soft and cozy under his palm.

Aithen promptly got hold of the ruffled collar of Voron's shirt and pulled at it, aiming to stick the priceless lace into his mouth.

Sauria chuckled from the doorway of the now-visible tiny cabin. "You may rethink wearing fancy clothes around that boy, Your Majesty."

Voron smiled, not minding the berry juice stains one bit.

A wing popped out from his baby's back. The feathers on it were small and soft but just as black as his own.

"He does that, randomly." Sparrow stroked the tiny wing gently. "Sauria says he's learning to control them."

"We'll learn together, then," he said. "Wings are new to me, too, little friend."

At the sound of his voice, Aithen looked up, startled. His tiny features crumpling, he appeared ready to cry.

"It's all right, Aithen." Voron spoke softly, bouncing his son in his arms. "From now on, I'll always be around. We'll be friends. I'll make sure of it."

He tapped the baby's chin with his finger. The sparkling sapphire in one of his rings caught the baby's attention. He stopped crying and busied himself by figuring out how to stick the ring into his mouth, along with Voron's finger or even the entire hand if necessary.

Deep laughter rolled between the trees of the forest. It took Voron a fraction of a second to realize the laughter was his. It'd been a long time since he'd laughed like this, with pure joy.

He tilted his head up to the sky. Tiny shimmering snowflakes descended from a fluffy cloud above, like specks of diamonds. Other than a few light clouds, the sky was clear. The sun was shining. The air was so still, the snowflakes slowly fluttered straight down, frosting the fallen leaves on the ground with brilliant glitter.

Sparrow looked up, too, catching a few snowflakes on her rosy cheeks.

"It rains when the Sky King cries," she said. "A storm means anger. Sun means happiness. What does it mean when it snows like this? With the sun shining and the complete stillness in the air?"

He inhaled deeply.

What was it that he was feeling?

He met the eyes of the woman he loved while holding their son to his chest.

"Peace," he said. "When it snows like this, the Sky King is at peace."

Epilogue

VORON

The Throne Room was filled with people. The walls had been expanded. The vines of the ceiling opened like a giant flower to provide amphitheater-style seating for all the highborn of the palace and beyond. The marble floor of the room held rows upon rows of seats for those who couldn't fly up to the branches. *Taureans, ariens,* and *snakanas* sat in the velvet seats in the middle or stood along the walls.

It was Sparrow's idea. By tradition, a royal wedding ceremony had to take place in the Throne Room. But she wished to invite the entire palace, including the servants, as well as some merchants from the city and the nearby villages. So, with her usual ingenuity, she had found a way to accommodate everyone by expanding the room and opening the ceiling in a new fashion.

He didn't object to any of it. During his reign, he'd modified the palace to his liking, making it far more practical. Now, it was Sparrow's turn to add whatever features pleased her.

Standing on the dais, in front of the throne, he could see his entire court, the servants of the palace, and the many guests who had come from Elaros City and beyond.

Brebie and Kanbor were sitting in one of the front rows. The burly *taurean* appeared squished from the sides in the chair way too small for him, his shoulders rolled in with his arms folded in front of him. He looked uncomfortable. But then again, Kanbor was uncomfortable very much anywhere indoors. He preferred to be outside in the gardens.

Brebie had her slim arms wrapped around her husband's thick bicep. Which didn't stop her from turning and twisting around to chat with people close by.

Alcon stood at the foot of the platform, always a man of duty. Though, Voron noticed his most loyal councilor's head twitching to the right every now and then, his gaze drifting up to a certain court lady.

Lady Dove sat on one of the lower branches above, her long legs dangling in the gauzy tendrils of her poofy skirt shaped like an upside-down chrysanthemum. She twirled one of her snow-white curls around her dainty midnight-dark finger, batting her long eyelashes at Voron's fierce but bashful councilor. A ruddy blush seeped through Alcon's skin on his cheekbones.

It would do Alcon good to loosen up a bit, hopefully, with the help of the pretty courtier. Though, judging by the toys she'd sent to Sparrow, Lady Dove might tie Alcon up first in order to loosen him up.

Beautiful music floated through the room, rising to the sunny sky. The bright daylight cast shadows onto the marble floor. They were sharp, like ink drawings.

The Sky Kingdom was shadowless no more.

The high double doors opened, and Sparrow entered the room, carrying Aithen in her arms.

She was a vision, taking Voron's breath away. The wide skirt of her pale-blue dress was dusted with tiny, crystalized snowflakes that wouldn't melt. Her dress sparkled like fresh snow on a bright, sunny day. The spider silk veil, stitched with raindrops by a *taurean* woman, lay over her chestnut hair under a silver circlet— an exact copy of his crown.

As she reached the dais, she passed their son to Alacine, his new nanny, who then sat next to Sauria in the front row. Aithen gleefully chewed on a wooden toy dipped in *dail*-tree resin. The little guy was getting his teeth one after another, faster than a baby dragon. According to both Alacine and Sauria, who had officially become the apprentice of the royal hag now, chewing on the ring helped soothe the discomfort for teething babies.

He made a few steps down in his impatience to have Sparrow at his side. She took his hands, with a smile brighter than the sun, and ascended the dais with him.

The High Priest began the ceremony. Only Voron hardly listened to the ancient words of the script. His attention fully absorbed by Sparrow, he studied her face, wishing to commit to memory the spark of happiness in her hazel eyes and the way they made him feel inside, like he was soaring even with both feet firmly on the ground.

"You may now gift your bride the ring, Your Majesty." The High Priest spoke the part Voron had personally written into the ceremony.

"A ring?" Sparrow's eyebrows rose up in surprise.

"I read that is the custom in many parts of the human world for the man to present his woman with a ring," he explained, pleased he managed to find this information buried in an old scroll in the Royal Archives.

"You read that?" Her smile grew wider.

He raised his hand and flicked his fingers.

Magnus soared into the Throne Room from above. The bird had a smart silk cravat tied around his neck for the occasion, looking even more important than ever.

Sparrow laughed as the crow made a wide circle over their heads, showing off, no doubt. Voron held out his hand and Magnus dropped a large sapphire-and-diamond ring into his palm.

"With this ring, I marry you," he repeated the words he'd read in one scroll about human customs and slid the ring on Sparrow's finger.

"It's truly breathtaking!" she gasped, stroking the image of open wings carved into the sapphire.

"The state seal," he explained. "For you to use as you wish. You are the queen, my Sparrow, in every sense of the word."

Sweet and caring, Sparrow provided a perfect balance to his often swift and ruthless way of ruling. People gravitated toward her, both courtiers and servants alike.

She was his queen. His bride. The mother of his child. The love of his life. With her by his side, he felt invincible.

"I love you," he whispered.

His skin tingled with anticipation as he waited to hear these three little words back from her.

She tilted her head, gazing at him with adoration but said nothing in reply.

He raised an eyebrow.

"Are you going to make me beg, little bird? On our wedding day?" There was nothing he wouldn't do just to hear her say those words again and again.

She laughed softly. "I'll tell you 'I love you' a thousand times, my king. Only somehow no words seem big enough to encompass all my feelings for you right now."

The High Priest hadn't said he should kiss his bride yet, but he suddenly didn't give a fuck. He needed it. He needed her. Gathering her into his arms, he gave her a kiss, hungry and passionate, the kind that he usually reserved for their bedroom.

"I love you, Voron," she panted when he finally let her come up for air. "I love you with all my heart. And I'll love you for as long as I shall live."

Not every day in their future would be filled with sunshine, but he vowed to fill it with love now and forever.

Afterword

Remember this from the afterword in Hearts on Fire?

"Flapping of wings woke me up. The room was still dark. The sky outside our open bedroom windows was just beginning to lighten with a new sunrise.

It was too early for the gargoyles to wake up. Yet I was certain I'd heard the sound of someone flying.

Or *something?*

A large, black bird landed on a windowsill. I'd recognized the crow. I just couldn't believe it would fly all the way from the Sky Kingdom.

With a tendril of worry curling around my heart, I climbed out of our bed where Elex had spread out in his warm stone form.

The crow had a tiny scroll in its beak. I held out my hand, and it dropped the scroll onto my palm.

"Did you carry it all the way here? You are a smart bird, aren't you?"

The crow cawed once before taking off and quickly disappearing into the graying sky.

I opened the message, already knowing who it was from.

"I have a confession to make," it read. *"When I said I never*

wanted to see you again, I lied. How do you feel about having a glass of wine at the Sky Palace with me, dear Amber? Bring your royal spouse, too, of course."

It was signed simply.

"Voron."

The note was short, but it made me smile.

I studied the puffy silver clouds in the sky, wondering which one of them might be hiding the mysterious Sky Kingdom high above us."

I know you may be wondering why Voron never told Sparrow about the human woman he met in the Kingdom of Dakath in the Below.

Of course, he never forgot Amber and Elex. And of course, he told his wife about the other human woman currently living in Nerifir. I didn't put that conversation in *Crownless King*, because Sparrow would have a lot of questions about Amber, and by answering her questions Voron would give spoilers to those who haven't read yet the Fire in Stone duet.

I do, however, plan to write a follow up story to both duets. In it, Amber will come to Sky Kingdom for a visit and she will meet Sparrow in person. I hope to have it done sometime this year, and it will be exclusive to my Patreon for a period of time.

You can join my Patreon here:

What's next? I love visiting Nerifir and have many more stories to tell in the world of the River of Mists.

The next one is called *Somber Prince*. It will be the first book in a new trilogy, structured similarly to Madame Tan's Freakshow, with three complete love stories of three different couples. I happened to have three exciting heroes I want to write about. And yes, we'll be going all the way down to the world of Under in Nerifir.

Please join my Patreon or subscribe to my newsletter to follow the updates on these and other stories.

Call of Water

MADAME TAN'S FREAKSHOW

Excerpt

With a bracing breath, I squeezed through the gap and into the fragrant semi-darkness of Madame Tan's menagerie.

Just one look, then I'd get out before Fleur was back. We would get some ice cream afterwards, and no one would ever need to know where I'd gone while she was using the bathroom.

Inside, I found myself in a dark, stuffy place behind yet another fabric partition. Just about three feet wide, it appeared to be a corridor, stretching along the outside wall in each direction. Following the music, I headed right, grateful for the rubber soles of my sandals that allowed me to pad along noiselessly.

The sound of music intensified, then the murmur of voices mingled in. One stood out above the rest—the melodious voice of Madame Tan who sounded as if she was telling an enchanting tale of old.

"Water Fae would probably be referred to as 'sirens' in your world. They are known for their enthralling voices and ethereal looks…"

Up ahead, I came flush with the thick velvet curtain blocking my way. Eerie, blue-green light cut through the darkness in the narrow gaps on each side of the curtain where it met the canvas walls of the corridor.

"Although their appearance closely resembles humans, Olathana Ocean Fae are not intelligent or even self-aware," Madame continued with her narration. "In fact, their IQ level is below that of a dog..."

Something must have happened behind the curtain because a series of loud gasps and murmurs reached me. The light in the gaps intensified.

Unable to stand the suspense of not knowing any longer, I leaned closer, tugging the curtain aside a little, just enough for me to peek through.

A large, tall water tank stood in the middle of the next room. Shimmering green and blue light shone from it, piercing through the waves of the fragrant smoke that curled over the heads of six people sitting at the bar in front of the tank.

They were having drinks and hors d'oeuvres while watching a figure floating in the water.

Judging by the shape of his body—wide shoulders of a swimmer, well-defined chest, and narrow hips—he was a male, despite the halo of long white hair streaming around his head in the water and the silver skirt with high slits on each side. The skirt was actually a long, loin cloth, I realized, upon a closer look. And it was the only clothing the male was wearing.

Madame stood next to the bar.

"Hear the siren's voice." She waved her arms in the air dramatically, and the sound of a somber but breathtakingly beautiful voice filled the space.

It was a wordless song—no lyrics—the emotions conveyed through the melody alone. Yet the suffering in it was so clear, my chest ached, and my eyes burned with tears.

The man in the tank remained upright, as if suspended in the glowing water. The glow appeared to be coming from him, his pale skin highlighted by the delicate blues, greens, and pinks, which shimmered through his long, silvery hair, too.

Suddenly, a few deep notes of the song sliced through me with recognition.

I knew this voice.

It was the same sound that had enchanted me back in the cabaret in Paris.

Some of the songs he sang back then might have been soulful and sad, but none had been this sorrowful.

Yet I had no doubts. This was the voice of the man with fascinating blue eyes and a warm smile that hid in the corners of his mouth, even when he was singing a song meant to make you cry.

Zeph.

I shot my gaze back to the tank, examining closely the face of the person inside it. He seemed paler than I remembered, his hair much longer. There was not a hint of a smile in his features this time. But it was certainly the same man, the one I'd spent a night with and hadn't been able to forget ever since.

My heart thundered so loud, I pressed both hands to my chest, afraid that the people at the bar would hear it.

"He's gorgeous!" A young woman exclaimed, raising a tall glass with luminous liquid to her lips.

A man sitting next to her gave her a side glance. "Looks rather human to me."

Madame leveled him with a stare. The next moment, however, her face lit up with another wide smile.

"But he is *not* human." She gestured somewhere behind her.

The same dark-haired girl with big, soulful eyes who sold us our tickets entered from the side, carrying a large crystal decanter filled with a shimmering cocktail. She refilled the man's glass with it.

"The differences between sirens and humans are not that apparent at a first glance," Madame continued the moment the girl had left.

I spotted Radax, the large, bearded man who had escorted me out of this tent earlier. Now he stood in the entrance where the girl with the decanter had departed. Another man, who looked nearly identical to Radax except that this one was clean-shaven, stood on the other side of the entrance. The arms of both were folded across their enormous chests.

"However, there *are* differences." Madame made another theatrical gesture toward the man in the tank...*Zeph*. "Aside from the ability to breathe underwater, as you can see, Water Fae swim better than any fish and infinitely better than a human. They can also regulate their body temperature and are not affected by cold."

"Still, looks human to me," the man at the bar retorted gruffly.

"No regular man could be this beautiful," a woman objected.

"So..." The man shrugged, dismissively. "A *pretty-boy* human, then."

With another gesture from Madame, a ripple ran through the water, carrying something that made Zeph's body arch. He threw his head back, his features crumbling into a grimace of pain, mouth open in a soundless scream.

This couldn't be right. Bounced around in my head.

Why would Zeph be here? How did he end up in that tank?

Zeph's jaw flexed as he bared his teeth. The singing never stopped, however, making me realize it must be a recording. He shot his hands to the side, his arms and legs rigid and straight.

Two pairs of magnificent fins opened, fanning out from his arms—elbow to wrist—and from the back of his legs—knee to ankle. The multi-colored glow in the water broke into iridescent swirls as Zeph slowly rotated inside the tank. When he turned with his back to the audience, they all broke into awed gasps.

A large, dorsal fin opened on his back like a shimmering sail of gossamer silk stretched between sharp spikes. It reflected the multicolored lights running through the water.

"But how is this attached?" A few people rose from their seats, leaning forward.

"It looks too real," someone said, their voice guarded.

"He doesn't seem to be very comfortable in there." An older woman reached over the counter.

Madame quickly slid in behind the bar, positioning herself in front of Zeph's tank.

"Please take your seats, ladies and gentlemen. Remember the rules. You cannot touch the glass," she reprimanded sternly.

With puzzled murmurs and gasps of awe and bewilderment, the audience settled down.

"Enjoy the refreshments," Madame prompted. Obediently, the six at the bar went back to drinking their cocktails and munching on the food.

Madame's smile returned. "I assure you, like all animals in my menagerie, the siren is kept in the utmost comfort. I make sure to maintain the optimal conditions for the wellbeing of my exhibits. Many would not have survived in the wild for as long as they do in my collection."

I stared at Zeph as he completed his rotation, facing the audience once again. His expression was now blank, the clear blue eyes gazing vacantly straight ahead. If I had not seen this face vividly animated when he was singing, talking, laughing a year ago, I would have been inclined to believe there was no thought, no self-awareness behind those eyes, just as Madame had claimed.

But I *did* know better. Because I did remember everything from that night. I knew that Zeph was a real man—smart, fun, and intelligent.

It did not matter right now how things had ended between us. Locking him in that tank was not right. Keeping him there could not be legal.

Fervently, I tried to decide on the best course of action. I should run back, find Fleur, and call the police.

As the light inside the tank dimmed. Radax and his beardless twin left. The people around the bar continued to eat and drink, with Madame telling them some out-of-this-world trivia about the food on their plates.

I had to get out of here before anyone spotted me. I was not looking forward to facing Madame if I were discovered trespassing on her property. Something about that woman made my skin crawl.

I was about to turn around, back to the gap in the wall I had used to enter, but the noise of footsteps and sounds of a conversation coming from that direction made me freeze in place.

Huddling into the shadows, I felt thankful for the darkness between the stuffy fabric walls. Whoever was approaching from the other end of the corridor wouldn't be able to see me right away. Yet the sounds traveled easily enough through the fabric, and I crouched down, afraid to breathe.

The footsteps were heavy, the conversation stilted. Not a real dialogue, but an abrupt exchange of cut-off sentences and short phrases. The strangled voices and some low grunts made me think that the men talking must be also carrying something heavy.

The loud thud of a load being set down on the ground confirmed that.

The footsteps then moved again.

In *my* direction!

Trying to keep the panic from rising, I checked both walls on each side of me. The inside partition was stretched over a frame. Taut fabric did not leave me enough space to crawl under. The bottom edge of the outside wall was weighed down by the sandbags outside. My attempt to raise it made a rattling sound of a tarp crinkling.

"What's that noise?" Radax's voice asked, close—way too close—to me.

"Sounds like someone is trying to sneak under the wall again," another deep male voice replied. The two would catch me before I managed to crawl half-way through any opening I could find or make.

"Cheap assholes," Radax grumbled. "No one wants to pay anymore. Everyone wants free entertainment."

Panic spiked hot in me, making it hard to think clearly. Glancing behind the velvet curtain again, I found the room there nearly empty now. The VIP clients had left. Madame was gone, too. The dark-haired girl carried out a pile of dirty dishes from the bar.

With not a second to lose, I slipped behind the curtain as the footsteps of Radax and his companion approached.

With the girl now gone, the VIP room was completely empty. Zeph's water tank was dark, too. It was hard to tell whether he remained inside. With the footsteps right behind me, I crouched low to the ground and scurried behind the bar. The curtain swished open, with the heavy stomping coming in a moment later.

"And?" Radax asked.

"Nope. No breach," the second voice answered. "Someone must be just poking around from the outside."

"Good. Let's help Amira spruce this place up. Madame already went to get the second group of VIP clients. They'll be here any minute."

The sound of chairs being re-arranged around the bar jolted me with another shot of alarm through my system. Next, someone would certainly come behind the bar to wipe the counter top off or to get some clean glasses, maybe.

Scrambling for a more secure hiding spot, I padded around the stand with the water tank. There was just about enough of a gap between the floor and the stand for me to fit under. Getting down on my belly, I wiggled from the rug behind the bar onto the packed dirt under the water tank. Trying my darndest not to sneeze in the dust, I fit my body between the tubes and hoses running from the bottom of the stand.

"Welcome to my special exhibit," Madame's pleasant voice greeted, followed by shuffling noises of people entering.

Another group of VIP clients.

How many did she have scheduled for today?

Listening to her speech about the Ocean Fae again, I wondered how *did* Zeph breathe underwater. It would be impossible for anyone to hold their breath for that long, and I didn't notice any tubes or masks inside the tank.

His fins appeared so incredibly realistic, as if they were a natural extension of Zeph's body. Were they some ingenious mechanical invention? A sophisticated costume? Or a crazy surgical modification?

The last possibility made my stomach churn.

Watching the reflection of the green-and-blue glow from the water tank on the floor in front of my hiding place, I wished I could see his face. The heart-breaking sound of his singing floated through the room once again. The wordless pain and longing of the song filled my chest with sorrow and compassion.

If it hadn't been for Radax and his buddy out there, I would have been on my way to get help for Zeph right this very moment. Instead, there I was, lying in dirt while he was being ogled and tortured up there.

Fleur must be losing her mind outside, looking for me.

The thought of her brought my cell phone to mind. With Zeph's magical voice filling the space, the risk of me being heard was less. Carefully, I slipped my hand to the phone in the back pocket of my shorts. Sliding it out, I quickly turned the ringer off, finding no messages from Fleur yet. Could she still be in the bathroom? Then I realized, I had absolutely no signal here.

Disheartened, I shoved the phone back in my pocket and remained still, listening to Madame's voice spinning her tales.

Apparently, Madame had two more groups of VIP clients scheduled for that evening. Unless she'd lied to me about the ten-thousand-dollar admission, which I didn't see any reason for, she'd made a lot of money today. And if she'd had but half that many visitors for each day of CNE, she'd make a fortune during this fair.

Did I rush to assume that Zeph was forced into that tank? Considering the amount of money involved, he could be a business partner of Madame or her employee, performing to earn enough money to buy that place by the ocean he'd dreamed about.

How well did I know him, anyway? Compassion made me initially view him as a victim, but now I questioned that. He could very well be performing willingly.

Showing up with the police would be stupid in that case. If anything, I risked being charged with trespassing.

Another question roamed my mind while I lay there. Why would people pay this much money just to see an actor float in the tank, no matter how handsome or talented he was?

"To see the things not found on Earth." Madame's words came to mind.

For the words to make sense, though, I'd have to believe that Zeph indeed was not of this world.

My legs started to fall asleep, and my back ached after lying in pretty much the same position for nearly two hours. The dust and the smoke that slithered under the tank made me incredibly thirsty, too.

Finally, the last group of VIPs had departed. The sounds of clinking dishes then the sweeping of the broom told me someone must be cleaning the place.

More people entered.

"It was a good day, but I'm tired now," Madame's voice announced. "Amira, bring my dinner to my trailer once you're done here. Then start packing up."

No audible reply followed, but I wondered if that was the name of the dark-haired ticket-booth girl. She seemed to do pretty much everything around here, from selling tickets, to waitressing, to cleaning up.

"Radax," Madame ordered to another one of her mostly silent helpers. "You have a few hours. We're leaving at sunrise."

A good few minutes passed in silence after Madame had exited. Then I heard the deep voice of Radax, "Go, get her dinner now, Amira, then take a nap for an hour. I'll manage without you for now."

As brief as the statement was, I caught a warm note in his voice I didn't expect from someone like him.

"Thank you," came in a barely audible whisper from the girl, Amira, then the soft padding of her shoes sounded as she left.

Radax stomped around the tank for a while as I lay still as a mouse, praying he wouldn't decide to check under it.

Once he finally left, I waited for a few more minutes, listening for any sound out there. This room must be deeper inside the group of the tents, with numerous walls and partitions effectively muffling the outside noise. All seemed quiet.

It was time to get out of here.

With a deep breath to calm my nerves, I crawled out onto the rug behind the bar. A faint glow from the streetlights filtered through the roof of the tent above, barely making a dent in the darkness.

Poking my head around the bar, I made sure no one was nearby then got to my feet and scurried to the velvet curtain, the way I had come in.

Before lifting it, though, I paused, staring back at the water tank. All the lights inside it were off, and the dark water made it impossible to see anything inside.

I hadn't heard any sound of Zeph getting out of it. Did they leave him inside for the night? That wouldn't be an appropriate way to treat a business partner or an employee.

Clutching the curtain in my hand, I recalled Zeph's listless expression and his wordless cry, more harrowing because it was soundless in the water. Was all of that an act?

Something didn't feel right about this place. Regardless of Zeph's position here, I decided to call the police the minute I got out of here if Fleur hadn't already.

A noise somewhere inside the tents snapped me back to the moment. Madame's people must have started to pack up as she'd ordered. Someone would come here, too, sooner or later.

Drawing back the curtain, I peeked into the corridor behind it to make sure no one was there. Then, I carefully started on my way back to the support pole and the gap in the wall I'd used to sneak in.

Right in the spot where it was, though, a massive wooden crate now stood, blocking my way. Frantically patting with my hands around the corner of the crate, I realized there simply was no space for me to squeeze behind it.

Unable to get out the way I'd came in, I searched for the bottom end of the canvas wall. If I yanked at it hard enough, I might be able to free it from the sandbags outside so I could crawl under it.

The canvas wall, edged with tarp, made the crinkling noise again when I tugged at it.

"Who's there?" A deep male voice suddenly boomed nearby, startling me into panic.

One of Madame's tattooed guards shuffled from around the crate.

Holding my breath, I pressed my back to the crate, frantically scrambling for an idea of what to do next as the guard moved my way.

Should I run back to the room with the tank and try to hide again? Or scream, in hope that someone outside would hear me?

Maybe I could just stay still, hidden by the crate?

A loud growl, accompanied by weird hissing noises, suddenly came from right behind me. I jumped forward, unable to hold back a strangled gasp of alarm, then realized too late that the sounds were coming from inside the crate.

The guard saw me.

"Hold there!"

The ray of light from the flashlight in his hand landed on my face, blinding me for a moment. Breathless from terror, I pivoted on my heel and ran as fast as I could back to the VIP room.

With his heavy steps gaining on me from behind, there was no time to stop and check if the space behind the curtain was still free of Madame's people. I rushed in at full speed and bumped into the hard-as-rock chest of Radax.

"What's going on?" he roared, catching me by the scruff of my t-shirt and lifting me up as if I were a cat.

"Found her snooping around the gorgonian's crate," the one chasing me replied, quickly catching his breath.

"Who are you?" Radax gave me a shake.

"Nobody," I panted, my heart lodged in my throat, choking me with panic. "Please, let me go."

"What the fuck were you doing by the crate?" the one with the flashlight demanded.

"Just, um…" I remembered Radax speaking about people sneaking in to see the show for free. "Wanted to see what you have here, without having to pay for the ticket." It wasn't even a lie. "I'll give you the twenty bucks right now." I patted the back pocket of my shorts. "Just let me go, please."

"What *did* you see?" Radax narrowed his eyes at me.

With my shirt in his firm grip, I could only stand on my tiptoes.

"Nothing," I lied, desperately hoping it came out convincingly enough. "Nothing at all."

"Weren't you the one I escorted out of here earlier?"

My heart dropped, he'd recognized me.

Denying felt stupid at this point, so I just kept quiet, scrambling for what to do next.

"You wanted to see the VIP exhibit, didn't you?" Radax asked next.

He was way too smart for his size.

"No. I have no idea what you're talking about…"

"Well, she's seen it, now." The other one scowled, tipping his head toward the tank.

A pale shape was clearly visible in the water. With both hands pressed against the glass, Zeph appeared to be watching us, although his eyes stared into the void unfocused, his expression remained impassive.

"She didn't eat *camyte*." The man with the flashlight scratched his bald head. "She can cause trouble if we let her go."

"I won't," I rushed to assure him. "I want no trouble. Promise. I just want to go home."

Getting the police involved felt absolutely necessary now, but I tried not to think about that, afraid it would reflect on my face somehow.

"Trez, go get Madame," Radax ordered to the other man.

"Oh God, no please," I whimpered, hating him for bringing her into this. "Not her. Just let me go, and she would never need to know about any of this. Please."

"This is her property." Radax dragged me to the exit of the room. "Her show and her business. She gets to decide what to do with you."

Yawning, her hair wrapped in a silk turban, Madame arrived in a smaller room somewhere inside the tents where Radax had brought me. Dressed in a pink kimono painted with golden birds, she tossed but one glance at me.

"Kill her."

AVAILABLE NOW

More in the River of Mists

Joyless Kingdom Trilogy

Somber Prince, book 1, Fall 2023

Wingless Crow

Crownless King

Fire in Stone

Hearts of Fire

Serpent's Touch

Serpent's Claim

Madame Tan's Freakshow Trilogy

Call of Water

Madness of the Moon

Power of Rage

More by Marina Simcoe

SCIENCE-FICTION ROMANCE

My Holiday Tails

Married to Krampus

My Tiny Giant

My Birthday Getaway

New Year, New Planet

Mail Order Mom

My Pumpkin

What Makes an Alien a Dad? – Summer 2023

Dark Anomaly Trilogy

Gravity

Power

Explosion

Stand Alone Novels

Experiment

Enduring (Valos Of Sonhadra)

About the Author

Marina Simcoe likes to write love stories with human heroines and non-human heroes who just can't live without them. She firmly believes that our contemporary world could always use a little bit of the extraordinary.

She has lots of fun exploring how her out-of-this-world characters with their own beliefs, values, and aspirations fit into our every-day life.

She lives in Canada with her very own extraordinary hero, their three little offspring, and a cat who is definitely out of this world.

facebook.com/MarinaSimcoeAuthor

instagram.com/marinasimcoeauthor

amazon.com/author/marinasimcoe

bookbub.com/profile/marina-simcoe

patreon.com/MarinaSimcoe

goodreads.com/MarinaSimcoe

tiktok.com/@marina.simcoe